Vasily Shukshin / SNOWBALL BERRY RED & OTHER STORIES / Edited by Donald M. Fiene, with translations by *Donald M. Fiene, Boris Peskin, Geoffrey A. Hosking, George Gutsche, George Kolodziej, and James Nelson*, with a **Chronology** of the Life and Works of Shukshin, and with a **Filmography** of Shukshin, a **Bibliography** of Shukshin, and with three **Critical Articles** on Shukshin's Works. *Published by* **Ardis, Ann Arbor.**

Published by Ardis Publishers,
2901 Heatherway,
Ann Arbor, Michigan 48104

Manufactured in the United States of America

TABLE OF CONTENTS

PREFACE AND ACKNOWLEDGEMENTS

This collection grew out of a friendship I struck up with Mr. Boris Peskin late in 1973, shortly after he had arrived in the United States—having emigrated some months earlier from the Soviet Union. A former librarian at Leningrad University, and a film critic, he had included in the many crates of books he shipped here several collections of stories by Shukshin and numerous articles about him. He insisted that I read Shukshin, whom he regarded—along with many other readers—one of the best writers in the Soviet Union. In this way an important cultural benefit was gained from the recent wave of emigrations out of the USSR.

In 1974 Mr. Peskin helped me translate the story "The Brother-in-Law," which was published in *Russian Literature Triquarterly* the following year (and reprinted in this collection). Then Carl R. Proffer, editor of Ardis, tentatively agreed to publish an anthology of Shukshin's work. Not until 1976, after I had been teaching in the Department of Germanic and Slavic Languages at the University of Tennessee for two years, was I able to commit myself seriously to the Shukshin book—this work being made possible by a Faculty Research Fund Award by the University of Tennessee that summer. This assistance is herewith gratefully acknowledged.

Meanwhile, Mr. Peskin was able to provide a valuable chronology of Shukshin's life and work, and a list of his films. (Mr. Peskin is continuing to do research for a monograph, to be published separately later, on Shukshin's contributions to Soviet film as an actor, director, and scenarist.)

Just as I was about to make my final decision about the contents of the Shukshin collection, Geoffrey Hosking, Senior Lecturer in History at the University of Essex, inquired through Carl Proffer about the possibility of contributing to the book. Professor Hosking, interested in the turn toward rural subject matter in recent Soviet literature, had published an article in the *Slavic Review* (Dec. 1973) entitled "The Russian Peasant Rediscovered: 'Village Prose' of the 1960s." And, as Senior Fellow at the Russian Institute of Columbia University in the spring of 1976, he had completed a chapter on Shukshin for a book he is currently writing: *Beyond Socialist Realism—the Search for an Image of Man in Contemporary Soviet Russian Fiction.* He graciously agreed to revise his Shukshin chapter for a critical introduction and to bring his working bibliography up to date for the end pages. He had already translated the story "In Profile and Full Face" for the anthology *Soviet Writing Today,* edited by M. Dewhirst and R. Milner-Gulland for Penguin Books; he obtained permission to include the story in the present anthology. (Grateful acknowledgement is herewith made to Penguin Books and the editors of *Soviet Writing Today* for permission to reprint, in slightly revised form, "In Profile and Full Face.") In addition, Professor Hosking translated four other stories.

Then a story that Professor Hosking and I agreed ought to be included in the book was submitted by chance to *Russian Literature Triquarterly* by James Nelson, Assistant Professor of Russian at Cornell College, Iowa. Carl Proffer asked if I wanted it for the book. I did. Also, in early autumn of 1976, three colleagues agreed to translate one story each: George Kolodziej, an instructor of Russian and Polish at Ohio State University; W. G. Fiedorow, Assistant Professor of Russian, Knox College, Illinois; and George Gutsche, Assistant Professor of Russian, University of Tennessee. When a second general essay on Shukshin was submitted at the last minute by Michel Heller [Mikhail Geller], Assistant Professor *(maitre-assistant)* of Russian at the University of Paris (Sorbonne), Mr. Gutsche agreed to translate that essay from Russian into English for the collection. Mr. Heller, who studied history at Moscow State University and left the Soviet Union in 1969, is the author of numerous articles and a widely translated study of Soviet Literature.

It is thus apparent that I can take little credit for acting on an over-all master plan in preparing this book of writings by and about Shukshin. At best, I seem to have been selected by chance to be a sort of coordinator for a more or less spontaneous (if belated) response to Vasily Shukshin in the West. The basis on which the stories translated were chosen was primarily their appeal to the various translators; but a special effort was made to include nothing that had already appeared in English in various issues (1964 through 1975) of the journal *Soviet Literature* (published in Moscow) or in the Shukshin collection *I Want to Live* (Moscow: Progress Publishers, 1973). As far as I know, nothing else by Shukshin has been published in English. The one exception to the policy of not duplicating a translation is the title story (actually, a film script), which appeared in *Soviet Literature*, No. 9 (1975) in a translation by Robert Daglish under the title *The Red Guelder Rose*. I had already translated a considerable portion of the work (generally regarded as Shukshin's best), before I learned of the existence of Daglish's translation. However, since the earlier version appeared in a journal not read regularly by many English-speaking people, and since the dialogue in it often seems to lack idiomatic authenticity (although the translation as a whole is otherwise quite accurate), I decided to continue with my own version.

Although I was initially disappointed at not being the first to present *Kalina krasnaia* in English, I can now express only sincere relief that Daglish preceded me. His easy understanding of what for me was often difficult Russian (with its Siberian colloquialisms, theives' jargon, and collective-farm and labor-camp slang) has saved me from a number of errors. Although I had my own native-informant in Mr. Peskin, I did not ask him to read my entire text, but only to explain a number of specific questions that I presented him. It was the errors I had not been aware of making that Mr. Daglish helped me to discover, as I compared my finished text with his. I am deeply grateful to him, as well as to Mr. Peskin.

I have tried to edit this entire book, with respect to translation of dialogue, to sound authentic to the American ear, but not to be too dependent on contemporary idiom and slang. The various translations done by different translators still have their considerable differences, however—and perhaps this is just as well. The non-Russian reader needs to be reminded that the author's original voice is bound to be different from what it appears to be in translation; perhaps that original voice is more easily heard by somehow searching for an "average" of the different voices presented here. It should be kept in mind that one of the translators, Geoffrey Hosking, is English. He was kind enough to allow his translations to be edited so as to yield a more American sound, though his British accent was not eliminated altogether, out of consideration for the needs of British readers of Shukshin.

It is hoped that this book is a sufficiently authentic and stimulating introduction to Shukshin to induce other translators and editors in the West to bring out the remaining work of this remarkable artist—who published over 130 stories (including six collections), two novels, six film scripts and one play; directed six films; and played major roles in over a dozen other films before his tragic death in 1974 at the age of forty-five.

Donald M. Fiene
Knoxville, January 1977

A CHRONOLOGY OF THE LIFE AND WORK OF VASILY SHUKSHIN
Compiled by Boris N. Peskin

1929 — Born July 25 in the village of Srostki, Altai Territory, Siberia. Father dies when S. very young; subsequently his stepfather dies at the front during the war.

1943 — Finishes seventh year of school, attends Biiskii Automobile Technical Training Institute for about one year.

1944-45 — Works on a local collective farm.

1946-48 — Works as carpenter-scaffolder and unskilled laborer in construction of factories in Kaluga and Vladimir.

1949 — Called up for service in the navy; while in the service, participates in amateur theatrical performances both as an actor and director.

1951-53 — On special assignment in Sevastopol as radio operator.

1953 — Released from navy because of illness; completes secondary school by correspondence.

1953-54 — Teaches history in school for rural youth in home village of Srostki; appointed director of the school.

1954 — From this time on lives in Moscow; begins to writes poems and stories.

1954-60 — Studies at the All-Union State Institute of Cinematography, in the studio of movie director Mikhail I. Romm.

1955 — Joins the Communist Party.

1958 — Still a student, plays first role (Big Fyodor) in M. Khutsiev's film "The Two Fyodors"; publishes first story in magazine *Smena.* Continues writing stories for publication on the advice of Romm.

1960 — Presents and plays lead role in his first (short) film—for his diploma at the Institute—based on his own scenario: "Report from Lebiazh'e" ("Iz Lebiazh'ego soobshchaiut").

1961 — Graduated from the Institute.

1963 — First collection of stories published: *Country Folk (Sel'skie zhiteli).*

1964 — Completes first full-length film, based on his own scenario: "There Lives Such a Fellow" ("Zhivet takoi paren' "); film receives Golden Lion of St. Mark award at the 16th annual Venice Film Festival; the script is published as a book.

1964-65 — During the filming of "What Is It Like, the Sea?" ("Kakoe ono, more?"), playing the role of the fisherman Zhorka, S. becomes acquainted with his future wife, the actress Lidia Fedoseeva.

1965 — Completes film "Your Son and Brother" ("Vash syn i brat"), based on themes from his stories "Stepka," "Ignakha Has Arrived" ("Ignakha priekhal") and "Snake Venom" ("Zmeinyi iad"). Receives Vasilev Brothers State Prize of the RSFSR for this film. Publishes novel *The Liubavin Family (Liubaviny).*

1966 — Publishes novella "Over Yonder" ("Tam, vdali") in a journal; marries

Lidia Fedoseeva (an article about her appears in *Aktery sovetskogo kino*, Vypusk 12 [M. 1976] , 178-89).

1967 — Awarded the Order of the Red Banner of Labor

1968 — Publishes screenplay about Stenka Razin (17th-century peasant rebel), "I Have Come to Give You Freedom" ("Ia prishel dat' vam vol'iu"), and a second volume of stories, *Over Yonder.*

1969 — Completes film "Strange People" ("Strannye liudi"), based on his own script. Conferred the rank of Honored Worker in the Arts of the RSFSR. Publishes article "Morality is Truth" ("Nravstvennost' est' pravda"). "As an artist I cannot deceive my people by showing life only as happy; the truth is also bitter."

1970 — Publishes third collection of stories, *Fellow Countrymen (Zemliaki).* Interview in *The Literary Gazette* published November 4, on plans for making the film "Stepan Razin." ("How did it happen that you have suddenly turned to such a remote historical theme?" —"Not suddenly. In 'Stepan Razin' I am governed by the same theme with which I started long ago and which occupies me now: the fate of the Russian peasantry.") —This film was never made, but permission was given Shukshin to go ahead with it one month before his death.

1971 — Plays leading role in S. Gerasimov's film "At the Lake" ("U ozera"); awarded State Prize of the USSR. Publishes the novel *I Have Come to Give You Freedom* in the journal *Sibirskie ogni.*

1972 — Completes film "Happy-Go-Lucky" ("Pechki-lavochki") based on his own script.

1973 — Publishes film script "Snowball Berry Red" in the April issue of *Our Contemporary (Nash sovremennik);* begins shooting the film (in which he also plays the leading role) in Vologda in the summer. Also plays minor role in a film directed by G. Panfilov (not released until 1976). Fourth collection of stories, *Characters (Kharaktery)*, appears. Falls ill in November, hospitalized; but leaves hospital against doctors' advice to complete the editing of "Snowball Berry Red."

1974 — "Snowball Berry Red" released in April; triumphant success; film later received the Lenin Prize. Publishes article in *Pravda* on May 22: "The Most Valuable Discovery." ("Now I must enter upon a path of broader reflection requiring new strength and the courage to reveal new depths and complexities in life.") *I Have Come to Give You Freedom* published as a book; fifth collection of stories appears: *Conversations under a Clear Moon (Besedy pri iasnoi lune).* Play "Energetic People" ("Energichnye liudi") published in *Literaturnaia Rossiia;* the Bolshoi Dramatic Theater in Leningrad presents this play under the direction of G. Tovstonogov. The Mayakovsky Theater in Moscow presents a dramatic performance of "Characters," based on stories by S. In July publishes film script "Brother of Mine" ("Brat moi") and novella "Point of View" ("Tochka zreniia"). During the summer and autumn works on set of S. Bondarchuk's film (based on Sholokhov's unfinished novel) "They Fought for the Motherland" ("Oni srazhalis' za Rodinu"); plays role of Lopakhin. On October 2 dies of a heart attack on set (at Kletskaia Station, in the district of Volgograd [Stalingrad[); buried in Moscow; survived by wife and two young daughters by her, Olga and Maria, and by a third daughter, Katerina, by a woman he had known before his marriage. (He had taken Katerina into his family after his marriage.)

1975 — Novella "Till the Cock Crows Thrice" ("Do tret'ikh petukhov") published in *Our Contemporary*, and film script "Call Me to the Bright Beyond" ("Pozovi menia v dal' svetluiu") in *The Star*. Sixth collection of stories appears: *Brother of Mine*. Also a two-volume edition of works and a collection of film scripts.

VASILY SHUKSHIN

Geoffrey A. Hosking

THE FICTION OF VASILY SHUKSHIN

A prominent feature of the life of the Soviet people in the last generation or two has been sheer uprootedness. People have been torn from their moorings by war, urbanization, political oppression and the creation of a modern industry and a collectivized agriculture. In their millions they have been swept into factories, building sites, army barracks, labor camps, and then often pushed back out again into a world ill-prepared to receive them. Their education has been scrappy, their work experience harsh, and little in the way of culture or settled family life has cushioned them against the bewildering peripetia of this existence.

These are the people for whom Vasily Shukshin speaks. Indeed, he was one of them himself (like many writers of the middle generation born in the late twenties and early thirties). Born in the Altai region of Siberia in 1929, he worked as a lad on a collective farm, but soon migrated to the building sites of the town, and then did his military service in the navy. His education came in dribs and drabs in the interstices of these peregrinations. Not until the age of twenty-five did he finally settle in the town, when he entered the State Institute of Cinematography to study under Mikhail Romm, an experience he thanked for his debut in literature:

> Romm had an outlook on the film that one would hardly expect in a well-known film director: he connected it directly with literature—good literature. He used to make us write sketches and short stories, sometimes on set themes, sometimes on whatever we liked. I had seen a lot of good in life—a lot of good people. So I started to write about them. Romm was pleased with my work. He said, "Vasya, you've got it in you, keep it up!" And I'm still writing.[1]

For all his later successes, both in the cinema and in literature, he remained to the end of his life with the feeling that he was a latecomer to urban culture, and he lacked confidence that he had really established himself in it. A few years ago he wrote:

> Now that I'm nearly forty it turns out that I'm not yet really a citizen of the town, but I don't belong to the country any more either... That's worse than falling between two stools: it's like having one leg on the shore and the other in a boat. You can't stay where you are, but you're afraid to jump into the boat.[2]

He was also torn between the worlds of literature and the cinema. They did not always complement each other as in the early days (indeed, Romm had foreseen that they would clash), and towards the end of his life he was trying to bring himself to give up the cinema and settle down to writing.

He admired Vasily Belov for sitting there in Vologda and doing just that.[3] But arguably he could never have done it himself: indeed, his widow has described how at the end of his life he had plans for further films, especially the long cherished project of one on Stenka Razin.[4]

Most of his literary creations have the same ambiguity about them. They are the children of the Soviet Union's whirlwind years of social change, in which tens of millions of people were torn away from their backgrounds and homes. Shukshin's heroes are the uprooted, who have left one milieu and never quite settled in another: village truck drivers and chauffeurs, construction workers, demobilized soldiers, taxi drivers, casual workers, all part of the seething demimonde which is neither of the country nor of the town. Even where his characters are firmly rooted in the village, then the village itself is changing, as urban culture, habits and concepts take hold, imperfectly understood and reflected in distorted forms. Neither proletarian nor peasant, Shukshin's people strive after a goal or an ideal without having the strength or confidence, the inner personal resources, to attain it. They are disoriented and bewildered, by turns aggressive and timid, arrogant and insecure; and their relations with their parents, spouses, children, workmates and superiors are correspondingly unstable.

Not surprisingly, therefore, the archetypal Shukshin situation is the *skandal*, the all too human conflict situation which brings out in raw and painful form the deepest feelings of the actors. One or two plot outlines will given an impression. A young man discovers that his unmarried sister is pregnant and goes like a medieval knight to demand satsifaction from her boy friend—but lights upon the *wrong* boy friend.[5] A shop assistant mistakes a customer for a drunk whom she threw out the previous evening, and the other customers, sick of waiting in the line, agree that it must be him and add their own insults, until in the end he goes to get an axe to kill someone and has to be forcibly restrained by his wife.[6] An elderly widower, anxious to propose marriage to a pious old lady in the village, asks a girl friend of his youth to act as matchmaker, but she uses the occasion to vent years of frustrated loneliness by denouncing both the prospective partners for immorality.[7] A country woman comes to visit her son in a prestigious urban hospital, but is not admitted by the concierge because it is not the right day for visiting; her son, instead of bribing the concierge or appealing to his doctor for help, discharges himself from the hospital in protest, and thus misses a vital operation.[8] A middle-aged man takes his prospective bride to a family feast to introduce her, but constantly, almost obsessively, seeks quarrels on well-worn themes with his relatives, until she walks out in embarrassment.[9] This is the stuff of Shukshin's human comedy: human feelings thrashing about, spilling out in all sorts of inappropriate, ridiculous and hurtful ways. People dream of the impossible and use unsuitable means to attain it. Semi-coherent words and phrases tumble out and form up in uncertain sentences. One sometimes has the impression that both society and language are being torn apart.

4

One can see Shukshin's world in microcosm in the story "In Profile and Full Face" (included in this collection).[10] Ivan plays out his internal drama before two audiences: first the old man, then his own mother. Both dialogues are examples of imperfect communication: with the old man because the latter has had an entirely different life experience and does not understand what is biting Ivan, with his mother because of her desperate desire to persuade him to stay in the village with her. The old man, who has struggled all his life to have enough to fill his belly, does not understand why Ivan cannot be satisfied with the modest but sufficient living he would make as an ordinary farm worker. Ivan refuses to do this, not only out of professional pride as a skilled worker, but also because he wants his work to have some purpose. The old man's generation he sees as "cavemen" (*dremuchie*) with no "horizons." The two of them conduct a dialogue which fails to meet in the middle. Ivan's most important profession of faith, "Ia ne fraer" (I'm not a sucker—not a chump) goes over the old man's head because it is couched in slang he does not even understand. Ivan's real feelings break out in snatches of song accompanied by explosive chords on the guitar. The two of them have only one thing really in common: the bottle of home-brewed vodka. Their drinking together constitutes a minimal human contact.

Ivan's dialogue with his mother is no more coherent, this time because the emotional charge is so great that it constitutes a barrier to communication. In the mother's conception of the world, as in the old man's, one yields to authority, begs and bribes where necessary, but takes one's lot and does not assert oneself. Her son's abrupt sense of his own worth she sees simply as an unfortunate mode of communication, not as part of his essence—especially since her aim for him, as a quiet and loving companion to her old age, is quite different from his own. Ivan, for his part, responds sufficiently to her love to want to shut himself off still further and not take any part in the dialogue beyond the muttering of discouraging monosyllables. Only once does he break out with "Ma, this is hard for me too."

At the center of Ivan's personality, what we see here in these two dialogues, as it were, "in profile and full face," is an alienation which he expresses in the following image:

> I was a bystander once: one fellow punched another in the glasses and ruined his eyesight. And there I was sitting in the court and couldn't understand what I was doing there. All over a stupid fight. All right, so I saw it happen—so what? I was in a terrible state throughout the trial.... It's just like that now. I sit here and think "What am I doing here?" The trial was a long one, but at least it eventually came to an end and I went away. But where can I go from here? There's nowhere to go.

Characteristically, the old man understands this image in the light of his own concerns: "There's only one way out of here: to the other world."

But the image actually captures much of contemporary Soviet society: indeed it is the one which Terts uses in *Sud idet* [The trial begins]. The leading positions in the Soviet power hierarchy and in the media are occupied by people who see life as a kind of trial conducted by those who are in the right against those who are in the wrong. The majority of the population, not feeling themselves to be in either category, can only stand by and observe with a strong sense of non-involvement. Ivan, for his part, embraces this non-involvement as his fate, and strides out of the village, kicking aside, metaphorically and literally, the only two beings who care for him in the world, his mother and his dog. "One must live alone in this world. Then it will be easy."

Shukshin's technique as a narrator is largely to let his characters speak for themselves. But he does not entirely remove himself from the text. Indeed, the very opening paragraph is unequivocally an authorial comment:

> An old man was sitting on the bench by his front gate. He felt as weary and dull as the warm evening which was drawing on. Long ago he, too, had known his morning sunshine, when he had stepped out boldly and felt the earth light beneath his feet. Now, however, it was evening and peaceful, with a touch of mist over the village.

Having established this explicit correspondence between the old man's mind and the state of the external world, Shukshin can allow the acrid smoke and the occasional bursts of flame from the bonfire to suggest the mood of his personages. Similarly the smell of the morning smoke, dry, wooden and unstoked, corresponds to the overnight change in Ivan's mood as he faces the prospect of immediate departure. These authorial interventions are couched in a language which the characters would not actually have spoken but which they would have understood, and whose image content is wholly within their comprehension and experience. In effect they are a kind of meeting point between the author and his characters. I think they are quite effective in this function, though it is arguable that Shukshin should have confined himself to a minimum of scene-setting and let his characters do the bulk of the communication of mood as well as the narration.

The best known of Shukshin's uprooted heroes by now is certainly Egor Prokudin, the chief personage of *Snowball Berry Red [Kalina krasnaia]* (included in this collection), which as a film has made a name for its author, director and principal actor all over the world. Egor is a classic victim of Soviet social experimentation. Brought up as a small child in a Siberian village, he became separated from his mother probably during the famine of 1932-34, and has never seen her since (till the events of the story). When the old people of the villages round about get together, they discuss the fates which befell their families at the time of the "dekulakization," so we know this is a memory which is still living, indeed dominant, in the villagers' lives, rather as the unemployment of the thirties continued to dominate the social and political outlook of American and British working people long after the Second World War. The collectivization, dekulakization and famine form the setting in which Egor's life must be seen.[11]

We do not know what Egor has done since early childhood (though the novel *Krazha* [The Theft], by Viktor Astaf'ev, with its depiction of a Siberian orphanage or *detdom*, might fill in some of the details), except that he fell in with a gang of criminals, and, when we first meet him, is just finishing a spell in a labor camp. We first see him awkwardly but conscientiously booming out the line of the bass bell in a chorus: a kind of symbol for his subsequent clumsy efforts to find harmony in social life outside. The main plot is concerned with his attempt to break way from the life of crime and settle down, in a village not far from his birthplace, with a woman to whom he has been writing from the camp. He fails. The gang catches up with him and murders him. But even apart from the harsh laws of the underworld, he has not the inner constancy to tolerate a settled way of life. The roots, the traditions, the sense of identity, are lacking.

This is apparent from the very start, when, in conversation with the camp commandant, he reveals that he knows virtually nothing about cows.[12] His desire to settle down with a cow and a plot of land sounds simply quixotic. Later on he shows that he has not the faintest idea how to take a bath in a village bathhouse— one of the fundamental rituals of the Russian peasant way of life: instead of pouring boiling water on the stones in order to produce steam, he pours it directly over the shoulders of his bathing companion, who rushes out naked into the yard shrieking.[13] His country childhood was so brief and broken off so prematurely (we are not told at precisely what age) that it has left him with none of the peasant's customs or skills, only with a few memories that form the one untroubled portion of his mind. He finds a certain distant echo of this serenity when he is ploughing on the tractor, but he does not believe he can really find peace again—as indeed he does not: the birch copse at the end of the furrow is the place where the gang kills him.[14] He resumes his unity with the soil, in the narrator's eyes, only after death:

> And there he lay, a Russian peasant on his native steppe, not far from home... He lay with his cheek pressed to the earth, as though he were listening to something that only he could hear.[15]

For most of the story, Egor is seen as a person perpetually unable to form stable relationships with others, though he has a yearning for such stability, and even a distant inkling of what it might be like if he could attain it. He tries to find stability with Lyuba, the woman to whom he has been writing from the camp, but it is symptomatic that he only goes to see her after his criminal associates have been raided by the police and he has not found anyone else to take him in. Half-measures and sharp changes of direction characterize all his actions. Furthermore, when Lyuba declines to let him into her bed on the very first night, he rushes off to the nearest town, not necessarily intending to return, and organizes a "debauch" with his release money and the help of a friendly waiter. This is just another variant, another attempt to find what he is looking for. And it does not work, because the fellow debauchees whom the waiter finds for him are so repulsive. "All the good-looking ones," he tells Egor, "are married, with families." Egor sees the force of this and rushes back again to Lyuba who, a forgiving woman battered already by life with an alcoholic husband, takes him in once more.

Egor's attempt to find stability in a job is no more successful. He has a great piece of luck, landing the prestigious job of chauffeur to the sovkhoz director, but abandons it on the first day because he cannot stand the limited and convention-bound relationship of driver and passenger ("I feel all the time as though I'm laughing at you.").[16] The tractor-driving job, which is broken off by his murder, does at least have the advantage of solitude, and who knows... We are left to speculate whether he could have found peace that way.

Most painful of all is Egor's relationship to his mother. When he goes with Lyuba to see her, he has to do so incognito and in dark glasses: without these protections the return of feeling would be too agonizing. Strong emotions express themselves in him not in tears, but in a steely set expression of the face (which Shukshin as actor conveys excellently on the screen) and a vice-like grip of the hand (the film unfortunately has him beat the earth and weep after leaving his mother, which is quite inconsistent with the rest of his character, and does not figure in the published text). Tears he cannot stand in anybody, and he gives his feelings dynamic expression only in occasional snatches of song, or in ridiculous professions of love addressed to birch trees.

Egor does not, then, really succeed in breaking out of the pattern which has dominated his life. Good relationships for him are brief ones, as with the taxidriver who drives him out of the prison settlement. The criminal community, with its tense goal-oriented relationships, embroidered by a little noncommittal sex, is his logical home, and the fact that it reclaims him violently at the end is not simply the intervention of an external force: indeed, he submits more or less voluntarily to his death.

* * *

Some of Shukshin's stories take us further than the portrayal of personalities torn about by rapid social change. Indeed a changing society is not necessarily essential to their peculiarities. This becomes clear if one reads Shukshin's two long novels, *Liubaviny* [The Liubavin family] and *Ia prishel dat' vam voliu* [I have come to give you freedom] ,[17] which, though springing from very different periods of Russian history, also portray restless, explosive personalities. *Liubaviny* depicts an Altai village in the 1920s, where the Soviet system has as yet scarcely even taken hold. Traditional village life continues more or less as it has for generations, and the major changes are still to come.

8

Yet the impression one has is not of harmony and mutual cooperation as, say, Vasily Belov might have described it, for example, in his novel *Kanuny* [The eve]. It is true, there is a long description of communal haymaking and of the evening singing and dancing which follow it, so that one is given some idea of the solidarity of inherited rural culture. But by and large it is the divisions within the village which are emphasized. Routine agricultural life is seen as austere and restricted, demanding from the peasants a degree of self-denial such that from time to time lusty and violent impulses cannot but break out. After the particularly hard labor of the harvest period the peasants

> imperceptibly turned into animals. There was a thudding of clubs and a crashing of broken crockery. An evil spirit welled up and broke out. At one end of the village sons rose against fathers, at the other end fathers against sons. Grudges going back a year were dredged up.[18]

What the peasant yearns for is *volia,* freedom from work, from cares and from the continuous repression which his way of life demands. This *volia* can take many forms. At times a sunset, or the sounds and smells of spring, can lift the grey pall which hangs over peasant perceptions to reveal something beyond. At one stage the villagers are shown rehearsing a play for presentation at the village club (with the purely utilitarian purpose of shaming rich peasants into parting with their grain), but, in the course of acting, the imaginary world they are thinking themselves into takes on a life of its own:

> They did not want to leave the village Soviet building. They wanted to stay on and think up ever new twists, to go on laughing and playing the fool. They were all in such a good mood. They had suddenly discovered a source of joy.[19]

But these interludes are rare. In general, the continual self-imposed privation leads to an accumulation of longing for freedom and spontaneity which makes the peasant a subconscious brother of the bandit. And indeed, whenever there is trouble in the village, violence flares up and someone gets killed, the murderer has to go off to the hills and become an outlaw. There is a persistent mutual symbiosis between the village community and the gang of bandits in the hills: each is necessary to the other for its way of life. The party and the Soviet government are trying to break into this vicious circle by building a village school and eradicating illiteracy, but the progress they make in the course of the novel is not encouraging. Indeed, Kuz'ma, the youth who is supposed to be representing the party, gets himself involved in the old round of feuding by marrying a village girl whom others have coveted.

The more one reads Shukshin, the more one discovers that most of the heroes of his short stories share, in one way or another, this longing for *volia,* or for something analogous to it. They are seeking to break out of the here and now, the immediate and empirical, the always imperfect, into some other, imagined world of freedom and perfection. This transcendent world can appear to them in many different forms. For the peasants of *Liubaviny*, singing, dancing and play-acting offer moments of release. For other characters it takes different forms: for young men, love, a worthy job, dreams of the future, of building a better world (the mode of transcendence sought by the traditional Socialist Realist hero), for old men reflecting on death and musing about the past, for all men story-telling, art and religion. If there is nothing else, then there is, of course, always drink, a very prevalent form of the search for transcendence.

In this sense, an archetypal Shukshin character is Stepka (from the story of that name),[20] who escapes from prison a mere three months before his sentençe expires (though he knows he is bound to be caught and sentenced to two further years) simply because it is springtime and he wants to see his village and family. He spends an intoxicating afternoon and evening among his loved ones, and then tells the policeman who comes to arrest him:

> "It doesn't matter... I've charged up my batteries now *(podkrepilsia)*, and I can take prison for a bit longer. My dreams were tormenting me—every night I would dream about the village... It's fantastic here in spring, isn't it?"

But of course he has not taken into account the suffering his premature dash for freedom will cause his family. The pain of joyful celebration followed by instant parting is expressed at the end in the large eyes and clumsily passionate gestures of his dumb sister.

This search for freedom is an amoral force. Another of Shukshin's springtime escapees is the unnamed youth of "Okhota zhit' " [I want to live]. Like Stepka he has given no forethought to his escape, and finds himself wandering through the taiga without a gun, facing certain death if he should chance upon a bear. An old forester gives him haven in his hut, they talk together, and the young man tells him what induced him to make his break:

> "You don't know how bright the lights are in a great city. They beckon to you. There are such dear, sweet people there, and it's warm and comfortable, and there's music playing. People are very civil there—and very afraid of death. Now, when I walk through a city, it belongs to me, see? So why should they be there while I am out here?... It's me who ought by rights to be there, because I'm not afraid of anybody. I'm not afaid of death, so life belongs to me."[21]

This Kirillovian position has its own terrifying logic. The old man feels compassion for the young man's youth, strength and beauty, and lends him a gun so that he can shoot his way out of the taiga if necessary. This gun the lad uses to kill the old man, so that there will be no danger of his escape being reported. The lad may not be afraid of his own death, but other people's deaths certainly do not worry him either.

The search for transcendence can also be funny, as in the case of Bronka Pupkov, the incongruously named hero of "Milles pardons, madame" (included in this collection). Bronka is the eternal *neudachnik,* the man who makes a mess of everything. The missing two fingers on his right hand ought by rights to be an honorable war wound, but in fact he blew them off when trying to get a drink in winter by breaking the ice on the river with the butt of his rifle.

The highly improbable story which Bronka recounts to his tourist charges is really only a luxuriant embroidery on his own nagging sense of personal failure, and after its recital he sits for hours by the riverside, in an almost mystical trance, and thereafter has to drink continuously for two days in order to recover. But the story deeply impresses his urban listeners, not brought up on the rich rural traditions of *vran'e,* and this is a catharsis for him, a public acting out of his personal inadequacy which perhaps is all that preserves him from permanent drinking. It is arguable that *vran'e* is a characteristically Russian mode of seeking the transcendent.[22] As Abram Terts has commented: "The Russian people drink not from need and not from grief, but from an age-old requirement for the miraculous and the extraordinary—they drink, if you will, mystically, striving to transport the soul beyond earth's gravity and restore it to its sacred non-corporeal state." And, in a less obsessive and self-centered form, it lies at the basis of imaginative literature.

The theme of creative art is one which Shukshin explores in the story "The Master" (included in this collection). Haunted by the beautiful church he has discovered, Semka Rys reflects on the aspirations of its original builder:

> What had he wanted, that unknown master, in leaving behind this fairy tale in weightless stone? Was he honoring God, or was he merely displaying his talent? But one who wishes to show off his talent does not stray far away from the crowd; he strives to get as close as possible to the high roads, or better yet, right in the middle of the crowded city square—there he'd be noticed for sure. But this one had been concerned about something else—beauty perhaps? Like the man who sang a song, sang it well, and went on his way. Why had he done it? Perhaps he himself did not know. Something to satisfy his soul... He too had felt happy about his work; he too had felt moved inside, and had understood that it was beautiful. But what of it? Nothing. If you know how to be happy, be happy. If you know how to make people happy, make them happy. If you can't do that, go ahead and make war, be a leader or something like that. You could even destroy this fairy tale here: put about two kilograms of dynamite under it, and it would be shattered and gone. To each his own.[23]

This extended reflection contains the kernel of the whole story. The transcendent world of the artist and the empirical world of the soldier and politician are directly counterposed to one another, and their collision is played out in the rest of the story. The chief architect's blunt utilitarian judgment has a shattering effect on Semka. His creative impulses are thwarted; what he had thought to make partly his own is taken away from him altogether. What he had considered beautiful and pristine is officially stated to be merely derivative and expedient. Semka takes offence as against a living person, never goes again to look at "his" church, and even avoids the village in which it is situated.

For old men, release and greater understanding come with looking backwards. Reflections, memories reveal the meaning of a whole life, and sometimes uncover an unexpected beauty in it. "Dumy" [Thoughts] [24] portrays the reminiscences of an elderly collective farm chairman, provoked by the nightly recurring (and initially infuriating) serenade of a village lad courting his girl. This sound inexplicably lifts Matvei right out of the everyday world of work and worry, and back to a night in his early teens when he had rushed on a horse from the meadows back to the village at night to fetch milk for his sick brother.

> Man and horse became one and sped together into the dark night. And the night sped towards them, the heavy scent of dew-damp grass meeting their face. A kind of wild rapture seized the lad, the blood coursed thumping through his head... He wasn't thinking about his brother's being ill at that moment. He wasn't thinking about anything at all. His spirit soared, and every vein in his body thrilled.

In his memories of that night, Matvei is conscious of penetrating into a strange region which has little in common with his ordinary life as chairman of a farm:

> He would hear the accordion playing far off down a side street. And immediately a kind of malaise would come over him. A strange, even welcome malaise. Without it something was missing.

This mood leads to reflections on love and death, subjects which either do not exist for him in his everyday life, or have turned into prosaic equivalents: love into marriage, death into the mere cessation of life, a dull fear at the back of everyone's mind. This dichotomy is suggested in Matvei's intermittent attempts to convey his feelings to his sleepy wife.

Then, when the accordion player duly gets married and no longer uses public means to woo his beloved, the vital trigger disappears, and Matvei loses touch with his malaise, relapsing into the everyday world where he smokes, sleeps badly and drinks too much.

Death is an important theme in Shukshin's work, a final frontier which forces—and enables—his old and sick to understand more about their lives. It is presented in its simplest form in "Kak pomiral starik" ("How the Old

Man Died"—included in this collection).[25] The old man dying is concerned with practical, this-worldly things: instructions to relatives, the question of who will dig his grave in the frost. At the same time, he is already abstracted from this world in a way that gives its affairs a new meaning. He has a "severe" and "solemn" expression on his face, a look of "other-worldly peace" (nezdeshnii pokoi). He is not a believer, and refuses extreme unction, but nevertheless an utterance that starts as a routine profanity turns into an invocation: " 'O Lord, O Lord...' The old man heaved a deep sigh. 'Lord, maybe you do exist, forgive me, a sinner.' " Not something he would have said in the prime of life: whether it is weakness or insight we are left to speculate.

In death the real meaning of a man's life, his work, his beliefs, his worth, stand out with greater relief. In "Diadia Ermolai" [Uncle Ermolai] [26] the narrator stands at his uncle's grave and remembers how he once lied bare-facedly to him as a boy, thinking him fussy and officious. Now he thinks quite differently about him and his peasant existence, and these thoughts turn into a re-evaluation of his own life:

> "He was an unsparing worker, and a good, honest man. Like everybody here, when you come to think of it... Grandad, grandma. Simple enough, really. But somehow I can't think it through, what with college and all my books. *Did* their life have some great meaning? Can it be found in the way they lived it? Or was there no meaning, just work and more work...? They worked and they bore children. I've seen lots of different people in my life since then, not idlers, no, but... Somehow they all see their life differently. And so do I. Only, when I look at these grave mounds I wonder which of us is right, which of us has really understood things better."

In "Dozhd' na zare" [Rain at dawn] [27] death brings the final confrontation of two long-established enemies, Efim, a party activist and former dekulakizer (now dying in a village hospital) and Kirill, a peasant whom he once expropriated and exiled. Their dialogue is bitter, but the sharp edge has been abstracted from their conflict by the passing of time. Kirill is not a believer—he understands man's peace of mind in terms of a purely secular conscience: "He who has hurt people in his lifetime does not die easy." From the position of moral superiority this implies he asks Efim what *he* had lived for. Efim replies: "So that there should be fewer fools around." Kirill counters:

> "You're a fool yourself. You used to keep on and on about a 'new life,' 'a new life'... You didn't know how to live yourself, and you prevented others from living. You made a mess of your life, Efim."

This judgment is delivered with cheerful, unrancorous finality. Some kind of attraction, even compassion, brings Kirill back to the hospital to see how his old enemy is getting on, and in fact he is present when Efim dies. He

13

feels a certain genuine sorrow for him, and as he goes off into the early morning, a warm rain breaks a long sustained drought. There is no real reconciliation between the two men, but the ending (reinforced by the story's title) suggests the author's hope that the burning hatred which has parched so much of the Soviet Union's social and political life may be passing as death takes away some of the old enemies and helps to bring others together. This is a hope which Shukshin has not been alone in feeling: it underlies, for example, the semi-senile reconciliation of Olesha Smolin and Aviner Kozonkov in Vasily Belov's *Plotnitskie Rasskazy*. On the other hand, Shukshin himself denies it in a later story, "Osen'iu" [Autumn],[28] in which the central figure is another activist, Filipp. Filipp in his youth refused to marry the girl he loved, Marya, because she insisted on a church wedding, and that was against his principles. Now, in his old age, he meets Marya's funeral procession and quarrels bitterly with her widower, till they have to be almost forcibly separated by the other mourners.

If death throws new light on the meaning of life, then it naturally poses religious questions. In facing this dimension, however, Shukshin's touch is less sure. This, one may surmise, is an area which he was probing tentatively through his characters. His vision of human beings certainly makes religious answers natural, yet for the most part he actually presents religion in eccentric or neurotic forms. A kind of manichean pantheism seems to emerge as a corollary of Shukshin's selecton of plot and character, and it is directly expressed by one or two of his heroes. In " 'Veruiu!' "[29] (" 'I Believe!' "—included in this collection) Maksim is affected by what might be called a distillation of the ills of Shukshin's "seekers," a world-weariness which he calls *dusha bolit* [my soul aches], and which will not be appeased by getting into a fight, drinking or attempting suicide, or any of the other palliatives which Shukshin's characters normally apply. In the end he goes to a priest—but a highly unusual priest, who lays before Maksim a vision of life which excludes neither belief in God nor acceptance of Communism, a kind of exuberant pantheism, in which good and evil co-exist eternally, and in which each man does his own creative thing as best he can. The apotheosis of the story comes with the priest dancing a wild gopak, singing, clapping and yelling incoherent credos:

> "I believe... in aviation, in the mechanization of agriculture, in the scientific revolution. In space and weightlessness! For they are objective!... I believe that soon everyone will gather in huge stinking cities. I believe that they will suffocate there and rush back to the open fields...."

There is certainly here an element of satire on the implicit official Soviet religion, yet the vision also fits Shukshin's own outlook. He is a Soviet aware of and uneasy about his own Sovietness. The same vision is repeated in more pessimistic form in "Zaletnyi"[30] ("A Bird of Passage"—

14

included in this collection). Sanya's philosophy, worked out in sickness and repose, is one which sees both beauty and bitterness in the foundation of human life:

> "Man is an accidental, beautiful and agonizing attempt on Nature's part to understand itself. But a fruitless attempt, I assure you, because in Nature along with man there lives a canker. Death! And death is unavoidable, but we will ne-e-ever take that in. Nature will never understand itself... So it gets mad and takes vengeance in the form of mankind."

This vision illuminates the vigorous yet tormented characters who people Shukshin's stories. Man appears as a flaw in the universe, and the conflicts of Soviet society as just another confirmation of this inescapable incongruity.

Towards the end of his life, Shukshin was preoccupied with the problem of literature as society's reflection upon itself (standing towards society perhaps in the same relationship as man to nature?). The preoccupation led him to seek a new form, which he was still elaborating when his evolution was cut short. In place of the anecdotal type of story related in close identification with the principal character, he was introducing strong elements of fantasy and satire, and distancing himself from his characters. The fantasy [Povest'-skazka] "Tochka zreniia"[31] [Point of view] is an example of this. It is a satire on the Soviet literary process. The framework is the presentation of a matchmaking from two points of view, that of the Optimist and that of the Pessimist, the two of whom cannot settle their differences among themselves and go to a magician who stages the two scenes as a kind of competition. The Pessimist shows the two families obsessed with material problems, especially that of living space (zhilploshchad'); besides, the young cople accuse each other of looking for extra-marital liaisons, and the match falls through. In the Optimist's version both the families are too principled to be bothered by material questions. They are the soul of generosity: indeed the bridegroom's father proposes to give the couple a second-hand Pobeda car. The only problem is that the son's unrestrained joy at this prospect brands him as a "property-lover" in the eyes of the bride, and so, once again, the match falls through. In each case the bride's hand is won by a certain *Neponiatno Kto* (It's Not Clear Who), who silently accompanies the bridegroom's party, ignores the matchmaking, and contents himself with business-like questions about the size of the apartment. Each side of the story is presented, largely in dialogue, in a cliche-ridden language approriate to its narrator: on the Pessimist's side ragged, slangy, abusive, on the Optimist's replete with the overblown sentiments of ideological journals. The mother of the Pessimist bride reproaches grandfather, "You don't half put your grub away, Pop!"—but in the Optimist's version that comes out as 'Ah, you *do* enjoy your food, Pop!" The Pessimist's bridegroom has a clear view of how marriage generally works: "I know those tricks only too well: today you say

15

you'll think it over, and tomorrow you'll be up to all kinds of hanky-panky with the bloke next door." The Optimist's bridegroom, on the other hand, has just filled in a questionnaire on marriage which he is only too happy to quote from: "I gave special attention to the spiritual characteristics (*dukhov-nyi oblik*) of the young family, and expressed what I feel to be an interesting idea: that is, that the young family of today cannot exist without mutual understanding and friendship."

The level of perception on both sides is entirely summed up by these excerpts, and the two writers cannot settle their differences among themselves. They need an external authority in the person of a Magician to appeal to. And he, for his part, needs an "assistant for organizational matters," a grey Certain Someone who looks like a Malyuta Skuratov to the Pessimist but to the Optimist is a "tranquil, perspicacious kindly man." The two writers' ultimate banalities and contradictions are poured out to this administrative genius. He it is who turns out in the end to have been It's Not Clear Who, the figure who in each episode pulled the chestnuts out of the fire while the writers were busy distorting people's fates in their own preconceived ways. In the final scene a neighbor drives out the writers and the Magician, the families settle down to their matchmaking undisturbed, and the Certain Someone, clearly superfluous, makes his apologies and goes. As an indictment of the distortions which writers have imposed on society this could hardly be clearer.

"Do tret'ikh petukhov" [Till the cock crow thrice] [32] continues this satire, this time more unequivocally through the medium of the traditional *skazka* or fairy tale. The main personalities are some of the most familiar fairy-tale heroes, Ivan-Durak, Baba Yaga, the Wise Man, but they are reinterpreted in the light of the contemporary Soviet social and cultural situation. One night, after lights-out in the library, some of the principal figures of classical Russian literature jump down off the shelves and hold a meeting to discuss whether they can allow Ivan-Durak to remain one of their number, or whether they should expel him. (The most decided in her opposition to him is Bednaia Liza, who shares his peasant origins, but has since moved up in the world.) Eventually they take a compromise decision: that he must go and obtain from the Wise Man a note certifying that he is "intelligent" (*umnyi*). This posing of the problem indicates the direction of the satire: it is not wisdom (*um-razum*) that Ivan seeks, as in the traditional tale (and the subtitle of this work), but merely a piece of paper, a formality. Such is the nature of contemporary cultural life. And, in the event, he does not even get that: he succeeds instead in purloining a rubber stamp which satisfies the formal requirements of his quest, though nobody knows what to do with it when he brings it back. The Wise Man in the monastery turns out to be a time-server whose citadel has just been taken over by devils dressed in blue jeans, singing pop songs and dancing shameless modern dances. He is busy adapting himself to his new masters, and makes cautious statements about

16

"the possible beneficial effect of ultra-diabolical tendencies on certain well-established norms of morality..." In his spare time he visits a circle of decadent youth, headed by his world-weary "queen," Nesmeiana, to whom he takes great pleasure in presenting Ivan as a specimen of something really *narodnoe*—"of the people."

On his journey Ivan also meets Baba Yaga, who tries to use him as free labor to build herself a new hut, her daughter, who tries to seduce him, and Gorynych the three-headed serpent whose wily use of his authority nearly thwarts Ivan's quest: he regards him alternately as food to be eaten, as a peddler of folk-tales with improper endings, and as a harmless subordinate whose caprices can be satisfied along with a kick on the backside.

The one sane person in this fairy-tale is Misha the bear (always a good-humored and common sense figure in the *skazka*). But he has been ousted from his traditional lair by the devils' batterings, and has taken to drink, abandoned his family, and is now preparing to leave the countryside altogether, go into town and sell himself to a circus as the only way to survive in the modern world.

Everything speaks here of the corruption of inherited customs and culture by literary administrators and commentators, by the incursion of "diabolical" ideology and cheap mass culture, and by the natural pliability of man. Ivan himself has no defense against these influences, and if he survives it is only because he is rescued from outside: the *deus ex machina* is the only element that has survived unchanged from the traditional *skazka!*

These last works clearly represent a new departure for Shukshin, and it would be wrong to look for any general lessons or conclusions in them. By incorporating the fantastic into his repertoire of contexts he has added a certain sharpness to his perceptions. However, I am not sure that his work gains thereby. In many respects, his better works are those which are more ambiguous, and where the minus signs are a little less readily doled out. Perhaps Shukshin's great forte is the ability to present, with both humor and sympathy, the sheer *confusion* in which most people live most of their lives in most societies, moved by passions and goals often grotesquely out of key with the reality around them. When this confusion is tidied up a bit, then his characters lose some of their aura. His strength is therefore anecdote, not satire. As befits a teller of anecdotes, he gives a picture of man which is fragmented and often contradictory. He achieved no synthesis—not even in his long novels—not so much because he died young as because it was not in his nature as an artist to fashion syntheses. But he probed some of the most delicate and thorny questions about the functioning—and malfunctioning—of the individual in society, and he even sketched out a metaphysical context for hazarding some answers. He has pushed out the frontiers within which human beings can be conceived as far as any writer regularly published in the Soviet Union.

1. *Molodaia gvardiia*, 3(1962), p.110.

2. "Monolog na lestnitse," in *Kul'tura chuvstv*, ed. V. Tolstykh, (Moscow: Iskusstvo, 1968), p. 119.

3. Vasilii Shukshin, "Poslednie razgovory," *Literaturnaia gazeta* (13 XI 1974), p. 8.

4. L. Fedoseeva-Shukshina, [untitled biog. note], *Zvezda*, 6(1975), 3-4.

5. "Drugi igrishch i zabav," *Nash Sovremennik*, 9(1974), pp. 2-11.

6. "Obida," *Literaturnaia Rossiia* (12 II 1971), pp. 18-19.

7. "Svatovstvo," *Novyi mir*, 7 (1970), pp. 42-8.

8. "Van'ka Tepliashin," *Zvezda*, 2(1973), pp. 3-7.

9. "Vladimir Semenych iz myagkoi sektsii," *Literaturnaia Rossiia*, (30 III 1973), pp. 18-20.

10. "V profil' i anfas," *Novyi mir*, 9(1967), pp. 88-94.

11. *Nash sovremennik*, 4(1973), pp. 105-6, 124.

12. Ibid., p. 88.

13. Ibid., pp. 104-5.

14. Ibid., pp. 126-7, 131-2.

15. Ibid., p. 133.

16. Ibid., p. 121.

17. *Sibirskie ogni*, 6(1965), pp. 3-39; 7(1965), pp. 24-71; 8(1965), pp. 28-102; also 1(1971), pp. 3-95; 2(1971), pp. 3-122.

18. Ibid., 8(1965), pp. 70-1.

19. Ibid., p. 102.

20. *Novyi mir*, 11(1964), pp. 64-72.

21. V. Shukshin, *Tam, vdali* (Moscow: Sovetskii pisatel', 1968), pp. 15-16; in English in V. Shukshin, *I Want to Live* (Moscow: Progress Publishers, 1973), pp. 87-122.

22. There is no adequate English equivalent of the word *vran'e*, which marries the concepts of "lies," "fantasy" and "story-telling." See Ronald Hingley's superb article on the subject "That's No Lie, Comrade," *Problems of Communism*, 2 (1962), pp. 47-55.

23. *Sibirskie ogni*, 12(1971), p. 12.

24. *Novyi mir*, 9(1967), pp. 94-7; in English in *I Want to Live*, pp. 191-200.

25. Ibid., pp. 97-100.

26. *Nash sovremennik*, 9(1971), pp. 57-60.

27. *Sibirskie ogni*, 12(1966), pp. 3-7.

28. *Avrora*, 7(1973), pp. 38-41.

29. *Zvezda*, 9(1971), pp. 24-30.

30. V. Shukshin, *Besedy pri iasnoi lune* (Moscow: Sovetskaia Rossiia, 1974), pp. 135-41.

31. *Zvezda*, 7(1974), pp. 108-35; after this article was written it was learned that Shukshin might have written "Tochka zreniia" as early as 1967.

32. *Nash sovremennik*, 1(1975), pp. 28-61.

SNOWBALL BERRY RED
AND OTHER STORIES

IN PROFILE AND FULL FACE[1]

An old man was sitting on the bench by his front gate. He felt as weary and dull as the warm evening which was drawing on. Long ago he, too, had known his morning sunshine, when he had stepped out boldly and felt the earth light beneath his feet. Now, however, it was evening, and peaceful, with a touch of mist over the village.

A thin gangling youth with a lined face sat down on the bench beside him. Young men like that look spindly, but actually they have the stamina of a horse. And they sweat well in a steambath, too.

The lad sighed deeply and lit a cigarette.

"Not working?" the old man asked.

"Well, I'm not exactly merry-making, grandad," Ivan said, after a pause. "It's enough to make you weep. Have you got a ruble-fifty on you?"

"Huh, what a hope!"

"Ugh, my head's splitting."

"How's working going, then?"

"It ain't. 'Get yourself a pitchfork,' he says, 'and report to the cowshed.' "

"Who, the director?"

"Yes, the director. And me with three different job certificates and nearly nine years of school as well. So I told him, 'Sweat it out yourself, if you're so eager.' "

"Hm. How long did they confiscate your driver's license for?"

"A year. And I only drank a mug of beer. Well, and a glass of red wine. But he was on to me like a shot... He'd been watching his chance for months, the pig. So I told him where to get off, and then he really turned nasty..."

"Ah, you know, lad, you're mighty hard to get along with... You should watch your step. What'll you do with them now? They're the bosses."

"Well, and so what?"

"You'll just have to stay where you are, that's what. You may have three certificates, but that won't help. You should learn when to hold your tongue."

In the garden plots they were burning the old stalks in preparation for ploughing. Every year it was exactly the same, yet one would never tire of breathing in the acrid, mouldering smell

21

of smoke and damp earth.

"Aye, you should learn when to hold your tongue, son," repeated the old man, gazing at the bonfires in the gardens. "That's our lot in life."

"But I don't really swear at them or anything," Ivan grumbled. "At least, only if one of them really gets his teeth into me... And anyway, the thing is, I didn't even break the law!" he shouted out exasperatedly. "How can you confiscate somebody's driver's license for a year just for a mug of beer and a glass of wine? The bastard."

"Take a look over the fence. Is my old woman in the garden?"

"Why?"

"Under the stove I've got a bottle of my home brew. I could bring it out to cure your hangover."

Ivan got up quickly and looked into the garden.

"She's there," he said. "In the far corner. She's not watching."

The old man went into the house and returned with a bottle of his spirit and a bunch of spring onions. And a glass.

"Why didn't you say straight away you had some of this?" asked Ivan impatiently. "Sitting there keeping quiet about it." He poured a glass and threw it back in one gulp. "I prefer the real home-made brew to the factory stuff: it has a good strong smell, like petrol. You don't pussy-foot around in front of it. Kkha! There, have one yorself. In one gulp, mind."

The old man drank unhurriedly, nibbling at an onion.

"Like petrol, isn't it?"

"What do you mean, like petrol? It's ordinary, home-made vodka."

"Well, there we are!" Ivan slapped his chest. "Now life seems worth living again. Thanks, grandad. Want a smoke?" He held out a packet of "Pamir" cigarettes.

The old man took one, fumbling with his stiff fingers, rolled it over and over again, stared at it, and then took a light from Ivan.

"Does Petya write?" Ivan asked him.

"Uh-huh. But I'll be dead soon, anyway, Ivan."

Ivan looked up at him in surprise: "Come off it!"

"There's no getting round it." The old man spoke calmly.

"Have you got a pain then somewhere?"

"No. I just feel it. When you're my age, you'll feel it too."

Ivan was in a good mood from the vodka, and didn't feel like talking about death.

"Come off it!" he said. "You've got plenty of life in you yet. Would you like me to fetch my accordion?"

"Aye, you do that."

Ivan crossed the road, went into his house... and did not return for a long time. Eventually he appeared with his accordion, but once again frowning.

"My mother," he said. "Of course, you can't help feeling sorry for her..."

"You're still bent on leaving, then?"

"Well, what else can I do?" Ivan had evidently just said the same thing to his mother. "I can't work in that... Oh, to hell with it, why talk about it? You know something?—I've already sailed the Northern Sea Route... and I'm a motor mechanic, and a grade-five metalworker... Okay then, I won't drive for a year, but do they really expect me to... Oh, what's the point, to hell with it," he squeezed the accordion, struck up a tune, and then abandoned it. He became downcast. "I get all the rotten luck, grandad, I really do. I got married in Eastern Siberia, remember? We had a little daughter... But then my wife pulled a surprise act—cleared off home to her ma in Leningrad. What d'you make of that?" He would often tell the story of his marriage.

"Why to Leningrad?"

"Oh, she was only working off her college years in Eastern Siberia. I don't care about the wife, to hell with her, but I do miss my daughter. I dream of her sometimes."

"Are you going to see her now when you leave?"

"My wife?! She's been married again for more than a year... She's young and good-looking, the bitch."

"Where are you off to, then?"

"To see an old mate... In the mines. Maybe not for good. Maybe for a year or so..."

"Young people don't seem able to go away just for a year nowadays. They all seem to leave for good now, without a second thought."

"Well, what would I do here?" Ivan flared up again. "Go and work in the... oh, to hell with it!" He pulled out the accordion and started to play, singing with a forced, almost vindictive gaiety:

So I was living with this woman,
Tarum-tarum-tum-tum,
And this woman, see, she left me,
She left me just like that!
Got frightened, did you, darling,
When the fun came to an end?

The old man still sat peacefully listening.

23

"I make 'em up," Ivan said. "As I go along. I can sing the whole night though."

So we won't take up our poses—
In profile and full face;
In a little golden frame...

"You ask for trouble, you do, Vanya," the old man broke in. "You could just as well put in a year here, looking after the pigs. You should think of your mother. She's been alone all her life."

Ivan broke off and sat silent awhile.

"That isn't the point, grandad. What galls me is that they could perfectly well have found me a job. D'you think they couldn't do with another metalworker? I ask you!.. The point is, the director's got a grudge against me as well. I took his daughter home a couple of times from the club, and he started to get up-tight. With good reason: she's fair game for anybody. And I know how to handle a woman... I could have given him quite a surprise. Pity I didn't."

You mean, got her in the family way?"

"Uh-huh. A nice little surprise for Mother's Day."

"Aye, you could have done that in style."

"Ah, I feel really low, grandad. I don't know why. I just don't feel like doing anything, like I'm just a... what d'you call it... a bystander. I was a bystander once: one fellow punched another in the glasses, and ruined his eyesight. And there I was sitting in the court and couldn't understand what I was doing there. All over a stupid fight. All right, so I saw it happen—so what? I was in a terrible state throughout the trial." Ivan looked over at the bonfires in the garden plots, sighed and fell silent. "It's just like that now. I sit here and think, 'What am I doing here?' The trial was a long one, but at least it eventually came to an end and I went away. But where can I go from here? There's nowhere to go."

"There's only one way out of here—to the other world."

Ivan poured out another glass and drank it.

"There's no happiness in life," he said and spat. "Shall I pour you some?"

"No, that's enough."

"Well, was your life a happy one?"

The old man sat in silence for a time.

"At your age I didn't think like that," he began quietly. "I used to do enough work for three people. Why, if you were to take just the grain I grew, you could probably feed the whole village for a year. I had no time to think the way you do."

"But I don't know what I'm working for. Do you understand? I was taken on, I do my bit. But if you ask me why, I don't know. Just to stuff myself? Well, okay, then, my belly's full—now what?" Ivan's question was serious: he paused to see what the old man would say. "Now what, eh? I feel like a damp rag."

"When you've got enough to eat, you start getting choosy," the old man explained.

"You don't know how it is with us. You had no horizons in your day, so you were satisfied... You were cavemen. I could live the way you used to, but I need something more."

"Pour me one," the old man asked. He drank and then spat. "Centipedes," he suddenly burst out. "You scamper hither and yon, and where does it get you? Look at all the cars they make nowadays—ugh! Where d'you think cancer comes from? From your bloody petrol, from the fumes. Soon you'll forget how to produce children..."

"Huh, that's not likely."

"You realize there's something wrong with your lives, but you still insist on your 'hori-i-izons'! Well, what are you belly aching about, then?"

"Ho, what's biting you? Sore because I called you a caveman? Well, what are you, then?"

"You're layabouts. Think yourselves clever! Look how a young fellow behaves nowadays: they offer him a ruble-twenty-five a trip—okay, so he could easily earn four rubles a day, but not on your life: he does two trips and unharnesses his horses. A great strapping lad, bursting with health. Now, I only used to get a quarter of a labor-day per trip, and I used to do five a day, sometimes with three or four carts behind me. And even when I'd earned my labor-day, I'd have to wait a year to see how much I'd get paid for it. Often it was only chicken-feed. And you complain you don't know what you're working for! You can't be bothered to earn fifteen hundred rubles a month, while I used to break my back right through the summer for a few miserable kopecks."

"But I don't need that much money," said Ivan, as though to provoke him. "Don't you see that? It's something else I need."

"You don't need the money, yet you haven't a ruble-fifty to your name for a drink. So you go scrounging instead... Don't need it, indeed. While your mother shrivels up working. It's criminal... Layabouts. The sun's still way up in the sky, and they're already coming back from the fields. In lorries, singing!.. There's workmen for you! All they do is whistle at the girls and make little surprises for Mother's Day..."

"No, life'll never be... I suppose in theory you're right, but after all a horse works, too..."

25

"You think it's a disgrace to work for a while in the pigsty! But it's not a disgrace to eat meat, I dare say?"

"You'll never understand, grandad," sighed Ivan.

"How can we understand?"

"As I say, I've eaten as much as I want already. So what now? I don't know. But I do know this doesn't suit me. I can't work just to fill my stomach."

Just to fill my stomach, oh,
Tum-tarum-tum-tum...

He sang.

The old man gave a laugh.

"You, rascal. Why did your wife leave you? Did you drink, eh?"

"The thing is, grandad, I'm not a chump. I was a first-grade specialist in the navy. Why did she leave?.. I don't know. Probably because I wasn't a chump."

"What's that again?"

"Doesn't matter." Ivan put his accordion down on the bench, lit a cigarette, and sat silent for a while. Suddenly he said without any flippancy and with a certain veiled alarm, even anguish, in his voice: "It's true I don't know what I'm living for."

"You should get married."

"It's crazy. I'm no fool, am I? But how do I find peace of mind? I don't even know where to look. How stupid can one get?"

"Get married. That'll stop you fretting. You'll have other things on your mind."

"No, that's not right either. I've got to be consumed by love. Fat chance of that here!.. I don't get it. Am I the only fool that feels this way, or does everybody—only they all keep quiet about it?.. You know, at night I lie awake thinking and thinking, and I feel so rotten I could cry. What's it all for?"

"Ugh!" the old man shook his head. "People are going to the dogs."

Meanwhile the day gently declined, melting away in the damp warmth. It was getting darker and darker. The flames in the gardens flared brighter. And the smell of smoke grew sharper. Far into the evening people would burn the old stalks and leaves and chat to one another. Their voices would carry clearly and the noise and bustle of the village would die away. Then it would get completely dark. The flames in the gardens would go out. And somewhere, very near, a man's deep voice would say:

"Oh, well, let's call it a day."

26

* * * * * *

The next day dawned as noisy, bright and full-throated as the previous one had faded peacefully, gently and sadly. The cocks crowed all over the village. People bestirred themselves and bustled about, losing no time.

Ivan got up early. He sat on his bed and stared at the floor. He felt sick and tense. He started to get dressed.

His mother was fanning up the stove, and he smelt smoke again, only now it was different: woody and dry, a morning smell. When his mother opened the door and went into the street, the air from outside smelled fresh from puddles covered by bright, glassy ice, from clods of earth dappled with touches of hoarfrost, from yesterday's bonfires, whose ash was now grey, moist and heavy, and from fallen leaves which had dampened in the spring but still rustled loudly whenever anyone walked through them.

"What if I went to the director and asked him?.." his mother began.

Ivan was shaving.

"You're joking. Why don't you go on bended knees: he'll be really tickled."

"Well, what's to be done, then?" His mother was trying not to whine, and to make her points as telling as possible, realizing that this was probably their last conversation. "People do go and ask for things. My tongue won't drop off..."

"I've been. And asked."

"I know you, son. You don't ask. You put your nose in the air and bark out orders..."

"Stop it, ma."

His mother could stand it no longer. She sat down on the step, began to cry quietly and wailed: "Where do you think you'll finish up? In some god-forsaken hole... Was I condemned from birth to suffer all my days? Why do you think only of yourself, my son?"

Ivan had known there would be tears. That was why he had felt so lousy. And tense. And why he had frowned in anticipation.

"Anyone would think you were seeing me off to war. What's so dreadful?.. Ah, damn it all! Always tears, whatever I do. I can't get away from them."

"I could easily go and ask—he isn't made of stone, he would find you something. Or why don't you see the inspector? Why leave straight away like this? When they confiscated Kolya Za-vyalov's license, why, the lad went and had a word with them... A quiet word is all that's needed..."

27

"But the police already have my license. It's too late."

"Well, you could go to the police station, then..."

"Oh-ho!" exclaimed Ivan. "Just catch me going there!"

"O Lord, O Lord... All my life it's been like this. Why have I been singled out for this misery? Am I damned?.."

It was getting too much for him. Ivan went out to the yard, washed at the hand-basin, and stood for a moment at the gate in his undershirt... He looked at the village. He knew everything in it. He had waited longingly in those alleyways on moonlit nights... And now he didn't feel in himself the firmness he would have liked before a long journey. Not that he was afraid to go, but he would have preferred to have a proper grip on himself, and to feel a bit more cheer in parting.

His dog, Dick, appeared from nowhere—a good-looking dog, but a mongrel—and jumped up to lick him.

"Down!" Ivan brushed him off and went inside.

His mother was setting the table.

"Why don't you try it just for a bit in the pigsty?"

They are persistent, mothers are. And helpless.

"Not a hope," said Ivan firmly. "I'd have the whole village laughing at me. I know why he wants to shove me into the pigsty. Well, it won't work."

"O Lord, O Lord..."

... They ate breakfast.

His mother packed everything in a suitcase, and then sat on the floor in front of the open lid and started to cry again. This time without saying anything.

"I'll work for a year or so and then come back. What's the matter with you?.."

"Let me go and try, son?" She looked up at her son, and her eyes were full of grief, entreaty, hope and despair. "I'll get round him. He's a good sort."

"Oh, ma... This is hard for me, too."

"Or perhaps you could slip one of the policemen something. You think they'd refuse? Of course, they wouldn't! D'you think Kolya Zavyalov didn't slip them something? Of course, he did... And they returned his license to him just like that."

"It'd be more to the point if *they* bribed *me*."

The next stage was to say goodbye to the stove. Whenever Ivan left on a long journey, his mother made him kiss the stove three times and say: "Mother stove, as you have given me food and drink, bless me for my long journey." And each time she would remind him of the words, though he had long known them by heart.

28

Ivan pecked the stove's warm brow three times and repeated: "Mother stove, as you have given me food and drink, bless me for my long journey."

... And they set off down the street, mother, son and dog.

Ivan didn't want his mother to see him off, didn't want people to stare out of their windows and say: "Vanya's off somewhere, is he?"

On the way they meet the old man with whom Ivan had talked the previous evening. Ivan stopped. It occurred to him that his mother, after chatting awhile, would not walk on, but turn round and go back with their neighbor.

"So you're off."

"Yes, I'm off."

They both lit cigarettes.

"Been fishing?"

"I've put the nets out just in case. But it's early yet."

"Yes, that's true."

His mother stood to one side, clutching her hands in her apron, not listening to the conversation, but gazing thoughtfully, or perhaps unthinkingly, in the direction her son was about to take.

"Don't start drinking there," grandad advised. "You know what the town is like: everyone's a stranger there. Feel your way first..."

"What d'you think I am, an alcoholic?"

They stood still a moment.

"Well, God be with you!" said the old man.

"You, too."

The old man went on his way. Ivan glanced at his mother... Staring in front of her as before, she strode out in the direction they both had to go. Ivan walked beside her.

They went a little way.

"Ma... you go home now."

His mother stopped obediently. Ivan put his arm around her... Her head quivered against his chest. That was always the worst moment. He must push her away, turn around and go.

"Right, then, ma... You go on back. Nohing will happen to me! People are always going on journeys. So off you go."

His mother made the sign of the cross over him... And then just stood there. But Ivan walked on. His stupid dog started to chase after him. It always went to work with its master.

"Go away!" said Ivan angrily.

Dick wagged his tail and went running on ahead.

"Dick! Dick!" Ivan called.

Dick ran up to him. Ivan kicked him hard. Dick bared his teeth and ran off to one side. And stared at his master in astonishment. Ivan turned. Dick gave a wag of his tail and made as if to follow him, but stayed where he was, still staring at his master in astonishment.

A little further off stood Ivan's mother...

"No, one must live alone in this world. Then it will be easy," thought Ivan, clenching his teeth. And he strode out along the road—towards the bus.

His mother was still standing there... watching him go.

1967   —Translated by Geoffrey A. Hosking

NOTES

1. Original Russian: "V profil' i anfas," *Novyi mir*, 9(1967), 88-94; reprinted: *Tam, vdali* (1968); *Zemliaki* (1970); and *Izbrannye proizvedeniia v dvukh tomakh* (1975), Vol. 1, pp. 88-97. This translation is reprinted, with slight changes, from *Soviet Writing Today*, ed. M. Dewhirst and R. Milner-Gulland. (Harmondsworth: Penguin Books, 1977).

HOW THE OLD MAN DIED[1]

The old man had been suffering since morning. An agonizing weakness had come over him... He had already been feeling weak for a month, but today the weakness was especially acute—such an anguish in his heart, he felt bad enough to cry. It wasn't frightening so much as surprising: he had never felt this weak in his whole life. First it seemed that his legs were paralyzed... Was he able to wiggle his toes? Yes, they wiggled. Then his left arm began to get numb—he moved it back and forth and could hardly feel a thing. But O Lord, what a weakness had come over him!

Until noon he just endured it, waiting patiently: maybe it would go away, or his heart would begin to feel a little better—perhaps he would even want to smoke or take something to drink. But then he realized what it was: it was death.

"Mother... Oh, Mother!" he called his old wife. "It's happened... I'm dying..."

"God be with you!" exclaimed the old woman. "What won't you think of next, lying there like that?"

"Get me down from here somehow. I feel terrible bad." The old man was lying on the stove. "Take me down."

"How can I do it alone? Should I go fetch Pronka?"[2]

"Yes, get him. Is he home?"

"He was bustling about in his yard a while ago... I'll just go over there."

The old woman put on her coat and went out, letting a frosty white cloud into the hut.

"It's always in the winter when people die," thought the old man, "making all that trouble for everyone."

Pronka, a peasant from the neighboring house, walked in.

"Christ, but it's freezing out!" he said. "Wait a minute, Uncle Stepan, till I warm up a little and then I'll tend to you. Or else I'll get you all cold. What's the matter, have you got worse?"

"Really bad, Pronka. I'm dying."

"Shame on you, saying such a thing!.. You shouldn't panic like that!"

"Panic or don't panic, it's over. It's terrible cold out, is it?"

"Almost sixty below." Pronka lit a cigarette. "But there's hardly any snow in the fields. They're scraping it up with tractors—only who can stand it out there?"

"Maybe it'll snow some more."

"It's not likely to now. Well, let's get you down from there..."

31

The old woman fluffed up the pillow on the bed and straightened the feather mattress. Pronka stepped up on the ledge at the base of the stove and put his arms around the old man.

"Now hold me around the neck... Yes, like that. My, how light you've got!.."

"From being sick all that time..."

"You don't weigh no more than a child. Even my Kolka is heavier..."

They put the old man on the bed and covered him up with a sheepskin coat.

"Do you want me to roll a cigarette for you?" suggested Pronka.

"No, I don't feel like smoking. Ah, Lordy," sighed the old man. "It's always in the winter when people die..."

"Stop that, now!" said Pronka seriously. "Just put all those thoughts out of your head." He moved a taboret over near the bed, sat down. "When I was at the front I really got it good. I also thought I was done for. But the doctor says to me: if you want to live, you will; if you don't, you won't. And I was so bad off I couldn't even talk. I just laid there and thought: 'Who wouldn't want to live, except maybe for some crazy person?' So you just lie down now and keep saying to yourself: 'I'm going to live!' "

The old man smiled weakly.

"Let me take a drag on your cigarette," he asked.

Pronka gave him the cigarette. The old man took a drag, then began to cough. He coughed for a long time...

"I'm completely done in," he said. "That smoke, though, it went into my belly."

Pronka laughed shortly.

"Where does it pain you the most?" asked the old woman, looking with pity and also, for some reason, with displeasure, at the old man.

"Everywhere... All over. I feel such a weakness... as if all my blood had been drained off."

All three were silent for a while.

"Well, I have to go now, Uncle Stepan," said Pronka. "Got to water the livestock and give them some feed."

"Okay, go on then."

"I'll drop by and see you in the evening."

"Yes, drop by."

Pronka went out.

"This weakness, you know what it's from? You don't eat, so you get weak," remarked the old woman. "Should we kill a chicken, maybe—and then I'll make you some bouillon? It'll be tasty and fresh... Won't that be nice?"

The old man thought a minute.

"Never mind. If you make it for me, I probably won't be able to drink it—but the poor chicken will already be dead."

"Lord above! Worrying about a chicken..."

"Never mind," repeated the old man. "Give me half a glass of vodka instead... Maybe it will quicken my blood a little."

"It might make you worse..."

"Don't matter, as long as it quickens my blood some."

The old woman took a quarter-liter bottle stopped with a rag out of a cabinet. The bottle was a little over half full.

"Watch out you don't get worse..."

"Damn it, when did anyone ever feel worse from drinking vodka?" The old man was quite vexed. "You've been keeping track of our vodka all your life, and you still don't understand: vodka is the best medicine there is! What a blockhead..."

"Just don't get all huffy!" said the old woman, vexed herself now. " 'Blockhead.' He's got one foot in the grave, and he's still making a fuss. The doctor certainly didn't order you to get all worked up."

"Doctors! They don't order you to die, either—but people die anyway."

The old woman poured out half a glass of vodka and gave it to the old man. He drank it down—and almost choked on it. It all came up again. He lay there a long time, white and motionless. Then he said with an effort:

"No, it's better to drink while you still feel like it."

The old woman looked at him bitterly and pityingly. She gazed at him for a long time, then suddenly sobbed:

"If you really do die, God forbid, what am I going to do when I'm all alone?"

The old man said nothing for a long while, just stared severely at the ceiling. It was still difficult for him to talk. But he wanted to speak well and not leave anything out.

"The very first thing," he said, "ask Mishka to give you money regular. Tell him: 'When your father was dying, he said for you to feed your mother to the end.' Tell him that. But, damn him, if he doesn't do what's right, then apply for relief money. A shameful thing—but you have to live. Better to let him feel ashamed. And write Manka that she should make sure her little boy gets an education. He's a bright boy, knows the whole 'Internationale' by heart. Tell her: 'Your father said to educate the boy.' " The old man was tired now. He again lay back for a time and stared at the ceiling. The expression on his face was solemn, severe.

"And what should I say to Petya?" asked the old woman, wiping away her tears. She also made an effort to speak seriously, without crying.

"Petka? Don't bother Petka—he can hardly make ends meet himself."

"Should I make the bouillon now? Pronka can kill a chicken..."

"Never mind."

"What's the matter? Are you getting worse?"

"Yes. Let me catch my breath a minute." The old man closed his eyes and slowly, quietly breathed in and out. He seemed, in fact, to be already dead: a look of aloofness, of some sort of other-worldly peacefulness, came over his face.

"Stepan!" the old woman called out.

"Hm?"

"Don't lie there like that..."

"What do you mean by that, you simpleton! A man is dying, and she tells him not to lie a certain way. How do you want me to lie, on all fours?"

"Should I get Mikheevna, to give you extreme unction?"

"Don't be silly!.. What good has your God ever done me? You'd be giving your Mikheevna one of our chickens for nothing... You'd do better to give the chicken to Pronka—at least he'd dig out a grave for me... Who will dig the grave, by the way?"

"Oh, they'll probably find somebody..."

" 'Probably find somebody!'—You'll be flapping around the whole village before you ever find anybody who wants to dig in this cold weather. It's always in the winter that people die. If only it was summer!"

"Why have you put yourself in the grave already? Maybe you'll get better."

"Sure, get better! My feet are freezing... O Lord, O Lord!" The old man heaved a deep sigh. "Lord... maybe you do exist: forgive me, a sinner."

The old woman again began to sob.

"Stepan, try to brace up a little. Remember what Pronka said: 'Put all those thoughts out of your head.' "

"What does he know? He's as healthy as a bull. If you tell him not to die, well of course he won't!"

"Well, then, Stepan, forgive me if I've wronged you..."

"God will forgive you," said the old man, uttering the oft-heard phrase. He wanted to say something else, too, something very necessary, but he began to stare strangely off to the side, and was overcome by anxiety. "Agnyusha," he said with an effort, "forgive me... I was always a little too hot-headed... And the bread... holy, holy![3] Look, in the corner... Who is it? Who's there?"[4]

Pronka came by in the evening...

On the bed lay the old man, his white nose pointing straight up. The old woman stood at the end of the bed, sobbing quietly.

Pronka took off his cap, thought for a moment and then turned toward the icon in the corner and crossed himself.

"Yes," he said. "He felt it coming."

1967   —Translated by Donald M. Fiene

NOTES

1. Original Russian: "Kak pomiral starik," *Novyi mir,* 9(1967), 97-100; reprinted with changes, most of them minor, in *Tam, vdali* (1968); *Zemliaki* (1970); *Besedy pri iasnoi lune* (1974), pp. 110-113; and *Izbrannye proizvedeniia v dvukh tomakh* (1975), Vol. 1, pp. 111-115.

2. In the anthologized version of the story, the name Egor is substituted for Pronka.

3. The original Russian here is: "A khleb-to—riasnyi-riasnyi!..." This makes little sense, indicates onset of delirium. The repeated adjective *riasnyi* (modifying *khleb* 'bread') has a religious or ritualistic quality and in fact it is derived from the word *riasa* 'cassock.'

4. In the only significant change in the anthologized version of the story, the following sentences are inserted at this point:

" 'Where, Stepan?'

" 'Over there!' The old man raised himself up on one elbow and with a fierce look on his face stared into the corner of the hut, toward the entrance way. 'There she is,' he said, 'over there, sitting down.' " [The pronoun here probably refers to "death," a word of the feminine gender in Russian.]

"A STOREY"[1]

Ivan Petin's wife had left him. And the way she did it! Just like in one of those good old novels—she ran off with an officer.

Ivan had gotten back from a long haul, pulled the truck up at the fence, unlocked the house, and found a note on the table:

"Ivan, I'm sorry, but I can't live with a slob like you anymore. Don't try to find me. Ludmila."

Big Ivan, not even looking around, sank heavily onto a kitchen chair as if he had taken a blow straight to the forehead. Somehow he knew right away that this wasn't any joke, that this was the truth.

Even with his ability to endure patiently anything that came up in life, it seemed to him that this was something he would not be able to endure, it hurt so much. He was seized by a feeling of such anguish and sadness that he nearly cried. He tried to think, but couldn't. Thoughts just wouldn't come; all he could feel was a terrible heartache. One short but clear thought did flash through his mind: "So that's what really bad trouble is like." That was all.

Forty-year-old Ivan was very nearly bald, unlike the men one usually sees in the country, and he looked a lot older than he was. His gloominess and taciturnity were not a burden to him; it was just annoying that people always noticed. But he never could see that a fellow should be judged for qualities like that, for whether he was always cheerful or whether he was a good talker. "Why, how could they?!" his very own Ludmila would say to him. He loved her even more for that... and said nothing. "That's not the important thing, after all," he would think. "I'm her husband, not some lecturer on politics!" And now how do you like that! It turned out that she really had been unhappy because he was so taciturn and undemonstrative.

Later Ivan learned how it had all happened.

A small military detachment with an officer had come to the village to help set up an electric substation. They were there all told only about a week. They set up the substation and left. And the officer set up a wife for himself besides.

For two days all Ivan could do was fret about it. He tried getting drunk, but that only made it worse, and nasty. So he quit that. On the third day he sat down to write a story for the district newspaper. He had pretty often read stories in the newspapers by people who had been hurt even though they'd done nothing at all. Now he, too, wanted to ask how could that be allowed to

36

happen to him.

A Storey

It was this way: I come home and theres this note on the table. I aint going into it exept to say she just gives me hell in it. Mainly I know why she pulled a trick like that. Everyone kept telling her she looked like some actriss. I forget which one. But shes a fool and didnt understand. Whats the big deal in that? I look like a lot of people but I dont go jumping around like I got ants in my pants. But when theyd tell her she looked like one it made her real happy. She even signed up for nightschool on account of it, she said so herself. If you told someone he looked like Hitler would he go and grab a rifle and shoot up everybody right on the spot? We had a guy like that at the front—the spitting image of Hitler. Later they sent him somewhere to the rear on account of you just cant have it. Nope, she just had to move to town. There she said everyone will recognize me. What an idiot! In general shes no idiot, just a little too impressed with her own fizionomy. Anyway theres lots of pretty girls—what if they *all* up and ran away from home! I know he told her, You sure look like some actriss! And of course she just lit all up. Hell they sent you to school and the govermint spent money on you and now you've hung yourself on society's neck and glad of it! And the govermint takes a loss.

Ivan laid down his white-hot pen, got up, and walked around the house a little. He was pleased with what he was writing, only he thought maybe he shouldn't bring the government into it. He sat down at the table again and crossed out "govermint." He continued:

Well the hell with you! You think just because Im a truckdriver I dont understand nothing? Well I see right through you! We benefit the govermint with these here hands Im writing with right now and if we meet I can give you a belt right between the eyes with these here hands like some guys would be layed up a week with. I aint threatening nobody and I cant be stuck for threatening nobody but if we meet I can let you have it a time or two. On account of that aint right neither: he sees some broad whose kisser aint too bad and right away he's trying to sweet-talk her. Believe

37

me even if I am bald I could beat the crap out of some guys because you meet all kinds of people on long hauls. But I dont do it however. And so what if she's somebodys wife! There the kind of people what can skip right over a little detail like that. What do I look like to the guy whose got my woman? I dont do nobody no harm.

Now look what happens she up and wagged her tail and took off following her nose. Right? So now our marriage is broke up. And can she be completely sure theyll get a new one going? Nope. All together she knew this guy a week while me and her spent four years together. Now you tell me she aint no idiot! And the govermint spent money on her schooling. So wheres all that learning now? After all they didnt teach her to do bad. And I know her folks, they live in the next little town fine people. Incidently she has a brother an officer too first lieutenant, but you dont hear nothing but good about him. Has ribbens for combat and political training. So howcome she's so full of stuff and nonsense? Im surprized myself. I done everything for her. Got real attached to her. Every time I come home from a haul I just get all glad on account of Ill see her soon. And dammed if they dont go and run off together on me! Well she can go to hell if she couldnt hold out when a fella showed up so sneaky she lost her head in ten minutes. I would of got over it somehow. But howcome she left for good? I dont understand that neither. Just cant get it thru my head. Anything can happen in life, maybe a person does something bad, but why wreck you whole life all at oncet? Its easy to wreck it but hard to put it back together. And she's thirty herself. Im hurt real bad right now which is why Im writing my storey. As far as that goes Ive got three ribbens and four medals myself. And Id of been a Shockworker of Communist Labor a long time ago exept Ive got this one little weakness when Ive had a few too many I start swaring at people. Cant get that thru my head neither, sober Im a completely diffrent person. But nobody never saw me drunk behind the wheel and never will. And in all four years I never oncet swore in front of my wife Ludmila she can tell you that. I never said a bad word to her. And now dammed if she dont up and run off on me with some other guy! Aint nobodys feelings that wouldnt be hurt. Im not made of stone neither.

Your's truely
Ivan Petin. Chauffer 1st Class.

38

Ivan took his "storey" and set off for the newspaper office, which wasn't far away.

It was spring all around and that made him feel even worse: cold and bitter. He recalled how just recently he and his wife had walked along that very street from the club. Ivan would meet her after rehearsals, and sometimes he accompanied her to a rehearsal. He hated the word "rehearsal" ferociously, but he never once showed his hatred; his wife worshipped the rehearsals and he worshipped his wife. He liked walking down the street wth her. He was proud of his pretty wife. Besides that, he loved spring; when spring was just barely getting started, but even the mornings could already be felt coming on strong, his heart would feel a sweet pang as though it were expecting something. That something was spring. And now it had come, spring itself, nude, spattered all over, and tender, promising the earth soon-to-come warmth and sun. It had come... And now—it hurt him to look.

Ivan wiped his feet carefully on the begrimed doormat on the porch of the newspaper office and went in. He had never been in the newspaper office before, but he knew the editor. They sometimes met fishing.

"Is Ageev here?" he asked a woman he had often seen at home and who was always running off to rehearsals at the club, too. In any event whenever he had occasion to hear her talk with Ludmila it was always the same old "rehearsal" and "sets." Seeing her now he decided not to say hello; he felt a painful jerk at his heart.

The woman looked at him with curiosity and, for some reason, as though she were enjoying herself.

"Yes. Do you want to see him?"

"Yes. I need to take care of some business here." Ivan looked straight at the woman and thought, "She's probably run off on somebody, too; she looks like she likes to have a good time."

The woman went into the editor's office, came out, and said, "You can go in."

The editor, a short little fellow, was enjoying himself, too. He was a little bigger around than he should have been for his height, plumpish, roundish, and bald, too. He got up from behind his desk.

"So!" he exclaimed and pointed out the window. "Time's aworking for us! Have you tried it with nets yet?"

"No." Ivan wanted to show by his whole look that he didn't have any time to talk about fishing nets right now.

"I want to try Saturday." The editor couldn't seem to cast off his cheerful mood. "Or don't you advise it? I just don't have

39

the patience..."

"I brung a story," said Ivan.

"A story?" The editor took surprise. "Your story? What about?"

"I told it all here." Ivan handed over his notebook.

The editor leafed through it... He looked for a second at Ivan. Ivan was looking at him seriously and somewhat somberly.

"You want me to read it right now?"

"Right now'd be best..."

The editor sat down in his chair and began reading. Ivan remained standing. He kept looking at the editor and thinking, "Probably his wife goes to rehearsals, too. But he don't care— let her go! He'd know what to say about all them 'sets.' He'd know what to say about anything."

The editor began laughing loudly.

Ivan clenched his teeth.

"Hey, that's great!" exclaimed the editor. And he began guffawing again, so that his springy little pot belly even began bouncing up and down.

"What's great?" asked Ivan.

The editor stopped laughing. He even got a little embarrassed.

"I'm sorry... Were you writing about yourself? Is this something that happened to you?"

"Yes."

"Hm. I'm sorry, I didn't understand."

"That's all right. Keep reading."

The editor buried himself in the notebook again. He didn't laugh any more, but it was apparent that he was amazed and that he found it funny anyway. In order to hide it he knit his brows and pursed his lips in an understanding way. He read to the end.

"You want us to print it?"

"Well, yes."

"But this can't be printed. It's not a story..."

"Why not? I've read things like it."

"Why do you want to print it, anyway?" Now the editor was looking at Ivan seriously and sympathetically. "What good will it do? Will it make your, uh, grief any easier?"

Ivan took a while to answer.

"Let them read it... there."

"But where are they?"

"I don't know yet."

"Then our little newspaper won't reach them!"

"I'll find them... And I'll send it."

"No, no, that isn't what I mean!" The editor got up and

paced around his office. "That isn't it. What good will it do? You think she'll come to her senses and come back to you?"

"Their consciences will be hurt."

"No, no!" exclaimed the editor. "Lord... I don't know how you... I sympathize, but this is stupid. What can we do? Even if I edit it."

"Maybe she'll come back."

"No!" the editor said loudly. "Oh, Lord." He was clearly agitated. "Better you write a letter. Shall we do it together?"

Ivan picked up the notebook and began making his way out of the newspaper office.

"So long."

"Wait!" exclaimed the editor. "Let's do it together—in the third person..."

Ivan passed through the reception room of the newspaper office without even glancing at the woman who knew so much about "sets" and "rehearsals."

He headed straight for the tearoom. There he got a pint of vodka, drank it straight down without any chaser, and set off for home—out into the emptiness and dark. He walked, hands in pockets, looking nowhere but straight ahead. The calm he was seeking in his soul wouldn't come. He walked and cried to himself. The people he met looked at him in surprise. But he kept on walking and crying. And he wasn't ashamed. He felt a great tiredness.

1967   —Translated by James Nelson

NOTES

1. Original Russian: " 'Raskas'," *Novyi mir,* 9(1967), 100-103; reprinted: *Sovet-skaia Kirgiziia* (5 XII 1967); *Tam, vdali* (1968); *Zemliaki* (1970); *Besedy pri iasnoi lune* (1974), pp. 245-250; and *Izbrannye proizvedeniia v dvukh tomakh* (1975), Vol. 1, pp. 83-87.

"MILLE PARDONS, MADAME!"

Whenever townsfolk came to these parts for a spot of hunting and asked who could act as guide and show them around, the answer was always:

"Ah, you want Bronka Pupkov. He's our expert at that sort of thing." And people would add, with an odd smile, "He'll entertain you, all right."

Bronka (that is, Bronislav) Pupkov was still a burly figure of a man, blue-eyed and smiling, light of feet and tongue. Being in his fifties, he had fought in the war, but the two fingers missing from his right hand were not a war wound: once, when he was still a boy, he had been out hunting in the winter, and, wanting a drink, had hacked at the ice along the shore with his rifle butt. He was holding the gun by the barrel, with two fingers over the muzzle. The breech-block of the old Berdan rifle was on safety, but it broke loose—and one finger was blown clean off, the other left dangling by the skin. Bronka tore that one off himself. He brought both of them, his index and middle fingers, home to bury in the garden. He wanted to put up a cross over them, but his father wouldn't let him.

Bronka looked for trouble all his life. Often he would fight and get badly beaten up, but then afterwards he would spend a while in bed, recover, and start careering around once more on his deafening motor scooter, without a grievance against anybody in the world. A carefree sort of life.

Bronka always looked forward to the hunting parties as a kind of festival. And whenever they came, he was always willing to take off as much time as they liked—a week, a month. He knew the area as well as his eight fingers, and he had a real flair for hunting. As for the townsfolk, they were generous with their vodka, and sometimes they would tip him as well, but even if they didn't he never minded.

"How long would you like?" he would inquire briskly.

"Oh, three days or so."

"Right. It'll all be arranged. You'll be able to relax and calm your nerves."

So off they would go for three or four days, or sometimes even a week. Bronka enjoyed it. Townsfolk were always respectful, and he felt no urge to get into fights with them, even after a drink. Besides, he loved telling them his hunting yarns.

It was on the last day of each trip, when they held a farewell

42

party, that Bronka would launch into his favorite story. He could scarcely wait for the day, and he used to prepare carefully for it. When at last it came he felt a pleasant tingle in the pit of his stomach and held himself gravely aloof.

"What's up with you?" they would ask.

"Oh, nothing," he would reply. "Where shall we have our party? On the river bank?"

"Yes, let's."

So as evening drew near they picked a cozy spot on the bank of the fine, fast-flowing river and laid their fire. While the carp broth was cooking, they took their first glass and started to chat. Bronka drained a couple of tin mugsful and lit up.

"Were you ever at the front?" he asked casually. Almost everyone over forty had been at the front, but he asked the young folk too, just to get his story started.

"Is that a war wound?" they rejoined, pointing at his two missing fingers.

"No. I was a medical orderly at the front. Aye... Things were tough then..." Bronka fell silent. "Have you heard about the attempt on Hitler's life?"

"Of course."

"No, no, not that one. The othe one."

"What other one? Was there another?"

"Yes, there was." Bronka placed his tin mug under the bottle. "I'll have another drop, if you please." He drank it down. "Yes, there was, my friends, there was another attempt. The bullet missed his head by so much." Bronka held up the end of his little finger.

"When was that."

"July the twenty-fifth, nineteen forty-three." Bronka became pensive again, as if recalling something very personal, distant and dear to him.

"Who fired at him?"

Bronka did not hear the question. He sat smoking and staring at the fire.

"Where was this attempt?"

Bronka did not answer. Everyone exchanged surprised glances.

"I fired at him," he said suddenly. He spoke quietly, gazing at the fire for a while, and then looked up. "Are you surprised?" his eyes seemed to say, "I'm surprised myself." And he smiled wistfully.

At that point everyone stared silently at Bronka, who sat there puffing away and poking brands back into the fire with his

43

stick. This was the great moment for him, a moment when pure alcohol seemed to course through his bloodstream.

"Are you serious?"

"What do you mean? Do you suppose I don't realize that distortion of history is a serious matter? No sir! I know all about that."

"Go on, you're making it up!"

"Where did you shoot at him? How did it happen?"

"I used an automatic. Look, like this: I squeezed with my finger and—bang!" Bronka looked up earnestly and sadly—how could people be so disbelieving?

Those same disbelieving people asked in bewilderment: "How come nobody knows about it?"

"Even a hundred years from now a lot of things will remain shrouded in darkness. You get my meaning? Or perhaps you don't know... That's the whole tragedy, that so many heroes remain unsung."

"Why, you sound like..."

"Wait! Wait! It's coming back to me now."

Bronka knew that, come what may, they would want to hear his story. People always did.

"You won't tell anyone about it?"

Consternation again.

"No, we won't tell."

"Word of honor?"

"Of course we won't tell! Come on, out with it!"

"No, I want your word of honor as Communists. You know what country folk are like."

"Everything'll be all right." They couldn't wait to hear. "Do tell us about it!"

"I'll take another little drop first," said Bronka, holding out his mug again. He looked absolutely sober. "Well, as I say, it happened on July the twenty-fifth, nineteen forty-three." He coughed. "We were on the offensive. When you're on the offensive, there's always more for the medical staff to do. That day I brought at least a dozen people into the field hospital. I brought in one lieutenant—right heavy he was—and found him a bed in one of the wards. Now there was a general in that ward. A major general, that is. His wound was nothing special, only a graze above the knee, and they were just bandaging it. The general caught sight of me and said: "You there, orderly, don't go away!"

" 'Oh no,' I thought to myself, 'he needs to go somewhere and wants me to escort him.' So I waited. Life is much more interesting with generals. You get the whole picture with them."

44

His audience listened attentively. Now and then a sprightly flame would flare up with a little rustle; darkness was creeping up out of the forest, but the middle of the river, where the current flowed, was still light, and it flickered as though an enormous long fish were swimming along, flashing its silvery tail in the dusk.

"Well, when they finished bandaging the general, the doctor said to him: 'You must rest a bit.' 'The hell with that!' the general answered. We were all afraid of the doctors, mark you, but the generals didn't take much notice of them. So, anyway, the general and I got into a car and drove off. The general asked me where I was born, where I'd worked, what education I'd had. I explained it all to him: how I was born in such and such a place—right here, as it happens—and how I was attached to a kolkhoz but did more hunting than farming. 'That's good,' said the general. 'Are you a good shot?' 'Yes,' I said, coming straight to the point, 'I can dowse a candle with a rifle at fifty paces. Now, as far as my education goes,' I told him, 'that never amounted to much: my father used to take me out on his trips to the forest when I was a nipper.' 'That's okay,' he said, 'you can do this job without a college degree. If you can dowse one particular deadly candle which has sparked off a fire all over the world, then,' he said, 'your country will never forget you.' A delicate hint. You get me? But I still couldn't see what he was driving at."

"We arrived at a big dugout. The general kicked everybody out and went on asking me questions. 'Any relatives abroad?' he asked. 'Not likely,' I answered. 'We're born Cossacks, the same line that built Bii-Katunsk fortress not far from here. That was under Tsar Peter. Pretty well the whole village descends from them.' 'Where did you get the name Bronislav?' 'The priest thought it up when he was drunk. I sloshed the long-haired bastard for that once, when I escorted him to the GPU in 1933.' 'What's that? Where did you take him?' 'Into town. We'd taken him prisoner collectively, but there was no one to escort him. So they said to me: 'What about you, Bronka, you've got a grudge against him, you be his escort.' "

"Why, it's a perfectly good name, isn't it?"

"With a name like that you've got to have the right kind of surname. But mine! Bronislav *Pupkov*—I ask you—why, in the army there were roars of laughter at every roll-call. But in the village we have a *Vanka* Pupkov—and nobody turns a hair."

"Hm, yes. So what happened then?"

"Well, then... Where was I?"

"The general was asking you questions."

"Oh, yes. Well, he got through his questions and then said:

'Comrade Pupkov, the party and the government have decided to entrust you with a very responsible mission. Hitler has come to the front line incognito, and we have a chance to bump him off. We've captured one German bastard who was sent across to us on a special mission. He carried out his mission all right, but he got caught. Now, he was due to cross the front line right here and hand some very important documents to Hitler. Personally. And Hitler and his hangers-on know the man by sight.' "

"Where do you come in?"

"Ask me no questions, and I'll tell you no lies. Another drop, if you please. Hr-r-rm! Let me explain: the point is, I resembled that Fritz like two peas in a pod. And that, my friends, is where life really started!" Bronka abandoned himself to his memories with such voluptuousness and such ill-concealed euphoria that his listeners couldn't help smiling. "They put me into a separate room right away, in the hospital, and laid on a couple of order-lies. One of them was a sergeant—attending me, a mere private! 'Right there, comrade sergeant,' I said, 'hand me my boots!' And he did. An order is an order, right? So he obeyed. Meanwhile I was doing this here training course..."

"Which training course?"

"Ah... a special training course. I'm not allowed to disclose any of the details yet. I signed an agreement not to talk about it for fifty years, and so far only..." Bronka counted under his breath, "So far only twenty-five have gone by. But, of course, you know all about that. Anyway, the good life went on. Every morning I got up to a three-course breakfast. If the orderly brought along any old cheap wine, I would send him away with a flea in his ear, and he would come back with spirits—gallons of it, there was, lying around that hospital! I would dilute it to taste and leave the cheap wine for him. A week went by, and I began to wonder how much longer it could go on. Well, in the end, the general summoned me to his office. 'How's it going, Comrade Pupkov?' he asked. 'I'm ready to carry out my mission,' I answered. 'Go to it,' he said. 'God be with you. When you get back we'll make you a Hero of the Soviet Union. But be sure you don't miss!' 'If I miss,' I said, 'I'm a vile traitor and an enemy of the people. Either I find death along side Hitler, or the man you rescue will be Hero of the Soviet Union, Bronislav Ivanovich Pupkov.' You see, they were planning a huge offensive at the time, with infantry advancing on the flanks and tanks mounting a powerful frontal assault."

Bronka's eyes glowed and flashed like live embers. He even forgot to hold out his tin mug.

46

"Comrades, I will not recount to you how I was conducted across the front line and how I got through to Hitler's bunker. But I did get through!" Bronka rose to his feet. "Yes, I got through all right! I took my last steps down the staircase and found myself in a large reinforced concrete room. A bright electric light was shining, and there were masses of generals milling about. I quickly sized up the situation: but where was Hitler?" Bronka tensed up, his voice broke and became a hoarse whisper, a grating, painful croak. He spoke unevenly, choking and often breaking off half way through a word.

"My heart was in my mouth. Where was Hitler? I had studied his fox's snout under the microscope and had decided in advance where to aim—at his moustache. I saluted, 'Heil Hitler.' I was holding a large package with an automatic inside, loaded with poisoned dum-dum bullets. A general came up and reached for my package, but I brushed him politely aside: 'Mille pardons, madame—for the Fuhrer in person.' I was speaking perfect German, mark you: 'For the Fuhrer!' " Bronka swallowed heavily. "And then... out he came. It was like an electric shock. I remembered my distant homeland, my mother and father—I had no wife then..." Bronka broke off a moment, as though ready to howl, to burst into tears, to tear the shirt from his breast. "You know how it is: your whole life flashes through your mind. The same as when you're face to face with a bear. Hr-r-r-rm!' "

"Well?" someone asked quietly.

"He came up to me. The generals all stood to attention. He smiled. And then I burst open the package. 'So you're smiling you rat! Well then, take this for our sufferings!' " Bronka was shrieking, holding up his arm as if about to shoot. No one knew what to think. " 'So you were laughing, were you? Well, now you can bathe in your own blood, you crawling vermin!!' " This was a heart-rending howl. Then followed complete silence, and a hurried, almost imperceptible whisper: "I fired." Bronka looked down and wept silently, shaking his head unconsolably. When he raised it, his face was furrowed with tears. Then quietly, very quietly, he said, with horror in his voice:

"I missed."

No one said anything. Bronka's state affected them so much that they didn't feel like speaking.

"Another drop, if you please." Bronka said quietly but insistently. He drank it and walked off to the water. And there he sat for hours, alone on the bank, in the grip of his traumatic experience. Occasionally he would sigh or cough. He declined the fish soup.

... It usually didn't take long for word to get around the village that Bronka had once again told his "assassination" story. Bronka himself would come home in a foul mood, prepared to be mocked and to return the mockery in kind. His wife, an unattractive thick-lipped woman, went for him straight away.

"So here you are with your tail between your legs. Been at it again, have you?"

"Get lost!" Bronka rejoined half-heartedly. "Gimme something to eat."

"Huh! Something to eat! To eat. What you need is a good knock over the head with a lead weight!" his wife yelled. "People are always pestering me, I don't get a moment's peace."

"Well, stay home then, don't wander the streets."

"Oh, no! I'm getting out of here! I'm going to the village Soviet right now. It's time they gave you another talking to. If you don't watch it, you chicken-clawed squirt, you'll find yourself up before a judge one of these days. For distorting history..."

"They can't do anything. It's not a published work. Don't you understand? Now gimme something to eat!"

"People laugh in your face, but what do you care? If they spit in your eye, you'd call it God's dew. You unwashed lout! You lickspittle! Have you any self-respect, or has it all been knocked out of you? Pah!" she spat. "Shameless toady. Bronislav Pupkov, huh!"

Bronka gave his wife a stern and angry look. Then he said quietly but forcefully: "Mille pardons, madame. I'm about to hit you so hard you'll..."

His wife slammed the door and went off to grumble about her "lickspittle."

But she was wrong if she thought Bronka didn't care. On the contrary, he suffered each time, got really worked up and fuming. For a couple of days he would sit at home drinking. He wold send his teenage son to the liquor shop for vodka. "Don't listen to anybody," he would say, guiltily and aggressively. "Just get a bottle and bring it straight home."

He had in fact been summoned several times to the village Soviet, where they had appealed to his conscience and threatened to take measures. When sober, Bronka would say angrily and incoherently, avoiding the chairman's eye: "Oh, come off it!.. Look, drop it!.. All this fuss... All right then, I won't..."

Then he would go for a drink in the pub, sit on the front steps a moment to let it take effect, and stand up, rolling up his sleeves and declaring loudly: "All right then! Who wants to take me on? Please don't take offense if I knock you about a bit.

Mille pardons..."
It's true, though, that he was a first-rate marksman.

1968   —Translated by Geoffrey A. Hosking

NOTES

1. Original Russian: " 'Mil' pardon, madam!'," *Novyi mir*, 11(1968); reprinted: *Zemliaki* (1970); *Besedy pri iasnoi lune* (1974), pp. 162-169; *Izbrannye proizvedeniia v dvukh tomakh* (1975), Vol. 1, pp. 115-122.

THE BROTHER-IN-LAW[1]

Guests had arrived at the house of Andrei Kochuganov: his wife's sister and the sister's husband. The sister's name was Roza and her husband's name was Sergei, that is, "Sergei Sergeevich," as he announced himself—swarthy, snub-nosed, with round, bottle-green eyes.

The sisters wept a few tears of joy and then quickly went to the guest room with the suitcases.

"And now they'll spend half the day looking at each other's fancy duds," said Sergei Sergeich condescendingly—but not without pride, since the suitcases were bursting with clothes. He stood there like a young lieutenant who has just got home on leave and is ceremoniously dragging ten-rouble notes out of his pocket. But the lieutenant may be excused on account of his youth, while here was a forty-year-old, smacking his lips with pride.

The two brothers-in-law lit cigarettes.

"How much time do you have off?" asked Andrei.

"Where I work we get a long vacation. We're in a privileged position." Again—arrogance and pride. There wasn't a modest spot on his entire body. He was like a quilt, with every patch bragging and swaggering. "Special privilege."

"Special how?"

"With respect to salary and vacation."

"What, a real high salary, huh?"

Sergei Sergeich chuckled at Andrei's ignorance. "For example, up to four hundred roubles!"

Andrei was duly amazed: "Oho ho!"

"Do you know how much a professor gets here?"

"Where?"

"Why, here—in the middle of Russia!"

"And how am I supposed to know that?"

"Look, the highest-paid professor gets five hundred roubles. Maximum!"

"Well, and so?"

"Well, so I never made it through grammar school!" Again Sergei Sergeich laughed his little laugh. "That's the way we live... I've already got one leg into Communism, so to speak."

"That's good then. Great."

"Can't complain, can't complain. Say, is there anything to do around here?"

Andrei shrugged his shoulders. "Sure, why not? You can find something to do anywhere."

"I'll bet... I told the wife, let's go to Yalta. No, she says. She wants to go back home. Okay, okay, I say, we'll go there if you want to so much. As for me, I'll take Yalta every time. I don't like these villages at all. There's nothing in the stores... As a matter of fact, I just now stopped at your little store here. 'Give me some champagne,' I say. She looks at me like a sheep staring at a new gate. 'What kind of shampoo?' she says. 'Cham*pagne*,' I say. 'Just ordinary champagne: dry, extra dry or sweet... What kind do you have?' 'Well, we don't have any kind,' she says. Nor any good wine, either. Just plain old vodka."

Andrei got to his feet. "I'm going to split some wood. No doubt you'd like me to heat up the bathhouse?"

"A steam bath—good. Do you do it country style?"

"Yes, country style, with smoke."

"Hey, that's great. Some people are surprised at that. 'Do you really like to bathe country style?' they ask me. But I really do. The smell of the smoke is nice. Only dump in more water than usual, will you?"

Andrei went out into the yard.

Soon his wife Sonia went out also. "Oh, what presents they brought!" she gasped in rapture, with a kind of holy reverence. "Two shawls she gave me, lovely ones—all flowery, with fringes, and a satin dress and two table cloths—also with fringes!"

"Fringes," said Andrei. "Drop that, now. We've got to haul more water. Your brother-in-law likes to bathe in a regular flood of it."

"Well, of course. My Lord, what's a little water? And you, Andrei, *please* try... Be a little more cheerful. You're walking around like an I-don't-know-what... like an old crab. They'll think we're not happy to see them! But I'm in seventh heaven! Oh, what shawls! I've never in my life seen anything like them, not even in my dreams. Oh, how some people live!"

It was already dark by the time they took their baths.

Sergei Sergeich basked in the steam, poured basins of water over himself, and moaned blissfully. Andrei was struck by the number of tattoos on his brother-in-law's lean body.

"Yeah, I did a little time," Sergei Sergeich cheerfully admitted when Andrei asked him about the tattoos.[2] "Four years... When I was young and stupid. My brother worked in a co-op. He was hauling stuff there in a truck... Hoo, ow, that's hot!.. At a certain place I hopped into the truck, tossed out two bales of crepe de Chine—and we got caught... Hey, toss another dipper on the stones, will you?"[3]

Andrei complied. Sergei Sergeich again furiously lashed himself with the birch twigs, again groaned and cried out...

"So what happened?"

"Huh?"

"With the crepe de Chine."

"Like I said—we got caught. They gave me four years and my brother seven. They didn't even consider his military decorations. He had twelve of them. And medals, too."

"What'd they get your brother for?"

"For putting me up to it. They got it out of me on the first interrogation. But he didn't serve his full time—only five years. He got out on the amnesty...[4] Hey, more steam! Two dippers!"

"Are you sure it won't be too hot for you?"

"C'mon, this is nothing. Just toss it on there!"

The hot stones snorted viciously and another violent, surging cloud of steam struck the ceiling and swirled downward... The heat took your breath away and boxed your ears for you. Andrei squatted down away from it. Sergei Sergeich underwent wriggling torments on the shelf, his swarthy, painted body glistening in the semidarkness. Finally he scrambled down from the shelf and ran out into the dressing room to catch his breath.

Andrei climbed up on the shelf for a minute and switched himself a little on the legs and waist. He was not a lover of steam. Then he also dropped down to the floor.

"Let's have a smoke," called Sergei Sergeich.

They lit up in the cool dressing room. Sergei Sergeich returned to his earlier topic. "So give me an example of what there is to do around here."

"For crying out loud," said Andrei. "Just lie down and spit at the ceiling... Or see a movie when they bring around a film. Or go fishing... 'What is there to do?' he says."

"Have you got any fish in your river?"

"A few. The guys around here fish upstream. There it's probably a little better."

"Do you have a boat?"

"Yes—but no motor."

"What's the matter? No motors around here?"

"Yeah, sure—over in the store... But who's got that kind of money?"

"At home I've got a motorcycle. On Saturdays around four a.m. I'll take off down the highway at a hundred kilometers an hour. What a beast that machine is! We drive out to the lakes to go fishing."

"Do you catch anything?"

"Well, not to lie about it, I usually bring home about half a sackful. Rozka hardly knows what to do with them all. She fries them, pickles them, makes chowder... But mostly we fertilize our garden with them."

"What?!" exclaimed Andrei.

"Sure. I really like onions—grow them in a hothouse. I use fishmeal for fertilizer... You should see the onions I grow! Nobody in our town has onions like that! This big... And sweet, my God... Just recently I got on the waiting list for a Volga. I was advised to wait for a Fiat, but the way I figure, they'll be fooling around with that Fiat for five more years—and in that time I can get a Volga. Hoo, boy!... I think I'll go get steam-blasted some more."

After that the women bathed.

Meanwhile, the men sat down over a bottle of *kalgan* vodka and got into a bad quarrel. Sergei Sergeich had begun to brag again about how terrific everything was turning out for him in his life... Then he began to reproach Andrei for not knowing how to live properly. "And you don't even have a television set?"

"Nope."

"Well, listen. You're nothing but a mangy muzhik. Do you mean to say you can't even afford a television set?"

Andrei got offended. "Not all of us get a professor's salary, you know."

"But surely you can buy a TV set!"

"What do I need one of those things for? And I don't need a Fiat, either. Understand? And if you keep on making remarks against me, I'll talk to you in a way you won't like..."

"Yeah? Like how?"

"You'll find out."

"Tell me now!"

"One good punch in the forehead!"

"Yeah?"

"Yeah! Who the hell do you think you are?... You no sooner arrive than you start spouting off—this is no good, you don't like that... I didn't ask you to come here. But now that you are here, hold your tongue. Act like a man."

"So you are suggesting that even if I see something that's inferior, I still have to say it's okay? Is that it?"

"Is it my fault there's no champagne in the store? And who needs champagne anyway? Around here nobody ever drinks that piss..."

"I didn't criticize you personally about the champagne—

only about the television. I can drink *kalgan* vodka just as well."

"And do you by any chance have a combine?"

"What kind of 'combine'?"

"The usual kind, that reaps the harvest."

"What do I need one of those for?"

"So okay—I don't need a TV set any more than you need a combine. Only I don't make remarks about you not having a combine."

"But a television set is an absolute necessity! Say you've got a son growing up: instead of scratching around in the garden in the evenings, he could be looking at TV!"

Andrei fell silent. "I've got some onions hanging up over there, whole bunches of them. Do you want some?"

"No. You're still just a poor yokel... Don't take offense of course."

Andrei gazed at his brother-in-law for a long time without blinking his eyes... "If you call me that again... Do you see that fist? I'll smash it right between your eyes!"

"Oh yeah?" Sergei Sergeich suddenly sat up. "Are you aware that I can throw my right faster than I can think? Do you see that nose?" He pressed a finger on his flattened beak. "Broken!... My stepfather did that. Do you know how me and my brother handled him when we grew up? Any way we felt like it... I'd walk up to him and—powie!" Sergei Sergeich reached out to show Andrei how he used to punch his stepfather—but Andrei unexpectedly let loose with his right and gave Sergei Sergeich a jangling blow on the forehead. Sergei Sergeich flew back off his chair, loudly cursing using "mother" words.

"Hey, I was only trying to *show* you! What a parasite! Up your ass with a steamboat!" Sergei Sergeich sat on the floor and rubbed his forehead with one hand and waved the other in the air. "I only wanted to show you, and you thought..."

"Two young louts ganging up on an old man," said Andrei. He was feeling a little sorry that he had reacted so fast. He had indeed thought Sergei Sergeich had meant to hit him. "Aren't you ashamed?"

"But you don't know how he used to thrash us. You..."

Just then a door opened in the passageway. Sergei Sergeich hopped up from the floor and began to talk rapidly.

"Andryukha! Close your mouth! Hush up! We're just sitting here drinking vodka. Nothing happened, understand? Or else I'll be in for it. She'll really give me hell, the bitch... We'll just be sitting here peacefully drinking our vodka, okay?"

Sergei Sergeich quickly gurgled out two glasses and pulled

his chair up to the table.

When the sisters came into the house, the husbands were just clinking their glasses. "Ahh," shouted Sergei Sergeich, "you look fresh as daisies!"

"I see you've already broken the ice," said Roza pleasantly.

"Everything's going great," said Sergei Sergeich. "Just great. Ask him."

"Great," affirmed Andrei.

"How come you aren't waiting for us?" Sonia scolded the men. But she scolded only for form's sake: both women were in a perfectly splendid mood.

Soon the four of them were amicably singing songs at the table. Sergei Sergeich began to sing in a thin, quavering voice. He closed his eyes and gently shook his head...

"I know you'll not wait for me,
My letters you'll not even read..."

Then they all joined in:

"You'll not even come when I call.
If you do, you won't know me at all.
Oh, you'll not even come when I call..."

Andrei didn't know the words and waited while Sergei Sergeich and Roza sang it through once, and then he joined in with the others, yodeling mournfully. He really loved that song, and deep down he was very sorry that he had punched his brother-in-law.

The next day Sergei Sergeich pulled a stunt that Andrei simply could not understand for the life of him.

Andrei returned home from work in the evening... Sergei Sergeich was waiting for him on a bench by the gate. Spotting Andrei, he got up, thrust his hands into the pockets of his trousers, smugly squinted his eyes, and queried his brother-in-law: "What's up jerk?... All done with your work?"

Andrei couldn't believe his ears. "Are you at it again?" he drawled menacingly.

"Follow me, citizen!" And Sergei Sergeich set off, without glancing back, toward the shed.

"What the hell do you want?" asked Andrei, not budging an inch.

"March! Can't you hear me?" shouted Sergei Sergeich. "You really are a jerk!"

Andrei glanced around. There was no one in the garden. He walked toward Sergei Sergeich. The look on his face promised nothing good. Sergei Sergeich yanked open the door of the shed... And there, on a wooden block, all oily and gleaming, lay a boat

55

motor. Brand new—right out of the store. Sergei Sergeich kicked it with the toe of his boot.

"Take it. Put it on your boat."

"What?.."

"Say 'Thanks' and take it away, before I change my mind. Understand? I'm giving it to you."

"How can this be?" Andrei still couldn't figure out what was going on.

Sergei Sergeich laughed out loud, very satisfied with himself.

"Look at his mouth hanging open, the simple jerk... C'mon, take it. It's yours."

"But it costs a fortune," said Andrei. "Damn it..."

Sergei Sergeich went up to Andrei and painfully, almost with malice, patted him hard a couple of times on the cheek. "Take it... I can buy you a dozen of the things. And remember Serga Neverov. Let's go."

When Andrei stepped over the door sill of the shed, Sergei Sergeich suddenly leaped on his back and shouted merrily, "Giddyap! Ride me up to the porch!"

"Hey, get off!" Andrei shook his shoulders. "What the devil."

But Sergei Sergeich sat firm. "Come on, up to the porch!.. Well?" Sergei Sergeich impatiently spurred Andrei in the side. "Come on!... It's a great joke. Hop, hop! Faster! What's the matter? Am I too heavy for you?"

That damned motor! It's the devil's work, no doubt about it. Metallic carrion... Andrei came close to throwing Sergei Sergeich over his head and knocking him onto the steps, because his brother-in-law was still yelling as they galloped along: "Yahoo! And the Cossack rode into the valley!.. Hop! Hop!"

Luckily, no one came out of the house, and no one could see from the street the kind of animal that the Kochuganovs' guest was riding "into the valley."

Andrei went into the house, opening the door with a kick... But there on the table he saw again the bottle of *kalgan* vodka, and he smelled the aroma of broiling meat... Everything in the cottage was neat and tidy, the radio was purring, his wife, Sonia, happy beyond all measure, was bustling about in the kitchen... Ah, the devil with him. So he'd given him a ride on his back—was it really all that bad? Anyhow, he'd gotten a motor out of it. To hell with him.

"Well, how do you like the motor?" asked Sonia.

"Oh, you should have seen him!.." Sergei Sergeich jumped in ahead of Andrei. "He glued his eyes on it and just sta-a-red...

56

I nearly split my sides." Sergei Sergeich and Sonia burst into laughter, pleased with themselves. "I tell him: 'Take it quick, before I change my mind. Hurry up, now!..' Well, come on, let's drink a toast: To the new acquisition... What are you standing there for? Haven't you come to yet?" Sergei Sergeich again burst into laughter. He sat down at the table. He had returned to the same tone he'd been using when he arrived the day before.

1969   —Translated by Donald M. Fiene and Boris N. Peskin

NOTES

1. Original Russian: "Svoiak Sergei Sergeich," *Novyi mir,* 10(1969), 67-94; reprinted in *Kharaktery* (1973), pp. 212-221, and in *Brat moi* (1975), with changes (including the respelling of the last word of the title as *Sergeevich*). The present translation is a slightly revised reprinting of that published in *Russian Literature Triquarterly,* 11(1975), pp. 168-174. The notes to that text, pp. 174-178, indicate in detail the differences between the original and anthologized versions of the story.
2. The connection between tattoos and serving time in prison is that it is chiefly in prisons and labor camps where tattoo artists do their work.
3. Steam in country bathhouses is produced by dashing hot water onto stones or bricks heated on top of a brick stove.
4. The amnesty of 1953 following the death of Stalin.

THE BASTARD[1]

Spirka Rastorguev was thirty-six, but looked no more than twenty-five.

He was strikingly handsome; on Saturday he would go to the bathhouse, thrash himself in the steam, draw off the dirt accumulated in a week of driving, put on a clean shirt—and behold, a young god! Bright, intelligent eyes... Effeminate lips, blossom-red on a dark-skinned face. His knitted brows, like a pair of crow's wings, swing into an uncertain curve. Damn good-looking!.. Nature, it seems, can be funny sometimes. But what does he care! He himself says: "It means little to me." Everything to him "means little." Thirty-six years old with no family, no real home. He knows his business—swearing and straying off nights to single women... He strayed off to all of them in order, without being picky. To him this too "means little." As luck would have it, he liked the older and uglier ones best.

"Spirka, you fool, do your mug a favor! Who do you fall for—pockmarked Liza, the grater! Haven't you any shame?"

"You don't drink water from the face," Spirka reasonably answers. "She's a 'grater,' but a better person than all of you."

Spirka's life got off track early. He was only in the fifth class when all kinds of stories about him got started. The German teacher, a quiet and overly sensitive old woman from among the evacuees, was staring at Spirka one time, and said with surprise: "Byron!.. It's striking, what a resemblance!"

Spirka hated the old woman.

They were just coming to the part "Anna und Martha baden," he was feeling sad, and again she comes to him: "No—it's striking. The very image of little Byron." Spirka couldn't stand it. Once, when the old woman began in her usual way:

"It can't be, no one will believe it: a little By...."

"And you go to..." Spirka let loose a stream of profanity that would make a drunken peasant ashamed.

The old woman's eyes started out of her head. She said afterward:

"I wasn't frightened, no, I was a hospital-train nurse in 1914, I've seen and heard a lot... But it surprised me: how does he know these words?! And what a handsome face!.. Lord, what a face he has—a little Byron!"

"Byron" was mercilessly whipped by his mother. He stayed in bed awhile, then set off for the front. In Novosibirsk he was

58

caught and sent home. Again his mother cruelly beat him. And at night she tore her hair and howled over her son; she had begotten Spirka from a "fine fellow" passing through, and that "fine fellow" she painfully loved and hated in Spirka. Spirka was the image of his father, and even matched him in character, though he had never laid eyes on him.

He didn't go to school any more, however much his mother tried to make him, and no matter what she thrashed him with. He threatened to jump from the roof onto a pitchfork. His mother retreated. Spirka went to work on the kolkhoz.

He grew up insolent, didn't obey his elders, made trouble, and got into fights... His mother was finally worn out by him, and she gave up.

"So let others handle him if they want."

And, indeed, they handled him. It was after the war. He and a buddy, a worthless trouble-maker, borrowed a general-store cart from the neighboring village while it was standing at the tavern, and they took a box of vodka from the driver... They got the better of that peasant! And they gave him a thrashing besides. For twenty-four hours they lived it up recklessly at the home of one of Spirka's girlfriends. And it was here that the police found them. Spirka had time to grab his rifle and hide in the bathhouse, and for almost two days they couldn't take him—he kept firing back. They sent his girlfriend to him—Vera the chatterbox—to persuade him to surrender peacefully. The playful chatterbox secretly, under her skirt, brought him a bottle of vodka and some cartridges. She was in there a long time with him... She came out and proudly declared:

"He won't come out!"

Spirka kept shooting through the window, singing:

Our proud 'Varangian' won't give in,
No one wants mercy from anyone!

"Spirka—each shot is an extra year!" they screamed at him.

"Count—how many?!" answered Spirka. And from the little window spurted a swift long flame and the shots rang out. Then he sobered up and felt deathly tired... He threw out his rifle and walked out.

He "sweat" for five years.

The same boldly handsome, insolent, and unexpectedly good Spirka came back. He struck people by his goodness and his good looks as well. He could take the shirt off his back if someone needed it. He could go into the forest on his day off, cut wood there till evening, and late at night bring a load of firewood to some old folks. He'd cart it there, unload it, and take it into the

59

house.

"But what would you like, Spirka, our angel? What would you like for this?" the old people would fuss.

"Just something to drink." He looks with curiosity. "It's nothing, I'm a peasant."

So Spirka came back from prison... He had no buddies, they all had scattered, and his girlfriends had married. People thought he, too, would leave. He played around a bit, gave money to his mother, and began to work as a driver.

That's how Spirka lived.

Two new people—teachers—came to the village of Yasnoe in the spring: Sergei Yurevich and Irina Ivanovna Zelenetsky, husband and wife. Sergei Yurevich taught physical culture, and Irina Ivanovna taught singing.

Sergei Yurevich was not tall, but he was muscular and broadshouldered... He walked with resilience, jumped lightly, and did somersaults; it was pleasant to watch him go through his exercises, with seriousness and enthusiasm, on the horizontal bar, on the parallel bars, and on the rings... He had an unusually wide, kindly mouth, a fat nose with a lump on it, and uncommon, very white, enormous teeth.

Irina Ivanovna was small, pale, and slender in a girlish way. There was nothing quite like it when she threw off her teacher's cloak, entered the room, and stood up on tiptoes in order to get from the shelf the heavy accordion—from which harmony would then come, and refinement. People couldn't help admiring her to the point of distraction.

This pair (they were about thirty or thirty-two) arrived in Yasnoe during the warm days at the end of April. They were settled in the big house with the old Prokudins.

Spirka was the first to visit the newcomers. Even before this he had always visited new people. He would come, sit for a while, drink with his hosts (incidentally, it should be said that, though he drank, Spirka seldom did it to the point of drunkenness), talk a little, and then leave.

It was getting on toward evening. Spirka washed, shaved, put on his holiday suit, and went to the Prokudins.

"I'll go take a look, see what kind of people they are," he told his mother.

The old Prokudins were having supper.

"Sit down, Spiridon, join us." Spirka sometimes helped the old people; they liked him and they felt sorry for him.

"Thank you, I just finished eating. Are the new people at home?"

60

"They're over there." The old man nodded at the door of the adjoining room. "They're resting."

"What are they like?"

"Not bad, respectful. They brought some cheese and sausage. Why don't you sit down and try some?"

Spirka shook his head and went to the other room. He knocked on the door.

"May I?"

"Come in!" they invited, behind the door.

Spirka entered.

"Hello!"

"Hello!" said the couple. And involuntarily they got lost in contemplating Spirka. So it always was.

Spirka went to introduce himself.

"Spiridon Rastorguev."

"Sergei Yurevich."

"Irina Ivanovna. Sit down please."

Pressing the warm small hand of Irina Ivanovna, Spirka openly, with curiosity, looked at all of her. Irina Ivanovna frowned slightly at the hand-pressing, smiled, hurriedly removed her hand for some reason, hurriedly turned, and went to get a chair... She brought the chair, and looked at Spirka not so much surprised as extremely curious.

Spirka sat down.

Sergei Yurevich looked at him.

"Welcome," said Spirka.

"Thank you."

"I've come to visit," explained the guest. "Or else you could wither away before our people stirred themselves."

"Are they unsociable?"

"Like everywhere: they prefer to stay in their own corners."

"Are you from around here?"

"I'm from the area—Chaldon."

"Serezha, should I prepare something?"

"Go ahead!" readily responded Serezha, and again he looked cheerfully at Spirka. "We can celebrate our new home with Spiridon."

"A little glass is allowed," agreed Spirka. "Where will you get it from?"

"Not far."

Irina Ivanovna went into the old people's room; Spirka accompanied her with his glance.

"How is life here?" asked Sergei Yurevich.

"Life..." Spirka grew silent, but he was not looking for a

word; suddenly he had begun to feel sorry that that little woman, the hostess, would not hear him tell about life. "A man, after all, lives by periods. A good period, a bad period..." No, he didn't want to talk. "Why did she go? Just tell the old people, they'll do what has to be done."

"Why? She's the hostess. So what kind of a period are you having now?"

"Well, a little of each. Not bad in general..." But he really didn't want to talk while she was preparing that stupid food. "May I smoke?"

"Go ahead."

"Are you a teacher?"

"Yes."

"What does she teach?"

"Singing."

"Does she sing well?" Spirka grew animated.

"She sings..."

"Could she sing for us?"

"Well... ask her, maybe she will."

"I'll go tell the old people... There's no need for her to be out there."

And Spirka left the room.

They returned together, Irina Ivanovna and Spirka. Irina Ivanovna brought cheese on a little plate, sausage, and salted lard...

"I agreed not to make anything hot," she said.

"It's fine that you agreed."

"But what a good treat it is!" Spirka nearly strained himself using the customary expression here. "Nice, isn't it—cucumbers and a piece of lard." Spirka glanced at the host.

"You know best," said Sergei Yurevich rather sharply—using the intimate pronoun, however.

Spirka was pleased that the host had gotten more informal with him—so much the better. He didn't notice the couple exchanging glances: he was beginning to feel good. Now a glass of vodka and we'll see what happens then.

Cognac appeared on the table instead of vodka.

"I'll down mine right away, and then that's all: I'm used to doing it that way. Is it all right?"

They obligingly gave their permission to Spirka.

Spirka drank his cognac, took a small piece of sausage...

"Here we are..." he hesitated. "We've reached the level of eternal frost, as they say."

The married people emptied their wineglasses. Spirka looked

62

at the woman's quivering, tender little throat. And then—whether it was the cognac so soon, or his blood—something heavy and hot threw itself toward his heart. He felt so strongly the desire to touch and to stroke that little throat that his hands itched. Spirka's look brightened and grew wiser... He began to feel good inside.

"Great cognac," he praised, "only it's expensive."

Sergei Yurevich began to laugh; Spirka didn't notice him.

"Home brew, now—that's nice stuff, isn't it?" asked Sergei Yurevich. "It's cheap but good."

"What cheerful thing can I talk about?" thought Spirka.

"Home-brew is rare nowadays," he said. "We had that during the war..." He recalled distant, difficult years, famine, back-breaking, adult work in the field... And he felt like talking cheerfully about all this. He threw up his handsome head, looked steadily at the woman, smiling:

"So, should I tell about how I've lived?"

Irina Ivanovna hurriedly took her gaze from him and looked at her husband.

"Tell us, tell us, Spiridon," asked Sergei Yurevich. "It'll be interesting hearing how you've lived."

Spirka began to smoke.

"I'm a bastard," he began.

"How is that?" Irina Ivanovna hadn't understood.

"My mother brought me in in the hem of her skirt—she wasn't married. There was a guy in these parts, quite a fellow. He collected hides in the region as a government purveyor. When he was getting his goods, he got me too."

"You know him?"

"Never saw him. When my mother got a tummy he didn't come near her any more. And then he was arrested for something—and not a word of him. He was probably put away. So that's the way I began to live..." And just as he had so suddenly wanted to talk about something cheerful, he suddenly didn't feel like it any more. That's enough of the cheerful stuff. Should he talk about the camp? Spirka looked at Irina Ivanovna, and again that irrepressible desire in his heart was pushing: to touch that woman's little throat, to stroke it.

He got up.

"I'm off to work now. Thanks for the hospitality."

"You drive at night?" Irina Ivanovna was surprised.

"We do here. Good-bye. I'll come again to see you."

Spirka left the room without looking around.

"A strange fellow," said the wife, after a short silence.

"You meant to say handsome?"

"Handsome, yes."

"Handsome... You know he's in love with you."

"Yes?"

"And you, it seems, got excited. Didn't you get excited?"

"Where did you get that idea?"

"Exci-ited."

"Did you want me to get excited?"

"Why should I?... Only, it won't happen with you."

The woman looked at her husband.

"You're frightened," he said. "You need courage for this."

"Stop," the wife said seriously. "What are you doing?"

"Courage and, of course, strength," continued the husband. "One has to be in good shape, so to speak. This one, he could do it. By the way, he was in prison."

"How do you figure that?"

"You don't believe me? Go ask the old people."

"If you have to know, you go ask."

"Why not?.."

The husband went out to the old people's room.

He returned in five minutes... And with feigned solemnity he declared:

"Five years! In strict-regime camps. For robbery."

The cool air, which had grown damp toward evening, did a good job freshening his hot face. Spirka walked along smoking. He suddenly wanted a heavy rainfall, so that the sky would be cut by fiery zig-zags, and so that thunder would come from above... And then he might begin to yell.

Spirka set out for Nyura Zavyalovaya's, the "den" next in line.

He knocked at the window.

"What is it?" asked the sleepy Nyura with displeasure, while dimly looming behind the window like a white patch.

Spirka was silent, thinking about Nyura: once during the war, when Nyura was about twenty-three and a widow with two little brats, Spirka (who was in his fourteenth year), at night, threw a sack of grain off his cart into her garden (they were traveling in a string of carts to the city for milling). It seemed like it was this very window at Nyura's that he had knocked on and said:

"Look in the garden, by the bathhouse... And hide it further away."

And when he came to Nyura two days later, also at night, she thew herself on him:

"Why, Spirka, you striped snake, did you want to put me in jail?! Why do you walk about filled, and throw things secretly to others?"

Spirka explained:

"But it wasn't for me! Why are you raising such a fuss?"

"Who was it for, then?"

"For you. They have to eat you know!.." The "they" referred to Nyura's children. "They sit there hungry..."

Nyura howled like a cow, and rushed to embrace Spirka. Thrown into confusion, Spirka swore.

"Well there you are!.. You'll pound it in the mortar for them, and bake flat cakes in the ashes... And you can have them with eggs, very, very good..."

That's what he suddenly remembered.

"Why are you standing there?" asked Nyura. "The door is open... Don't wake the old folks."

Spirka stood there. There was a cruel curiosity in his character: what will she do now?

"Spirka?.. Well, what's with you?"

Silence.

"Mindless fool... He wakes me and then begins... Well, then, go to hell!" Nyura went toward her bed.

Without a noise Spirka stole through the entrance room where Nyura's old folks were snoring, and found himself in her room.

"Why are you playing games?"

Spirka began to feel unbearably sorry for Nyura... What the hell's going on? It would've been better not to come in then.

"That's enough, Nyurka, let's sleep."

Three days later, in the evening, Spirka went to the Prokudins'. The new people weren't at home. Spirka talked with the old folks for a while. He told how the earthly Mother-of-God appeared before a certain soldier...

Irina Ivanovna arrived. Alone. She was fresh: she brought into the house the cool of the street on a spring evening. She was surprised and, it seemed to Spirka, pleased.

Calm and decisive, Spirka walked into the room.

"A little bouquet," he offered. And he handed the woman a blood-red flaming bouquet of fire-flowers.

"Oh!"—the woman was pleased—"Oh, what nice ones! What are they called? I never saw any like these..."

"Fire-flowers." There was a cheerful ringing in Spirka's chest: so it always was when there was a prospect of fighting or embracing a woman he wanted. He didn't hide his love. "I'll bring them to you often now."

"But no, why?.. After all, it's extra trouble..."

"Oh," Spirka flirted, "it's really trouble! I go right by, you just cut them with a scythe." Spirka thought for a moment that it was after all a good thing that he was handsome. Another would've been finished long ago, and that's all there is to it. He smiled; it was easy for him.

The woman also began to laugh and grew confused. Spirka was delighted, just as he was when on a very hot day he drank very cold water from a spring, putting his whole face in it. He drank and drank—and like a little flame through his body, an agonizing warmth flowed. He took the woman by her hand... As in a dream!—only he would not wake up.

The woman tried to withdraw her hand... Spirka didn't release it.

"Why are you doing this?.. You shouldn't."

"Why shouldn't I?" Everything that Spirka was capable of, everything that always worked smoothly with other women, all this he now wanted to use on this dear weak being. He prayed in his soul: "Lord help me! Let her not put up a fight!" He drew the woman to him... He saw her surprised eyes, close to him, widen. Now—so that her hand wouldn't tremble and weaken— "Lord, I don't need anything else now—I'll kiss her and that'll be all." And he kissed her. And he stroked the white, tender, little throat... And again he kissed the soft pliant lips. And then her husband entered... Spirka didn't hear him come in. He saw the woman's head jerk up and fright splash in her eyes... Spirka heard behind him the derisive voice:

"There they are. And the husband."

Spirka released the woman. There was neither shame nor fear. It was sad. Such disappointment took hold of that neat, composed, confident man... The host arrived! And they have everything, the devils, and they are everywhere—these charmed people. He looked at the husband.

"Bold fellow. Well, what happened, did you make it?" Sergei Yurevich wanted to smile but a smile wouldn't come; only his eyes narrowed badly, and his fat lips trembled in an offended way. He looked at his wife. "Why are you silent? Why have you turned pale?!" A scream—malicious and sharp—lashed the woman like a whip. "Slut!.. Did you have enough time?" The husband stepped toward her...

Spirka blocked the way. He saw up close his dark eyes blazing with hurt and anger... And Spirka caught in addition a subtle Eau-de-Cologne chill emanating from Sergei Yurevich's

66

cleanly shaven cheeks.

"Calm down," said Spirka.

In the next instant a short, strong arm drew Spirka from the room.

"Well, now, my handsome fellow, let's go!" Spirka could do nothing with this arm: it was as if welded to the nape of his neck, and the strength of the arm was almost inhuman, exactly like being pushed back by a connecting-rod.

Spirka was dragged like this through the old people's room; they looked wide-eyed both at their neighbor and at Spirka.

"I caught a mangy cat," explained their neighbor.

The horror that Spirka experienced!.. The shame, the pain, the malice—everything was mixed inside of him and was suffocating him.

"Animal, snake," Spirka said hoarsely, "What are you doing?.."

They came out on the porch... The connecting-rod went into motion, and Spirka flew down from the high porch and sprawled out on the damp, dirty straw, where people wiped their feet.

"I'll kill you," flashed in Spirka's head.

Sergei Yurevich came down towards him...

"Get up."

Spirka jumped up before he was ordered... And immediately he again flew to the ground. With horror and disgust he understood: "He's beating me!" And again he jumped up and tried to slip under the monstrous connecting-rod to get to the physical culture teacher's throat. But a second connecting-rod quickly got him in the jaw from below.

Spirka was thrown backwards; he tasted copper in his mouth. Again he threw himself on the teacher... He knew how to fight, but his rage, pain, shame, and consciousness of his helplessness before the connecting-rods—all this deprived him of his former deftness and composure. Blind rage kept throwing him ahead, and the connecting-rods continued to work. It appeared that he never once reached the teacher. He didn't get up from the last blow. The teacher bent over him.

"I'll get even with you," Spirka said unclearly, weakly, seriously.

"Let's consider this a lesson in courtesy. You have to get rid of your camp tricks." The teacher was also speaking seriously, and not maliciously.

"I'll kill you," repeated Spirka. In his mouth there was a painful mishmash, as if he had chewed up a bottle of Eau-de-

67

Cologne—it cut and burnt everything: "I'll kill you, I tell you."

"For what?" calmly asked the teacher. "What will you kill me for?.. Rascal."

The teacher went back to the house, slammed the door behind him, and put the latch in place.

Spirka tried to get up but couldn't. His head buzzed, but he was thinking clearly. He knew how he could get into the Prokudins' storeroom through an opening in the roof of the house. The storeroom wasn't kept locked: a twine rope was slipped in a loop over a small nail, and that's all, so that the door wouldn't come open itself. The door into the old people's room was also never locked at night. In the other room there was no lock at all. He knew so much about the Prokudins' house because their son Mishka had been Spirka's comrade since youth, and Spirka often visited and even stayed overnight there. Now Mishka wasn't there, but everything, of course, remained just as it was before.

With difficulty Spirka finally raised himself, climbed to his feet, and held on to the wall of the house... He went toward the river. His strength was returning.

He washed his beaten face, and examined his suit and shirt with the help of matches... He couldn't let his mother see the blood and suspect something was wrong when he went to get his gun. He could get his gun for any reason: To go into the woods with grain, and sit there in the morning by the lake.

His mother was already sleeping.

"Is that you, Spirka?" she asked in a sleepy voice from over the stove.

"It's me. Sleep. I have to go to work now."

"Get the baked potato in the stove, and the milk in the entrance room... You can eat on the road."

"O.K., I'll take it with me." In the dark Spirka took his gun from the wall: then he busied himself in the entrance room for a while... He came back into the room where his mother was sleeping (he left his gun in the entrance room). He got up on the stove platform, found his mother's head in the dark, and stroked her thin warm hair. He often caressed his mother when he'd been drinking; she didn't stir.

"You've been drinking... How can you go out now?"

Spirka's mother loved him more and more with the years; she felt sorry for him, and was ashamed that he would not in any way settle down with a family—the way good people do! She was waiting, perhaps, for some independent widow or divorcee to latch onto their house.

"It doesn't matter, I'm going."

"Well, Christ be with you." His mother made the sign of the cross over him in the darkness. "Drive carefully, now."

"Everything will be all right." Spirka was cheerful and wanted to leave right away and somehow forget about his mother: she was the one whom it was painful for him to leave in this life, his mother.

He walked down the dark street, firmly pressing his gun. He kept wanting to get loose from thoughts of his mother. She wouldn't live through it. They'd lead him away tied up, and she would see... Spirka quickened his pace. "Lord, give her strength to bear it," he prayed. He almost ran. And toward the end he even began to run. He was excited, as if he were running not to kill anyone but to the bed of Irina Ivanovna, to warmth and harmony. She rose before his eyes, Irina Ivanovna, but somehow immediately disappeared. He remembered her lips, soft and half-closed, but the taste of blood in his mouth prevented him from enjoying the recollection—as well as the Eau-de-Cologne breeze from Sergei Yurevich's smooth cheeks. He remembered that scented breeze now for some reason.

Spirka was running and quietly singing to himself to keep his spirits up:

"Will the black horse really
Bite through the bit?
Really will my dear one..."

The whole house is dark. "Yes, yes..." Spirka was soon speaking thoughtfully to himself. "We'll take the ladder... we'll set it up, and into my dear one's... Quiet now." He made it safely to the storeroom, and listened there—it was quiet. Only his heart was knocking against his ribs. "Calm down, Spirya!" The rope, too, broke almost noiselessly, only the nail sprang out and hit with a delicate tinkle. After extending his free hand forward, Spirka soundlessly moved through the entrance room touching the wall along the way until he located the door. "Yes, yes..." He bent down, stuck his fingers under the bottom of the door as far as they would reach, lifted it, and pulled it out toward himself. The door opened with a quiet and pleasant sigh: "P-akh." It opened the rest of the way without a sound. It smelled like old people were living there, a sheepskin coat that had got damp, a warm stove, dough... And this was the place where he had been dragged out by his skin. "Carry me through, Lord, so the old people don't wake up." It was terrifying: something was bound to get in his way! "Oh, how he beat me, how he beat me! He really knows how."

Spirka was himself surprised at his lightness, his skill. He

69

didn't even hear himself. He groped for the door of the second room, and raised it, too, from below... The door creaked. Spirka quickly, carefully closed it after him... He was in their room! In the darkness of the room, weakly diluted by the light of the street lamp, the bed creaked. Spirka found a switch on the wall and clicked it. Sergei Yurevich was sitting on the bed looking at him. Irina Ivanovna raised herself... At first she stared at her husband, then, from his look, she turned to Spirka and his gun. Silently she opened her mouth... Spirka understood that Sergei Yurevich wasn't sleeping: he was watching, very knowingly, motionless, with his dark eyes.

"I warned you I'd get even," said Spirka. He tried to pull back the hammers of the double-barrelled gun, but they were already raised (when had he raised them?).

"Do you remember? I told you."

Spirka was not disturbed by the fact that Irina Ivanovna was sitting in a woman's undershirt, that one strap had slid down over her shoulder, and her breast, dull white and firm (and which had not nursed children), was completely visible up to the nipple.

The couple was silent. They looked at Spirka.

"Get out of bed," ordered Spirka.

"Spiridon... you'll get the firing squad..."

"I know. Get out."

"Spiridon! Really..."

"Get out!"

Sergei Yurevich jumped from the bed—in his shorts and undershirt.

Spirka put his gun to his shoulder.

Sergei Yurevich turned deathly pale...

And at this point Irina Ivanovna suddenly began to scream, and so horribly, so loudly, furiously, insistently, as to be quite unlike herself—she was so small and quick, with warm soft lips—somehow quite inhumanly she screamed, bitterly and despairingly. Then she fell from the bed and crawled, extending her arms...

"You shouldn't! O-o-oh! You shouldn't! O-o-oh!.." And she tried to grab the gun—on her knees—she tried...

Then Sergei Yurevich leaped on Spirka with his arms spread wide. He got a blow in the chest from the butt of the gun, and he fell.

"My darling!.. You shouldn't..," wailed the little woman. It was as if she had forgotten Spirka's name. "O-o-oh!..."

In the other part of the house, behind the door, the old people were roused and they too began to yell.

"You shouldn't!" screamed the woman, and she shook her

head and kept trying to embrace his legs. She was crawling without underpants—she didn't notice that her undershirt had slipped down her back, and she kept trying to grab Spirka's legs.

Spirka lost his head, tried to shove the woman away... And somehow it suddenly came to him clearly that if he shot now, then later it would be impossible for him either to pray away this shot, or to cover it with wine. "If only she wouldn't wail so!.. But how much strength she has!"

"Your mother!" cursed Spirka.

He walked out of the room and strode away from the dark house. Somehow he immediately became very tired. He remembered his mother, and he ran a little in order to escape from this thought of his mother. From all kinds of thoughts. He remembered Irina Ivanovna again, naked, and both pity and love for her burned his heart. It became light for a moment—as if he had not made a mess of it. Lord, how she howled!.. As if she were grieving for a dead husband! And again—his mother... Here's the one who will howl! Spirka ran faster. He ran to the cemetery and sat on the ground. It was dark. He aimed the barrels at his heart... He reached for the hammers. He thought: "Well!.. Is that all?!" His fingers groped for the two cold thin triggers...

"Now's the time," he thought again. And suddenly he saw himself clearly, lying with chest opened up, arms spread, looking with empty eyes into the clear morning sky... The sun will rise, and above him—his cold body—blue flies, fat and greedy, will buzz. Then the whole village will come running—to look. Some will say "Maybe we should cover him." "What?.. Nuts to that!" Spirka shuddered. He sat down. "Wait a moment, fellow, wait. Wait, wait. Just stand there, stupid, don't fool around! I ask you: what is this? Lord!—I was thrown out. Haven't you ever been beaten? What's the big deal?" "What is this?" Spirka asked aloud. "Well?" With disgust and with caution he pushed aside the barrels, regripped the gun, and carefully let forward the hammers. He sighed deeply and gladly. And he began to speak loudly, foolishly, experiencing great relief and gladness.

"What is this now, Spirya? Ai-yai! How can this be? Was it a little boy who was beat up? Beat up... Bad, right? I want to blow my brains out—pook!.. How stupid!" Spirka even began to laugh, and touched his lip; his lip had been split by the teacher's fist, and there was pain when he laughed. "What were you doing? What were you doing? (His smashed mouth could not get the sounds right.) "It is really possible? Ai-yai! That's no good. You're beaten up and right away you've got to shoot yourself. Oh-oh!"

Spirka lay down on his back on the cool earth, and spread his arms... This is how he would've been lying tomorrow. Here where a heart now beats—Spirka placed his hand on his chest—here there'd be a hole ripped open from two shells—bigger than a cap. Perhaps he would've caught fire and his jacket and shirt would've been turned to ashes. He would lie there naked... Oh, shit! How disgusting to look at him! Spirka sat up, lit a cigarette, and inhaled with delight. He had hurried so much to drive those two charges into himself that he didn't even think of having a little smoke until afterwards. Even those who are to be executed, Spirka had heard, ask to smoke for the last time. He remembered a little girl, his niece: when she felt that her father was getting tired of carrying her on his back, she puckered her face in a funny and pleading way and said: "Hay-eater! Giddyap, hay-eater!" Spirka remembered the girl and laughed. Again he lay down, smoked, and looked at the stars; it seemed that they were almost quivering and ringing: a very thin bell sound; and he too felt like whimpering quietly, like a puppy... He screwed up his eyes and felt the earth carry him smoothly, powerfully. Spirka jumped up. He had to do something, anything at all. "I'll do something now!" he decided. He picked up his gun and began to walk quickly—without knowing where. Only away from the cemetery, from those crosses and the silence. He began to swear at the corpses aloud, though not unkindly.

"Are you down there? Well, then stay there! Lie there—that's your fate. What am I doing here, then? You're lying there, but I can still run a bit over this earth. I'll get around a little."

Now he wanted to run from thoughts of the cemetery, of how he had lain there... He wanted to run anywhere, to anyone. Perhaps he'd tell everything... Maybe, to have a laugh. If only he had a drink! But where now? Where? But doesn't Verka serve refreshments at the tea-room? Aha... one can always eat there! Besides, I can stay the night there as well.

Spirka turned down an alley.

At first Vera grumbled. "What is it—it's not night, it's not day..." Spirka lit a match and illuminated his face.

"Take a look. I was nearly killed, and you're making a big deal out of the time." Vera was frightened. Spirka quietly began to laugh, satisfied.

"And where did all of this happen?" asked Vera.

"At a place... did they do a nice job?"

"My God, Spirka!.. One of these times you'll be beaten to death. Where did it happen?"

"I can't say. It's a secret."

They went into Vera's room. Vera began to draw the curtains

72

closer together and she lit a light. Once again she looked at Spirka... she touched the burning scratches on his face with her warm hand, smelling of cream.

"Oh!.." Spirka exclaimed affectedly. Again he began to laugh and to walk about the room.

"These single women are great people! Somehow it's always cozy and nice at their places. You can walk in straight away if you don't make the floor creak. You have time to think a little... And meanwhile you can fondle your hostess and press her hand... Everything is right to the point and sensible. They tremble, because they're not used to it, and they look at you affectionately and searchingly. They're dear people. They're good. I feel sorry for them."

Vera found a bottle of vodka. She even went down into the cellar and brought up some cucumbers. Only she returned frightened...

"You have something there, a gun maybe? I stopped..."

"A gun. Let it stand there."

"And why do you have a gun?"

"I just do."

"Spirka... why are you doing this?"

Vera had had a good husband, a good peasant, who had died in 1940. God knows what happened. Cancer, probably.

"Spirka!"

"Yes?"

"Are you fighting with someone... or maybe you're running?"

"I'm fighting. Look, I've been wounded." Spirka again began to laugh. Something seemed funny to him. It was nice.

"You're a strange fellow. Perhaps you killed someone?"

"No. Afterwards I'll kill. Later."

"Spirka, I'm afraid. Perhaps you're in trouble... then me as well, as a witness... Well, go to hell!"

"Everything is all right, dear little fool. Why are you so frightened? I didn't kill anyone. I was almost killed myself... and I still have to plan how I'll kill."

"Drink and leave." Vera got angry. "Leave, Spirka. That's the limit for me."

Spirka got serious.

"Calm down. Am I really the kind of person who gets innocent people into trouble? How could you think that? You know me... I'd never come here if... Forget it."

"Carrying your gun at night..."

Spirka emptied the glass and took a bite of cucumber. Vera

hadn't begun to drink.

"I don't want to."

"Why?"

"I don't want to. You frightened me with that gun. Who beat you up?"

"Some strangers. Stop asking about it. It's not necessary." He remembered the teacher... Pale, in his shorts. Spirka shrugged his shoulders, driving out the unpleasant, wicked thought. His gladness was disappearing. "Okay, okay," he said hurriedly. "Don't ask any more about it." And he poured out another half a glass, so he wouldn't have time to think again about the woman teacher, so he wouldn't remember her. But she did come to mind—small, half-naked, scared to death... He remembered all the same.

In the morning Spirka jumped out early. He left his gun at Vera's. "I'll drop back tonight and get it."

"And where are you going?"

"To work, that's where. That... don't chatter about that gun."

"Well, now I'm off to tell everyone: Spirka and his gun spent the night with me..."

"Very clever. Some strangers beat me up... At a tavern. I tried to chase them with my gun, but couldn't catch them."

Vera looked at Spirka with distrust; while Spirka did not even try to seem especially truthful.

"Will you have something to drink?"

"No. Good-bye."

Spirka went to the teachers' house. He went down curving alleys, through backyards, in order to meet fewer people. All the same he ran into two or three. He met the kolkhoz foreman, Ilya Kitaitsev. Ilya maliciously, knowingly, began to smile in the distance.

"Say! Quite a night you had!"

Spirka gave a broad smile, too, overcoming the pain which ran through his whole face like needles. He said:

"Yes, it was, Ilyukha! It was some night. Let's have a smoke."

"How did it happen?"

"Just happened—I fell." Shame, disgrace... His tongue went dead, the tip, from shame. Ilya's subtle little grin cut his heart like a blade. "Let's smoke, how about it?"

"Let's smoke, let's smoke. You had a good fall... From high up probably. How did it happen?"

"Well, Ilyukha... it just happened—people fall. If I shove you

74

now, you'll fall too. Well, don't you think so?" Ilyukha stopped smiling.

"What's with you?"

"And what's with your yapping? Hell, right away you're being sarcastic! You can't say a word without sarcasm. Let me pass!"

Now he couldn't live in the village for a while. "For a single disgrace you have to go to the end of the world... All kinds of lip-flappers will have a good smile... Oh, teacher, teacher... How you learned to work your hands! Very well, very well. It would be nice to hang you by your feet to the ceiling... No, before your eyes... to kiss your wife, all of her, till she was sore, so that she would scream."

Cruel feelings drove Spirka ahead, as if something were shoving him from behind. He didn't notice that he was hurrying again. But he knew that now he wouldn't throw himself on the teacher, no. That would come later... Steady now. It's horrible. That's afterwards.

Later, recalling that morning conversation with the teachers, Spirka experienced no satisfaction.

He appeared like some ragged, dark figure stepping out from behind a tree with an axe... He stood on the threshold. The teacher was already dressed, shaved... he was fresh from the electric shaver and was standing in front of the mirror. It hummed near his face. The other teacher, swollen from sleep and yesterday's screaming, tender, white, was preparing breakfast. She, too, froze, with a plate in her hands.

"A single warning," Spirka began to say in a business-like manner. "What happened here with us—not a sound to anyone. Pass that warning to the old people yourselves. I'm disappearing from the horizon for a time, but, Sergei Yurevich, all the same, excuse me, I'll get even."

"What is this 'get even'?" Irina Ivanovna stupidly asked again.

"I got an advance. I must work it off." Spirka didn't know when this would take place, but sometime he would come—calm, handsome, well-dressed—and say: "I've come to pay you." And whatever the situation was like and no matter what Spirka himself was like then, only the teacher would lose his composure and become pitiable. And he would plead: "Spiridon, I was stupid, I beg your forgiveness..." "Well, well," Spirka would say politely, "you shouldn't be on your knees now. Your woman is here now... your wife, she must respect you."

"What advance?" Irina Ivanovna could not understand at all.

75

"Taken from whom?"

"He will take his revenge on me. He'll avenge himself," clarified the teacher. "Fine, Spiridon, I've accepted your offer for a meeting. We won't tell anyone anything."

"Okay... Good-bye for the time being." Spirka went out.

"But where is this place I'm disappearing to?" he thought. He even stopped. Only now, suddenly, the realization distinctly came to him that he had, it seemed, decided to leave.

"But where? Where?" It turned out that he knew this too: the city of B—sk, which was fifty kilometers away. When he had decided this, he didn't know, but it was in him already. Only an inborn caution demanded that the decision be checked again.

Passing his house, Spirka went on to the garage. There he still had to endure the amused glances of the drivers. He was annoyed and nervous. He took his route assignment and then quickly drove off.

The road calmed him down a little. He began to think. Again he tried to generate in his imagination the sweet picture which had brightened his outlook when he was talking that morning with the teacher: he would come to him—polite, well-dressed... But the picture he wanted for some reason didn't come. Annoyed, Spirka wanted to get himself excited, to help it along; wait now— it'll come... "Hello!" No... it's not coming. It's repulsive to think about all this. It suddenly struck him—though he renounced what he saw in himself—that he had no real, all-consuming malice toward the teacher. All those visions: the teacher with his head hanging down, or the teacher, pale, pitiable, crawling at his feet— Spirka had wanted this so much that they, those pictures, became dear to him, sweet. He could calm down then, and maybe even sometime do what he planned to do: hang the teacher with his head down. After all, you have to plan something for a fierce enemy! You have to see him, if only in your thoughts, as humbled, crushed. You have to! But... Spirka even began to fidget in his seat: he understood that he found no malice in himself for the teacher. If he had figured it out, if he had thought about his whole life as well, he would also have understood, would have remembered, that in general he never harbored ill-will toward anyone. But he didn't think of that and desperately resisted, trying to stir up malice within himself.

"Well, chump!.. You're trash, aren't you? Thrown out like some mangy creature, and you... Well, now! How I was beaten! Laughing and playing... I was dragged out, trampled. But what kind of a person are you? After all, people will laugh at you. And the teacher will be the first one to laugh. What are you?

Not a single old woman would allow herself to be treated like that." There was no malice.

"And what now?" Spirka didn't know how to answer this question. And later, in the course of the day, he still tried to understand: "What now?" And he couldn't.

His personal life in general suddenly grew hateful, and seemed monstrously devoid of sense. And Spirka grew more and more convinced of this. At times, he even felt loathing for himself. He had never felt that before. Peace came to him, but a kind of deathly peace, such a peace that a man who has gone astray understands before the end, when he realizes that he has gotten lost and sits down on a stump. He doesn't scream any more, he doesn't look for the path, but sits down and stays seated, and that's it.

Spirka did just this: he turned off the road into the forest, and pulled into a meadow, turned off the motor, stepped out, looked around, and sat on a stump.

"Here's a place to shoot oneself," he suddenly thought calmly. "Or else at the cemetery. But here it's pretty."

In truth it was pretty. Only Spirka did not especially examine this beauty, but somehow immediately understood all of it.... And he sat. He bent over, picked a blade of grass, bit it between his teeth, and began to listen to the birds. Small proprietors of the forest whistled, peeped, and chirped somewhere in the bushes. A pair of handsome woodpeckers, beetle-black with little white aprons on their breasts, flew out of the thicket, selected a young pine, ran along it up and down, flashing with their red crests, pecked a little, didn't find anything, took off, and again, in a low flight, hid in the bushes.

"They, too, fly in pairs," Spirka thought. He thought again that people envy birds... They say: "Like a heavenly bird." You could envy them. Spirka thought again about the teachers: he probably threw out those flowers Spirka brought her; they were probably lying under the window, withered.... Such pretty little flowers, those red ones. Spirka smiled. Spirya the fool... There are little flowers here too. Blue, white, yellow ones... There's a lily flowering, there's some lungwort... And over there a bunch of white caps had sprung up. Spirka loved the fragrance of white caps. He got up, tore off a tight little bundle of the small white flowers which had collected together in a compact circle as large as a saucer. He sat down again on the stump, spread the flowers on his hands, sank his face into them, and began greedily to inhale the cool, damp-astringent, marsh fragrance of this modest, unspectacular local flower. He covered his face with his hands and

77

remained sitting that way. For a long time he sat motionless. Maybe he was thinking. Maybe crying...

... Spirka was found three days later in the forest, in a cheerful meadow. He was lying with his face buried in the earth, clinging to the grass with his hands. His gun lay next to him. No one could understand how he had fired it. He was hit in the heart, but he was lying face down... Somehow he managed to get it out from under him.

They brought him back, they buried him.

Many people were there. Many cried...

NOTES

1. Original Russian: "Suraz," 1970; reprinted with changes: *Zemliaki* (1970); *Kharaktery* (1973), pp. 66-91; and *Izbrannye proizvedeniia v dvukh tomakh* (1975), Vol. 1, pp. 186-199. Note: *Suraz* is not the usual Russian word for 'bastard'; it is a Siberian dialect word that also carries the connotation of 'distressing event.'

A BIRD OF PASSAGE[1]

The blacksmith Filipp Nasedkin—a peaceful man and an unflagging worker, respected by everyone in the village—suddenly took to drink. That is, he didn't really take to drink, but he started to enjoy the odd drop. It was his wife, Nyura-the-Nuisance, as she was known, who called it "taking to drink." It was she who stormed into the kolkhoz office and created such a stink that everyone decided Filya must indeed have taken to drink. They also decided they must take him in hand.

What made them most suspicious was that Filya had fallen in with Sanya Neverov. Sanya was a very curious individual. Consumed by various diseases (pleurisy and a perforated stomach ulcer and liver trouble and colitis and God knows what, including piles), he lived, as he said himself, from day to day, never knowing what the morrow might bring. Of course, he didn't work, but he did have a little money from somewhere. People would gather at his place to drink, and he would always make them welcome.

Sanya's hut was at the edge of the village; it was subsiding at the back over the steep river bank, while its two little window-eyes looked out far, far away—across the river to the blue hills. Around the hut was a little enclosure with some old logs and a couple of birch trees growing—a place where one could really relax.

Who knows, perhaps Sanya had seen and learned a lot in the course of his life (he never talked much about himself), but he certainly had a way of making searching comments about life and death. He was a genuinely kind man, too. People felt drawn to him as to a close friend who was lonely and ill. You could sit for hours with him on the old warm log outside his hut gazing at the hills together. You could think about things or not, as you wished: either way you felt better, more clear in your head, as though you had suddenly become an immense, free being, able to fathom the beginning and end of your life, or as though you had taken the measure of priceless things and understood them all. "Well, what does it all come to?" You would reflect. "Things are good, that's all."

The married women had hated Sanya from the moment he first appeared in the village. That had been in the spring, when he took a fancy to a broken-down gypsy hut, made a bid for it, bought it, and moved in. As was the custom, he immediately received a nickname—the Bird of Passage; and he was also called

Sanya, properly enough, seeing his name was Alexander. Filya, whenever he went to see Sanya, felt as though he were cradling in his hands a weak but still warm sparrow with drops of blood on its wings—a little bundle of undying life. And all Filya's feelings—good and evil—were aroused when people slandered Sanya. As he said at the kolkhoz board meeting:

"Sanya's a human being. Get off his back. Stop pestering him."

"He's a drunkard," interjected the bookkeeper, a middle-aged but still smart-looking woman activist.

Filya looked at her and was suddenly struck by the fact that she had lipstick on. Somehow he'd never noticed that before.

"Silly fool!" Filya said to her.

"Filipp!" the kolkhoz chairman barked sternly. "Watch your language."

"I do go to see Sanya, and I shall keep on going," Filya repeated, feeling a vicious force within him.

"Why?"

"What business is it of yours?"

"You'll go out of your mind there! Why, he can't have more than a year or eighteen months to live. It doesn't matter to him how he lives them. But for you it's different."

"He'll outlive you all," Filya asserted, rather haphazardly.

"All right, suppose he does. But why should you be driven to drink?"

"You just try driving me to drink," chuckled Filya. "I know who would get drunker. Have you ever seen me really drunk?"

"That's what they all say to start with," shouted the chairman, the bookkeeper, and the agronomist in unison, supported by the brigade-leader, Naum Sarantsev, who was no mean drinker himself. "That's the thin end of the wedge!"

"That's what makes the drug so dangerous," the chairman began to expatiate. "At first it doesn't seem very frightening—indeed, it leads you on. Did you ever happen to play cards at a public market soon after the War?"

"No."

"Well, I did. I was returning from the front, bringing with me a bit of loot: a Paul Bouret watch, an accordion... I had to change trains at Novosibirsk, and rather than kick my heels I went off to the market, where I saw some people playing cards. The old game, guessing three cards. 'Come on, soldier boy,' they said, 'try your luck!' I'd already heard from the lads how we soldiers would get cheated at that kind of thing, so I said: 'No, count me out.' 'Oh, come on, give it a try!' 'We-e-ell,' I thought to myself, 'all right then, I'll risk thirty rubles.' " The chairman warmed to his theme, and his audience listened, smiling. Filya sat thumbing his cap between his knees. " 'All right then,' I said, 'but don't play me any tricks, you crooks!' You had to guess one card out of three. First of all he shows them to you, then he shuffles them in front of you and lays them face down. All three. You have to guess one of them, the ace of diamonds, let's say. Does it all right there in front of you, the bastard! Okay, so he showed me all three face up—'Remembered them?' he asked. 'Yes,' I said. 'Right, then: watch!' One, two, three, he shuffled them around. I tried to follow the ace of diamonds. 'Now, which one?' he asked. I prodded a card with my finger and he turned it over: the ace of diamonds. I won! And they let me win another three or four... But no more: by evening I'd lost my accordion, my watch and all my money—just like that! Lost the whole lot! I was going to try and fight for them, but there turned out to be a whole crowd of them. So I arrived home empty-handed. And that, Filipp, is how every plague starts—almost from nothing. They let me win a few to begin with, and only then started to clean me out. And all the time I kept wanting to win back my losses, you see, I kept on hoping... That's how I lost it all. Now, vodka works by that very same method: first of all it lulls and soothes you, then it gets a proper grip on you. So you just watch your step, Filipp, don't delude yourself."

"I'm not eighteen any more, you know."

"Vodka doesn't ask to see your birth certificate! It doesn't give a damn what age you are. Now you're a good worker, and your family's still in good shape... So we're just warning you, stop going to see Sanya! He may be a good man and all that, but see how our womenfolk have complained about him."

"They're fools," repeated Filya.

"You drum away like a woodpecker: 'Fools! Fools!' Is your Nyura a fool, then?"

"Yes, she's a fool too, What's the point of making a fuss?"

"She doesn't want to let the family be broken up."

"Nobody's breaking it up. She's the one who's doing her damnedest to do that."

"Well, that's your affair. We've warned you. And that Sanya of yours, we'll simply run him out of the village, that's all... It's high time."

"You've no right to. He's a sick man."

"We'll find a way round that. If he's sick he shouldn't drink. Off you go to work, Filipp."

* * * * * *

"Did they summon you?" asked Sanya that evening, his left eyelid quivering nervously.

"They did." Filya felt ashamed for his wife, the chairman and the whole board.

"Did they tell you to stop coming?"

"Yu-u-up... What do they think I am, a child?"

"Ah, yes," agreed Sanya. "Of course." His eyelid was still quivering. He gazed at the distant hills as if he were expecting the setting sun to turn round and rise again from behind them. "At night, some time after eleven, the nightingales sing. Ah, the little devils, how they put on a show. To impress one another, I suppose."

"They're attracting the females," Filya explained.

"Well, they certainly do it beautifully. My, how beautifully. Men don't have it in them. Men are strong by nature."

"You?.. Strong?" thought Filya.

"I respect strong people," Sanya went on. "When I was a child there was a little boy who used to bully me—he was stronger than I was. My father advised me to do some training, some weight-lifting, and in a month I'd be beating *him* up. So I started lifting the axle of a freight wagon. I practiced for three days, and ruptured myself. I got an umbilical hernia."

"You should have got a dumb-bell, if you were weaker—fastened it to a strap and clouted him over the head with it. I was a quiet little boy, too, and when a bully once started to pester me I let him have it, just once, with the pendulum of a grandfather clock. I never had any more trouble from him."

Sanya was becoming intoxicated. His gaze was clouding over, descending from the distant hills and settling on the river, the road and the wild raspberry bush by the fence. His eyes warmed and became joyful.

"You see, Filipp, I'm fifty-two. Let's ignore the first twelve years, when I wasn't fully aware. That leaves forty. Forty times I've seen the spring, forty times!.. And I have only just realized how wonderful it is. Previously I kept on putting it off, I never seemed to have time, I was always bustling around acquiring more knowledge, trying to become a big name... But now, whoa! Hold it! Let me take it all in. Let me feast my eyes on it. It's a good thing I still have a few springs left. Because I understand a great deal now. That's all! One can't understand more. One shouldn't try."

A chill breath came from the river below, advancing upwards

82

almost imperceptibly—just a gentle, marshy current of air, stifled by the immense, calm warmth of the earth and the sky.

Filya did not understand Sanya, and did not try. He, too, felt that life on earth was good. Out of politeness he kept the conversation going.

"Tell me, are you quite alone in the world?"

"Not at all. I have relatives, but you see, I'm ill." Sanya was not complaining, not even in a veiled way. "Besides, I got into bad habits—drinking... I'm an embarrassment to them. That's natural."

"You must have had a difficult life."

"It's been varied. At times I gave the blows, at times I received them. But now it's all over. Or rather, no... Right now I am conscious of eternity. When it starts to get dark and it's still warm, then I am conscious of eternity."

That was quite beyond Filya. Another peasant was sitting with them, Egor Sinkin, who had a beard because of a wartime jaw injury. He couldn't make anything of it either.

"Did you do time in prison, then?" Egor inquired.

"Bless you, you're very anxious to make a convict of me! No, it's just that I was alive and didn't realize how wonderful it is to live. Oh, I did this and that... Rushed pointlessly about. But I'm at peace now. I was an artist, if you really want to know. But at the same time I wasn't an artist." Sanya laughed softly, sincerely, and with good humor. "Now, I've really confused you. Don't worry. There are plenty of queer folk around, eccentrics... My brother sends me money. He's rich. Or at least, no, not exactly rich, but he has enough to live on. And he gives me some."

That the two peasants could understand: his brother pitied him.

"If only I could start all over again!" On Sanya's thin, dark face his muscles and his sharp cheekbones stood out in ridges. His eyes shone feverishly. He was worked up. "I would explain what I know now: that man is an accidental, beautiful and agonizing attempt on Nature's part to understand itself. A fruitless attempt I assure you, because in nature along with man there lives a canker. Death! And death is unavoidable, but we will ne-e-ever take in that fact. Nature will never understand itself. So it gets angry and takes vengeance in the form of man. Like an evil... mm..." Sanya's further words were inaudible. In effect he was talking to himself, for the peasants got tired of straining to hear him and began to discuss their own affairs.

"Love? Yes," Sanya muttered. "But love only complicates and confuses everything. It makes the whole attempt painful,

83

that's all it does. Hooray for death! Even if we can't comprehend it, nevertheless death enables us to realize that life is wonderful. And that's not at all sad, no... Perhaps it's senseless, yes... Yes, it's senseless all right..."

The peasants realized that Sanya was by now thoroughly drunk, and made off home. Filya wandered along the alleys and footpaths, and gradually the ardent faith that life was wonderful faded from his breast. There remained only a heart-rending sense of pity for the man still sitting there alone on his log, muttering away to himself about something he considered vital.

* * * * * * *

A week later Sanya died.

He died sober. At night. Filya was with him.

The whole time Sanya knew very well that he was dying. Only occasionally did his mind wander, as though bent on some reflection of its own, and then he would stare at the wall, ignoring Filya.

"Sanya," Filya would call, "don't let your mind wander. That makes things worse. Perhaps you could get up and walk about a bit? Let me take you for a walk round the hut, eh?.. Sanya?"

"Mm?"

"Force yourself. Stretch yourself a bit."

"Filipp, go and... go and fetch a raspberry branch. It's growing by the fence. Mind you don't shake the dust off. Bring it here."

Filya stepped out into the darkness, and it overwhelmed him with its immensity. A silent spring night, dark and melancholy—it was infinite. Filya had never been afraid of anything in his life, but now for some reason he felt apprehensive. He hastily broke off a fresh raspberry branch, damp with night dew, and hurried back into the hut. He thought: "How can there be dust on it? It's too early—the roads are still muddy. Where could dust come from?"

Sanya propped himself up on his elbow and stared hard in Filya's direction. He was waiting, and Filya saw nothing but those eyes in the hut as he came in. They flickered with pain, beseeching, appealing to him.

"I don't want it, Filipp!" he said quite distinctly. "I know just what it looks like. No, I don't want it."

Filya dropped the branch.

Sanya, exhausted, let his head fall back on the pillow and

84

then said in a low, restless voice: "My God, what an eternity... Another year, six months! I don't need more."

Filya's heart tightened. He knew now that Sanya was on the point of death. Any moment. He said nothing.

"I'm not afraid," whispered Sanya, hastening with his failing strength. "I can face it... But if I could have another year, then I'd accept death. After all, one has to accept it anyway. But it can't happen just like this... This isn't an execution. So how can it happen just like this?"

"Have a little vodka, Sanya."

"Another six months! The summer... I don't need anything, I'll just gaze at the sun. Do you know I can't remember a single blade of grass? Who needs my death, when I don't want to die?" Sanya was weeping. "Filipp..."

"Yes, Sanya."

"Who needs my death? It's so stupid, so stupid. Like a great mindless wheel rolling over you."

Filya was weeping too: he could feel the tears trickling down his cheeks. He wiped them angrily away with his sleeve.

"Sanya, don't call Death names, and perhaps he'll... er... go away. Don't swear at him."

"I'm not swearing at him. But this is so stupid! So hard... and no one can help. Blockhead!"

Sanya closed his eyes and fell silent. He said nothing for a long time. Filya even began to think it was all over.

"Turn me..." asked Sanya. "Turn me over." Filya turned his friend towards the wall.

"Blockhead," said Sanya once more very quietly, and then fell silent again.

Filya must have sat for about an hour in his chair, waiting for Sanya to ask for something. Or even to speak. But Sanya did not speak again. He was dead.

* * * * * * *

Filya and the other men of the village buried Sanya. They buried him quietly, without unnecessary words, just a brief remembrance.

Filya planted a birch at the head of the grave. It took root. And whenever the warm southerly winds blew, the birch would bow down and quiver with its multitude of little green hands— as if it were trying to say something. And could not.

1970   —Translated by Geoffrey A. Hosking

1. Original Russian: "Zaletnyi" (1970); reprinted: *Zemliaki* (1970); *Besedy pri iasnoi lune* (1974), pp. 135-141; and *Izbrannye proizvedeniia v dvukh tomakh* (1975), Vol. 1, pp. 179-186.

"I BELIEVE!"[1]

Every Sunday a mood of depression would descend upon him. Real, deep-down, gut-rot depression. Maksim could feel it physically, as if a slovenly, slightly diseased peasant woman with bad breath were pawing him shamelessly all over, caressing him and trying to kiss him.

"Again! It's come over me again!"

"Oh, Lord! You're just like a soap bubble: hither and thither, wherever the wind blows. Depression, indeed!" mocked Maksim's wife Lyuda, a surly working woman who had never in her life known what depression was. "What have you got to be depressed about?"

Maksim Yarikov looked at his wife with black eyes shining fiercely. He gritted his teeth.

"Aye, that's right, swear at it. Use foul language, and perhaps my depression will go away. Go on, you're good at cursing."

Sometimes Maksim would restrain himself from fighting because he really wanted to be understood. "You won't understand."

"Why not? Explain and I will understand."

"Well, look, you've got all the normal parts of the body—arms, legs... and what not. What size they are is another question, but they're all more or less in the right place. If your leg hurts, you feel it. If you're hungry, you get something to eat. Okay?"

"Well?"

Maksim got lightly to his feet (he was a slight forty-year old, pugnacious and impetuous: he never managed to wear himself out at work, though he put a lot into it) and he walked up and down the parlor, his eyes flashing aggressively.

"But a man has a soul too! Here it is, here, and it aches!" Maksim pointed to his chest. "I'm not making it up. I can feel it elementally—it aches!"

"Have you got any other aches?"

"Listen!" Maksim yelped. "If you really want to understand me, listen! Even if you *were* born a blockhead, try to grasp the fact that some people do have a soul. After all, it's not as if I were asking you for three rubles for vodka, what I want is... Oh, you idiot!" Maksim suddenly broke off, losing his self-control. He realized that he would never be able to explain to Lyuda what was going on inside him, that she would never understand him.

Ne-e-ever! Not even if he were to cut open his breast with a knife, take out his soul and present it to her in his open hands. She would just say "Ugh! How gruesome." Anyway, he didn't believe in a fleshly soul of that kind. So what was the point of talking and getting worked up? He went on: "Ask me who I hate more than anyone in the world, and I'll tell you: people who have no soul. Or a rotten one. Talking to you is like knocking my head against a brick wall."

"Huh! Windbag!"

"Oh, get lost!"

"Why are you so irritable, anyway, if you've got a soul?"

"What d'you think a soul is, a currant bun? You could never understand why I bear this burden everywhere—my soul, that is—and why it aches. That's why I'm irritable. I get worked up."

"All right, then, be like that, damn you! Normal people wait for Sunday to come round so they can relax in a civilized fashion. They go to the movies or whatever. But you, if you please, you get worked up. You soap-bubble!"

Maksim stopped at the window and stood there for hours gazing out at the street. It was winter, and frosty. The village sent its columns of grey smoke up into the clear sky—people warming themselves. If a woman went by with buckets yoked over her shoulders, her boots could be heard crunching on the firm, crusty snow, even from behind double window panes. Or a silly dog would start barking and then fall silent again—all because of the frost. Everyone was sitting at home, in their own warmth. Chatting, making dinner, discussing relatives... Some would be drinking, but that was scarcely any more exciting.

When Maksim got depressed, he didn't philosophize or start thinking about who he could ask for what, he just felt hurt and aggrieved. Not about anyone in particular—there was no one he wanted to punch in the face. He didn't want to hang himself, either. He didn't want to do anything—that was the worst of it, damn it! He didn't want to lie on his backside and do nothing. And he didn't want to drink vodka—he hated making himself ridiculous. Occasionally, when he did drink, he would start accusing himself repentantly of such dreadful sins that people would get embarrassed—and he would, too, afterwards. Once after drinking he had beat his head against a police-station wall with all kinds of posters on it and bellowed out some story about how he and another peasant had invented a powerful engine the size of a matchbox, and then sent the plans abroad. He declared that he was guilty of base treachery, and that he was a "scientific

Vlasov," and he begged to be marched under armed guard to Magadan—barefoot, he insisted.

"Why did you send the plans abroad?" the sergeant pressed him. "And to whom?"

Maksim didn't know. He only knew he was "worse than Vlasov." And wept bitterly.

* * * * * * *

On one of those dreadful Sundays Maksim was standing at the window looking out at the road. As usual it was a clear, frosty day, and the chimneys were smoking.

"Well, now what?" thought Maksim angrily. "A hundred years ago it was just like this. Nothing's new. And it'll always be the same. There goes a boy—Vanya Malafeev's son. And I remember Vanya walking along just like that, and I looked just the same. Now those children will be having their own children. And those children will have their own... Is that all there is to life? What's it all for?"

Maksim felt really sick. Then he remembered that Ilya Lapshin had a guest, a relative of his wife, and that that relative was a priest. A real live priest—with long hair and all. He had something wrong with his lungs, and had come to take a cure. He was taking badger grease, from badgers Ilya caught for him. The priest had plenty of money, and he and Ilya would often drink. Only home-brewed spirits: the priest never drank anything else.

So Maksim went to call on the Lapshins.

As he expected, Ilya and the priest were sitting at the table, drinking booze and talking. Ilya was already pretty far gone: his head was nodding and from time to time he would proclaim that next Sunday—not this Sunday, next Sunday—he would bring home a dozen badgers in one swoop.

"I don't need that many. I just need three good, fat ones."

"I'll bring a dozen and you choose which ones you want. My job is to bring 'em home. And you choose the best ones. The main thing is that you should get better. So I'll bring home a dozen of 'em."

The priest was bored with Ilya, so he was pleased when Maksim showed up.

"What is it?" he asked.

"My soul aches," said Maksim. "I've come to ask whether believers' souls ever ache."

"Want a drink?"

"Just don't think I came especially to have drink. Of course, I could do with one, but that's not why I came. What I'd like to know is: does your soul ache sometimes or not?"

The priest poured some spirit into the glasses and pushed one towards Maksim with the water jug.

"Dilute it to suit yourself."

The priest was a strapping sixty-year old, with broad shoulders and huge hands. It seemed incredible that there was anything wrong with his lungs. And his eyes were clear and intelligent. He looked at you keenly, even challengingly. Not the kind to be waving a censer: he looked more as though he spent his time dodging alimony payments. There was nothing pious or austere about him: how could someone with a mug like that disentangle the living trembling threads of people's sorrows and troubles? But still, Maksim sensed it instantly, he wouldn't be boring, this priest.

"So your soul aches?"

"That's right."

"I see." The priest took a big drink and wiped his lips with a corner of the starched tablecloth. "Well, let's take this gently. Listen carefully and don't interrupt." He settled back in his chair, stroked his beard and started with evident pleasure: "As soon as the human race appeared, evil appeared too. And as soon as evil appeared, so the desire to struggle with it also appeared— with evil, I mean. So good appeared. In other words, good only appeared when evil did: if evil exists, then so does good; if evil doesn't exist, then neither does good. Are you with me?"

"Sure, sure—go on."

"Now, don't put the whip to me, I'm not even in harness. yet." This priest obviously loved to expound his views in this strange, roundabout, non-committal way. "Who is Christ? He is Good incarnate, called to destroy evil on earth. For two thousand years he has existed in people's minds and struggled with evil."

Ilya fell asleep at the table.

The priest poured another glass for himself and Maksim and nodded for him to drink.

"For two thousand years people on earth have been trying to destroy evil in the name of Christ. But the end of that war is not in sight. Please don't smoke. Or go over to the vent window and make your fumes there."

Maksim put out his cigarette on the sole of his boot and continued listening intently.

"What's the matter with your lungs?" he inquired, to be civil.

90

"They ache," the priest explained curtly.

"Does the badger grease help?"

"Yes, it does. Now let's continue, my smoke-breathing child."

"What?" Maksim asked in surprise.

"I asked you not to interrupt me."

"I was only asking you about your lungs."

"You asked why a person's soul aches, and I'm giving you an elementary outline of the structure of the universe so that your soul may regain its composure. So listen carefully and take in what I have to say. The idea of Christ, then, arose from the desire to overcome evil. Otherwise, we wouldn't need it. Imagine that good has triumphed, Christ has triumphed. Then what need have we of him anymore? None. Then the idea would be not something eternal and immutable, but a mere temporary instrument, like the dictatorship of the proletariat, for example. Protracted, but still temporary. Whereas I want to believe in eternity, in an eternal immense force, an eternal order, which will come one day."

"Communism, you mean?"

"What about Communism?"

"You believe in Communism?"

"I'm not allowed to. You're interrupting again!"

"All right, I won't do it again. But you... er... make yourself a bit clearer. Take your time."

"I am making it clear: I would like to believe in eternal goodness, eternal justice, in an eternal higher force, which started everything off on earth. I would like to understand that force and to hope that force will one day triumph. Otherwise what's the point of it all? Eh? Now, where is that force? Does it exist?"

Maksim shrugged his shoulders.

"I don't know."

"I don't either."

"Well, that's a fine thing!"

"I'll go further than that. I don't know any such force. Maybe it's not given to me, as a man, to know and understand it. In that case I simply do not comprehend my existence here on earth. Now, those are exactly my feelings, so you came to the right person with your aching soul: my soul aches too. Only you came looking for a ready answer, while I'm trying to delve into the depths—but it's an ocean. And one can't empty it by the glassful. So we drink this loathsome brew..." The priest took another drink and again wiped his lips with the tablecloth. "When we drink this stuff we are drawing from the ocean, in the hope of reaching the bottom. But by the glassful, by the glassful, my friend! It's a

91

vicious circle—and we're doomed."

"Excuse me... Can I say something."

"Go ahead."

"You're a kinda interesting priest. I didn't know there were priests like that."

"I am a man—I count nothing human indifferent to me. A famous atheist once said that, and he was right."

"So, if I understand you right, God does not exist."

"That's what I said. But now I'm going to assert that he does. Pour another glass, my child, four parts of spirit to one of water, and pass it to me. And have one yourself. Drink up, my simple child—we'll see the bottom yet!.. He drank. "Now I will assert that God does exist. His name is—Life. That's the God I believe in. We have always imagined God as a wishy-washy, well-licked, hornless, sweet little calf. So much the worse for us: there is no such God. But there *is* a severe, powerful God—Life. He offers good *and* evil! Take them together and that's paradise. How did we figure out that good should conquer evil? Whyever should it? For instance, it would be in my interest to conclude that you have come to see me, not in order to discuss the truth, but in order to drink spirits. And that you're sitting there straining your eyes trying to look as if you were interested in what I'm saying."

Maksim stirred in his chair.

"It's no less in my interest to conclude that it's not a drink you need, but the truth. But most of all, I'd like to know which is correct: was it your soul or drink that brought you here? You see, I'm giving this matter serious thought rather than just taking pity on you as a poor little waif. So, as befits my God, I say to you: "Your soul aches? Good. Good! At least you're going somewhere, damn it! Otherwise, you'd be rooted to the fireside with spiritual composure! Live, my child—weep and dance! Don't be afraid of licking frying-pans in the other world, because you'll get your full measure of heaven and hell right here, in this world." The priest was talking loudly, his face glowing, and he was sweating. "You came to ask what to believe in. You're right: believers don't have aching souls. But what should one believe in? Believe in Life. Where it will all end I don't know. What direction it's all going in I don't know either. But I really enjoy running there along with everyone else, overtaking some of them where I can... Evil? Okay then, evil. If anyone in this magnificent race should stick his foot out and trip me up, then I will pick myself up and bash him in the mouth. None of your turning the other cheek: bash him and have done with it!"

"And what if his fist is harder?"

"Well then, it's my fate to stay behind him."

"And where are we all running?"

"Anywhere. What difference does it make where? The good and the evil are all going the same way."

"Somehow I don't feel I'm going anywhere at all."

"Then you're weak-kneed. You're an invalid. Your fate is to sit in one place and moan."

Maksim gritted his teeth. He glared angrily at the priest.

"Why was I dealt such a miserable fate?"

"You're a weakling. Weak, as a... as a half-boiled rooster. It's no use rolling your eyes like that."

"All right, then, your so-called holiness, and what if I thump you between the eyes, right now?"

The priest burst out laughing in his booming bass voice (lung disease, indeed!). "You see this?" he said, holding up his brawny arm. "It's pretty solid: a process of natural selection would follow."

"Well, then I'll bring a rifle."

"That'd mean the firing squad for you. You know that, so you won't be bringing any rifle, for you're a weakling."

"Then I'll stab you with a knife. I can do that all right."

"You'll get five years. I'll have a pain for a month and then it will heal. You'll still have your five years to sweat out."

"All right, then, why does *your* soul ache?"

"I am ill, my friend. I've only run half the course, and now I'm lame. Have you ever flown in an airplane?"

"Many times."

"Well, when I came here it was my first flight ever. It was tremendous! As I was getting on board I thought to myself: "If this contraption crashes, then that's how it should be. No point in worries or regrets." I felt fine the whole journey. When it lifted me from the ground and bore me aloft, I even stroked its flank— magnificent creature! I believe in airplanes. And in general, there's a lot of justice in life. For example, people regret that Esenin had such a short life. But his life was just the length of his song. If that song had been any longer, it wouldn't have been so moving. There's no such thing as a lengthy song."

"What about your church services? Why, once they get going..."

"That's not singing, that's moaning... No, Esenin's life was just the length of his song. D'you like Esenin?"

"Yes, I do."

"Let's sing some together."

"I don't know how."

"Well, fill in where you can without interrupting."

The priest boomed forth about the frozen maple tree, and his bass voice was somehow sad and penetrating, so that the song really was moving. When he got to the words, "And I myself, alas, have grown unsteady," he thumped his fist on the table, wept and shook his flowing mane.

"Oh wonderful, wonderful Esenin! How he loved the peasant! Yes, loved him! And I love you, my child! What about justice, then? Is it too late? Yes, it's too late..."

Maksim felt that he, too, was beginning to be drawn to this priest.

"Father! Father! Listen!"

"I won't."

"Listen to me, thickhead!"

"I won't! You're a weakling..."

"Huh, I leave people like you standing at the post. Weakling indeed. Fatface!"

"Let us pray!" the priest rose to his feet. "Repeat after me..."

"Oh, for goodness sake..."

The priest lifted Maksim with one hand by the scruff of the neck and stood him next to himself.

"Repeat after me: I believe!"

"I believe!" said Maksim.

"Louder! Solemnly: I believe! Together: I believe!"

"I belie-e-eve!" they yelled out together. Then the priest continued in the customary rapid monotone: "In aviation, in the mechanization of agriculture, in the scientific revolution. In space and weightlessness! For they are objecti-i-ive! Together now, after me!"

Together they roared:

"I belie-e-eve!"

"I believe that soon everyone will gather in huge stinking cities. I believe that they will suffocate there and rush back to the open fields... I believe!"

"I belie-e-eve!"

"In badger grease, the bull's horn, and the standing shaft! In bodily flesh and muscle!"

... When Ilya Lapshin forced open his eyes, he saw: the colossus-priest majestically hurling his huge frame around the parlor, thudding onto his haunches and slapping his thighs and chest:
Hey, I believe, I believe!

94

Oompa, oompa, oompa, one!
I believe, I believe!
Toodle, oodle, oodle, two!
I believe, I believe!

While around the priest Maksim Yarikov made little twisting steps and repeated in his high-pitched voice:

Gee-up, gee-up, gee-up, three!
I believe, I believe!
Haul up, haul up, four at last!

"I believe! I believe!"

Maksim brought up the rear, and together they completed a silent circle round the hut, before the priest again opened his arms and threw himself on his haunches, as if plunging into icy water. The floorboards sagged.

Hey, I believe, I believe!
Hiya, hiya, hiya, five!
Hitch her up there, man alive!
I believe, I believe!
Stick at six, six old sticks!
I believe, I believe!

Both of them, the priest and Maksim, were dancing with a kind of grim frenzy, so that one felt it was all quite natural: either they must dance, or else tear their shirts, weep and gnash their teeth.

Ilya watched awhile, then made as if to join in the dance. But all he could do was to pipe up weakly: "Hiya! Hiya!" He didn't know the words.

The priest's shirt was wet through at the back, while under it his muscles rippled powerfully; obviously, earlier in his life he had never known tiredness and illness had not yet consumed his tough sinews. Probably they wouldn't be that easy to consume: previously he would have eaten up any number of badgers. And if so advised, he would ask for the fat of a whole wolf to be brought—and he would make a good job of that too.

"Follow me!" he commanded again.

And all three, led by the ecstatic, feverish priest, set off dancing round and round the room. Then the priest, like a great heavy animal, leaped once more into the center of the circle, bending the floorboards under him. The plates and glasses vibrated on the table.

"Hey, I believe! I believe!"

1971   —Translated by Geoffrey A. Hosking

NOTES

1. Original Russian: " 'Veruiu!'," *Zvezda,* 9(1971); reprinted: *Kharaktery* (1973), pp. 159-170; *Besedy pri iasnoi lune* (1974), pp. 120-128; and *Brat moi* (1975).

"OH, A WIFE SAW HER HUSBAND OFF TO PARIS..."[1]

Every Saturday evening Kolya Paratov would give a concert in the courtyard. He would bring out his accordion, with its brightly colored squeeze-box, draw it open, and...

Oh, a wife saw her husband off to Paris,
With a pack of army rations at his side...

Then came the refrain. Kolya jerked to and fro, with his backside sticking out comically.

Diddy-dum, diddy-dum, diddy-dumm dum-dum,
Diddy-dum, diddy-dum, diddy-dum...

There was laughter from the old women who wandered out into the yard in the evening. And the children who hadn't yet been called in for bed—they would laugh too.

But she murmured to herself as he went,
"I hope you never come back no more!"
Diddy-dum, diddy-dum, diddy-dum, dum-dum...

Kolya was an engaging lad, with his grey eyes, high cheekbones, and a flaxen-yellow forelock. He was one of those stocky, reliable Siberians that Moscow had never forgotten since the time in 1941 when, bright-eyed and clad in white sheepskin coats, they had marched night and day through the streets, comforting an enormous city merely by their appearance.

"Kolya, give us a flamenco, then!"

Kolya, cheerful from his Saturday drinking, looked up smiling and called out:

"Valya, throw down my boots. The comrades here would like a gypsy number."

Valya, upstairs in the apartment, had no intention of responding. She was mad at Kolya. She was ashamed of his concerts and hated him for them. Kolya knew there was little chance she would come to the window, but he deliberately went on calling her, breaking into Tyrolean yodels for the entertainment of his audience.

"Valya, give a sign of life, my little dove! Show us an eye, or even a little finger! He-e-ey there!"

The people in the yard giggled and looked up, too. Eventually Valya could stand it no longer. The third-floor window flew open with a mighty crack, and she leaned her massive bosom on the sill and snapped furiously:

"I'll give you a sign of life all right—a good crack on the head with a saucepan, you moron!"

There was a burst of laughter from below. Kolya laughed, too, but... strangely. Kolya's eyes were not laughing: he was looking at Valya soberly and seemed glad to have made her lose control, to have provoked her into showing herself up as a stupid, vicious scold. It was as if he were getting his own back on her for something, which was not like him at all, and no one realized what he was doing: they thought he was just fooling around.

Meanwhile a fair crowd of people, some of them men and some mere boys, had gathered around Kolya.

"What's your size, Kolya?"

"Vier zwangzig—forty-two."

They gave Kolya dancing pumps (he was in gym shoes), and he started to dance... All at once he became serious, even a little solemn: he danced attractively and with abandon. The accordion seemed to cleave to his hands, assisting the flamenco where appropriate, then falling silent and letting his feet do the work. They sounded crisp and precise, heel and toe tapping a staccato rhythm on the asphalt. Again and again the accordion would strike up, and the soft, flaxen curl would dangle back and forth across his perspiring forehead. His audience fell silent, sensing perhaps that he was dancing out some—how should one put it?—some private anguished fantasy of his own. At the third floor window a corner of the expensive blind stirred: that was Valya taking a look at her "clown." She looked serious, too. Like everyone else she was held spellbound by the bitter, frenzied flamenco. Three years ago Kolya, with that same flamenco, had "captivated" the proud Valya, more proud in those days than... At moments like this, anyway, Valya loved her husband.

Kolya the Siberian had got to know Valya in the most idiotic way—by correspondence. He had done his military service with her brother, who at one point showed around a photo of his sister. Several soldierly hearts leaped at the sight, for Valya was pretty. Some of them asked for her address, but Valya's brother gave it only to his bosom pal, Kolya. Kolya sent a photo of himself to Moscow and appended to it a profusion of "diverse thoughts." Valya replied. Soon a regular correspondence was under way. Kolya was a year older than Valya's brother, so he was mustered out earlier and went to Moscow on his own. All Valya's relatives came along to look him over. They all took a liking to him—and so did Valya. The only trouble was that his one worldly possession was his forelock, and, even worse, he had no training of any kind. But they decided that would come with time. And so Kolya became a Muscovite without even going home to see his mother.

He and Valya settled down to their life together, and gradually it began to dawn on them that as people they were absolutely alien to one another. But by then it was too late: within a year a pretty, chubby little fair-haired daughter, Nina, was born to them. Kolya realized he was trapped. The family clubbed together and bought them a two-room cooperative apartment: Valya came from a line of tailors and was a first-rate dressmaker herself. Kolya, on the other hand, was always changing jobs, without ever making more than a hundred rubles, or a hundred and twenty at the outside. Valya would often pull down three hundred after tax. She worked as a telegraphist: she would put in a twenty-four hour shift, and then spend two days at home sewing.

Their "mutual understanding" began with Kolya's swift discovery of his wife's boundless appetite for money. He made a few attempts to reason with her, to point out that, well, really it wasn't proper to be quite so... But he simply met with a blunt rebuff.

"Even the women in the village were never as grasping as that..."

"Shut up about your village," Valya warned. "Why don't you go back there? You're no use to anybody here."

"My God, what have I let myself in for?" Kolya agonized. "What on earth have I let myself in for?"

Kolya had his head screwed on, for all that he came from the country, and it had never occurred to him that fate might deal him such a low blow. In the army he used to think a lot about what he would do after his discharge: first he would go to evening school to complete his tenth grade (he had nine already), then after that he would... And so on and so forth—but now that was all up the spout. The first year he wandered around looking for a suitable job—though, without realizing it, he was looking for one which suited his wife rather than himself. He couldn't find one, gave up, and stuck to loading trucks. Then his daughter was born and he had to devote all his spare time to her, because Valya was too mean to pay an old woman or someone to take her out for a walk. As for herself, Valya did nothing but sew. So much for Kolya's tenth grade. He would sit Nina on a bench in the courtyard and sing with a scowl:

> My dreams are not a wisp of mist
> That fades in midday's heat,
> But you went by, ignoring me,
> And smiling down the street.

The little girl would laugh away, but Kolya felt more like weeping—bitter and impotent tears. He would have left and returned to his village, except that he couldn't bear to think of being parted from his daughter... That was the one thing he couldn't bring himself to do, for all his Siberian toughness and endurance. Anything you like chum, but not that.

Six months earlier Kolya's mother had come to stay with them. Valya received her politely, but his mother was frightened of Valya just the same, frightened to put a foot wrong around the apartment, frightened even to pick up her little granddaughter. It pained Kolya just to look at her. When they were alone together, Kolya reproached her:

"What's up with you, Ma?"

"Hm?"

"I don't know, you're kinda... Why, you haven't even picked up little Nina."

"Oh, I'm scared, son, I might do something I shouldn't."

"Well, really, you..."

"It doesn't matter, honestly. I've seen how you live, let's be thankful for that. And it's a good life, son, very good. You don't have to pinch and scrape, thank the Lord! Make the most of it. She's not a bad girl. She's got a sharp tongue, it's true, but at least with that sort you know where you are. She'll run things. God bless you, I say."

So his mother left convinced that her son was well off.

After her departure husband and wife quarrelled about something, and Valya stung him on the raw:

"You're mother's a fine one. Comes here and sits around like a... Didn't get dinner ready once, never so much as took Nina for a walk. Quite the *grande dame*!"

At that, for the first time in his life, Kolya struck his wife over the ear. Without a word she walked out and went back to her family. Kolya took Nina to the liquor shop, had a drink and returned home to wait. When his mother-and-father-in-law appeared, he found it came naturally to give them a piece of his mind.

"Now you just watch it, my lad!" his wife's parents said in unison and thumped on the table. "You just watch it! We could get you on an assault charge and have you run out of Moscow in no time. D'you think we brought her up just for you to come along and lay your hands on her? You little squirt! Her boyfriends were engineers and people like that, you know, way above your level!"

"Well, why did you miss your chance then? You should have taken the first one by the scruff of the neck and marched him off to the registry office. Or were they too quick for you? Had their bit of fun, did they, and beat it while the going was good? How could you have been so negligent?"

At that point they struck up a vocal trio:

"Why, you swine! You moron!"

"We'll call the police! We'll call the police right away!"

"Filthy ragamuffin!"

"Little punk!"

Nina started to cry. Kolya blanched, grabbed a meat ax and advanced on his wife and in-laws. Quietly, but with conviction, he said:

"If you don't stop shouting at me, you bastards, I'll kill you all here and now!"

From that moment the Paratovs, husband and wife, realized it was all up with their marriage. They even pretended to feel freer and more at ease. Valya started to go off somewhere in the evenings.

"Where are you going?" Kolya would ask, gritting his teeth against the pain.

"To see my customers."

They still slept together, however.

"Well, how are you customers?" Kolya inquired one night, slapping his wife's bottom and chuckling. He wasn't pretending: he really did feel like laughing, though it came out a bit edgy.

"Idiot," said Valya calmly. "You needn't start imagining things. They're not that sort."

"No, they're not that sort," Kolya agreed. "They're the other sort."

Sometimes, on Sundays, the two of them would go for an outing with Nina. A couple of times they went to the Exhibition of National Economic Achievements. They dropped into the steak bar, and Kolya ordered shish-kebabs, a bottle of good wine, and some sweets for Nina. As they enjoyed their food and sipped the wine, Kolya would watch his wife out of the corner of his eye and think to himself: "What the hell is the matter with us? Are we both out of our minds? Life can be fun. Other people manage to get something out of it."

They looked at various oddments in the exhibition. Kolya loved to look at the farm machinery: he would stand for ages in front of the tractors, the seed drills, the mechanical mowers. The machines reminded him of his home village, and then he would start to feel wretched. He realized perfectly well that his present life was an absurd, disgusting, shameful travesty. His hands were atrophying from lack of work, his heart was drying up through constant overloading with petty, vengeful, caustic

101

feelings. He had got into the way of drinking with the shop assistants. Whether they had done any work or not, they would drain three or four bottles in the cellar, and sometimes the butcher boys would turn up as well, great brawny lads without a care in the world. As for the rest of his life, that really stank, and in order not to face up to it, he would fall instead to meditating about the village, his mother, the river... He would think about them all the time, on the job and at home, in the daytime and at night. But he could come to no conclusions: he only made himself miserable and felt more like drinking. "Well, what am I to do? People do leave their children sometimes. Is it my fault it's all turned out like this?"

People had long since gone off home, but Kolya still sat there, quietly trying out sad little snatches of tune by ear. He was thinking again, turning things over and over in his mind. In his thoughts he tramped over every inch of his village, looking into every alleyway and sitting on the bank of the pure, fast-flowing river. He knew that if he were to turn up there alone, his mother would start crying, would tell him it was a terrible sin to abandon one's own child, would beg him to return home, would say... O Lord! What on earth should he do?

The third-floor window opened.

"Are you going to go on wailing much longer out there? You've made yourself the laughing stock of the neighborhood, and now you stop everybody from getting to sleep. Cretin. They'll be talking about you in all the apartments round here."

Kolya remained resolutely silent.

"Do you hear? Nina can't sleep. You bloody buffoon!"

"Shut your trap. And the window too—give the kid a chance to sleep."

"Cretin."

"Bitch."

The window shut. But a minute later it opened again. "I'll report to somebody what you said at the Exhibition: 'I'd just like a little tractor, a little combine and twenty-five acres.' You're a kulak they forgot to finish off. Why *don't* you go back home? Don't want to work on the collective farm, eh? Oh no, you'd like a private farmstead just for you and your ma. The collective farm doesn't appeal to you, huh? Vermin! Petty bourgeois!"

That was monstrous. Why, Valya knew perfectly well that Kolya's father and grandfather and his whole family had always been poor peasants and were the first to enter the collective farm. Kolya had often told her about it.

He put his accordion down on the bench. That was quite

enough from her. It was time to put an end to it! Any more of this self-imposed torment, and he'd become a mental case or an alcoholic. There must be some way out.

He quickly leaped up the three flights of stairs and burst into the apartment. Valya, sensing something dreadful was going to happen, clutched Nina to herself.

"Just you dare! Just you dare lay a finger..."

Kolya was shaking all over.

"P-put the child d-down," he stammered.

"Just you dare!"

"One way or another I'm going to kill you today," Kolya said, shocked at himself. It was as though not he, but someone else had spoken those terrible words, someone with foresight and resolve. "You've asked for it. And you're going to get it. I'm going to put you to death this very night."

Kolya went to the kitchen and took the axe from out of the drawer. He did everything quite calmly, the shaking had gone. He gulped down some water and turned off the tap. He thought for a moment and then for some reason turned it back on.

"Let it run for the moment," he said out loud.

He went back into the sitting room. Valya was not there. He went into the other room. She wasn't there either.

"She's run away." He went out on the landing and waited a moment. Then he went back into the apartment. "That's as it should be."

He put the axe back in its place, walked up and down the kitchen and then got a half-empty bottle of vodka from a hiding place. He poured out a glassful and replaced the bottle. Then he stood for a moment with the glass... and poured the vodka down the sink.

"You'll be sorry, you bastards!"

He sat down, but stood up again immediately. The kitchen seemed very grubby, so he reached for the broom and began to sweep the floor.

"Right, then; where were we?" Kolya said to himself. "A wife saw her husband off to Paris, eh?" He closed the window and the ventilation pane. He shut the door, lit a cigarette, took three deep pulls on it and stubbed it out. He reached for a pencil and wrote in big letters on the margin of the newspaper: "My dear little daughter, your daddy's gone on a business trip."

He put the paper down where it would be seen. Then he turned on the gas, both burners.

When, first thing next morning, Valya came with her mother

103

and father, Kolya was lying on the kitchen floor, with his face in his hands. Even the staircase outside stank of gas.

"The pig! Even left the gas on..." At that moment Valya realized what had happened, and gave a shriek. Her mother clutched at her breast. Her father went up to Kolya and turned him over on his back.

Kolya's tears were not yet dry... And his light brown forelock was matted and dangling to one side. His father-in-law shook him and eased open his eyelids with his fingers... Then he put the body back in its former position.

"Better... er... call the police."

1971   —Translated by Geoffrey A. Hosking

NOTES

1. Original Russian: " 'Zhena muzha v Parizh provozhala...'," *Nash sovremennik,* 9(1971); reprinted: *Izbrannye proizvedeniia v dvukh tomakh* (1975), Vol. 1, pp. 232-239.

THE MASTER[1]

There once lived in the village of Chebrovka a man called Semka Rys, a rake, and also a carpenter second to none. Tall, skinny, with a big nose, he didn't look at all like a hero of ancient times. But when Semka took off his shirt, still wearing his sun-bleached undershirt... And when he merrily exchanged curses with his foreman while toying with his ax, then you could see all of Semka's frightening strength and power. It was in his arms. Semka's arms were not gnarled and musclebound; they were thick and smooth from his shoulders to his paws, as if they had been cast from a mold. He had splendid hands. The ax looked like a toy in them. Hands like that didn't look like they could ever tire, and Semka, just to show off a little, would holler: "What d'you think we are, machines? So come and wind me up, I'm out of juice. But be careful when you come up from behind, I kick."

Semka wasn't a bad man. But as far as he was concerned, as he used to say, "Everything went stiff and lifeless in this world," and so he wasted his "horse's strength" on whatever struck his fancy. To raise a little hell, pick fights, horse around—that appealed to him.

"You have a pair of golden hands," people would say to him. "You could, if you wanted to, have a real sweet life, live in clover!"

"I don't care for clover."

He gave all of his paychecks to his family. He drank only on what he made on the side. You ought to see the kind of cupboard he could make; it would dumbfound you. People came from afar, asked him to build things for them and offered large sums of money. Once a writer who spent his summers in Chebrovka took him to the provincial capital, where Semka remodeled his office for him. Together they hit on the idea of doing the office in the style of a village log hut. (The writer, you see, was born in the country; he pined for his native village).

"What a waste of money!" his fellow villagers said in amazement when Semka told them about the peasant hut they had built in a modern city house. Just think, right out of the sixteenth century!

"On the floors we put split logs, planed them, and that's all, didn't even paint them. The table, we knocked that together with boards. Along the walls we put benches, in the corner, a cot. No mattresses on the cot, no blankets either, just a piece of felt and a sheepskin coat, that's all. We smoked the ceiling with a blowtorch. Now it looks like the room had no chimney. The walls, we covered them with rough boards."

The village folk just shook their heads. "The fools couldn't find anything better to do."

"Right out of the sixteenth century," said Semka thoughtfully. "He showed me drawings, and I did it all from the drawings."

Incidentally, when Semka lived with the writer in the city, he didn't drink. He read various books about bygone times, examined old icons, spinning wheels... The writer had all kinds of things like that.

The same summer Semka became interested in a little church that stood in the village of Talitsa, about two miles from Chebrovka. He examined it carefully. In Talitsa there remained only seven households out of twenty. The little church had been closed for a long time. It was small and made of stone. It suddenly appeared before your eyes, right behind a slope that was skirted by the road to Talitsa... For reasons of their own the folk back then hadn't put it up high on the hill, as was the custom. Instead, they had built it on a low spot at the bottom of the slope. Semka remembered from childhood that if you were going to Talitsa and got lost in your thoughts, then at the turn of the road, near the hillside, you'd start up at the sudden appearance of the church; it was white and seemed to float amidst the heavy greenery of the poplars.

There was a church in Chebrovka, too, but obviously built in more recent times; it was big, with a tall bell-tower. It, too, had been closed for a long time; one of its walls was cracked. So, you had two churches, a big one standing on top of a hill, and aother that was small and hidden away at the bottom of a hill. Which one would you say is the winner, if you were to compare them? The little one, at the bottom of the hill. It was better in every way; because it looked so light and beautiful, and because it came to view so suddenly... You could see the Chebrovka church from three miles away, and that's what its builders had in mind. The Talitsa church was hidden as if on purpose from Philistine eyes. Only to those who came to it did it reveal itself, all at once, suddenly...

It happened that on his day-off Semka went again to see the Talitsa church. He sat on the hillside and began to look at it attentively. It was peaceful and quiet all around. The village was quiet, too. And the white beauty stood among the green leaves— how many years had it stood there!—saying nothing. How many

106

times had it watched the sun rise and set. How many rains had washed it, how many snows had buried it... And here it was, still standing. But for whom was it standing now? Its builders had long ago rotted in the earth; and the wise head that had first envisioned it had long ago turned to dust, and the heart that had rejoiced over it had long been one with the earth, a handful of soil. What had he wanted, that unknown master, in leaving behind this fairy tale in weightless stone? Was he honoring God, or was he merely displaying his talent? But one who wishes to show off his talent does not stray far away from the crowd; he strives to get as close as possible to the high roads, or better yet, right in the middle of the crowded city square—there he'd be noticed for sure. But this one had been concerned about something else— beauty, perhaps? Like the man who sang a song, sang it well, and went on his way. Why had he done it? Perhaps he himself did not know. Something to satisfy his soul. Ah, dear man!.. I don't know what to tell you, down there in your black, sinister darkness of non-existence, because you won't hear me. And what is there to say, anyhow? To be sure, it's nice, it's beautiful, it moves your soul, it makes you feel happy... But is that really the point? He too had felt happy about his work; he too had felt moved inside, and had understood that it was beautiful. But what of it? Nothing. If you know how to be happy, be happy; if you know how to make people happy, make them happy. If you can't do that, go ahead and make war, be a leader or something like that. You could even destroy this fairy tale here: put about two kilograms of dynamite under it, and it would be shattered and gone. To each his own.

Semka continued to study the church and noticed that four stones at the top, under the cornice, were different from all the rest. They were shining. He came up closer and examined them. Sure thing, the craftsman had wanted, one could see that, to polish the whole wall. The wall faced the east; if he had polished the whole wall, then, as the sun rose (it rose from behind the hill), the little church on clear days would glow with the sun's fire, from its summit on down, until it was entirely bathed in bright sunlight, from its cross to its foundation stone. So, he had began to polish the stones, but had stopped for some reason. Perhaps whoever was having the church built and was paying for the work had said: "That's enough; it'll do as it is."

Semka's interest grew. He wanted to know how the stones had been polished. Probably, in this way: first with rough sand, then with smoother sand, and finally with a piece of cloth or leather. That's a lot of work.

The church could be entered through its basement. This Semka had known since childhood. He had often crawled in with his friends. The entrance into the basement, once covered by a folding door (long ago carried off by someone), was half-crumbled and overgrown with tall weeds... Semka pushed himself with difficulty into the narrow opening between the church floor and the ground, and, sometimes crawling, sometimes only hunched over, made his way to the vestibule. The church was spacious and resonant. A light wind barely stirred a loose metal leaf hanging from the cupola; the rustle, barely audible outside, was loud and perturbing inside. The rays of light shining through the windows cut into the dark emptiness of the church with wide golden streaks. Only now, as he looked around and was touched by the beauty and mystery of the church, did Semka discover that the walls did not meet the floor at right angles, but instead bulged out at the bottom in an obvious curve. To put it simply, at the bottom along the walls ran a stone buttress about three feet deep at the base and some six feet high. At the top it neatly disappeared into the wall. Semka could not imagine what it was for at first. He only noted that the buttress stones, neatly cut and fitted together, were dark at the base. But higher up they turned lighter and then completely blended with the white wall. The dome at the very top was constructed out of some special stone; it, too, was probably polished. It was so light and festive under the dome. And this effect was achieved with just four narrow little windows.

Semka sat on the altar step and thought. What was the purpose of this stone buttress? And he explained it like this to himself: the master had done away with right angles and the square. Since the little church was small, he had to create the feeling of free space inside. Nothing so oppresses one, and confines the soul as a cube-like cage. He therefore put the darker stones at the base, and, as he was building up the buttress, narrowed it to merge with the wall. Thus, the walls looked as though they had been shifted back.

Semka went on sitting in the church, until the spot of light on the stone floor had stolen up to his feet. He crawled out of the church and went home.

The following day, having reported sick, Semka did not go to work. He went instead to the regional center where there was an active church. He found the priest at home, not far from his church. The priest sent his son away and said simply:

"I am listening."

The dark and lively eyes of the middle-aged priest, glinting with mischief, looked at Semka directly, steadily, expectantly.

"Do you know the Talitsa church?" For some reason Semka had decided that with writers and priests one must use the familiar form of address. "Talitsa is in the Chebrovka region."

"The Talitsa church?.. Chebrovka region... It's a small one, isn't it?"

"Right."

"I know it."

"Of what century is it?"

"What century? I'm afraid to say, for fear of getting it wrong... But I think it was built as far back as the reign of Aleksei Mikhailovich. You see, his son didn't pamper the people with churches. The seventeenth century, second half. Why do you want to know?"

"But it's so beautiful!" exclaimed Semka. "Don't you realize that?"

The priest chuckled.

"Thank God it is still standing. Beautiful, you say. Of course, it is. I haven't seen it in a long while, but I remember it. It stands on low ground, right?"

"Who built it? Does anyone know?"

"You should see the metropolitan about that. I couldn't say."

"You've got money, don't you?"

"Well, let's say I do."

"Sure, you do. Don't say you don't. You're independent of the government, aren't you..."

"What's all this to you?"

"Restore it—it's a marvel! I'll fix it up myself. I'll do it in one summer. I need two or three helpers. We'll be done before winter. You'd pay us about..."

"I, my dear son, have no authority in this kind of matter. I, too, have somebody to answer to... Go and see the Metropolitan!" The priest was also getting excited about it. "Go and see him; why not? Are you a believer?"

"That has nothing to do with it. I'm like everybody else, and maybe a little worse—I drink. It just makes me sad to see such a beautiful thing go to waste. Historical monuments are being renovated everywhere now..."

"Sure, but the government is doing it."

"But you have money, too."

"The government is doing the renovating. They have their reasons. Go, go and see the metropolitan."

"And where is he? Here?"

"No, you have to take a trip."

109

"To the provincial capital?"

"Yes, to the capital."

"I don't have any money on me. I had enough only to come and see you..."

"I'll give you some. Where are you from?"

"From Chebrovka, I am a carpenter, my name is Semen Rys."

"Here you are, Semen, go see him! He's a good man... very intelligent. Tell him everything. But are you doing this on your own initiative."

"What d'you mean 'my own initiative'?" Semka didn't understand.

"Did you come to me on your own, or were you chosen and sent by some group?"

"I came on my own."

"Well, it doesn't matter, go anyway! While you are on your way, I'll call him up. He'll know already why you are coming. He will receive you."

Semen thought for a moment.

"Give me the money. I'll pay you back later."

"Yes, we'll settle it later. On your way back from the metropolitan, stop by here again to tell me how it went."

The metropolitan, a solid, gray, eternally sober old man, wth an unexpectedly thin little voice, greeted Semka cordially.

"Father Gerasim called me... Well, tell me, what prompted you to think of renovating the church?"

Semka took a sip of hot tea from a beautiful cup.

"What prompted me? I don't know. I looked at the church—such beauty! And nobody needs it!"

The metropolitan chuckled.

"Yes, a beautiful church, I know it. It was built under Aleksei Mikhailovich, yes. I still don't know who the architect was... But that can be found out. The land belonged to the Boriatinsky boyars... Why do you want to know the master's name?"

"No reason, it would just be interesting to know. A man of real talent!"

"He was a great master. We'll find out later who he was. It's obvious he knew the churches of Vladimir and Moscow..."

"It's amazing what he thought up!.." And Semka began to tell how he succeeded in unraveling the secret of the old master.

The metropolian listened, nodding his head, and sometimes saying: "How d'you like that!" Meanwhile Semka was putting forth his own ideas: the far wall, the east one, should be polished the way the master had wanted it; the cupolas should be recovered and gilded; the top windows should be fitted with colored panes; then there would be such a glow, such a glow under the dome!.. The master had chosen for the dome some kind of special stone, with a touch of quartz in it... And if orange panes were put in...

"That's all very good, my son," interrupted the metropolitan. "But consider this now: if they say 'We'll give you permission to renovate the Talitsa church, just tell us who will do the work for you,'—well, I would name Semen Rys, the carpenter from Chebrovka, before you could blink your eye. Only.,. they won't allow me to renovate it. That's the way it is, my son. It's a sad business."

"Why?"

"I, too, will ask 'Why?' And they will ask me 'What for?' How many households are there in Talitsa? I'm asking that myself now..."

"In Talitsa, very few..."

"But that's not even the main problem. Just think what kind of war against religion there will be, if they start opening new parishes. Think about that for awhile."

"But no one would have to pray in it! Museums like that are everywhere..."

"But museums—that's the government's business, not ours."

"So what do we do now?"

"I suggest this. Write a letter from the whole village to the effect that there is a neglected church in Talitsa, going to waste. Say that it appears worthwhile, not from the point of view of religion..."

"Never in my life could I write such a letter. You write it yourself."

"I can't. Find somebody who can. If you can't find anyone, write it yourself, in your own words, that would be even better..."

"Wait a minute! I have just the man I need!" Semka remembered the writer.

"And take your letter to the people in charge. Go to the Regional Executive Committee. They will decide. If they turn you down, write to Moscow... But don't write to Moscow right away. Wait till they turn you down here. They might send down an investigating team..."

"It would make people happy, just to have it standing there!"

"So that's my advice. Don't write anything about our conversation. And don't talk about it anywhere. That would only ruin things. Farewell, my son. May God grant you success."

111

As Semka left the house, he took note of how the metropolitan lived. Holy God! His house had at least eight rooms. In the yard stood a "Volga" passenger car. That didn't sit well with Semka. He decided that it really would be better to deal with one's own Soviet authorities. These priests, all they do is confuse things... They want to do something, they itch to do it, but in the end their mamas won't let them.

But first Semka decided to drop in on the writer. He found his house, but the writer wasn't there.

"He's not in," said a young, heavy-set woman rather sharply, and slammed the door. When he had been building the "sixteenth-century hut," he hadn't seen this woman. But now he had a sudden passion to see his "hut." He rang again.

"I'm here alone," he heard a woman's voice say from behind the door. And the door opened again.

"Well, what now?" she said.

"Look, I'm the one who remodeled Nikolay Efimych's office... I justed wanted to see it..."

"My God!" exclaimed the woman, and closed the door.

"I think he's home," decided Semka. "And, I think they're having some kind of heavy conversation."

He waited a while, hoping the woman would blurt out in a fit of temper: "Some kind of idiot who remodeled your office," and the writer would perhaps come out himself. But he didn't come out. Maybe he wasn't at home after all.

Semka went to the Regional Executive Committee.

He got to see the chairman immediately, though in a rather strange way. He walked into the waiting room and the secretary jumped on him:

"Why are you late?! They either complain about not being received, or they don't show up on time. Where are the rest of you?"

"They're coming," said Semka. "They're coming!"

The secretary went into the office, stayed there for a while, came out and said angrily: "Go on in."

Semka went into the office. The chairman walked up to him to greet him.

"What a fuss you raised, what a fuss!" he said with a smile that included nevertheless a reproach. "We rock the boat, rock the boat, don't we, brothers? How are you?"

"I came about the church," Semka said, shaking hands with the chairman. "She got me all confused, your helper. I came alone, about the church..."

"What church?"

"In our village, no not in ours, but in Talitsa, there is a little seventeenth-century church. An unusual beauty. If it were repaired, it would... No, not to pray in. It's valuable, but not from the religious point of view. If you'd give me three helpers, I'd repair it before winter." Semka spoke hurriedly, because he couldn't stand it when people looked at him with bewilderment. He always got nervous then. "What I'm saying is that there's a church in Talitsa," he started to speak slowly, but he got annoyed again. "It must be repaired without fail. It's all run down. It's the pride of the Russian people, but everybody has given up on it. If it were repaired, it would stand there for another three hundred years and give joy to the eyes and to the soul."

"Hmm," said the chairman. "We'll make sense out of this right now." He pushed a button on the table. The secretary looked in. "Ask Zavadsky to come here. So, you have an old church in the village; it looks interesting to you as a seventeenth-century architectural monument. Is that it?"

"Exactly so. The important thing is that it doesn't need that much work done to it. All we have to do is touch up the cupolas, cement a few stones here and there, provide for expansion, raise the cross a bit..."

"Sure, sure, we have a colleague who takes care of such things. Here he is."

Into the office walked a man still young, handsome, sporting a head of wavy black hair and a dimple on his chin.

"Igor Aleksandrovich, please look after this comrade. It's along your line."

"Shall we go?" suggested Igor Aleksandrovich.

They walked down a long corridor, with Igor Aleksandrovich leading the way, and Semka half a step behind.

"I myself am not from Talitsa, I am from Chebrovka, Talitsa is..."

"In a minute, in a minute we'll take care of everything."

"They don't waste time around here at all," thought Semka.

They walked into an office, one a little less imposing than the chairman's. It was just a room, with a table, a chair, sketches on the walls, and a shelf with books.

"Well?" said Igor Aleksandrovich, and he smiled. "Sit down, take your time and tell me everything."

Semka told him the whole story in detail. While he was talking, Igor Aleksandrovich picked up a folder from the book shelf, leafed through it, found what he needed and, keeping the folder open with the palm of his hand, expressed noticeable impatience. Semka noticed this.

"That's all?" asked Igor Aleksandrovich.

"For the time being."

"Listen to this. 'Talitsa church of the N province of the Chebrovka region,' Igor Aleksandrovich began to read. 'Church of the Blood, so called. Assumed to have been erected in the eighties or nineties of the seventeenth century. One of the princes of the Boriatinsky family perished in Talitsa at the hand of the enemy...' " Igor Aleksandrovich raised his eyes from the paper and offered a supposition: "It's possible that some drunken brothers or godparents got into a fight. So, it says here that 'they perished at the hand of the enemy, and on that spot a church was built.' The architect is unknown. As an architectural monument it is of no value, since the author did not show anything new for his time, offered no unusual solutions or attempts at such solutions. It is more or less a good copy of the Vladimir churches. The dimensions of the church are worthy of note, but these were dictated not by architectural considerations, but, obviously, by the material means of the client. It ceased activity in 1925."

"Have you seen it?" asked Semka.

"Yes, and this," said Igor Aleksandrovich, pointing to an official letter in the folder, "is the answer to my inquiry. I, too, was deceived, as you were..."

"Did you go inside?"

"Yes, of course. I even took specialists from our province there..."

"Wait a minute!" said Semka ominously. "What did the specialists say? About the buttress..."

"Along the walls? The explanation for that, you see, goes like this. The Boriatinsky family were fond of burials in their church, and they completely undermined the foundation. The church, if you noticed, leans slightly to one side. One of the later descendants put a stop to this practice and had the buttress built... There are inscriptions on the buttress, if you look closely, at the places where there are tombs underneath."

Semka felt disheartened.

"But it's such a beautiful thing!" he insisted, not ready to give up.

"Sure, it's beautiful." Igor Aleksandrovich nimbly got to his feet, took a book from the shelf, and showed Semka a photograph of a church. "It looks like this, doesn't it?"

"Yes, it does."

"That's the Vladimir Church of the Protection of the Virgin, twelfth century. Ever been in Vladimir?"

"I am not a believer..."

Semka nodded his head at the official letter. "I think they fed you a lot of rubbish, your specialists. I'm going to write to Moscow."

"But this is the answer from Moscow. I'll tell you why I myself was misled. I, too, thought it was from the twelfth century... that somebody independently, all alone, perhaps from hearsay, copied the Vladimir architect's work. But miracles just don't happen. Who sent you, the village soviet?"

"No, I came on my own..."

Semka went home that day. He arrived in the regional center when it was still daylight. He went to see Father Gerasim. Father Gerasim was in his church serving mass. Semka returned to the servants the money that was left over, kept enough money for his ticket home and a bottle of red wine. He said he'd send back what he owed by mail... And he went home.

From that time on he never mentioned the Talitsa church, he never again went to see it, and if he happened to be on the Talitsa road, he would turn his back on the church at the hillside. He would look at the river and the meadows beyond the river, and he wouldn't say a word.

People noticed all this but nobody cared to talk to him about it. Nor did they ask him why he went to the provincial capital, and where he went while there. If he chose to be silent, that meant he didn't want to talk about it, so why ask him?

1971   —Translated by W.G. Fiedorow

NOTES

1. Original Russian: "Master," *Sibirskie ogni*, 12(1971); reprinted: *Kharaktery* (1973), pp. 41-56; *Besedy pri iasnoi lune* (1974), pp. 209-218; *Brat moi* (1975); and *Izbrannye proizvedeniia v dvykh tomakh* (1975), Vol. 1, pp. 244-253.

GENERAL MALAFEIKIN[1]

Mishka Tolstykh, a carpenter in the Construction and Installation Administration, a small man with prominent cheekbones and long hands, a Muscovite originally from the Trans-Baikal region, was coming home from a visit to his brother, a Leningrader. His brother had received him badly, immediately wanting to teach him what's what in life... Mishka was offended, got drunk, insulted his brother's wife, and set off for home—to Moscow.

He came to the train station early, went inside the sleeping compartment, threw his suitcase on the top shelf, and asked the car attendant for sheets and a blanket. She told him, "First we go, then you get your sheets." Mishka took off his shoes and, for the time being, lay down on the mattress on the upper berth. And he fell asleep.

He woke up at night. Below him, in the darkness, two people were speaking quietly. One of the voices sounded familiar to Mishka. And it was this voice, the familiar one, which was doing most of the talking. Mishka listened.

"No, no, really," the voice was saying quietly, "I can't agree with you. It happens to me constantly. You call him in, the scoundrel, to your office: 'Well, what are we going to do?' Silence. 'What are we going to do with you?!' Silence. He only shrugs his shoulders. 'Are we going to continue in this vein?' Death-like silence."

"They're masters at keeping silent," seconded the other voice, tired and no longer young. "That they know how to do."

"I should say! Standing there not saying anything, like someone with a mouthful of water. 'Well, now,' I ask, 'how long are we going to play this game of silence?' "

Mishka recalled whose voice the one below reminded him of: that of Semion Ivanovich Malafeikin, his neighbor in Moscow from house no. 37, an unsociable part-time painter and a disabled pensioner. Mishka once did some hack-work with that Semion Ivanovich; together they did some finishing work in an apartment for some sort of an important higher-up. They worked for about a week and a half, and in all of that time Malafeikin probably said no more than ten words. He wouldn't even greet him when he came to work. To the question, why was he so silent, Malafeikin responded: "It hurts my chest to prattle with you." But the one below, he, of course, was not Malafeikin... Though it was amazing

116

to what extent his voice was similar.

" 'I'll have you evicted from Moscow, you scoundrel!' you tell him. 'You just make me lose my patience and I'll evict you!' 'Please don't,' he begs. 'So, you've finally opened your mouth! You've started to speak?' "

"Does it happen that you evict them?"

"Not often. One does feel sorry for them, the scoundrels. What would they do there?"

"My God! But we need all the people we can get!"

"And what would you do with them? Make moonshine?"

The two below shared the quiet, preoccupied laugh of higher-ups.

"Well... yes. We've got trash like that around too. And how do you struggle with this problem?"

"How? Prevention plus police. It's torment, not a struggle. It's exhausting. You come to your dacha, light the fireplace, and as you're looking at the fire—I just love, by the way, to look at the fire—some ugly mug peers at you out of the fire. 'God,' you think to yourself, 'won't they ever leave me alone?' "

"What do you mean—peers at you?" His companion, the tired one, didn't understand. "You mean mentally?"

"Well, you know, you see so much of them during the day, and later they appear to you just about anywhere. Do you have a stone dacha?"

"I don't have a dacha at all. When I have a bit of free time, I go to my place in the country. It's quite close. And your dacha is made of stone?"

"Stone, two-story. You're making a mistake, not having á dacha. Such a convenience. You know, no matter how tired you get during the day, you get there, light the fireplace, and your soul is at peace."

"Is it yours?"

"The dacha?"

"Yes."

"No, of course not. How can you even think that? I have two drivers working in shifts. One of them has learned already; at a quarter till five he calls: 'Home, Semion Ivanovich?' 'Home, Petya, home.' We call the dacha home he and I."

On the top berth Mishka started tossing and turning. Why, the name of the person telling the story is also Semion Ivanovich! Just like Malafeikin's. What's going on here?

And the Semion Ivanovich below continued:

" 'Home,' I say, 'home, Petka. To hell with Moscow and all that racket!' We arrive and put a few logs in the fireplace..."

117

"And there is no one else to do that?"

"Oh, you mean servants? Oodles! But I like to do it myself. I put on the logs and light them myself. It's glorious! You know, sometimes you think to yourself, 'Why in the hell do I need all these honors, medals and benefits? I'd rather just live in the country and burn wood in the stove.' "

His tired companion laughed quietly in disbelief.

"What, you don't believe me?" exclaimed Semion Ivanovich in a low voice, probably also laughing. "I'm telling you truthfully: I'd give it up, I'd give it all up."

"Why haven't you done it?"

"Well... It's not all as simple as it seems. And who would allow it?"

"That's it, precisely," sighed his companion. "You know, I also..."

"On the contrary, they offer me a promotion. Oh no, thanks just the same, my head is already in a whirl from all these matters."

Just now, you were probably at that conference... I heard something about it in passing..."

"No, I was attending to other matters. We've got others who... So, tell me, do you also spend your vacations in your place in the country? In the summer, too?"

"Almost always. I go to my father's—we go fishing..."

"I spend mind in health-resorts."

"Where? In Kislovodsk?"

"Among others."

"In the main building?"

"No, we've got our own building there."

"Where?"

"Just before you get to Kislovodsk."

"But where? I know the area quite well."

Semion Ivanovich chuckled.

"Oh no, that building you don't know. It can't be seen from the road."

They were silent for a moment.

"It's behind a fence," explained Semion Ivanovich.

"Um-m..," said the tired companion rather vaguely, and fell silent again.

This silence seemed to make Semion Ivanovich somewhat uneasy.

"To tell the truth, it does get a bit boring," he continued. "I mean, there is a refreshment bar where you can get champagne, fruit, this and that... But that's not the point! It gets mono-

118

tonous."

"Of course," the tired one said very vaguely again. "I have nothing... Do they show films?"

"I should say! But you know what we do? We don't attend the ordinary ones, we get together—just the men—and order, you know, the ones... with nudity... Are you fond of those?" Semion Ivanovich laughed uncertainly. "They're quite interesting."

His companion failed to respond to this. He remained silent.

"Well?" asked Semion Ivanovich in alarm.

"Well, what?" said his companion.

"Are you fond of those with nudity?"

"Well, I've... ah... seen very few of them."

"Come, come, now! It's a real spectacle! One of them comes on built like... and starts shaking her, shaking her, you know... It's fascinating! No, it's a spectacle, a real spectacle no matter what you say."

"Completely naked?"

"Totally!"

"But how... do we really make films like that here?"

Semion Ivanovich, without a trace of apprehension, laughed with delight.

"But they're not ours. They're from over there."

"Aah!" said his compaion. "There. Yes... of course."

"Oh, they know how to make them, the devils. They know, all right. But you know, I'll tell you something about all this: it's beautiful!"

"I didn't say anything!" said his companion in alarm.

"Yes, but in your heart you probably condemned me."

"I? But why should I?"

"Oh, but you condemned me, condemned me. You shouldn't be in such a hurry to condemn me, to begrudge Semion Ivanovich... You can't possibly know how afterwards Semion Ivanovich works to exhaustion at his desk. You sit there, and you study matters on hand... Can one be candid with you?"

"But, certainly!" quickly, without any trace of fatigue, said his companion. "I understand perfectly. I myself have to..."

"Oh, of course! Of course, you also work without eating or getting enough sleep... We need so much sympathy! But then we turn right around and point our finger at some general and think: just look at his paunch hanging out. And do I have a paunch?"

"Why, no!" His companion was clearly taken aback. "On the contrary, I didn't have any... But that's not the point..."

"And what is the point?" asked Semion Ivanovich harshly.

119

"What do you mean?"

"What?"

"The point is not who is a general and who isn't. After all, ultimately we are all working for the same cause."

"You don't say! Would you just look! And here I didn't even know that. Can it really be? All?"

His companion was silent.

"Well?" Semion Ivanovich asked again. It was hard to understand why he was so angry.

His companion was silent.

"Silent? So we're also silent, are we?"

"Listen!" One could sense that his companion got up. "What is going on here? What have you got against me?"

"Heaven forbid!" immediately responded Semion Ivanovich with sincerity. "I haven't got the slightest thing in the world against you. I was just asking. I thought that you had something against *me*. You don't?"

"Of course not. Well, it's time to get some sleep. What time is it? Approximately?"

"Approximately, you say?.. Eh, I've left the one with a luminous dial... About two o'clock."

"Very likely. Maybe we should get some sleep, don't you think?"

"Yes, of course. I had a bit to drink today... saying goodbye to some comrades. Let's sleep."

And they immediately fell silent, and didn't speak any more.

Mishka didn't know what to think. Who was that below? The voice was strikingly similar to that of Malafeikin. And his name was also Semion Ivanovich. So what was all this? Mishka knew about Malafeikin just about everything there is to know about a neighbor, without taking any special interest in him. Some time ago Malafeikin took a fall from a scaffolding and suffered serious injury. He was alone then, and remained alone. Quiet and taciturn. On Sundays some woman older than he would come to see him with a little girl. Who they were to Malafeikin, Mishka didn't know. He would see how Malafeikin spent time with her in the courtyard: the little girl played in the sand, and Malafeikin read a paper. Maybe this was his sister with her daughter, because somehow it didn't seem likely that there was anything else in this. And that, essentially, was all that there was to Malafeikin. But the general below... No, that is a coincidence. It happens sometimes!

Mishka carefully climbed down from his berth, went to the

toilet, climbed back up, and closed his eyes. It was quiet in the compartment. Mishka fell asleep.

In the morning Mishka woke up later than the others, just as they were approaching Moscow. He opened his eyes, looked down, and below, by the window sat... Semion Ivanovich Malafeikin. Another person, about fifty, rosy-cheeked, sat by the window across from him. They sat there looking out the window. A girl in pants was sitting off to the side reading a book. They were silent.

Mishka had forgotten about last night's conversation, and was about to say, "Hello, neighbor!" when he remembered... and recoiled from surprise. He was dumbfounded. He lay there, remembering. Maybe he just dreamed about that conversation last night?

While Mishka was agonizing about what had transpired, the rosy-cheeked man stretched audibly and said, as people say after a long silence.

"It seems that we're almost there." He rustled some papers on the table, a newspaper perhaps, rolled it up, rose and walked out of the compartment.

Mishka leaned his head down. The girl glanced up at him, then out the window, and went back to her reading. Malafeikin, snub-nosed, with tiny lashless eyes, his hair parted, wearing a tie, and almost inaudibly tapping the table with the fingers of his right hand, was looking out the window.

"Hello there, general!" said Mishka above him quietly.

Malafeikin raised his head sharply... Their eyes met. Malafeikin's tiny eyes became round with surprise, and even, as it seemed to Mishka, frightened.

"So!" said Malafeikin disapprovingly. "Would you look who comes dragging in. Where you coming from?"

Mishka didn't say anything, but just looked at his neighbor. He tried to do it derisively.

"How is it that we're taking these... trips?" asked Malafeikin in a way that was somehow malicious, and quickly looked at the door.

Yes, it was really he who was talking nonsense about stone dachas, and how he was tired of awards and honors.

"Hey, what was that line of...," Mishka started to say, but the rosy-cheeked man walked in, and Malafeikin, in alarm, quickly turned towards him, and got up. And he started to speak.

"Well, are we almost there?" Fussing, he moved to the window, and smoothed the part in his hair. "So we are. There's Yauza already. So. So..." He stamped about momentarily, started

121

out of the compartment, but returned and bent over his suitcase.

"What a jerk!" Mishka thought in amazement. He could see from above how Malafeikin's ears had gotten red. He didn't pester the part-time painter any more, and only observed him from above with great curiosity.

"You don't happen to be going downtown?" asked the rosy-cheeked man. And he looked at Malafeikin respectfully.

"How's that?" said Malafeikin, startled. "I? No, no... Someone is... No, I'm going in another direction."

"I just thought that we could go together."

"No, no... I'm going elsewhere."

"We're going in the direction of Sbiblovo," said Mishka loudly, raised himself and sat up in his berth. He was bursting with suppressed laughter.

"Oh, I see that our fellow traveller has awakened!" said the rosy-cheeked man. "Good morning, young man! I envy your ability to sleep. I don't sleep well when I travel. I curse myself: get some sleep while there is a chance. But somehow I just can't seem to do it."

Smiling, Mishka was looking at Malafeikin.

"I wouldn't mind sleeping once again as much."

"Sleeping is for the young."

Malafeikin fastened his squeaky yellow suitcase, tightened the straps, lifted it up, and set it in the corridor. From the corridor, without entering the compartment, he reached in and took his leather coat off the hook, removed his hat from the shelf, and went out further into the corridor to get dressed.

"He's afraid I'll expose him," Mishka decided. "What the hell do I need you for?"

Malafeikin didn't come into the compartment any more. He got dressed, took his suitcase and went to the back of the railway car.

Mishka, however, lay in waiting for him outside, on the platform. He caught up, and walked in step with him.

"What's the matter, did you tie one on yesterday?" he asked amicably. "Why were you spinning those yarns last night? How come?"

"Beat it!" suddenly bellowed Malafeikin, and got as red as a beet. "Why are you pestering me?! Didn't sober up? Go sober up! Why are you pestering me?! Why are you pestering people?!"

People started to stare at them. Some even slowed down, expecting a scene.

Mishka, fearful of any such trifles which might require explanations, dropped back, but he didn't let Malafeikin out of

122

his sight. He got mad at him.

They got on the subway together. Mishka kept following Malafeikin; he just didn't know what means to use to unmask this scoundrel: he might call a policeman at the slightest provocation.

In the subway car Malafeikin turned around carefully and was confronted by Mishka's steady, scathing look. Mishka winked at him. Malafeikin's ears again bloomed a poppy red. The stiff collar of his leather coat propped up his hat from behind. Malafeikin did not turn around any more.

At the subway exit, on the escalator, Mishka once again came up to Malafeikin. He whispered in his ear,

"Just don't holler, don't holler. I only want to ask you one question, that's all. I've got this brother in Leningrad, he's also a bit crazy, he also pretends to be somebody else. Why try to be someone you're not? What are you trying to gain by that? I'm asking you seriously."

Malafeikin was silent. He looked up, then straight ahead.

"I mean, do you feel better after you do all this?"

Malafeikin was silent.

"Why did you lie to that guy last night?"

As the escalator levelled out and was about to discharge them, Malafeikin started searching for a policeman with his eyes. Mishka passed him and, looking back, he came to the bus stop first.

"I'll finish with you in the courtyard when we get home," he decided.

By the house, when they got off the bus, Mishka once again started walking up to Malafeikin, but the latter suddenly screwed up his face painfully, shook his head so violently that his hat almost slid off his head, stamped his foot, and shouted:

"Don't come near! Don't come near me! Don't come near!" He shouted this, turned around, and walked home quickly. He almost ran. The large yellow suitcase with straps pounded against his leg. His leather coat crinkled and crackled pleasantly. Straightening his hat with his left hand Malafeikin walked on... Not once did he turn around.

Mishka for some reason suddenly felt sorry for him.

"Windbag," he said quietly to himself. "He's got a dacha, you see. With a fireplace, you see. Now there's a windbag for you! They, you see, know how to live... Windbags."

And he also walked off. To the store. To buy cigarettes. He was out of cigarettes.

1972   —Translated by George Kolodziej

NOTES

1. Original Russian: "General Malafeikin," *Sever*, 3(1972); reprinted: *Izbrannye proizvedeniia v dvukh tomakh* (1975), Vol. 1, pp. 264-272.

SNOWBALL BERRY RED[1]

This story begins in a corrective labor colony lying somewhat
north of the city of N., in a region both beautiful and severe.

It was an evening after a working day. People had gathered in
the club.

A broad-shouldered man with a wind-burned face came out
onto the stage and announced:

"And now the former-recidivists' choir will sing for us the
pensive song 'Evening Bells.' "

The members of the choir entered the stage one by one
from the wings and arranged themselves into two groups: one
large, one small. The choristers gave remote resemblance to being
singers.

"Taking part in the 'bom-bom' group," the broad-shouldered
man continued, pointing to the large group, "are those whose
sentences are up tomorrow. This is our tradition, and we are
honoring it now."

The choir began to sing. That is, they started up in the small
group, but in the big one they bowed their heads until the re-
quired moment, when they rang out with feeling:

"Bom-m, bom-m..."

It is in the "bom-bom" group that we see our hero, Egor
Prokudin, about forty years old, with cropped hair. He is making
a serious effort; when it is time to "chime" he wrinkles his forehead and sways his round head, so as to make it seem that the
sound of the bell is rolling and floating in the evening air.

Thus ends Egor Prokudin's current sentence. Ahead—is
freedom.

In the morning, in the office of one of the superintendents,
the following conversation took place:

"So tell me, how do you intend to live, Prokudin?" asked
the superintendent. He had obviously asked this many, many
times—the words came out so readily, like a prepared phrase.

"Honestly!" Egor hurriedly gave out in reply—also, one must
suppose, prepared in advance, since the answer leaped out with
such remarkable ease.

"That I understand... But how? What do you imagine you
will do?"

"I plan to work in agriculture, citizen superintendent."

"Comrade."

"Huh?" Egor didn't understand.

"Now everyone is your comrade," the superintendent reminded him.

"Aha!" recalled Prokudin with pleasure. And he even laughed at his forgetfulness. "Yes, yes. I'll have many comrades!"

"And what exactly drew you to agriculture?" the superintendent inquired with genuine interest.

"Why, because I'm a peasant! That is, by birth. In general, I love nature. I'm going to buy a cow..."

"A cow?" The superintendent was astonished.

"A cow. With an udder like that." Egor made an outline with his hands.

"You don't choose a cow by its udder. Suppose it's young—then what sort of udder 'like that' would it have? Of course, if you pick an old cow, then it really would have an udder like that... But that's not the point. A cow should be... shapely."

"Now is it done then, by the legs?" asked Egor deferentially.

"What?"

"Choosing. Do you choose a cow by its legs, maybe?"

"And why by its legs? By its breed. There are different breeds—such and such a breed... For instance, the Kholmogorsky and the..." But the superintendent didn't know any other breeds.

"I love cows," Egor reasserted vehemently. "I'll lead her into the barn... put her into her stall..."

The superintendent and Egor were silent for awhile; they stared at one another.

"A cow, that's good," agreed the superintendent. "Only... well, you can't spend all your time with a cow. Do you have some sort of trade?"

"I have many trades."

"For instance."

Egor thought for awhile, evidently selecting from the multitude of his pursuits the least... how to say it—the one least accommodating to felonious intentions.

"Metalworker."

The telephone rang. The superintendent picked up the receiver.

"Yes. Yes. And what kind of class was it? What subject? 'Eugene Onegin'? So, and who did they ask all the questions about? Tatiana? And what was it about Tatiana that they couldn't understand? What I'm saying is, why did they..." The superintendent listened for awhile to the thin, clamorous voice in the receiver, glanced at Egor reproachfully. Then he barely nodded his head: it was all clear to him. "Let them... Listen to me: let them just knock off their clever heckling. What significance does that have—will there or won't there be any children?! As if the poem was written about that! Or else *I'll* come and explain it to them! You tell them... Okay, Nikolaev will come over immediately." The superintendent hung up that receiver and picked up another one. While he was dialing the number he remarked, annoyed, "Those wise guys... Nikolaev? They broke up the literature class of one of the women teachers: they began to ask questions. What? 'Eugene Onegin.' No, not about Onegin, about Tatiana—will she have any children by her old husband or won't she? Go and check it out. Okay? Those damned smart alecks!" The superintendent hung up the receiver. "They actually began to ask questions!"

Egor snickered, as he pictured to himself this literature class. "They just wanted to know..."

"And do you have a wife?" the superintendent interrupted sharply.

Egor pulled a photograph out of his shirt pocket and handed it to the superintendent. The latter took it and looked at it.

"Is this your wife?!" he asked, not hiding his amazement.

The photograph showed a rather pretty young woman, kind-looking, with clear features.

"Future wife," said Egor. He did not like it, that the superintendent had acted so surprised. "She's waiting for me. But I've never seen her face to face."

"How did that come about?"

"Pen pal." Egor reached over and took the photograph. "I'll just take that..." And then he himself became lost in contemplation of the sweet, simple Russian face. "Baikalova, Lyubov Fyodorovna. What trustfulness in her face, eh? It's amazing, isn't it? She looks like she could be a cashier or something."

"And what does she write?"

"She writes that she understands all my trials... 'But,' she says, 'I don't understand how you took the notion to land up in prison.' Nice letters. They make you feel peaceful... Her husband was a boozer. She kicked him out. And even so, she didn't get bitter about people."

"And do you understand what you're getting into?" the superintendent asked quietly and seriously.

"I understand," said Egor, also quietly, and hid the photograph away.

"First of all, dress properly! Going off like that—and showing up like some riff-raff." The superintendent looked Egor over with dissatisfaction. "What sort of clothes... why are you dressed in that outfit?"

Egor was wearing boots, a Russian blouse with the collar on the side, a short jacket and some sort of peaked uniform cap—making him look either like a country truck driver or a sanitation worker—or possibly also like an amateur actor in costume.

Egor gave himself a cursory glance and grinned.

"This was the way I had to dress for my role in the play. And afterward I didn't have time to change."

"Actors..." was all the superintendent said, and then he began to laugh. He was not a mean man, and he never ceased to be amazed at the unlimited inventiveness of the people he had to deal with.

And now here it was—freedom!

That is—a door slammed behind Egor and he found himself on the street of a small settlement. He took a deep, deep breath of the spring air, screwed up his eyes and twisted his head back and forth. He walked along for a bit and then leaned against a fence. An old woman carrying a handbag came by and stopped.

"Do you feel bad?"

"I'm okay, mother," said Egor. "It's good that I did time in the spring. One should always do time in the spring."

"Do time?" The old woman didn't understand.

"In prison."

Only then did the old woman realize with whom she was talking. She warily edged away and shuffled on. She looked at the fence beside her, then glanced back again at Egor.

But Egor was holding up his hand at a Volga. The Volga stopped. Egor began to dicker with the driver. The driver at first would not agree to give him a lift, but then Egor took a wad of bills out of his pocket and flashed it... He walked over to get in next to the driver.

Just then the old woman who had talked with Egor approached him again. She had even taken the trouble to cross the street.

"I beg you to forgive me," she began, bowing to Egor. "But why exactly in the spring?"

"What, do time? Well, if you do time in the spring, you get out in the spring. Freedom and spring! What more does a man need?" Egor smiled at the old woman and declaimed: "Oh, my skies of May, and the long blue days of June."

"My lands!" The old woman was astonished. She straightened up and stared at Egor the way people stare at a horse in the city that's going right down the same street where cars are traveling. The old woman had a rosy, wrinkled little face and clear eyes.

128

Without knowing it, she had given Egor a most pleasant and precious moment.

The Volga pulled away.

The old woman watched it leave. "Can you believe it? A poet—a regular Fet."

But Egor had completely given himself up to motion.

The settlement came to an end, and they leaped into open space.

"Do you happen to have any music?" asked Egor.

The driver, a young fellow, reached into the back with one hand and fetched out a transistor tape recorder.

"Turn it on. The button on the end."

Egor turned it on and some splendid music began to play. He leaned his head back on the seat and closed his eyes. He had waited a long time for such a moment. He had got tired waiting.

"Happy?" asked the driver.

"Happy?" Egor came back to consciousness. "Happy..." He seemed to be tasting the word to see how he liked it. "I'll tell you, kid, if I had three lives to live, I'd spend one in prison, give one to you, and live the third for myself. But since I only have one, then right now, of course, I am happy. And do *you* know how to be happy?" Egor was sometimes able out of fullness of feeling to ascend to the realm of beautiful but empty words. "You know how, right?"

The driver shrugged his shoulders, did not reply.

"Ah, that's a bad deal for you, son—if you don't know how."

"But what's there to be happy about?"

Egor suddenly grew serious, became lost in thought. That happened with him—he would suddenly for no reason fall to thinking.

"What's that?" asked Egor, from the depths of his thoughts.

"I said, what is there to be so all-fired happy about?" The driver was a sober fellow and rather dull.

"Well, that, brother, I don't know—what to be happy about," said Egor, returning with reluctance from his faraway inner world. "If you know how, then be happy; if you don't, then lump it. There's no use asking questions. But do you like poetry, for instance?"

The fellow again shrugged his shoulders vaguely.

"Well, see," said Egor with pity, "and you were expecting to be happy."

"No I wasn't."

"Well, you have to love poetry," Egor decisively ended this flaccid conversation. "Just listen to the kind of poetry there is in

129

the world." And Egor began to recite, though with omissions, to be sure, because he had forgotten parts:

"... into the snowy whiteness
The strident terror heaves.
Thou hast come, my black destruction—
Unafraid I rush to meet thee.

"O city, in your discord cruel,
You called us filth and liars.
And now the field in frozen sorrow...
"And something, something. I forgot a little there.
"Is choked by telegraph wires.

"There's another part I forgot. But it goes on:

"May your heart be pierced with pain
By this song of animals' rights!..
...As hunters torture a wolf,
While the beaters close in like a vise.

"The beast lies low, while deep in the brush,
A trigger will soon be pulled...
But a sudden leap... and the two-legged foe
Is ripped by the fangs of the wolf.

"My favorite beast, I salute you!
Though the knife you are certain to feel.
Like you I am everywhere hounded
By the menacing enemy steel.

"Like you I am always on guard—
And though the hunter's horn is loud,
With my final dying leap,
I will draw my enemy's blood.

"Deep in the fragile whiteness
I will fall and twist in the snow...
But this song of revenge for my death
Shall be sung on the other shore."[2]

Egor, stunned by the power of the words, sat silent for a time, staring ahead with his jaws clenched. There was a resoluteness in his gaze, intent on the far horizon, as though he himself had fearlessly thrown down such a challenge in the past and was

130

unafraid to do so now.

"How was the poetry?" asked Egor.

"Good."

"Yes, good. Like you've just slugged down a glass of pure alcohol," said Egor. "And you say you don't like poetry! You're still young—you should be interested in everything. Hey, stop! I just saw some sweethearts of mine."

The driver did not understand what sort of "sweethearts" Egor was talking about, but he stopped.

Egor got out of the car. All around was an unbroken birch forest. And such a pure, white world against the still black earth, such luminescence!.. Egor leaned against a birch tree and looked around.

"Well, will you look at what we have here!" he said with quiet rapture. He turned toward the birch tree and stroked it with the palm of his hand. "Hullo there! Ah, you look so... You're like a bride. Are you waiting for your groom? Soon, soon he'll come." Egor swiftly returned to the car. Now everything had become clear to him. He had to have some kind of release. And soon. Immediately.

"Step on it, kid. Put it to the floor. Or else my heart is going to jump out of my chest: I've got to do something. You don't have any alcohol with you, do you?"

"Hardly!"

"Well, keep rolling, then. How much did your music box cost?"

"Two hundred."

"I'll take it for three hundred. I like it."

When they reached the main city of the district, Egor commanded the driver to stop on the outskirts, before they had reached the house where his people would be. He paid off the driver generously, took his music box and, cutting across courtyards by a complicated route, walked to the "shanty."

The gang was in session.

A good-looking young woman was sitting with a guitar. Near the telephone, at which he stared stubbornly, sat a hulking bruiser with a face like a bulldog. Also sitting down were four young chicks with bare legs... A muscular young man strode about the room and kept glancing at the phone... In an armchair sat a fellow with protruding lips and stained teeth who was swigging champagne from a long-stemmed glass... Five or six other young men were scattered around the room—some smoking, others just sitting.

131

The room was dingy and ugly. Some sort of dark-blue wall-paper, torn and dirty, quite inappropriately called to mind by its color the spring sky, and this made that stinking, closed little world altogether unbearable and oppressive. Such habitations are called dens—an insult to animals.

They all sat as though in some sort of strange torpor. From time to time they glanced at the telephone. The room was heavy with tension. Only the young woman, so striking with her high cheekbones, ran her fingers lightly over the strings of her guitar and sang softly, beautifully, in a rather husky but tender voice:

> "Snowball berry red,
> Snowball berry ripe,
> A little birdie told me
> My sweetheart he had lied.

> "My sweetheart he had lied,
> Just wanted to be my lover.
> When I would not give in,
> He left me for another.

> "And I..."

At the front door sounded a prearranged knock. Every-one started, as though they had heard a scream.

"Hush!" said Fat Lip with a slight lisp. He looked at every-one in amusement, remarking, "Nerves!" And with a glance he sent someone to open the door.

"It was the muscular young man who went.

"Keep it on the chain," said Fat Lip. He put his hand into his pocket. And waited.

The muscular young man opened the door a crack. And then he quickly released the chain and looked around at everyone.

The door closed.

But suddenly from behind the door marching music blared out. Egor opened the door with a kick and marched into the room. Everyone jumped up from their places and tried to hush him.

Egor turned off the tape recorder and looked at them all in surprise.

They came up to him, greeted him, but all made an effort to keep quiet.

"Hey, Gore." (That was Egor's nickname—Gore.)[3]

"How ya doin'?"

132

"You got sprung, huh?"

Egor offered his hand, but could not figure out what was going on. A lot of his acquaintances were there—and others who were more than acquaintances: Lucienne (the girl with high cheek bones) for one, and Fat Lip for another. Egor was glad to see them. But what were they up to?

"How come you're all here together like this?"

"Some of our boys are knocking over a store," explained one, shaking hands with Egor. "They're supposed to call... We're waiting."

The girl with high cheekbones was especially glad to see Egor. She clung to his neck and covered him with kisses. Her eyes glistened with tears of unfeigned joy.

"Oh, my Gore!.. I dreamed about you today."

"Well, well," said the happy Egor. "And what did I do in your dream?"

"You hugged me. Oh, so tight."

"Are you sure you didn't confuse me with somebody else?"

"Gore!.."

"Well, turn around, little son!" said Fat Lip. "You've become a real Cossack."

Egor went over to Fat Lip and they embraced reservedly. Fat Lip did not even stand up. He looked at Egor merrily.

"I remember a certain evening in spring," began Fat Lip. And everyone got quiet. "The air was somewhat damp, and there were hundreds of people in the train station. There were so many suitcases that it dazzled your eyes. The people were all excited—couldn't wait to get on their trains. Among these nervous and excited people sat one lonely person... He was sitting on his old-fashioned trunk and thinking bitter thoughts. A certain elegant young man went up to him and asked: 'And why do you grieve, good man?' 'Oh, woe is me! I'm all alone in the world and I don't know where to go.' Then the young man..."

The telephone rang. Again everyone started, as though shocked.

"Yes?" said the one who looked like a bulldog, feigning indifference. He listened for a long time, nodding now and then. "Everyone is sitting here. I'm not going to leave the phone. They're all here. Gore showed up... Yes. Just now. We're all waiting." Bulldog hung up the receiver and turned toward the others.

"They've begun."

They all began to fidget.

"Champagne!" ordered Fat Lip.

133

Bottles of champagne were passed around.

"How big is the job?" Egor asked Fat Lip.

"Eight grand," said the latter. "To your health!"

They drank.

"Lucienne... sing something, to relieve the tension," asked Fat Lip. He was lean, calm and extremely insolent; very insolent eyes.

"I will sing about love," said the charming Lucienne. She tossed back her dyed hair and placed her palm with a flourish on the strings of her guitar. Everyone felt silent.

"Tittle-tattle, my magpie,
Spells of magic, eyes of night.
Those not gay and those in sorrow,
Go away now, out of sight.

"In the meadow, in the dark,
Love is free, and shining eye.
My heart is aching, lure me on,
Tittle-tattle, my magpie."

Again the telephone rang. At once a funereal silence descended.

"Yes?" said Bulldog, using all his strength to stay calm. "No, you called the wrong number. That's all right, don't worry about it. Yes, it could happen to anyone." Bulldog hung up the receiver. "She was calling a laundry, the bitch."

They began to fidget again.

"More champagne!" said Fat Lip. "Gore—whose greetings have you brought us?"

"Later," said Egor. "Let me just look at you all first. And here are all these young people I don't even know yet. I'll just introduce myself."

The young people respectfully shook hands with him for the second time. Egor, with a grin, attentively looked each of them in the eye. He nodded his head and said, "So, so..."

"I want to dance!" announced Lucienne. And she smashed her champagne glass on the floor.

"Lay off, Lucienne," said Fat Lip. "Don't start up with that, now."

"Go to the devil!" said Lucienne, half drunk. "Gore, our feature number!"

And Egor also dashed his wineglass to the floor.

And his eyes, too, began to flash.

134

"Okay, everybody, make a circle. Move it!"

"Cut it, Gore!" said Fat Lip, raising his voice. "You picked the wrong time!"

"But we can still hear the phone!" they shouted at Fat Lip from all sides. "Let them do their hop... What do you care? And besides, Bulldog is sitting right by the phone."

Fat Lip pulled out a white handerkerchief, and, though late with the gesture, pretentiously waved it at them in the style of Pugachev.

Two guitars struck up a *barynia* folk dance.

Lucienne stepped out... Ah, how she danced! She really know how, too. Not wildly, no, but precisely, lightly, with a fine sense of rhythm. She seemed to be hammering her crippled life into the grave with her heels, while her true self beat its wings like a bird trying to fly away. She put so much into her dance... She even became suddenly beautiful—sweet and natural.

Whenever Lucienne approached him, Egor would also dance, moving only his legs. He folded his arms behind his back, avoided fancy steps, did not prance like a goat—in short, he was also good. And they looked very good together. Their dance was imbued with something lasting and unforgettable.

"This is the moment my long-suffering soul was waiting for," said Egor with utter seriousness. Indeed, this was just what he had hoped for from his long-desired freedom.

"Wait, Egorushka, and I'll soothe your soul in another way, too," replied Lucienne. "Oh, how I will soothe it. And I will soothe my own soul, too."

"Soothe it, Lucienne, it's crying."

"I will. I'll press it to my heart like a little dove and say to it: 'Are you tired? Darling... darling... dearest, you're tired...' "

"Make sure that dove doesn't peck you," interjected Fat Lip into the sentimental conversation.

"No, it's not an evil dove," said Egor seriously, not looking at Fat Lip. And a grim shadow passed over his kindly face. But they did not stop dancing. They danced—and one wanted to watch them forever. The young people watched them anxiously, avidly, as though an ugly part of their lives, too, was being trodden into the grave—and afterward they would emerge into the bright daylight, and it would be springtime.

"It's weary in its cage," said Lucienne tenderly.

"It's crying," said Egor. "It needs a holiday."

"Switch it on its little head with a twig," said Fat Lip. "And that will calm it."

"What people, Egorushka, eh?" exclaimed Lucienne. "How

wicked they are!"

"Well, Lucienne, to wicked people, we ourselves are wolves. But my soul, my soul... it's crying."

"We'll soothe it, Egorushka, we'll soothe it. I'm an enchantress and I'll put all my spells on it..."

"Doves make good soup," said Fat Lip maliciously. He was thin as a knife blade, cool and terrible in his youthful insolence. His whole character was reflected in his eyes. His eyes glittered with malice.

"No, it's crying!" said Egor in a frenzy. "It's crying! It's smothering in there, so it's weeping." He tore open his shirt and stood in front of Fat Lip. The guitars suddenly fell silent. And the dance of Lucienne-the-enchantress suddenly came to a halt.

Fat Lip already had his hand in his pocket.

"Back to your old ways again, eh, Gore?" He spoke with an odd satisfaction.

"I'm telling you for the last time," said Egor calmly, wearily, as he buttoned his shirt. "Don't touch me on my sore place again. Next time you might not get your hand in your pocket in time. That's a warning..."

"I'll keep it in mind."

"Ahh," said Lucienne, distressed. "How tiresome. More blood, more corpses. Brr! Pour me some champagne, somebody."

The telephone rang. Somehow they'd all forgotten about it.

Bulldog lunged for the phone and grabbed the receiver. He put it to his ear—and dropped it almost at once, as though it were hot.

Fat Lip was the first to jump up. There was always an urgency about him, yet he was calm at the same time.

"They got burned," said Bulldog tersely in a horrified voice.

"Everybody split up!" commanded Fat Lip. "Spread out. And lie low for two weeks. Now!"

They disappeared one by one. This was something they evidently knew how to do. No one asked any questions.

"No two together!" added Fat Lip. "We'll meet at Ivan's place. No sooner than ten days."

Egor sat down at the table, poured himself a glass of champagne, drank it.

"What are you going to do, Gore?" asked Fat Lip.

"Me?" Egor thought for awhile before answering. "I think I might actually go into agricultural work."

Lucienne and Fat Lip stood over him in disbelief.

"What sort of agricultural work?"

But then Lucienne shook him. "What are you sitting there

for? We've got to leave."

Egor started, got to his feet.

"Leave? Time to leave again?... When am I ever going to arrive, citizens? Where's my amazing music box?.. Oh, there it is. Is it absolutely necessary to go? Perhaps..."

"What are you talking about? In ten minutes they'll be here. They probably tailed our boys."

Lucienne walked to the door.

Egor was about to follow her, but Fat Lip laid a restraining hand on his shoulder and said quietly:

"Better not. Let's talk a minute. We'll all be seeing each other again anyway..."

"Are you going with her, or what?" asked Egor bluntly.

"No," said Fat Lip firmly, with seeming honesty. "Take off!" he barked at Lucienne, who had lingered in the doorway.

Lucienne glowered at Fat Lip and left.

"Take a rest someplace," said Fat Lip, pouring out two glasses. "Take a rest, old buddy—with King Kolka maybe, or Vanka Samykin. Samykin has a real cozy place. And look—don't hold it against me for... today. But, Gore... you know, Gore, you sometimes press on my sore place, too, only you don't realize it. Well, drink up! To our next meeting! And for now, good-bye. Don't be unhappy. Have you got enough dough?"

"Yeah, they made up a collection for me before I left..."

"I can throw in some more."

"Well, okay," Egor changed his mind.

Fat Lip took a roll of bills out of his pocket and peeled off a thick sheaf for Egor.

"Where are you going to be, then?"

"I don't know. I'll find somebody. But tell me, how could you have screwed up so bad, anyway?"

Just then one of the young fellows slipped into the room, white with fear.

"They've surrounded the whole block," he said.

"What are you doing here?"

"I don't know where to go... I wanted to tell you..."

"His horns don't even show yet," laughed Fat Lip. "What made you come back here? Ah, you sweetheart, my sweetheart, my little calf... Follow me, brothers!"

They left by a back entrance and ran along a wall toward the street, but they could hear the heavy footsteps of a patrol coming toward them. They changed direction—and again heard footsteps.

"Damn," said Fat Lip, without losing his enigmatic gaiety.

137

"It looks like they've got us. What do you think, Gore?"

"Quick, in here!" Egor pushed his companions into some sort of recess in the wall.

The footsteps, coming from both directions, drew closer.

The beam from a powerful flashlight played along the wall to the right.

Fat Lip pulled out his revolver.

"Put it back, you fool!" said Egor sharply, angrily. "You psychopath. Maybe they won't even see us—but suddenly you're going to open fire!"

"But I know those bastards!" exclaimed Fat Lip nervously. He was finally beginning to lose his cool.

"Look, I'll rush out and lead them away. I've got my release papers," said Egor quickly, peering about to see the best direction to run. "The papers have today's date on them, so I'm covered. If they catch me, I'll just tell them I panicked. I'll tell them I was looking for a woman, when I heard the whistles— and just lost my head. I'm off. Don't remember ill of me!"

And Egor dashed away from them, running blindly with all his might. At once from all sides whistles began to blow and running footsteps resounded.

Egor ran exultantly, like a kid... As he ran, he urged himself on and even hummed a song. He spotted a patch of light, threw himself in that direction, crawled over some pipes—and triumphantly burst into song:

"Hip, hip, hooray! Oh, nothing saw I, no one do I know..."

He had already got past the pipes, but behind him in the darkness they were running up very fast. Egor dove back into one of the wide ducts and froze.

Overhead footsteps boomed on the iron pipe...

Egor squatted, hunched over, smiled contentedly and hummed:

"Oh, nothing saw I, no one do I know..."

He had undertaken a rather dangerous venture. When the booming footsteps had subsided, even though it would have been possible just to stay there and outsit them, he suddenly rushed out and began running again.

Again they scrambled after him.

"Oh, nothing saw I, and no one do I know... No one do I know..." Egor sang to embolden himself. He hopped over a low fence, ran through some bushes: he had gotten into some sort of garden. A dog began to bark close by. Egor abruptly changed direction... Another fence. He leaped over it on the run and found himself in a cemetery.

"Hello!" said Egor. And began to walk quietly.

The hullabaloo behind him gradually veered off to the side.

"Damned if I didn't outrun them!" marvelled Egor. "Too bad it's not always like that. When you really *need* to escape, then you get caught, like some kid."

And again Egor was overcome by the joy of being free and of being alive.

"Oh, nothing saw I, and no one do I know," he sang once more. He turned his tape recorder on low and walked along looking at the inscriptions on the grave stones. A street curved around the cemetery and the headlights of cars rounding the bend would light up the crosses for a considerable time. And the shadows of the crosses, long and deformed, would sweep over the ground, the grave mounds, and the fences... It made a rather eerie scene. Suddenly Egor's music seemed totally out of place. He shut it off.

" 'Sleep in peace till the bright dawn,' " Egor managed to read. " 'Merchant Neverov of the First Guild.' And how did *you* get here?!" Egor exclaimed. " '1890'—Ah, that explains it. Well, well—a merchant of the first guild. 'Riding with wares on the road from Kasimov,' " Egor began to sing softly, but stopped suddenly. " 'To my dear, unforgettable husband, from his inconsolable widow,' " he read a little farther on. He sat down on a low bench for awhile... Then he stood up. "Well, friends, you have to lie here while I move on. There's nothing we can do about it... I'll go off on my own, like an honest John. There's got to be some place where I can lay my head. There's just got to be, right? Right!" And he sang yet again: "Oh, nothing saw I, and no one do I kno-o-ow."

So he set out to look for a place to lay his head.

At the door of a wooden cottage on the very edge of town they yelled at him from inside:

"Go away! Or else I'll come out there and give you something to suffer about... I'll show you grief and suffering."

Egor was silent for a minute.

"Okay, come on out."

"I'll do it, too!"

"When you come out, tell me—is Ninka here or not?" Egor asked the man in a civil tone of voice. "But tell the truth! Because I'll find out, and if you've lied to me, I'll punish you severely!"

The man also fell silent. And then he, too, changed his tone of voice and said grumpily—but not threateningly:

"There's no Ninka here, I told you. Can't you understand

139

that? All you loafers, hanging around every night..."

"How would you like to get singed a little?" Egor spoke his thoughts aloud, rattling the box of matches in his pocket. "Hah?"

There was a long silence behind the door.

"Just try it,"the voice said at last—but now almost placatingly. "Just you try to start a fire... There's no Ninka here, I'm telling you the truth. She's gone away."

"Where to?"

"Somewhere up north."

"Why the hell didn't you say that at the beginning, instead of barking at me like a damned dog? What's the problem, anyway?"

"Because your kind only bring trouble. That's why she had to go away, because of people like you."

"Well, think of it this way—she's in good hands now, they'll take care of her. Good-bye now. Take it easy."

In a nearby phone booth Egor got angry again.

"What do you mean, it's forbidden? Why?!" he roared into the receiver.

Someone gave him a long explanation.

"You're all diseased," said Egor, his voice trembling. "I'll make a bouquet out of you sons-of-bitches and stick you in the ground head first... You bastards!" Egor slammed down the receiver. He fell into thought. "Lyuba!" he said with exaggerated tenderness. "That's it! I'll go see Lyuba." And he spitefully pushed the door of the phone booth as hard as he could and strode off toward the train station. He spoke to Lyuba, his dear one, as he walked along:

"Ah, my darling... Lyubushka, my little dove. You're my little Siberian potato cake! I'll at least put on a little weight at your place, and let my hair grow out. Oh, you dear little cupcake!" Egor got more and more frenzied. "I'm coming to eat you up!" he shouted into the silence of the night. He didn't even look around to see if he had startled anyone with his noise. His footsteps echoed in the empty street; it was already freezing, and the cold asphalt rang out. "I'll smother you with my embraces! I'll tear you into pieces and gobble you up! And wash you down with home-brewed vodka. To the last morsel!"

Egor had just arrived at the village of Yasnoe on the local bus.

Lyuba stood on a little rise of ground waiting for him. He spotted her from a distance, recognizing her at once. His heart

140

skipped a beat.

He walked up to meet her.

"Oh, man," he whispered to himself, in rapture. "She's absolutely gorgeous! Sweet as sugar and plump as a little bun. She's a regular Little Red Riding Hood."

"Hello," he said politely, affecting shyness, and extended his hand. "I'm Georgii." He warmly pressed her strong, countrywoman's hand. And, for good measure, he shook it as well, also warmly.

"And I'm Lyuba," she said. She looked at Egor evenly and somewhat thoughtfully. She was silent. Egor grew restless under her gaze.

"It's me," he said. He felt very stupid.

"I'm me, too," said Lyuba, and continued to stare at him calmly and thoughtfully.

"I'm not very handsome," said Egor inadvertently.

Lyuba burst into laughter.

"Let's go sit for awhile in the teashop," she said. "You can tell me about yourself."

"I don't drink," said Egor hastily.

"Oh, really?" Lyuba was sincerely pleased. She responded with complete simplicity and naturalness. Her innocence disconcerted Egor.

"Well, of course," he said, "I do take a drink in company. But I don't, you know, get plastered... I'm very temperate..."

"We'll just drink tea then. And you can tell me a little about yourself." She continued to gaze at her pen pal. She looked at him so strangely, that it seemed as though she was secretly laughing at herself, as if to say, astonished at her behavior: "You're a fool, aren't you? What have you gotten yourself into?" But she was obviously an independent woman—able to laugh at herself, yet did what she wanted anyway. "Let's go. Talk to me. You know, my mother and father—they're very strict—they say to me: don't come around here with your convict." Lyuba was walking somewhat ahead. As she said this, she turned around with a calm and cheerful look. "And I say to them: but he's a convict by accident. Through misfortune. That's right, isn't it?"

At the news that she had parents—and strict ones besides—Egor began to feel glum. But he didn't let it show on his face.

"Yes, yes," he said "intelligently." "It was all a matter of circumstantial coincidence. Incredible bad luck."

"That's just what I told them."

"Are your parents Old Believers?"

"Why, no. What in the world made you think that?"

141

"Well, they're strict... And there's something else they won't like. I smoke, for instance."

"Oh, heavens! My father smokes, too. Though my brother, it's true, doesn't smoke."

"So you have a brother, too?"

"Yes, we have a big family. My brother has two children—grown up already: his son is already studying at the institute and his daughter is finishing her tenth year in high school."

"Everybody studying... That's good," approved Egor. "Fine young people." He began to get a sour taste in his mouth from such kinfolk.

They stopped in at the teashop. They sat down at a little table in the corner. The teashop was crowded, people came and went continually... And they all looked Egor over with interest. This, too, made him feel ashamed and uncomfortable.

"Maybe we could get a bottle of something and go somewhere else," suggested Egor.

"What for? It's so splendid here... Oh, Nyura, Nyura!" Lyuba summoned the waitress. "Bring us something, dear... What should we get?" she said, turning to Egor.

"Make it red wine. Vodka gives me heartburn," said Egor, making a grimace.

"Red wine, Nyura!" Lyuba was making a rather puzzling impression, as though she were playing some sort of intellectual game. She played it calmly, gaily, as she studied Egor with curiosity. Had he guessed what was going on or not?

"Well, Georgii," she began, "tell me about yourself."

"Just like the third degree," said Egor, laughing weakly. But Lyuba didn't respond to that, so Egor got serious again.

"Well, what to say? I'm a bookkeeper. I was working in a supply house. The bosses, of course, were stealing... Suddenly—bang!—an audit. I was the one they reeled in. Naturally, I had to take the rap. Listen," said Egor, following Lyuba's example in using the intimate form of address, "let's get out of here. They all keep staring..."

"Oh, let them stare! What do you care? After all, you didn't run away..."

"Right here's my release papers!" exclaimed Egor, about to dig into his pocket.

"I believe you, I believe you, for heaven's sake! I only said what was true. All right? And how many years did you do, then?"

"Five."

"And so..."

"That's all... What else is there to say?"

"With hands like those—you're a bookkeeper? It's hard to believe."

"What? My hands?... Oh, well. They got that way from all the physical exercise I did while I was in..." Egor put his hands under the table.

"Hands like those would do better at breaking locks than keeping accounts," laughed Lyuba.

And Egor, rather disturbed, also gave a false little laugh.

"So what do you plan to do here? Are you going into book-keeping again?"

"No!" said Egor with alacrity. "I'm never going to be a book-keeper again."

"But what will you do, then?"

"I'll have to look around... But let me rein in my horses a little, okay, Lyuba?" Egor now gazed directly into the woman's eyes. "You want them to run full speed on the subject of work. But work is not something you rush into.[4] Let's drop that for awhile."

"But why have you been deceiving me?" asked Lyuba with equal directness. "The fact is, I wrote to your superior, and he replied that..."

"Ahh," sighed Egor, defeated. "So that's the way it is." And then he became relaxed, even cheerful. "Okay, then—whip the whole troika up the mountain. Pour me a drink."

And he turned on his music box.

"And you wrote such nice letters," said Lyuba regretfully. "They were more like poems—genuine poems—than letters."

"Really?" Egor perked up. "You like them? Maybe I've been wasting my talents." He sang: " 'He lost his youth and his talent behind those prison walls...' Let's have another one, Lyuba! 'Oh, those nights in prison, oh those nights of fire...' Another drink!"

"Why are you carrying on like that? Wait a minute... Let's talk."

"So, that damned superintendent—the craphead!" exclaimed Egor. "And he never said a word to me. Well, I showed up here as a law-abiding citizen, didn't I? A bookkeeper!" Egor roared with laughter. "Keeping accounts of consumer goods..."

"What were you intending to do, Georgii?" asked Lyuba. "You were lying to me... Does that mean you were going to rob me?"

"Jesus Christ Almighty! To come way the hell out here to Siberia to steal a couple of pairs of felt boots? You're insulting me, Lyuba."

143

"Well, what is it you want here, then?"

"I don't know. Maybe just find rest for my soul... But that's not it, either. Anyway, for me to find rest, that would be... No. I just don't know, Lyubov."

"Ah, Egorushka..."

Egor actually flinched and looked at Lyuba in fright—so much had she sounded like far-away Lucienne when she said his name that way.

"What?" he said.

"You really are like a horse on a mountain. You're exhausted. Your sides haven't started to heave yet, and you're not yet foaming at the mouth. But you'll surely drop. You'll drive yourself until you die. Is it true that you have no one? No relatives?"

"That's right—I'm just a poor little orphan. I wrote you that. Do you know my nickname? It's Gore—woe is me: my pseudonym. But let's not get into my private life, please. Forget that. I'm not a beggar yet. Maybe I'm not good for much, but I still know how to knock over a store. Sometimes I'm fantastically rich, Lyuba. It's too bad you didn't meet me during one of those times... Then you would have seen that I... completely detest that stinking money."

"You hate it, yet because of it you end up being crucified."

"It isn't because of the money."

"Well, why, then?"

"There's nothing else on this earth that I'm fit to be—except a thief." Egor said this with pride. He was feeling very much at ease with Lyuba. He had simply taken the notion to astonish her with something.

"Oy-ee!" said Lyuba. "Well, drink up and we'll go."

"Where?" asked Egor, surprised.

"To my house. You came to see me, didn't you? Or do you have another pen pal somewhere else?" Lyuba chuckled. She also felt very much at ease with Egor, very much...

"Wait," said Egor in confusion. "I thought we just made it plain that I'm not a bookkeeper..."

"That was certainly some profession you picked!" Lyuba shook her head. "Pig keeper would have been an even better one. You could have pretended that your pigs all got sick and they sent you to prison for it. You really don't act much like a swindler. More like a normal guy—even like one of our village types here. So, Mr. Pigkeeper, shall we go?"

"By the way," said Egor, with a touch of smugness, "for your information, I'm a truck driver of the second class."

"Do you have a license?" asked Lyuba skeptically.

144

"My license is in Magadan."

"See, you're invaluable—even if your name does mean grief. That grief needs to be whipped out of you. Let's go."

"Typical peasant psychology, like driving a cart horse," said Gore. "Listen—I'm a recidivist convict, you little fool. I'd steal the pennies off a dead man's eyes. I..."

"Hush! I think you're a little tipsy, aren't you?"

"Right. But what's going on?" Egor came to himself. "I don't understand. Explain it to me, please. We're going to your house. Okay. But what then?"

"Stay at my house. Take a rest, even if only for a week... I don't have anything worth stealing anyway... Just relax for awhile... Then after that you can start breaking into stores again. Let's go. Or else people will say, 'She no sooner met him, than she turned him away at the door. Why did she invite him, then?' That's the way we are here! We're always minding each other's business... But for some reason I'm not afraid of you, I don't know why."

"Good. But your daddy might decide to give me a love-tap... with an axe. There's no telling what ideas he'll get about me."

"Don't worry about that. From now on, just trust me."

The Baikalovs' house was a large one, built of logs. Lyuba lived with her parents in one half of it; on the other side of a partition lived her brother and his family.

The house was situated on a high river bank. Beyond the far shore was a limitless plain. The Baikalovs were well set up, with a large yard surrounded by trim outbuildings and a bathhouse down on the river bank.

The old people happened to be cooking little meat pies in the kitchen when grandmother Mikhailovna caught sight of Lyuba and Egor out the window.

"Oh, lookee, she's bringing him!" she said in alarm. "Lyubka—and that jailbird!"

The old man also pressed himself against the window.

"Now what sort of life will we live!" he said in a fit of temper. "He'll put his ways on us, like a knife in the heart. What has that girl brought down on us?"

They could see Lyuba telling Egor something as she pointed with her hand beyond the river, then looked around and pointed back, toward the village. Egor obediently turned his head, but he kept glancing at the house, at the windows.

Behind the windows there was total panic. The old people had never really believed that someone from a prison was going to visit them. Even though Lyuba had showed them Egor's telegram, they still didn't believe it. But now it had all turned out to be horribly true.

"Oh, that baneful wench!" the old woman wept. "But what could I do with that wanton girl?! I couldn't stop her no ways..."

"Don't let on that we're frightened," the old man instructed her. "We've seen such bandits before! It's Stenka Razin all over again."

"We're bound to greet him, though, aren't we?" said the old woman, after first giving the matter some thought. "Or what? My head's just all in a whirl, I can't think what to do..."

"Yes, we're bound. We'll treat him just like people, or else watch out—we'll lose our lives. All from our own daughter. Oh, Lyubka, Lyubka..."

Lyuba and Egor entered the house.

"Hello!" said Egor cordially.

The old people only nodded in reply and openly stared him up and down.

"Well, here's our bookkeeper," said Lyuba, as though everything were perfectly normal. "And he's not at all a highway robber, he only got in trouble because... because..."

"Because of a misunderstanding," prompted Egor.

"And how many years are they giving now for misunderstandings?" asked the old man.

"Five," said Egor tersely.

"Not enough. They used to give more."

"But just what sort of misunderstanding did he sit in prison for?" asked the old woman straight out.

"The bosses were stealing, and he was writing it off," explained Lyuba. "Well, have you asked all your questions? It's time to eat now—our guest has been on the road a long time. Take a seat, Georgii."

Egor uncovered his close-cropped head and sat down meekly on the edge of a chair.

"Sit down for now," commanded Lyuba. "I'll go heat up the bathhouse, and after that we'll eat." Lyuba went out. She seemed to have gone off on purpose, to let the three of them come to some kind of understanding with each other—by themselves. No doubt she was counting on her basically good-hearted parents.

"May I smoke?" asked Egor. He wasn't all that anxious—let them kick him out if they wanted to; but if they could get on peacefully together, it would be better—and more interesting. Of course, it wasn't simply for amusement that he wanted to settle in here, even if only for a short while. The thing was, he absolutely

146

had to find someplace where he could hole up and get his bearings.

"Feel free," said the old man. "What do you smoke?"

"Pamirs."

"Those are cigarettes, aren't they?"

"Right."

"Give me one, I'd like to try them." The old man sat down next to Egor. And all the while he kept looking him over and staring at him.

They lit up.

"So what kind of misunderstanding was it you had again?" asked the old man, as though just in passing. "Did you go to hit somebody on the forehead and accidentally break his skull?"

Egor stared at the sly old man.

"Yes..." he said vaguely. "We bumped off seven people in one place, but we didn't spot the eighth. He got away. And that's how we got caught."

The old woman dropped a piece of stove wood on the floor and sat down on a bench.

The old man proved to be less naive and remained calm.

"Seven?"

"Seven. We cut their heads clean off, put them in a sack and lammed off..."

"Oh, my Lord and saints above," muttered the old woman, crossing herself. "Fedya..."

"Quiet!" commanded the old man. "One fool talks non-sense, and the other believes him... And you, mutt, watch your tongue in front of elderly people."

"Well, what kind of elderly people are you, to call me a bandit right off the bat? You hear that I'm a bookkeeper, and all you do is snicker. Okay, I was in prison, but what do you think—the only people in prison are murderers?"

"Who's calling you a murderer? But that bookkeeper business, you're also... you're just going too far with that... Don't tell your lies here. Bookkeeper! I've seen a passel of bookkeepers in my day, and they're all quiet types, with a sort of hang-dog look. Your bookkeepers are all four-eyed, with weak voices... and I notice they've all got turned up noses, too. But what sort of bookkeeper are you? You—if they beat you on the head for six months, you still wouldn't feel it. Go tell Lyubka that book-keeper business, she might believe you. But not me. As soon as you walked in here, I could tell right off—this one either beat somebody up or stole a truckload of lumber. Am I right?"

"You ought to get a job as a police inspector, pop," said Egor. "You'd be worth your weight in gold. Are you sure you didn't serve with Kolchak in your young years? Like maybe in the White counterintelligence?"

The old man blinked his eyes rapidly. Somehow he was thrown completely off balance, though he wasn't quite sure why. Egor's accusations had taken an ominous turn.

"What's that for?" he asked. "Why are you talking that way?"

"And why did you get so shook up? All I did was ask a question... Okay, another one: you never stole any grain from the kolkhoz fields during hard years?"

The old man, stunned by such an unexpected reversal, kept silent. He had been completely thrown off the condescending tone of voice he'd been using and could not find a way to reply to this upstart. Egor, of course, had pursued his interrogation precisely with this in mind. He had seen real masters of this technique in his life.

"You're having difficulty answering," continued Egor. "Well, never mind... We'll now ask a question of a different sort, closer to home, so to speak: do you often take part in the meetings here?"

"What sly tricks are you trying to pull now?" the old man asked at last. He was on the verge of really losing his temper. He was ready to counter-attack profusely and angrily, but Egor suddenly jumped up from his chair, put on his uniform cap and began to stride around the room.

"See how cozy we've learned to live!" Egor rapped out, glancing sharply from time to time at the old man, who had remained seated. "The country is producing electricity, steam engines, millions of tons of cast iron... People work and strain with all their might. They literally drop from the effort; they eliminate all traces of sloppiness and stupidity in themselves, and they finally reach a point, you could say, where they are staggering from the exertion." Egor leaped on the word "exertion" and smacked his lips over it. "In the Far North people get old before their time and they have to go out and get themselves gold teeth... But at the same time there are other people, who, out of all the achievements of mankind, have chosen for themselves only a warm stove! Think of it! Really wonderful... They'd rather prop their feet up on the hearth than work in harmony with all those others who are killing themselves..."

"But he's been working since he was ten years old!" the old woman butted in. "He's been in the fields from childhood..."

"Rebuttals later," said Egor, cutting her short rather sharply. "We're all as nice as pie when our own interests are not at stake,

148

when our own pockets, so to speak, are not touched..."

"I've been a Stakhanovite all my life!" the old man almost screamed. "I've got eighteen commendations!"

Egor stopped, surprised.

"Well, why did you sit there without saying anything?" he said in a different tone of voice.

"What do you mean? You didn't give me a chance to get a word in edgewise!"

"Where are the commendations?"

"Over there," said the old woman, also utterly bewildered.

"Over where?"

"There, in the cupboard, all put away."

"They belong on the wall, not in a cupboard! In the cupboard! Everybody keeps hiding everything in the cupboard..."

At that moment Lyuba walked in.

"Well, how are you getting along?" she asked cheerfully. Her cheeks had got all red in the bathhouse and her hair had worked loose from under her kerchief... How pretty she was. Egor looked at her involuntarily. "Is everything okay? Nice and peaceful?"

"What a fire-eater you found!" said the old man with unfeigned delight. "Look how he's taken over here! A regular commissar!" he laughed.

The old woman only shook her head and angrily pursed her lips.

Thus Egor made his acquaintance with Lyuba's parents.

He got acquainted with her brother Petro and his family somewhat later.

Petro drove into the yard in a dump truck... The sound of its raucous engine rattled the window panes for some time. Finally Petro got the truck parked, and the motor sputtered into silence. Petro stepped down from the cab. His wife Zoya came out to meet him. She was a sales clerk at the village store, an articulate butterfly of a woman, quick and bustling.

"He finally got here... Lyubka's, you know, pen pal," she said at once.

"Oh, yeah?" said Petro with mild curiosity. Petro was a strapping fellow, somewhat morose, constantly preoccupied. "Well, what about him?" He kicked one of the tires of the truck, then another one.

"He says he was a bookkeeper—there was something about an audit, he says. But with that mug of his, he looks more like a bandit."

"Yeah?" said Petro, again rather lazily and incuriously. "So then what?"

"Oh, nothing. But we'll have to keep an eye on him for awhile... Go take a look at that bookkeeper! See for yourself! He'd stick a knife in you without a second thought, that bookkeeper."

"Yeah?" Petro continued to kick the tires. "You think so?"

"You just go take a look at him! Take a look and see what she found for herself! Go take a look—we're all going to live under the same roof with him now."

"Well, what of it?"

"Oh, nothing at all!" said Zoya, raising her voice. "We've got a daughter in school, that's what! Is that all you can think of to say, 'What of it'? You constantly leave us alone over night, that's what! You and your 'What of it,' you stump. His wife and daughter are going to have their throats cut, and he won't even stir himself!"

Petro went over to the house, wiping his hands on a rag as he walked along. As to his wife's remark about not stirring himself, this was indeed characteristic of him: he was an extraordinarily calm, even phlegmatic man, though he was suffused with massive, capable strength. This strength could be sensed in every movement that Petro made, especially when he turned his head and stared with his rather small eyes—with a steady, steely, unblinking fearlessness.

"Now you can go with Petro," said Lyuba, as she set about getting Egor organized to take a bath. "But what can we give you to change into? What made you do that—to come a-courting, and not even bring an extra pair of underclothes? Well? What in the world were you thinking of, to turn up like that?"

"You're talking about prison!" exclaimed the old man. "Not a health resort. It even happens that they come out of health resorts stripped clean. Why, Ilyushka Lopatin—you remember—went to take a cure for radiculitis. It cost him a whole cow—and he came back without a kopeck."

"Well, here's some of my husband's old things I just found. I hope they fit." Lyuba pulled out of a trunk a long white undershirt and a pair of drawers.

"What's this?" said Egor, not understanding.

"Clothes that belonged to my former husband," Lyuba stood there with the pair of drawers in her hand. "What's the matter?"

"Oh, no..." Egor was insulted. "I'm not some beggar who has to drag around in somebody else's old underwear! I've got money. I'll go buy some in a store."

"Where are you going to buy any now? The stores are already

150

closed. But why all the fuss? These have been washed..."

"Go ahead and take them," said the old man. "They're clean."

Egor thought it over for a minute, and took them.

"I'm sinking lower and lower," he muttered. "It's interesting even to me, what's happening to me. After awhile I'll probably even sing you a song: 'In the garden, in the garden—cabbages or flowers?' "

"Oh, go on now," said Lyuba, escorting him to the door. "By the way, Petro's not the tenderhearted type, so don't get upset: he treats everybody the same."

Petro was already taking off his clothes in the little dressing room of the bathhouse when Egor came down the river bank.

"Will they let in people with shaved heads?" said Egor, trying to be as cheerful as possible. He even stretched his lips into a smile.

"They let in anybody," said Petro, in the same unemotional tone of voice he had used with his wife.

"Let's introduce ourselves. I'm Georgii." Egor held out his hand. He kept smiling as he looked into Petro's somber eyes. In spite of himself, he wanted to be accepted by these people. He really felt it now. Was it on account of Lyuba, perhaps? "As I said—I'm Georgii."

"Okay, okay," said Petro. "Do you want us to kiss each other, too? So your name is Georgii. So what? Maybe I'll call you Zhora..."

"George, to you." Egor was left with his hand hanging in the air. He stopped smiling.

"What?" said Petro, perplexed.

" 'What?' 'What?' " repeated Egor heatedly. "Christ, I've been sucking around here like a beggar-whore all day!" He threw his underwear down on the bench. "The only thing I haven't done is wag my tail! What have I done to step on your toes, that you won't even shake my hand?" Egor was really agitated. He groped in his pocket for a cigarette, lit it, and sat down on the bench. His hands were almost trembling.

"What's up with you?" asked Petro. "What are you sprawling there for?"

"Go and wash," said Egor. "I'll go next. I've been in prison. Us convicts know our place. Don't worry about it."

"Oh ho!" said Petro. And he went into the bathing room without bothering to take off his shorts. Egor could hear him clattering around with the basins and the dipper...

Egor lay down on the bench and smoked.

"So that's the way it is!" he said to himself. "Just like a poor relation. Crap!"

The door of the bathing room opened and Petro glanced in at Egor out of a cloud of steam.

"What's the matter?" he asked.

"What do you mean?"

"Why are you lying there?"

"I'm just a foundling."

"Oh ho!" said Petro. And he went down into the bathing room again. He stayed in there a long time, pouring water in basins, moving benches around... Finally he got impatient and opened the door again. "Are you coming or not?!" he asked.

"I've got release papers!" Egor almost yelled in his face. "Tomorrow I'm going to get the same kind of passport you have! Exactly the same, except for one little remark that no one will ever read anyway. Understand?"

"In about one minute I'm gonna shove your head in a bucket," said Petro expressionlessly. "And sit your ass on the hot stove. Without a passport." Petro was rather pleased at his own wit. He added: "But you have to show your release papers," and chuckled briefly.

"Well, this is a different conversation altogether!" said Egor. He sat up on the bench and began to get undressed. "If I don't watch out, I'll have to show you my high school diploma."

Meanwhile, Lyuba's mother and sister-in-law had driven Lyuba into the corner with their questions.

"Whatever made you take him to the tearoom?" shrilly queried the highly vocal Zoya, a woman given to hysteria. "Why, the whole village knows already: some jailbird came to see Lyubka! They all told me about it at work."

"Oh, Lyubka, Lyubka!..." her mother persisted in a quaking voice. "Tell him this, see: if you came here just to put on some fat and then afterward go into the world again, then—tell him—he should go away this very day and not shame you in front of everyone. Tell him, if he..."

"How could it be possible that he doesn't have a family someplace? Think about it. He's not some kid of seventeen, is he? Use your head!"

"Tell him this: tell him, if he means to do something bad, then he should just gather up his things and..."

"What things? All he needs to do is tighten his belt and he'll be ready to go," put in the old man, who until then had been

152

silent. "What are you jumping on the girl for? What do you expect to get out of her? Let's just see what happens, see what sort of fellow he turns out to be. How in hell can she answer for him now?"

"Don't frighten me, for the love of Christ," was all that Lyuba could say to her mother and sister-in-law. "I'm already frightened. Do you think this is easy for me?"

"There! That's just what I'm trying to tell you!" exclaimed Zoya.

"Here's what to do, dearie... Are you listening, Lyuba?" the old woman continued with her pestering. "Tell him this: see here, my good man, go away today and spend the night someplace else."

"And where would that be?" asked Lyuba, feeling numb.

"In the village meeting hall."

"Phoo!" said the old man, disgusted. "Have you all gone completely off your rockers, or what? Look, you can't invite the guy here and then send him off to sleep at the village soviet. What a thing to do! It goes against Christ!"

"Tomorrow we can get a policeman to investigate him," persisted Lyuba's mother.

"What's to investigate? His face tells the whole story."

"I don't know," said Lyuba. "It seems to me that he's a good man. Somehow I can see it in his eyes. I already noticed it in a picture he sent me—his eyes—sort of sadlike. I don't care what you do to me—I feel sorry for him. Maybe I'm..."

Suddenly Petro leaped out of the bathhouse with a roar and rolled around on the damp ground, still holding a twig besom.

"He's boiling me!" yelled Petro. "He's boiling me alive!"

Egor ran out after him with a dipper in his hand.

They all ran out of the house toward Petro. The old man had an axe.

"Help! Murder!" screamed Zoya wildly. "Help, good people, murder!"

"Don't bellow like that," requested Petro in a pained voice, as he sat on the ground and rubbed his scalded ribs. "What's the matter with you?"

"What happened, Petya?" asked the sputtering old man.

"I asked this halfwit to splash on a dipper of hot water—to toss it on the hot stove—but instead he poured it all over me!"

"I couldn't believe my ears," said Egor, dismayed. " 'How will he ever be able to stand it?' I think to myself. The water was hot as hell. I tested it with my finger—it was boiling hot! 'How can he tolerate it?' I wonder. 'Well,' I think, 'probably he's hardened

153

to it. Probably his skin is all thick, like a bull's.' I had no idea I was supposed to throw it on the stove..."

" 'He tested it with his finger,' " mimicked Petro. "What are you, anyway—an absolute child? A little baby?"

"Well, I thought you wanted to rinse yourself..."

"But I hadn't finished my steam bath!" bawled the always calm Petro. "I hadn't even washed myself!.. What would I want to get rinsed off for?"

"We'll need to smear some kind of grease on it," said Petro's father, inspecting the burn. "It's not all that bad. All we need is some sort of grease... Who's got some?"

"I've got some rendered mutton fat," said Zoya, and she ran off to the house.

"Okay, let's go back inside," commanded the old man, "before all kinds of people start showing up."

"But how could you have done that, Egor?" asked Lyuba.

Egor hitched up his shorts and again began to justify himself:

"Here's the way it happened, see: he had already got the room filled with steam so that you couldn't breathe, and then he calls out: 'A dipper of hot water!' Well, I think, he wants to balance the temperature somehow."

" 'Balance the temperature,' " mimicked Petro again. "What I ought to do is balance you—with a dipper on the forehead! What a halfwit—he scalded my whole side! And suppose the water had really been boiling?"

"Well, I tested it with my finger..."

" 'With my finger,' he says. What you need is a good..."

"Okay, hit me on the forehead, then," pleaded Egor. "That'll make me feel better." He handed Petro a dipper. "Please. Hit me. I mean it..."

"Petro..." said Lyuba. "It was just an accident. Forget it now."

"Go on back to the house, for God's sake!" said Petro, now angry at everybody. "Look up there—people really starting to gather!"

In fact, there were six or seven curious neighbors standing at the Baikalovs' fence.

"What happened?" asked a man who had just come up.

"Petro, their son here, got drunk and fell on the stove," explained some old woman.

"Oy, oy!" said the man. "Is he still alive?"

"Sure he's alive—look, he's sitting there, just coming to."

"I bet he really yelled!"

"Oh, how he yelled! My window panes even began to rattle!"

154

"Naturally he yelled..."

"Where did he get it, on his hind end?"

"What do you mean, hind end? You can see he's sitting down!"

"Yeah, that's right... He probably fell on his side. And who's that with him? What man is that?"

"They really must have got drunk!" marvelled the old woman.

It was long past midnight, and they were all still sitting up.

The old people, slightly tipsy, were talking and arguing with friends about their various common interests. There must have been above a dozen of the old folks gathered around the table. They chatted away, constantly interrupting each other, two or three always talking at once.

"Who did you say? Who did you say? No, no—she's the one who went way off to get married in... where was it? In Kraiushkino!"

"That's right. And who did she marry, again? It was..."

"Mitka Khromov. She married Mitka Khromov!"

"Right—Mitka."

"It was the Khromovs who were kulaks, had their property taken away..."

"Who'd you say got dekulaked? The Gromovs? Not on your life!"

"No, no, not the Gromovs, the Khromovs!"

"Oh, I thought he said the Gromovs. I was gonna say... I went off with Mikhailo Gromov to go lumberjacking in the taiga."

"And when old Khromov got dekulaked..."

"That's right—he used to have an oil press."

"Who had an oil press? Khromov? What are you saying? It was the Voinovs who had an oil press! Khromov's the one who drove in sheep herds from Mongolia. It was a felting machine that he had—and the Voinovs had the oil press. They were dekulaked, too. They came and got Khromov right out of his pasture. I recollect how they started to tear down his storehouse, looking for felt boots—that's where they made their felt. The whole village, I recollect, came to watch."

"Did they find any?"

"Nine pairs."

"Did they do anything to Mitka?"

"No, Mitka was already off on his own by then. Yes, that's right! He had already married Klanka. His father had set him up. Nothing happened to them. Even so, when they took his father

155

away, Mitka moved off from Kraiushkino. It was too hard for him to live there after that."

"Wait a minute, which one of them got married in Karasuk?"

"That was Manka. And Manka's still alive. She's living in town with her daughter. It's hard for her now. I happened to meet her at the market. She's sorry she sold her house in the village. She says that while the kiddies—her grandchildren—were still little, they needed her to take care of them. But now they're all grown up and nobody needs her anymore. It's hard for her."

"That's how it is," said several of the old women at once. "When the children are little, you're needed, and when they grow up a bit, no one wants you anymore."

"It's all a matter of what kind of son-in-law you have... If he turns out to be an ingrate, then too bad for you..."

"Yes—the sort of husbands they marry nowadays... It's scandalous!"

Egor and Lyuba were sitting somewhat off to the side from the old people. Lyuba was showing him the family photograph album that she herself had made up and carefully preserved.

"And that's Mikhail," said Lyuba, pointing to her brother. "And that's Pavel and Vanya together. They were in the war together at first, but then Pasha got wounded. When he was all healed up, he went back. And that time he got killed. Vanya was killed last, in Berlin. His commanding officer sent us a letter... I feel the saddest over Vanya—he was always so cheerful. He took me around with him everywhere. I was little then, but I remember him so well... I still dream about him; he's always laughing. Look, he's laughing in the picture. And here's our Petro... Look how stern he is, and he was only... how old was he then? Eighteen? Yes, eighteen. He was captured, then our soldiers freed him. They beat him bad in the camp... But otherwise he never got a scratch."

Egor raised his head and looked over at Petro. Petro was sitting alone, smoking. You couldn't tell he'd had anything to drink at all. He sat there like always, pensive and serene.

"About what I did today... splashed him. It was like the devil had pushed my hand."

Lyuba leaned over closer to Egor and asked him quietly and slyly:

"Are you sure you didn't do it on purpose? It's hard to believe that you..."

"What do you mean!" Egor exclaimed sincerely. "I really thought he wanted it on himself—that he was calling down fire on himself, as they say."

"But you're from the country, you said. You must know all about bathhouses. How could you have thought such a thing?"

"Well, people have different customs..."

"Well, I'm ashamed to say that I thought Petro had said something to you that you didn't like and you were only pretending to be dumb when you splashed him."

"What? No! I swear it!"

Petro, sensing that they were looking at him and talking about him, glanced over at them... He met Egor's eye and gave him a friendly grin.

"So, Zhorzhik, you were about to boil me?"

"I'm really sorry, Petro!"

"Never mind! Turn on your music one more time, will you? It's really good music."

Egor switched on his tape recorder. It blasted out with the same march tune that he had used to announce himself to the gang. It was a joyful and life-affirming march. It sounded strange here in the peasant cottage—it broke into the peaceful conversation with a sharp and somehow incongruous rhythm. But music is music: gradually the conversation at the table died down... And everyone sat and listened to the lively march.

Late at night, utterly quiet... The moon shone brightly through the windows.

They had put Egor in the same room with the old people, behind a flowered curtain through which the moonlight easily penetrated.

Lyuba was sleeping in the front room. The door to the room was open. In there it was also quiet.

Egor couldn't sleep. The silence was maddening.

He raised his head and listened intently... All was quiet—except for the old man's snoring and the ticking of the wall clock.

Egor snaked out from under the blanket, dazzling white in his drawers and long shirt, and silently stole into the front room. Nothing banged or creaked... The only sound was the cracking of a little bone somewhere in Egor's foot.

He was already at the door. He took another step or two into the front room, when suddenly in the silence Lyuba's sharp and not-at-all-sleepy voice rapped out:

"Okay, march right back to bed!"

Egor stopped dead. He said nothing for a moment.

"What's the matter?" he whispered in a hurt voice.

"Nothing. Lie down and go to sleep."

"I can't get to sleep."

157

"Lie down anyway... think about the future."

"But I just wanted to talk for a little while!" said Egor, starting to get angry. "I wanted to ask you a couple of questions..."

"We'll talk tomorrow. What sort of questions do you need to ask at night?"

"One question!" said Egor at last in an angry voice. "That's all..."

"Lyubka, grab something—grab a frying pan!" suddenly rang out behind him the voice of the old woman, also quite wide awake.

"I've got a pestle under my pillow," said Lyuba.

Egor went back to his bed.

"Oh, how he crept along on his tiptoes, the tomcat," the old woman went on. "He thought nobody was listening. But I heard everything, and saw him, too!"

"Honest John!" hissed Egor behind his flowered curtain. "Wanted to give his soul a rest! And his body! Honest John with his release papers!"

He lay back quietly... Then he turned over on his side.

"The damned moon! It's shining like a son-of-a-bitch." He turned over on his side. "They've taken up defensive positions against me! Who are they trying to protect, I wonder?"

"Come on now, stop your grumbling," said the old woman in a placating tone of voice. "He's got to grumbling and can't stop."

Suddenly Egor began to recite in a loud, clear, almost frenzied voice:

"She wore a long underskirt of wide, red and blue stripes that looked as though it had been made from a theater curtain. I would have given anything to be in the front row, but the performance never took place." A pause. And then into the silence, from behind the curtain, a scholarly footnote followed: "Lichtenberg! 'Aphorisms'!"

The old man stopped snoring and asked anxiously:

"Who's there? What happened?"

"It's him over there, lying in bed and cursing," said the old woman in a disapproving voice. "He didn't get to sit in the front row," he says.

"It's not me that's cursing," exclaimed Egor, "but Lichtenberg!"

"I'll give you something to curse about," muttered the old man. "What the hell's going on?"

"It's not me!" exclaimed Egor in exasperation. "I was

quoting Lichtenberg. And he wasn't cursing at all, he was being witty."

"Also, no doubt, a bookkeeper?" asked the old man, not without malice.

"He was a Frenchman."

"What?"

"A Frenchman!"

"Go to sleep, everybody!" said the old woman irritably. "We've all had our say now."

It became quiet. All that could be heard was the ticking of the clock on the wall.

And the moon stared in at the windows.

In the morning, after everyone had eaten breakfast and Lyuba and Egor were sitting alone at the table, Egor said:

"So, Lyubov... I guess I'll go into the city and see about buying myself some clothes... and things. I need something to wear..."

Lyuba looked at him calmly, almost mockingly, but with a faint touch of sadness as well. She remained silent, as though she had understood more than what Egor had said to her.

"Go, then," she said softly.

"Why are you looking at me that way?" Egor found himself gazing at Lyuba as well, she looked so nice in her morning freshness. He felt a touch of alarm at the possibility of parting from her. And he also became sad. But that made him uncomfortable. He became agitated.

"What way?" she said.

"Don't you believe me?"

Lyuba was again silent for a long time.

"Do what your heart tells you to do, Egor. Why do you ask whether I believe you or not? Whether or not I believe you— that won't stop you from going."

Egor bent down his cropped head.

"I'd rather not lie, Lyuba," said Egor resolutely. "All my life I've hated it when I lied... And I do lie, of course—and that only makes life all the harder. I lie, and I hate myself for it. I even feel like I want to do away with myself, smash my life to bits. Only, I'd like to go out in style—with a smile on my lips and a glass of vodka in my hand. So right now I'm not going to lie. All I can say is that I don't know. Maybe I'll return, maybe I won't."

"Thank you for the truth, Egor."

"You're really nice," Egor burst out. Then he began to fidget and fret even more than before. "Ah, it's all a come-on. How many times have I said that to women! Slobbering over the words. Words are worth nothing! Why do people believe them?.. Look, here's what I'll do." Egor put his hand on Lyuba's hand. "I'll go off alone and search my heart. I have to do it that way, Lyuba."

"Do what you have to do. I won't say a word. But if you go away, I'll be sad. Really sad. Probably, I'll cry." At that moment tears came into her eyes. "But I won't say anything bad against you."

Egor became quite helpless: he could not bear to see tears.

"That's enough now, Lyubov. I have to go. It's too hard for me. I ask your forgiveness."

Egor stepped out into the wide expanse of a new field... It had not yet been plowed, and pointed little shoots of grass had just begun to break through. Egor strode along briskly, resolutely, stubbornly. That was the way he had gone through life—as he did through this field—resolutely and stubbornly. He would fall, then get up and again stride along. He would push on as though in that lay his only salvation, just to go and go, never stopping, never looking back, as though in that way he might escape from himself.

And suddenly behind him, as though out of nowhere, people began to appear. They would appear and follow along behind him, barely able to keep up. These were all his friends, shabby, crumpled men and women whose venality was revealed in their eyes. All were silent. Egor was silent, too, as he kept on walking. More and more people joined the throng behind him... They walked along that way for a long time. Then Egor stopped all of a sudden and, without glancing around, vigorously waved them all away and muttered angrily through his teeth:

"No more now! That's enough!"

He looked back. Only Fat Lip was there, striding up to meet him. He smiled as he walked along. And he kept his hand in his pocket. Egor clenched his teeth more firmly and put his own hands in his pockets... And Fat Lip disappeared.

... Egor stood by the road and waited to see whether a bus or some chance automobile might not come along and take him into the city.

In the distance a truck came into view.

Lyuba worked all that day in a daze... Her feelings kept getting the better of her. She unexpectedly confessed to her girl-

160

friend, after they had finished the milking chores and were walking out of the cattle yard:

"You know, Verka, I've really got stuck on the guy..." She surprised herself by saying such a thing. "I can't help it! My heart has been aching and aching all day."

"Did he leave for good or not? What did he tell you?"

"He said he didn't know himself what he was going to do."

"Tell him to go to the devil. He's not worth spitting on! 'He doesn't know himself.' That means he's got a wife someplace. What does he say about that?"

"I don't know. All he says is that he has no one."

"He's lying. Lyubka—don't be a fool: take your Kolka back and live with him again. They all drink nowadays anyway! Who do you know that doesn't? Mine came home the day before yesterday... that worm!" And Verka, a lively little woman, confided in a whisper: "He came inside, and crack!—I conked him with a rolling pin! I even frightened myself! In the morning he gets up and says, 'My head aches, I must have bumped it some place.' I say to him: 'You shouldn't drink so much!' " And Verka began to titter.

"But how did it happen in so short a time?" Lyuba continued to marvel at her own thoughts.

"What?" asked the puzzled Verka.

"How did I ever manage it, I say, in so short a time? Why, I saw him for only one day! How could it have happened? Is such a thing really possible?"

"What was he in prison for?"

"Burglary..." And Lyuba looked at her friend helplessly.

"Out of the frying pan, into the fire," said the latter. "A drunkard for a thief. What a terrible fate, poor thing. Live alone, Lyuba. Maybe somebody halfway normal will turn up. And this other one—won't he take to stealing again? What then?"

"What then? They'll put him in jail again."

"Bite your tongue! Have you gone crazy, or what?"

"I just don't know what's happened to me. I've completely lost my head. It's disgusting even to me... And here my heart is aching and aching for him as though I've known him for a hundred years. And it's only been a day. It's true, he did send me letters for a whole year..."

"Well, they don't have anything to do there, so it's easy for them to write."

"But you should see what letters they were!"

"Love letters?"

"Oh, no... All about life. He really must have seen a lot, that poor devil of a jailbird. When you read what he writes—it's enough to break your heart. I don't even know myself whether I love him, or pity him. All I know is that my heart is aching."

Meanwhile, Egor was attending to his affairs in the regional capital.

The very first thing he did was buy some stylish duds.

He walked down the wooden sidewalk of the wooden provincial town: brand new suit, necktie and hat, hands in his pockets.

He stopped in at the post office, got a telegram blank, wrote down an address, a sum of money to be sent and a few words of greeting. He handed in the blank, leaned on the counter near the window and began to count out the money.

"Give the money to fatlip," the girl behind the counter read out. "Fatlip—is that someone's last name, perhaps?"

Egor thought for a couple of seconds and said:

"Absolutely correct, someone's last name."

"Well, why did you write it with small letters then? And what a funny name!"

"There's others that are worse," said Egor. "Down at the plant we had a guy named Pistonov."[5]

The girl raised her head. She was as cute as could be, with great big eyes and a little turned-up nose.

"So?"

"Nothing. His name, he said, was Pistonov." Egor was very serious, to go with the hat he was wearing.

"Well, that's a normal enough name."

"Yes, in general, quite normal," Egor agreed. And suddenly he forgot he was wearing a hat and grinned. And then he became rather self-conscious. "Excuse me, please," he said, sticking his head in the window, "see... I just got in town from the gold fields, and I don't know a single soul here..."

"So?" said the girl, not following him.

"Look, do you have a boyfriend?" asked Egor bluntly.

"Why do you want to know?" The cute little snubnose did not seem to be very put off and even looked up from her work to stare at Egor.

"What I had in mind was, maybe you and me could paint the town red together."

"Citizen!" the girl admonished, raising her voice sharply. "Mind your manners! This is a public place. Either send your money order, or get out!"

Egor crawled back out of the window. He was insulted. Why the hell had she looked up at him with her big eyes, then? Egor

162

simply couldn't get it out of his head: one minute she was looking at him tenderly, and the next she was snapping his head off. What the hell was this phoney-baloney, anyway?

"Leading me on that way!" he grumbled indignantly. " 'Citizen!' How am I 'citizen' to you? To you I'm comrade, and even friend and brother."

The girl again looked up at him with her big gray eyes.

"Back to work, back to work," said Egor. "Don't be making eyes all the time."

The girl hmphed and bent over the telegram blank again.

"And what a stupid hat he put on!" she could not refrain from remarking, not looking at Egor.

She handed him a receipt, also without looking at him. She put the receipt on the counter and turned to other matters, from which she absolutely refused to be distracted.

"Ah, these broads," raged Egor, as he left the post office. "You just wait! You'll be doing the dance of the little swans for me yet! Cracow style!" He strode off toward the railroad station restaurant. "The butterfly polka!" Egor kept working himself up. In his eyes appeared an uneasy glint that bore witness to the hurt that he felt. It pained him inside his chest. He quickened his step. "No, dammit, it's too much! These dames, these Little Red Riding Hoods... Watch out, because I'm going to put on a little figure-skating show in this town! I'm going to electrify the atmosphere in this place and open up a whorehouse!" After that he mumbled nothing but nonsense, anything that flew into his head: "Ta-rum-pum-pum, ta-rum-pum-pum, ta-rum-pum-pum-pum-pum."

In the restaurant he ordered a bottle of champagne, handed the sharp-looking waiter a twenty-five rouble note and said:

"Thanks. Keep the change."

The waiter was overcome.

"Thank you very much, oh, thank you..."

"It's nothing," said Egor, and motioned for the waiter to sit down for a minute. The waiter took a chair. "I've just got in from the gold fields," Egor went on, as he studied the obliging young fellow, "and I wanted to ask you... is there someplace around here where we could organize a nice little whorehouse?"

The waiter automatically looked around behind him...

"Well, I'm expressing myself rather crudely... I'm worried, because all this money is burning a hole in my pocket." Egor pulled out a rather thick wad of ten-and twenty-five-rouble notes. "What say? I've got to use them up. What's your name, by the way?"

On seeing the money, the waiter began to lick his lips, but he restrained himself, held onto his dignity. He knew that people with dignity got paid more.

"Sergei Mikhailovich."

"Well, Mikhailych... I need a holiday. I've been up north a long time..."

"I think I can come up with something," said Mikhailych, after first putting on a thoughtful expression for a couple of minutes. "Where are you staying?"

"Nowhere. I just arrived."

"In all probability, something can be arranged... A nice little picnic, so to speak, in honor of your arrival."

"Right, right, right," said Egor, getting excited. "A cozy little cathouse. A nice private bordello... We'll have ourselves a party, right, Mikhailych? There was something about you I liked the minute I laid eyes on you! I thought to myself—here's somebody I can rumple up my money with."

Mikhailych broke into sincere laughter.

"What's so funny?" asked Egor.

"Hokay!" said Mikhailych gaily in English. "Got you."

Late that evening Egor was lying on a plush divan and talking on the telephone with Lyuba. Mikhailych was in the room, too, and a sharp-nosed woman with a wart on her temple kept walking in to consult with Mikhailych in a low voice.

"Hey! Lyubasha!" shouted Egor. "It's me! I'm in the military registration office. I didn't have time to get registered. What? It's late?... Well, they put in late hours here. Yes, yes..." Egor nodded at Mikhailych. "Yes, Lyubasha!"

Mikhailych opened the door of the room, slammed it noisily, and loudly stomped past Egor, shouting as he drew near:

"Comrade Captain! May I see you for a minute?!"

Egor nodded his head at Mikhailych in approval and continued to talk, while Mikhailych pretended to go off into gales of silent laughter.

"But, Lyubasha, what can I do? I'll probably have to stay over night here. Yes, yes..." Egor listened for a long time, kept saying "yes, yes" while grinning proudly and happily at the play-acting Mikhailych. He even covered the mouthpiece once and said: "She says she's worried. She's been waiting for me."

"Wait, wait..." began the accommodating Mikhailych, but Egor stopped him with a glance.

"Yes, Lyubushka darling!... Just keep talking. I love to hear your beautiful voice. It gets me all excited!"

164

"He's too much!" whispered Mikhailych in feigned delight. "It gets him excited!" He began to laugh again, but rather hoarsely, unconvincingly, as he bared his gold teeth. He was trying as hard as he could, since Egor had promised to pay well for the party.

"Where will I spend the night? Oh, right here someplace, on the couch, I guess... It's okay, I can sleep anywhere—I'm used to it. Don't you worry about it, now. Yes, my little darling, my little sweetheart!" Egor said this so sincerely and tenderly that Mikhailych even forgot to pretend to laugh. "I'll see you soon, dearest. So long, now. Here's a kiss for you... Okay, I understand, I understand. Good-bye."

Egor hung up the receiver and looked at Mikhailych strangely for a time—as though he didn't even see him. At that moment it was as if a tender, invisible hand were stroking Egor's face, which gradually lost its habitual look of hardness and truculence.

"Yes," said Egor, returning to himself. "Well, then, innkeeper, shall we get on with the orgy? How are things in back?"

"Everything's ready."

"Did you find me a dressing gown?"

"Yes, more or less... We had to borrow it from some old actor. Nobody had one!"

"Let's have it!" Egor donned the long, quilted robe which had several worn places. He looked down at himself.

"You can't get them anywhere anymore," said Mikhailych, trying to excuse himself.

"It's a good robe," approved Egor. "Well, have you followed all my orders?"

Mikhailych left the room.

Egor reclined on the couch with a cigarette.

Mikhailych returned and announced:

"The people have assembled for the orgy!"

"Let's go," nodded Egor.

Mikhailych flung open the door... And Egor in his dressing gown, just barely inclining his head, swept off like Caligula to debauch himself.

The "debauchers" were a strange group—most of them decidedly old. There were some women, but these were all remarkably homely and wretched-looking. They were all seated at a richly-laden table, staring at Egor in bewilderment. Egor was noticeably taken aback, but quickly composed himself.

"Why is everybody so sad?!" said Egor loudly and cheerfully, as he proceeded to the head of the table. He paused, gazing at

165

them all attentively.

"Yes," he said, the words tumbling out of him. "Tonight we'll tear out our sorrow by its tail! Pour the drinks!"

"Dear fellow," one of the guests addressed him, a middle-aged, almost doddering man. "Tell us, what are we celebrating here? Some special occasion, or what?"

Egor pondered for a moment.

"We are gathered here," began Egor softly, thoughtfully, as at a funeral, glancing at the bottles of champagne, "in order to..." And suddenly he raised his head and studied them all once more. Again his face was released from its harshness and tension. "Brothers and sisters," he said with feeling, "my soul has just been shaken by a tender experience. I realize my beautiful words mean nothing to you, but let me say them, nevertheless." Egor spoke seriously, forcefully, even ceremonially. He even paced up and down, as far as the room would permit, continuing to look at them all. "Spring..." he went on. "Soon the little flowers will begin to bloom. The birch trees will turn green." Egor suddenly choked up completely and had to stop. He could still hear the sweetly natural voice of Lyuba, and this distracted him.

"It won't be long until Trinity Sunday," said someone at the table.

"You can go out now and walk and walk," said Egor, "through a little clearing deep into the woods, down into a ravine where a brook is bubbling... Am I making sense? Because I'm talking away here, and it seems I'm ashamed of my own words, like a jerk!" Egor got genuinely angry at himself. And then the words began to pour out of him, loud and angry, as though a crowd of hecklers were standing in front of him. "You all took me for a fool, didn't you? Three hundred roubles, and I just threw it to the wind! But what if it just so happens that I love everybody today? I feel tender and loving today, like the most... like a cow that has just calved! So what if the orgy fell flat? Who needs it? Better off without it. But don't misunderstand me—I'm not stupid and I'm not a fool. And if anyone thinks he can do what he wants with me just because I'm tenderhearted—he'll get a surprise from me. Dear people! Let's love one another!" Egor was almost shouting now and beating himself on the chest. "Well, why are we rustling around here like spiders in a jar? Do you know how easily they die?! I don't understand you..." Egor walked down the length of the table. "I don't understand! I refuse to understand! And I don't understand myself, either—because every nght I dream about market stalls and suitcases. But no more! Go out and do your own thieving... I'm going to sit down on a

166

stump and I'm going to sit there thirty and three years. I'm just joking. I feel sorry for you. I also feel sorry for myself. But if someone else were to pity me or stupidly fall in love with me, I would... I don't know, I'd feel sad, I couldn't stand it. I feel wonderful, and my heart is bursting—but I feel terrible, too. I'm frightened! It's a hell of a thing..." confided Egor quietly, unexpectedly in conclusion. He paused with bowed head, then looked kindly at everyone and commanded: "Everybody take a bottle of champagne! Have you got them? Okay! Unseal them now—and shoot off the corks all at once!"

Everyone responded, began to chatter... Amid the sounds of approval and general hubbub, the bottles exploded.

"Pour it out quick, before it bubbles over!" ordered Egor.

"Ah, right... it's gushing away. Give me a glass! Hey, friend, a glass. Hurry!"

"Hey, damn you!... You spilled some!"

"Spilled some?"

"Yes—a pity, it's so good."

"What cheerful stuff it is. Look, how it bubbles and boils! From the fermenting. They must keep it a long time."

"Well, of course! With this stuff they try to..."

"And listen to it fizz!"

"My dears!" said Egor, with genuine tenderness and pity. "I am happy that you have perked up and started to smile, that you like my champagne. I love you all more and more!"

They were all too embarrassed to look Egor in the face, with all that muddle-headed nonsense he was spilling out. They got quiet while he talked and stared at their wine glasses.

"Drink up!" said Egor.

They drank up.

"Down the hatch—again! Drink up!"

Again they perked up and began to jabber. It was certainly a strange celebration—and all for free.

"Ooh, it just keeps on fizzing and fizzing."

"But weaker now. The strength is gone."

"And the taste—I can't quite place it."

"Yes, indefinite, sort of."

"Ah?"

"It looks like horse piss, but the taste of it, you can't tell what it is."

"And it sticks in your throat, kind of... Does it stick in your throat, too?"

"Yes, it feels like it's foaming all away in there."

"Right, and it gets all up your nose, too! Drink up—it's

167

good!"

"That's the proof that foams away like that."

"What do you mean, 'proof'? This stuff is no stronger than kvass. That's gas escaping, not 'proof.' "

"Okay, forget the champagne!" commanded Egor. "Now grab the bottles of cognac!"

"What's the hurry?"

"I want us to start singing some songs."

"That we can do!"

"Open the cognac!"

They opened it. Everyone did as he was told.

"Pour only half a glass each! You don't drink cognac in large amounts. And if anybody says that cognac smells like bedbugs, I'll hit him over the head with a bottle. Drink up!"

They drank up.

"Sing a song!" commanded Egor.

"But we haven't eaten yet..."

"They're starting in against me," said Egor, offended, and sat down. "Okay, then. Eat. All they want to do is stuff themselves. That's all they can think about..."

Some of the more punctilious guests put down their forks and stared in puzzlement at Egor.

"Eat, eat!" said Egor. "What's the matter with you?"

"But you should eat, too, or else you'll get drunk."

"I won't get drunk. You eat."

"Go to hell, then!" loudly protested a large, bald-headed man. "You invite us to a party and then you start criticizing us. But I know for myself—there's no way I can drink without eating, or I'll be under the table in a second. It's boring that way. Nobody wants to drink that way..."

"Well, eat then!"

Meanwhile, in the village, Lyuba's mother and father were pestering Lyuba with questions. They wouldn't let the poor thing alone.

"How could that be? Do you mean to say they don't close the registration office at night?" the old woman wanted to know.

Lyuba herself was lost in conjecture. She didn't know whether to believe that story about the registration office or not. Yet, she herself had talked with Egor, had heard his voice, listened to what he said... Even now, she couldn't stop talking to him in her mind: "Well, Egor, with you it's never boring. What are you up to now, I wonder?"

"Lyubka?"

"What?"

"What sort of registration office is that? You know very well all those places close up at night."

"Well, evidently not, since he said he was spending the night there..."

"A likely story! You can't believe what that one says."

"Here's what I think," said the old man. "They told him: 'Come tomorrow at eight o'clock—sharp.' That's the way those army people are. And he decided it was better to spend the night in town than have to go all the way out there again tomorrow morning."

"That's exactly what he said," said Lyuba joyfully. " 'I'm going to spend the night here,' he said, 'on the couch.' "

"But all those official places close up at night!" insisted the old woman. "Are you both daft? How could they leave him alone there all night? He'd steal one of their rubber stamps for sure."

"Mama!"

The old man also curled his lip at such stupidity:

"What in hell would he need a rubber stamp for?"

"Well, it appears I can't say a word around here! No sooner say something, than they jump down your throat!"

Egor was organizing the debauchers into a choir.

"We'll start up the melody," he said, pulling at the bald man, "and you all over there, as soon as I wave my hand, you start singing 'bom-bom.' Okay, start:

"Those evening bells... Those evening bells..."

Egor waved his hand, but the "bom-bom" group didn't respond.

"What's the matter with you?! I told you, as soon as I wave, you go 'bom-bom.' "

"But when you waved, you were still singing yourself."

"Just chime in anyway. I began to wail because I thought I was hearing church bells from long ago. I'm so homesick, I feel like I'm dying. So I started to sing real soft. But you just do your 'bom-bom' and don't worry about it... There's no way for you to know how sad I feel—that's not your problem."

"It's like someone in jail, pining like that," suggested Mikhailych. "Or in a prisoner-of-war camp somewhere."

"What sort of churches do they have in prisoner-of-war camps?" someone objected.

"Why not? They've got churches over there, too. Not exactly like ours, of course, but all the same—a church with a bell. Right,

169

Georgii?"

"Damn you all! All you know how to do is yammer!" said Egor, really angry now. "They start in talking and can't stop. I swear they've got diarrhea of the mouth!"

"Never mind. Let's start again. Don't get all worked up over it!"

"How can I keep from getting worked up, when I tell you something and you won't do it? Oh well, let's go now:
"Those evening bells... Those evening bells..."

"Bom... bom... bom." The bells in the tower rang helter-skelter and all off key, spoiling everything.

Egor waved his hands in disgust and went into the next room. He paused in the doorway and said despairingly:

"Sing anything you want. Don't get sore, but I can't take you all anymore. Just have a good time without me. Sing one of your own songs, why don't you?"

The "bom-bom" group, and all the others, too, fell into confused silence... But there was so much wine and fantastically tasty food on the table that their grief was short-lived—just enough to appease their consciences.

"What's with him?"

"You don't even know how to sing 'bom-bom!" Mikhailych chided them all. "What's so hard about that?"

"Yeah, it came out off key..."

"That was Kirill's fault... He started too soon."

"Who started too soon?" said Kirill, insulted. "I sang normal—just like somebody was ringing a bell. I certainly know you can't hurry that up. Because a bell—first you have to swing it."

"Well, who came in too soon then?"

"Forget it! Why hash that over now? Let's have a good time—like he told us to do."

"It seems like we didn't deserve to be yelled at—because maybe I don't even know how to sing. How am I going to sing like some canary, if I wasn't even born with a good voice?"

Egor, disgruntled, was reclining on the couch when Mikhailych walked in.

"I'm really sorry, Georgii, that we didn't do it right—with the bells."

Egor was silent for a minute, then asked peevishly:

"And how come they were all so ugly?"

Mikhailych was completely dismayed.

"Well, look, Georgii—all the good-looking ones are married, with families. I only got the single ones—like you told me."

Egor sat for awhile longer. Gradually his face began to

170

brighten. His heart seemed to beat faster, as though he were recalling some joyous thing.

"Can you get me a taxi?"

"Sure."

"To Yasnoe. I'll pay whatever he wants. Go ahead and call!" Egor got up, threw off the dressing gown, put his jacket on and straightened his tie.

"But why to Yasnoe?"

"I've got a friend there." And he again began to pace about in agitation. "My soul... I feel like turpentine's been poured on it, Mikhailych. It's going to lead me off God knows where. As soon as it smells freedom, I have to get moving. Call the taxi! How many people did you collect?"

"Fifteen. Seventeen counting the two of us. What about it?"

"Here's two hundred for you. Give each of them a ten spot and you keep the rest. Don't cheat! I'm going to come back and check up."

"Georgii, I wouldn't do that!.."

Egor flew through the bright, moonlit night along the wide highway—toward the village, toward Lyuba.

"What am I doing? What am I doing?" Egor tortured himself. "What's the matter with me?" He was possessed by anxiety and excitement. He couldn't remember when he'd been so shaken up by a skirt.

"Well, what's the story on family life these days?" he asked the taxi driver. "What's the latest thing they're writing about it?"

"Writing where?" asked the confused driver.

"In general—in books."

"In books they write all sorts of things," said the taxi driver with a frown. "In the books, everything's okay."

"And in life?"

"In life... What's the matter, don't you know how it is in life?"

"Bad, right?"

"Bad for who?"

"Well, you, for instance?"

The taxi driver shrugged his shoulders—very much like the fellow who had sold Egor the tape recorder.

"What's the matter with all of you!... Brothers, I swear I don't understand you. Why are you all so sour on life?" said Egor in amazement.

"What do you want me to do, giggle at you? What do I have to do to satisfy you?"

171

"Satisfy me! You'd better save that for your old woman! And make sure you know how to do it, too. Or else you'll crawl up on her and she'll say: 'Get away from me, you smell like a goat!' "

The taxi driver began to laugh:

"Is that what they say to you?"

"No. I don't like the way goats smell, either... Say, roll the window down a little, will you?"

The driver glanced at Egor, but kept silent.

Egor again returned to his own thoughts, which he simply could not get straightened out. His head was all in a muddle—on account of this Lyuba.

They drove up to the big, dark house and Egor sent the taxi on its way. Suddenly he panicked. He stood at the gate with his bottles of cognac and didn't know what to do. He walked around the house and entered Petro's gate; he walked through the garden, went up on the porch and kicked the door with his foot. It was quiet for a long time, but then a door creaked, someone in bare feet came walking down the entrance hall, and Petro's voice called out:

"Who's there?"

"It's me, Petro. Georgii. Zhorzhik..."

The door opened.

"What do you want?" said the astonished Petro. "Did they kick you out, or what?"

"No, no... I didn't want to wake them up. Listen, did you ever drink any Remy Martin?"

Petro stood silent for a long time, gazing into Egor's face.

"Drink what?"

"Remy Martin. Twenty roubles a bottle. Shall we go hole up in the bathhouse with it?"

"Why the bathhouse?"

"So we won't disturb anybody."

"Let's just sit in the kitchen..."

"No. I don't want to wake anyone."

"Well, let me get some shoes on, then... And I'll bring out something to eat, too."

"Don't bother with that! All my pockets are full of chocolate—I stink of it, like some college girl."

Into the small dark world of the bathhouse a moonbeam made its way through a window and left a patch of light on the floor. Petro and Egor also lit a lantern. They sat down by the window.

"Why the hell didn't you come home?" asked Petro.

"I don't know. You see, Petro..." Egor started to say, but then fell silent. He opened one of the bottles and set it on the window sill. "Look—cognac. Twenty roubles a bottle! Can you believe it?!"

Petro pulled two glasses out of the pocket of his old riding breeches.

Neither of them said anything for awhile.

"I don't know what to say, Petro. I don't understand what's going on with me myself."

"Well, don't say anything, then. Pour me a glass of your precious stuff... I used to drink a little of this during the war. In Germany. It smells like bed bugs."

"It does not smell like bed bugs!" exclaimed Egor. "It's bedbugs that smell like cognac. Where do they get that, anyway, that it smells like bed bugs?"

"Maybe the good stuff doesn't smell, but the normal kind does."

The night drew on. The moon kept shining. The entire village was bathed in its pale, greenish, cadaverous light. All was quiet. No dog barked, no gate creaked. Such silence prevails in a village just before dawn. And in the steppe, too, when just at dawn the fog and the damp imperceptibly collect in the low places. Quiet and chill.

And suddenly in this silence there was heard from the bath-house:

"I sit behind bars in the damp and the gloom..."

Egor sang first and then Petro joined in. It came out so un-expectedly beautiful, so sonorous and sad, that it made you want to cry:

"And feed a young eagle that lives in my cell—
My unhappy comrade who stretches his wings
And pecks at the meat that has brought him to hell..."

Early that morning Egor accompanied Lyuba to the dairy farm. He just fell in next to her and walked along. He was dressed in his fancy suit again and wearing his hat and tie. But he was rather quiet and pensive. Lyuba was overjoyed that he was walking with her—she was in a radiant mood. And the morning was lovely—cool and clear. It was springtime indeed, no doubt about it.

"Why so mournful, Egorsha?" asked Lyuba.

"Oh, just..." Egor mumbled vaguely.

173

"They hid away in the bathhouse," laughed Lyuba. "And they weren't even afraid! Ever since I was a little girl, you couldn't get me to go in there at night for anything!"

That surprised Egor:

"Why not?"

" 'Cause devils are there! That's where they hatch out, in the bathhouse!"

Egor looked at Lyuba in tender amazement... And quite unintentionally he brushed his hand along her back.

"That's right: don't ever go in the bathhouse at night. Or else those devils... I know all about them!"

"When you drove up last night in the car, I heard you. I thought it was my saintly Kolenka coming home."[6]

"What Kolenka?"

"Why, my husband."

"Ah. And does he come back now and then?"

"That he does."

"Well? What do you do then?"

"I lock myself in the front room and sit there. He never comes when he's sober, and when he's drunk I can't stand to look at him. He turns into a complete fool. It's disgusting. I begin to shake all over."

Egor's heart beat faster upon hearing these genuinely angry words. He could not bear despondency, spinelessness and abasement in people. Perhaps that was why he had been led so far off the beaten track in life, why he had always from early youth been attracted to people who were sharply drawn. Sometimes they were drawn with crooked lines—but always with sharp definition.

"Yes, yes, yes," said Egor, affecting sympathy with Lyuba. "It's a real affliction, with those alcoholics."

"Yes, an affliction!" affirmed the openhearted Lyuba. "But a very bitter one, with constant tears and cursing."

"An out and out tragedy... Oy, oy!" said Egor in surprise. "Look at all the cows!"

"The dairy farm... This is where I work."

Egor stood as though rooted to the ground upon seeing the cows.

"Look at them... those cows," he repeated. "Look, they saw you, didn't they? They're all excited. See how they roll their eyes at you..." Egor fell silent. Then all at once, in spite of himself, he began to talk in a rush. "All I can remember from my whole childhood is my mother and our cow. We called the cow Manka. One spring, in April, we let her out of the fence so she

174

could pick up old hay on the road. You know, it drops off the carts in the winter and then shows up along the roads and fences when the snow melts in the spring. Well, somebody stuck a pitchfork in her belly. She had gone inside somebody's fence—a few people still had some hay. They punched a hole in her—she came home dragging her guts on the ground."

Lyuba stared at Egor, much struck by the artless narrative. It was apparent that Egor was sorry he had come out with this story. He was displeased with himself.

"Why are you looking at me?"

"Oh, Egorsha..."

"Forget it," said Egor. "It's just words. Words aren't worth anything."

"You didn't make the story up, did you?"

"No, no! Why should I? But you shouldn't take people so seriously. Listen to them, but take what they say with a grain of salt. You're too trusting..." Egor looked at Lyuba and again tenderly, solicitously, hesitantly stroked her back. "Have you really never been deceived by anyone?"

"No—who would ever do that?"

"Hmmm." Egor gazed into the clear eyes of this woman and grinned. What a nightmare—all he wanted to do was touch her and look at her all the time.

"Oh, look, the director of the sovkhoz is coming," said Lyuba. "He must have been at our cow barn." She became quite animated and smiled broadly, without even fully realizing it.

Walking toward them came a well-nourished, sturdy-looking fellow, still rather young—perhaps about the same age as Egor. He walked with a firm, proprietary stride, looked with curiosity at Lyuba and her—who was he? her husband? a friend?...

"Why are you smiling all over your face like that?" said Egor in unpleasant surprise.

"He does a good job running things. We respect him. Hello there, Dmitry Vladimirovich! Have you come by to see us?"

"Yes, I have. Hello!" The director firmly shook Egor's hand. "You aren't one of our replacements, are you?"

"Dmitry Vladimirovich—he's a chauffeur," said Lyuba, not without pride.

"Oh, yes? Good. Can I put him behind the wheel right away? Does he have a license?"

"He doesn't have his passport yet," Lyuba's pride vanished.

"Too bad. He could have come with me right now. My own driver was called up by the military registration office for some reason. I'm afraid he'll be gone a long time."

"Oh, Egor!" said Lyuba, getting all excited. "Why don't you go with him? You'll get to see our district and have a chance to look around."

And that animated excitement, those absurd words—about "getting to see the district"—induced Egor to do something that five minutes earlier he would have laughed at the very thought of.

"Let's go," he said.

And he went off with the director.

"Egor!" Lyuba shouted after him. "You'll be eating dinner at a tearoom somewhere! Where will you be... Dmitry Vladimirovich, you'll have to suggest a place to him, because he doesn't know where to go."

Dmitry Vladimirovich laughed.

Egor looked back at Lyuba for a minute, then turned around and followed the director, who had been waiting for him.

"Where are you from?" asked the director.

"Who me? From around here. Your district—the village of Listvianka."

"Listvianka? We don't have any such village."

"What do you mean? Sure you do."

"No we don't. I know my district."

"That's strange... What happened to it?" Egor didn't like the director: smug and sleek. The smug part especially rubbed him the wrong way. He couldn't stand smug people. "There was a village called Listvianka here. I remember it well."

The director looked at Egor thoughtfully.

"Well, could be," he said. "Probably it burned down."

"Yes, it probably burned down. Too bad—it was a nice little village."

"So you're going to come along with me?"

"Yes. That's what we decided, if I understood you correctly."

And so they drove off over the wide-open fields of the giant sovkhoz—a state farm worth a million roubles.

"Why did you start off with me that way?"

"What way?"

"Pretending you were some local yokel. Why?"

"I don't like it when people start right in on your biography. What's a biography?—just words that anyone can make up."

"How do you mean? How is it possible to 'make up' your biography?"

"How? Like with me for instance: I don't have any documents except for one paper, and nobody knows me around here—so I just say whatever I please about myself. If you really want to

176

know, I'm the son of a public prosecutor."

The director gave a laugh. He didn't like Egor, either: too irrationally belligerent, somehow.

"What's the matter? I'm wearing a hat and a tie, aren't I?" Egor glanced at himself in the mirror. "Why couldn't I be a prosecutor's son?"

"I'm not going to ask you for any documents. I'm even letting you drive without a license. But what shall we do if we run into a police inspector?"

"You're the boss."

They pulled up at the apiary. The director jumped lightly out of the vehicle.

"I'll just be a minute. Or if you want to, you can come with me. The old man will give you some honey."

"No, thanks." Egor had also got out. "I'll just stay here... and admire the view."

"Look all you want." And the director went off.

Egor indeed began to admire the view. He gazed all around, and then he walked over to a birch tree and touched it.

"Well? Are you starting to get green yet? It won't be long now... You'll be able to put your clothes on. You must be tired of standing there naked. Soon you'll look beautiful—all dressed up."

The old beekeeper came out of his hut.

"Why don't you come on in?" he shouted from the stoop. "Come in and have a glass of tea!"

"Thanks anyway, pop. I don't feel like it."

"Well, look around then." And the old man went back inside.

Soon the director came out, accompanied by the old man.

"Drop in more often," the latter said politely. "Drink some tea for the road. You pass by here a lot."

"Thanks, dad, I appreciate it. Time to go now."

They drove off.

"Look," said the director, putting a package of some kind down between the seats. "This is interesting stuff—propolis, a sort of glue used by bees."

"For curing stomach ulcers?"

"Right. Have you had ulcers, then?" the director turned towards him.

"No, I've just heard about the stuff."

"Yes. Well, one of our men got an ulcer. I'm trying to help him—a good man."

"They say it really works."

A village came into view up ahead.

"Let me out at the club," said the director, "and then go to Sosnovka—seven kilometers from here—and pick up the brigade leader Savelev and bring him here. If he's not at home, ask where he is and find him."

Egor nodded.

He let the director out at the club and drove off.

Men and women, boys and girls all began to gather at the club. Some of the older people came up, too. They were getting ready to have some sort of meeting. They surrounded the director and he said something to them in his usual confident and self-satisfied manner.

The young people had gathered off to the side, where they were also holding a lively conversation. They frequently broke into laughter.

The old men stood smoking by the fence.

Large banners had been hung across the front of the club-house. Everything pointed to a familiar celebration.

The clubhouse was new, just recently built: near the foundation lay a pile of bricks and the bed of an old dump truck containing hardened cement.

Egor drove up with the brigade leader Savelev and went off to find the director. They told him the director was already in the club, sitting on the stage at the table reserved for the presidium.

Egor walked across the main room where the sovkhoz workers were sitting, climbed up on the stage and walked around behind the director.

The director was conversing with some broad-shouldered man and shaking a piece of paper. Egor touched his sleeve.

"Vladimirych..."

"Well? Did you bring him? Good. You can go now."

"No, it's not that..." Egor called the director off to the side, and when they had got to where no one could hear them, he said: "Can you drive a car yourself?"

"Sure. What's the problem?"

"I can't do it anymore. You'll have to drive back yourself. I'm not up to it. And there's no way I can make myself do it. That I know."

"But what's the matter... Did you get sick, or what?"

"I just can't drive people around anymore. I agree—I'm a fool, irresponsible and politically backward... I'm just a worthless

178

ex-con—a *zek*—but I still can't do it. I feel all the time as though I'm laughing at you. It would be better if I drove a dump truck. Or a tractor! Okay? Don't be sore at me. You're a good guy, but... The thing is, I really feel bad right now, so I'm going." And Egor quickly stepped down from the stage. As he walked across the auditorium, he berated himself for having prattled away like a fool to the director. He'd become a regular chatterbox... all that apologizing. But why apologize? Just tell him I can't, and that's the end of it. But no, he'd had to go and explain, and justify himself and even slobber about his "backwardness." Phooey! Egor had a rancid taste in his mouth. This was the way you became an ass-kisser—little by little. By going up and looking them in the eye... Tfoo! What a bitter pill to swallow!

The director, meanwhile, was watching Egor as he walked across the room. He didn't fully understand what had happened. That is, he understood nothing.

Egor passed through a little wood on his way back.

He came out into a clearing, crossed it, and entered another wooded area where the trees were thicker.

Then he walked down into a little ravine where a brook was bubbling. He stopped above the brook.

"I knew you had to be here!" he said.

He stood there for a long time, then jumped over the stream and climbed up the hill on the other side...

And there spread out before his eyes was a birch grove: the entire numerous family of trees seemed to run up and greet him.

"Ah, you!" he said.

And he walked into the grove.

He strolled among the birches... He took off his necktie and tied it around one of the most beautiful, one of the whitest and most graceful trees. Then he noticed a high stump right next to it and placed his hat on it. He stepped back and admired them from the side.

"What a pair of squares!" he said. And he walked on farther. But for a long time he kept looking back at this natty couple, smiling the while. He felt a lot better now.

Back at Lyuba's house, Egor walked from one corner of the room to the other, completely lost in thought. He was smoking. From time to time he would suddenly begin to sing: "Tell me, pretty maidens, why do you love the handsome lads?" Then he would stop singing and stand still, gazing out the window or staring at the wall... And then he would start pacing again, seized once more by fretful impatience—as though he had just about made up his mind about something, but couldn't make the final decision for the life of him. He kept stewing and stewing and fretting.

"Don't worry yourself to death, Egor," said the old man. He was also pacing the room—over to the door and back, braiding unbleached thread into a trot line. He drew the line through an old mitten. "It's no worse to be a tractor driver. Probably even better. Look at all the money they make now!"

"I'm not all that worried."

"I'll be done braiding this soon. Then when the water clears a little we can go down and set out the trot line. That's something I really like to do."

"Yeah, me, too. Nothing I like better than setting out trot lines."

"Right. Some people would rather use a seine. But a seine, I don't know... They get caught too easy, and after awhile you get worn out with the damned thing, untangling it, tossing it out again—it takes up too much time."

"Yeah, it's not easy casting those nets... 'Tell me, pretty maidens...' Will Lyuba be back soon?"

The old man looked at the clock.

"She should get home soon. Right now they're delivering the milk. As soon as they get that done, she'll be home. Listen, Gore—don't hurt her. She's our last one. Somehow you always worry more over the baby. When you have kids of your own, you'll remember what I'm telling you. She's a nice girl, a good girl—but she's had all this bad luck. Her husband turned out to be a drunk, and we only barely managed to get rid of him."

"Yeah... These alcoholics are a complete disaster! Whenever I see one, I want to put every last one of those devils in prison! Give each of 'em five years, right?"

"Well, prison's a little harsh, isn't it? But maybe for a year someplace"—the old man brightened—"in strict isolation—I'd go for that. Put all of them there together in one heap."

"And will Petro be back soon?"

"Petro? He ought to be home soon, too... Let those drunks sit there for awhile and think things over."

"Sit—nobody would mind that! Let them do a little work!" said Egor, adding wood to the fire.

"You're right! Let them go in the forest and chop trees!"

"No, down in the mines! In the forest—out in the fresh air—any fool would agree to that. No, it has to be the mines! The pits! The bottom of the shaft!"

At this point Lyuba walked in.

180

"Well, look who's here!" exclaimed Lyuba in surprise. "I thought they'd be gone till dark—and here he is back already."

"He left off driving the director," said her father. "Don't yell at him, though—he explained why. He gets sick when he drives a passenger car."

"Let's go talk for a bit, Lyuba," said Egor. And he led her into the front room. He seemed to have made up his mind about something.

Just then Petro drove into the yard in his dump truck and Egor walked out to meet him. He didn't get to tell Lyuba what had got him so upset.

Lyuba watched from a window while Egor and Petro talked for quite some little time; but then Egor beckoned to her and she went running out. Egor climbed up into the cab of the dump truck and got behind the wheel.

"Are you going far?" called out the old man. He had also seen Petro hand over the truck to Egor and realized that Egor and Lyuba were evidently getting ready to drive off.

"I don't know... Egor has to go someplace," Lyuba barely had time to say as they drove off.

"Lyubka!" shouted the old man, wanting to add something, but Lyuba had already slammed the door.

"What is that Zhorzhik up to?" the old man wondered aloud. "Everything's gone to hell with us now, never know what's going on..."

And soon he went over into his son's half of the house to find out where Egor had taken his daughter.

"There's a village called Sosnovka," Egor explained to Lyuba in the truck as they drove along—"nineteen kilometers from here."

"I know Sosnovka."

"An old woman called Kudelikha lives there. She lives with her daughter—but the daughter had to go to the hospital."

"Where did you learn all this?"

"Well, I just found out—I was in Sosnovka today. But that's not the point. This guy I know, see, he asked me to go see her and find out about her children—if they're still alive, where they live and so on."

"And why does he want to know all that."

"Well—she's some kind of relation to him, an aunt or something. But here's what we'll do: when we get there, you go in... No, we'll go in together, but you ask her the questions."

"Why?"

181

"Let me explain things first and then you can ask questions!"
Egor almost shouted. He was obviously very agitated.

"All right, Egor. But just don't shout at me, okay? I won't
ask anymore. So then what?"

"You have to talk to her, because if she sees that a man is
asking her questions, then she'll guess that, you know—he was in
prison with her son—I mean her nephew. And then she'll start
asking all kinds of questions. But my friend warned me that I
mustn't tell her he's in prison... Whew! It's complicated. Anyway, do you understand now?"

"I understand. But what excuse can I give her for asking all
the questions?"

"We'll have to think of something. For instance, you're from
the village soviet. No, not from the soviet, but the district.. what is
that again, where they give out the pensions?"

"The district social security department."

"Right, social security. You tell her you're from that office
and you're checking up to see how the old people are getting
along. Ask her where her children are, and if they write to her.
Okay?"

"Okay. I'll do it the way you want."

"Don't be too abrupt with her."

"I'll do it right, you'll see."

Egor fell silent. He was unusually serious and intent. He
forced a smile and said:

"Don't be offended, Lyuba, but I don't feel like talking now,
okay?"

Lyuba touched his hand with hers.

"Don't say anything more. Do what you know you have to
do. I won't ask any more questions."

"And I'm sorry I shouted at you," added Ego. "I don't like
it myself when people yell at me."

Egor drove along at a good clip. The road followed the edge
of a forest. The dump truck bounced heavily as the wheels rolled
over bared roots and stumps. Lyuba clung to the door handle
as the truck jolted along. Egor gazed straight ahead, his lips firmly
compressed, his eyes narrowed almost to a squint.

They pulled up to a roomy log house. It had a Russian stove,
benches, and a pine floor that had been scrubbed, scraped and
scrubbed again. A simple table with a painted top. In the holy
corner, an icon of St. Nicholas.

The old woman Kudelikha peered and peered at Lyuba and
Egor through her half-blind eyes... Egor was wearing dark glasses.

"Why have you covered your eyes, sonny?" she asked. "Can't you see with them?"

Egor shrugged his shoulders vaguely, said nothing.

"Well, Granny," said Lyuba, "they've sent me around to find out all about you."

Kudelikha sat down on a bench and folded her brown, withered hands over her apron.

"Well, what do you want to know? They pay me twenty roubles..." She looked up at Lyuba trustingly. "What else?"

"And where are your children? How many did you have?"

"I had six, dear. One still lives with me—Nyura, and three are out away... Kolya's in Novosibirsk, he's a train engineer. Misha's there, too—he builds houses. And Vera's in the Far East. She got married out there, husband's in the service. She just sent me a photograph of the whole family. The grandchildren are already getting big. There's two of them—a boy and a girl."

The old woman fell silent, wiped her mouth with the edge of her apron, nodded her little, birdlike head, sighed. She was plainly accustomed to wandering far back in her memories. She was there now, no longer noticed her guests. But then she came to herself again and looked at Lyuba, said something just to break the awkward silence. After all, they seemed to be concerned about her...

"So... They're alive, you see." And then she stopped talking again.

Egor was sitting on a chair by the door. He seemed to have turned to stone, never moved a muscle while the old woman talked, just stared at her.

"And the other two?" asked Lyuba.

"Well, those... I just don't know if they're alive, bless their hearts, or if they passed away long ago." The old woman again began to nod her tiny, wrinkled head, in an effort to compose herself and keep from crying. But tears began to fall on her hands and she quickly wiped her eyes with her apron.

"I just don't know. They went out into the world during the famine time... Now I don't know where they are. Two more sons... two brothers... And I don't know anything about them."

A heavy silence descended in the house... Lyuba couldn't think of anything else to ask. She felt sorry for the old woman. She glanced at Egor. He sat there like a statue, still staring at Kudelikha. And his whole face, with those dark glasses, also seemed to have turned into stone. Lyuba began to feel very strange.

"That's all right, Granny." She completely forgot she was

183

from "the social security" and went over to the old woman, sat down next to her in the most simple and natural way, as she knew how to do, put her arm around her and cuddled her. "You just wait, dear. Don't cry. There's no need to cry. You'll see. They'll still be found. We just have to look for them!"

The old woman obediently wiped away her tears and nodded her head.

"Maybe they'll be found... Thank you. Are you from peasant people yourself? You seem so natural, like."

"Yes, indeed I am. And we must certainly try to find your sons..."

Egor stood up and went out of the room.

He walked slowly across the entryway. He stopped at the front door and ran his hand over the doorpost. It was smooth and cold. He leaned his forehead against it and stood as if frozen. He stayed that way for a long time, gripping the doorpost with his hand until his fingers turned white. Lord—if only he were still able to cry in this life—things would be a little easier. But not a single tear moistened his eye. Only his cheekbones turned to stone and his fingers were squeezing whatever they could with all their strength. And there was nothing else that could have helped him in this awful moment—not tobacco, not vodka— nothing. Nothing would have done him any good. He suffered openly, groaned aloud in torment; he felt as though his soul was being seared in a slow fire. Over and over he repeated to himself, like a prayer: "That's enough! Stop it now. That's enough!..."

Egor heard Lyuba's footsteps coming, swung away from the doorpost and stepped down from the low front stoop. He walked away quickly along the fence, glancing back at the house. He again fell into concentrated thought as he walked around to the other side of the truck, kicked at the tires... He took off his glasses and stared at the house.

Lyuba came out.

"Lord, how sorry I felt for her," she said. "She just broke my heart."

"Let's go," commanded Egor.

They turned around... Egor glanced at the house for the last time and then drove off.

They were both silent. Lyuba thought sadly about the old woman.

After they had driven beyond the village, Egor stopped the truck, laid his forehead against the steering wheel and tightly closed his eyes.

184

"What's the matter, Egor?" asked, Lyuba, frightened.

"Wait a minute... I want to stop here for a minute," said Egor with a catch in his voice. "You know... she broke my heart, too. That's my mother, Lyuba. My mother."

Lyuba gasped quietly.

"What were you thinking of, Egor? How could you not tell her?"

"It's not the right time," said Egor almost angrily. "I need a little more time... But I'll tell her soon. Soon."

"What do you mean, you need time! We're going to turn around right now!"

"I can't now!" shouted Egor. "I have to at least let my hair grow out... I want to at least look like a human being." Egor put the truck into gear. "I sent her some money," he added, "but I'm afraid she'll go off to the village soviet with it and demand to know who it's from. She might even not take it. I beg you, Lyuba—go by and see her again tomorrow, say something to her. Think of something. Right now I just can't. Not right now. My heart would crack in half."

"Stop the truck," ordered Lyuba.

"Why?"

"Stop."

Egor stopped.

Lyuba leaned over and embraced him, as she had just embraced his mother, tenderly and capably... She laid his head on her breast.

"Oh, God!... Why are you like this? Why are you both so loveable?" She burst into tears. "What am I going to do with you?"

Egor freed himself from her embraces and coughed a few times in order to clear his throat. He put the truck into gear and declared in a near frenzy of joy:

"Don't worry, Lyubasha!... Everything will turn out all right! I'll put my head on the block if I have to, but you'll have a good life with me, I swear it."

When they got back home Petro met them at the fence.

"He's obviously worried. About the truck," guessed Lyuba.

"But why? I told him..."

Lyuba and Egor climbed down from the cab and Petro approached them.

"He showed up again here... your..." Petro broke off, speaking in his customary reluctant manner.

"Kolka?" said Lyuba in unpleasant surprise. "How dreadful!

What does he want? He's torturing me to death, that whining slob..."

"Maybe I'll just go and get acquainted with him," said Egor, glancing at Petro. Petro barely nodded his head.

"Egor!" said Lyuba in alarm. "He's certain to be drunk. He'll start a fight. Don't go, Egor!" Lyuba moved to stop him, but Petro held her back.

"Don't be afraid," he said. "Hey, Egor..."

Egor turned around.

"There's three more waiting for you, behind the fence. Keep on your guard."

Egor nodded and went into the house.

Lyuba struggled with all her might to free herself, but her brother held her tightly.

"But they're going to beat him up!" said Lyuba, almost crying. "What's wrong with you? Let me go, Petro!"

"Who are they going to beat up?" said Petro calmly in his deep voice. "Zhorzhik? It won't be so easy to whip him. Let them talk for a bit... And then your Kolya won't be coming around here anymore. Let him understand that once and for all."

"Ah," said Kolya, stretching his mouth into a forced smile. "Here's the new master." He got up from the bench. "While I'm the old one." He walked up in front of Egor. "We need to have a little talk." Kolya was not so much drunk as hungover. He was a tall fellow, rather good looking, with intelligent blue eyes.

The old people looked fearfully at the "masters"—the old one and the new one.

Egor decided not to dally. He immediately grabbed Kolya by the collar and dragged him out of the house...

He led him with difficulty onto the porch, then pushed him off it.

Kolya fell down. He hadn't expected they would begin so soon.

"If you ever show up around here again, you piece of carrion... This here was your last visit," said Egor from above. And then he started to walk down the steps.

Kolya scrambled up from the ground and began agitatedly to threaten Egor: "First let's get away from here. Follow me, now... Come on, now, you dog! Come on, now!"

They were already on the other side of the fence. Egor was walking ahead, Kolya following. Kolya kept making nervous threatening moves, once pushed Egor from behind. Egor looked back and shook his head reproachfully.

"Keep going, keep going," repeated Kolya, his voice shaking.

The three Petro had warned Egor about came up to meet them. "Not here," commanded Egor. "Let's go on farther."

They walked on. Egor again found himself in front.

"Listen," he said, stopping. "Let's walk together, so it won't look like you're leading me to the firing squad. They're watching us..."

"Keep moving, keep moving," repeated Kolya, hardly able to contain himself.

They walked on for a short way.

When they reached a high wattle fence, where they were less visible from the road, Kolya no longer restrained himself and leaped on Egor from behind. But Egor quickly twisted to the side and tripped Kolya. Kolya again ignominiously fell down. Then one of the others came to the attack, but Egor smashed his fist into the fellow's stomach. That one sat down. The other two stood dumbstruck by this turn of events, but Kolya jumped up and ran over to the fence to break loose a long stake.

"Okay, you dog!" said Kolya, choking with anger. He pulled out the stake and rushed at Egor in a rage.

Egor knew from long experience that a man almost never completely forgets himself—always, even at the last possible moment, he somehow manages to consider the consequences. If he kills you, it means he meant to do it. He will seldom kill you by accident.

Egor stood with his hands in his pockets and looked at Kolya. Kolya ran head-on into that calm—that somehow ominously calm—gaze.

"You won't have time to hit me with it," said Egor. He paused for a second, then added sympathetically: "Kolya..."

"Why are you threatening me? What have you got to fight with?" shouted Kolya, still trying to bluff. "A knife, maybe? Okay, take it out, then! Take out your knife!"

"You shouldn't drink so much, you jerk," said Egor with sympathy. "You tore the stake loose, but now your hands are shaking so much you can't hold it. Don't ever come to this house again."

Egor turned around and walked back. He heard someone make a move toward him from behind—no doubt Kolya—but the others stopped him:

"Let him go! The piece of shit. Some jerk from the city. We'll take care of him some other time."

Egor neither stopped nor turned around.

187

Egor was plowing a furrow for the first time in his life.

He stopped the tractor, jumped to the ground, and walked along the freshly plowed furrow, quite amazed at himself: was this really his own work? He kicked a lump of dirt with his boot and grunted with satisfaction.

"Well, well, Zhorzhik. There's no doubt about it—if you keep on this way, you'll become a real shock-worker!" He gazed out over the steppe, breathed in the vernal smell of the new earth and closed his eyes for a minute. He stood there without moving.

When he was a kid he had loved to listen to telegraph poles. He would press his ear to the pole, close his eyes, and listen to the humming of the wires—a sensation that always stirred him deeply. He never forgot it: that eerie humming sound, as though it came from another world—from the devil knew where. If you shut your eyes even more tightly and entered that powerful, resonant sound with your whole being, then it would seem to be coming from within you—from somewhere in your head, or your chest—it was hard to say where. It was scary, but fascinating. How strange it was: that part of his life had been quite long and varied, yet the things from it that he remembered well were so few: the cow Manka, the birch saplings he and his mother would chop down for stove wood... But these precious memories still lived within him, and when his life became unbearably oppressive, he would recall that far off village, the birch forest on the river bank, and the river... This did not make things any easier for him, it only made him feel a deep sense of loss and sadness, and his heart would ache in a different way—with sweetness as well as pain. And now, when such calm seemed to emanate from the freshly plowed field, when he could feel the warm sunshine on his head, and he was able to rest from his ceaseless running, he could not understand how it could ever happen—that he would stop his running for good and find peace. Was that really possible? In his heart was the premonition that his days of rest would be short.

Egor again surveyed the steppe. He would be sorry to lose this too. "What kind of freak am I," he thought involuntarily, "that I don't know how to live! God damn it! You have to live! Is life good? Yes, it's good. So enjoy it then, be happy!" Egor drew a deep breath.

"You could live for a hundred and forty years, breathing air like this," he said. And only now did he notice a birch copse at the edge of the field. He walked toward it.

"Ah, my beauties, standing here all by yourselves at the edge of the field. Well, have you got what you were waiting for? You've finally turned green..." He caressed one of the trees. "What pretty dresses! Oh, my little brides, what beautiful clothes you've put on—but you stand here saying nothing. You could have shouted and called me, but all you did was get dressed up and stand there. But now I've finally seen you. You're all beautiful. I must go back to my plowing now. But I'll be right near by, and I'll visit you again sometime." He walked some distance from the birches, looked back and laughed: "Look at them, standing there like that!" And then he returned to his tractor.

As usual, he talked aloud as he walked along.

"If I stand around with you, I'll never become a shock-worker. And the thing is... Well, it's all the same to you, anyway—and I really must work hard from now on. That's the way it is." And Egor began to sing:

"Snowball berry red,
Snowball berry ripe,
A little birdie told me,
My sweetheart he had lied.
My sweetheart he had lied,
Just wanted to be my lover..."

Still singing, he climbed into the cab and put the huge iron mass into motion. He continued to sing, but the song could no longer be heard over the roaring and clanking of the tractor.

In the evening they all ate supper together—the old people, Lyuba and Egor.

Some nice songs were playing on the radio and they were all listening to the music.

Suddenly the door opened and an unexpected guest appeared: a tall young fellow—the same one who had come rushing back the night of the police raid.

Egor was rather taken aback.

"Oh ho!" he said. "We have a guest! Sit down, Vasya!"

"Shura," corrected the guest, smiling.

"Oh yes—Shura! I keep forgetting. I keep mixing you up with Vasya, remember him? That big guy—the first sergeant..." Egor chattered on while making an effort to regain his composure: the guest was indeed most unexpected. "Shura and I were in the service together," he explained. "Under the same general. Sit down, Shura, eat supper with us."

"Sit down, sit down," invited Lyuba's mother as well.

And her father even moved over on the bench to make room: "Here, sit down."

"Thanks, no, I can't, I have a taxi waiting for me. I just need to tell you something, Georgii. And give you something..."

"Now you just sit down and eat!" insisted Egor. "The driver will wait for you."

"No, I can't," Shura glanced at his watch. "I have to catch a train..."

Egor got up from the table. He kept on chattering away, so that Shura would have no opportunity to let something slip from his tongue. Egor, who hated empty and trivial words himself, nevertheless knew how to confuse people by inundating them with a stream of words. Sometimes he did the same thing when he himself was confused.

"Well, tell me, do you ever meet any of the guys? Man, we really had the good times, didn't we? I still dream about those days in the army. Well, let's go. What do you want to give me? I guess it's in the taxi. I wonder what it is the general sent me. What do I have to do, sign for it? Did you come here direct, or did you have to change trains? Well, let's go, then..."

They went out.

The old man fell silent. All he could think about, with his honest peasant mind, was one thing.

"Say," he said, "how much does it cost to go riding around in a taxi? What do they get for each kilometer?"

"I don't know," said Lyuba distractedly. "Ten kopecks." She had sensed something very unfriendly in this guest.

"Ten kopecks? Let's see, ten kopecks times thirty-six versts... how much is that?"

"Well, that would be thirty-sixty kopecks," said the old woman.

"Don't be an idiot!" exclaimed the old man. "Ten versts, that would already be one rouble. And thirty-six would be three-sixty—that's how much it is! And three-sixty and three-sixty is seven-twenty. That's seven-twenty just for the round trip from town. And I used to work a whole month for seven-twenty..."

Lyuba couldn't stand it anymore and also got up from the table.

"I wonder what they're doing out there?" she said and left the room.

She went out into the entryway and saw that the outside door was open. She could hear Egor and Shura talking. She froze.

"You tell him that. Got it?" said Egor harshly, angrily. "Remember what I said and tell him."

"I'll tell him—but you know him..."

"I know. But he knows me, too. Did he get the money?"

"Yeah."

190

"Okay. You guys and me are quits. If you come looking for me, I'll get the whole village after you." Egor laughed shortly. "I wouldn't advise it."

"Gore... Don't get pissed off at me now, I'm only doing what he told me. He said, 'If he's out of money, give him some.' So here—take it."

And Shura, evidently, handed Egor a packet of bills. Egor must have taken the money and hit Shura in the face with it— once, again, a third time. And then he said quietly, through his teeth:

"You son-of-a-bitch—you were right. I did get pissed off."

Lyuba made a deliberate noise and then walked out onto the porch.

Shura was standing there with his hands at his sides, his face white...

Egor handed him the money and said in a quiet, almost hoarse voice: "Here you are. I'll be seeing you, Shura. Be sure to give them my regards. Do you remember what I told you?"

"I remember," said Shura. He gave Egor one last glance, full of evil promise, and went to the taxi.

"Well, well," said Egor as he sat down on the step. He watched the cab turn around... He followed it down the road with his eyes and then glanced up at Lyuba.

Lyuba was standing above him.

"Egor..." she started to say.

"Never mind," said Egor. "Just some old business of mine. Debts, you might say. But they won't come here anymore."

"I'm afraid, Egor," confessed Lyuba.

"Of what?" said Egor in surprise.

"I heard that when you try to... quit a gang... well, they..."

"None of that now!" said Egor sharply. "None of that," he repeated. "Come on, sit down now and don't talk about that ever again. Sit down..." Egor took her hand and pulled her down. "Why are you standing behind me like that? That's not nice, to stand behind somebody's back. It's impolite."

Lyuba sat down.

"Well?" asked Egor cheerfully. "Why then do you grieve, my pretty dawn?[7] What we need to do is sing a song!"

"Lord, I can't sing now..."

Egor ignored her.

"Come on I'll teach you... I know a real good song." And Egor began to sing:

    "Snowball berry red,
    Snowball berry ripe..."

"Oh, I know that!" said Lyuba.

"Okay then, sing along with me. Now...

Snowball berry..."

"Egor!" beseeched Lyuba. "Please, for the love of Christ, tell me they're not going to do anything to you."

Egor clenched his teeth and said nothing.

"Don't be angry, Egorushka. Why are you acting that way?" And Lyuba burst into tears. "Why is it you can't understand me? I've been waiting and waiting for happiness—and now it's going to be taken from me... What's the matter with me? Have I been cursed? Will I never be allowed to find joy in life?!"

Egor put his arm around Lyuba and wiped away her tears with the palm of his hand.

"Don't you believe me?" he asked.

"Believe, believe... What does that mean when you don't want to talk? Just tell me, Egor. I won't be afraid. Maybe we can go away somewhere..."

"Oh, no!" howled Egor. "Are you sure you want me to be a shock-worker? I'll tell you the truth, Lyuba, I'll never make it this way. I just can't bear it when people cry. I can't bear it. Have pity on me, Lyubushka."

"Okay, I'm sorry. Everything's going to be all right, then?"

"Everything's going to be all right," said Egor carefully and precisely. "I'll swear it by anything you want, by all that's holy. Now let's sing a song." And he began:

"Snowball berry red,

Snowball berry ripe..."

Lyuba joined in and they sounded just terrific together, really beautiful. For a minute she forgot everything and became calm.

"A little birdie told me,

My sweetheart he had lied.

My sweetheart he had lied,

Just wanted to be my lover.

When I would not give in,

He left me for another."

Petro watched them from behind the fence.

"Write down the words for me," he said mockingly.

"Oh, Petro," said Lyuba in an offended voice. "You've ruined our song."

"Who was that that came to see you, Egor?"

"Just a friend of mine. Are we going to heat up the bath house?" asked Egor.

"Sure we are. Come here a minute, I've got something to tell

192

you."

Egor walked over to the fence. Petro leaned over and said something quietly in Egor's ear.

"Petro!" shouted Lyuba. "I know what you're up to. I know. After the bath!"

"I asked him to take a look at the jet in my carburetor," said Petro.

"I'm just going to see what's wrong with the carburetor," said Egor. "Probably needs to be blown out."

"I'll carburetor you! After the bath, I said." And with these final words, Lyuba went into the house. She felt much calmer, but just the same a worrisome fear had crept into her heart. It was the sort of persistent fear familiar to women in love.

Egor climbed over to Petro's side of the fence.

"Brandy—that's shit," he said. "I prefer either champagne or Remy Martin."

"But you just try this."

"I have—and everything else, too. One thing I rather like, for instance, is whisky and soda..."

They continued their conversation as they walked toward the bathhouse.

Now Egor was sowing the field that he had plowed earlier. That is, he was driving the tractor and towing a seeder, upon which stood a young woman with a trowel who saw to it that the seed was spread evenly.

Petro drove up in his dump truck, which had been modified to carry seed. Egor helped him fill the seeder. They talked briefly:

"Are you going to eat dinner here or at home?" asked Petro.

"Here."

"I can take you back if you want. I have to go home anyway."

"That's okay. I brought everything with me... Why do you have to go back?"

"The motor started missing. It's undoubtedly the carburetor jet."

They laughed, recalling the "carburetor" they had "blown out" together that last time in the bathhouse.

"I've got another one at home. I've been keeping it ready."

"Do you want me to take a look and see if something else is making it miss?"

"Nah, just a waste of time. I know it's the carburetor jet. It's been giving me trouble for a long time. I just hated to throw it out. But now I'll change it."

"Well, I'll see you." And Egor returned to his tractor. Petro left to distribute seed to the other sowers.

The tractor roared to life and lurched forward.

... Egor was distracted momentarily from the instrument panel, glanced ahead, and noticed in the distance that a Volga had stopped near his little birch grove at the edge of the field. Three people stood near the car. Egor stared hard at them... and finally recognized them. They were Fat Lip, Bulldog and the tall fellow. And Lucienne was in the car. Lucienne was sitting in the front seat; the door was open. Although her face was hidden, Egor recognized her from her skirt and legs. The men stood by the car, waiting for the tractor.

Nothing had changed in the world. The day was warm and clear, the birch copse at the edge of the field stood all green and freshly washed from yesterday's rain... The soil gave off such a rich odor, such a rich, thick, damp smell, that it made one feel slightly dizzy. The earth had assembled all its vernal forces, its living juices, and was getting ready again to bring forth life. And the faraway dark-blue stripe of forest, a cloud above it, white and fleecy, and the sun high aloft—all of this was life, spilling out everywhere, concerned about nothing, afraid of nothing.

Egor throttled back very slightly... He leaned down and picked out a wrench—not too heavy a one, but one he could handle deftly—and stuck it in the pocket of his trousers. He glanced down to see if it was visible under his jacket. You couldn't tell it was there.

When he drew even with the Volga, Egor stopped the tractor and turned off the engine.

"Galya, go eat dinner," he said to his helper.

"But we've only just filled up the seeder," said Galya uncomprehendingly.

"Never mind. Just go. I've got to talk with my comrades here—from the central committee of the trade union."

Galya set out toward the brigade shack, just barely visible in the distance. She turned around two or three times to look at the Volga, at Egor...

Egor also glanced across the field unobtrusively... Two other tractors with seeders crawled along the far side; their steady rumble somehow did not disturb the silence of the vast bright day.

Egor walked over to the Volga.

Fat Lip began to grin while Egor was still quite a ways off.

"Look how dirty he is!" exclaimed Fat Lip with a smile. "Take a look at him, Lucienne!"

194

Lucienne climbed out of the car and looked seriously, unsmilingly, at the approaching Egor.

Egor walked awkwardly through the soft plowed earth. He looked at his guests. He did not smile.

Only Fat Lip smiled.

"By God, I never would have recognized you!" he continued in his mocking tone. "If I had just run into you someplace, I never would have known who you were."

"Please don't touch him," said Lucienne suddenly in her husky voice, looking demandingly, even angrily, at Fat Lip.

While Fat Lip was all agog with a kind of vengeful joy.

"Lucienne! What are you saying! He's the one that shouldn't touch *me*! Tell him not to touch me! Or else he's liable to hit me on my damned neck with his holy fist..."

"Don't touch him, damn you!" Lucienne blurted out. "You'll be dead yourself soon, so why...."

"Shut up!" hissed Fat Lip. And his smile was gone in an instant. It was obvious—you could see it in his eyes—that his vindictive impotence had turned to black rage: the man was permanently deaf to any suggestion of justice. If he had no one to bite, he would turn like a snake and bite his own tail. "Or else I'll lay you out next to him—and put your arms around him. I'll add another statute to my list of offenses: desecration of corpses. What the hell difference does it make to me?"

"Please, I beg you," said Lucienne, after a pause. "Don't touch him. It will soon be all up with us, anyway—let him live. Let him plow the earth—he likes it."

"For us it's the end—but he's going to plow the earth?" Fat Lip smiled, showing his rotten teeth. "Where's the justice in that? Did he do less than we did?"

"He got out of the game... He has his release papers."

"He hasn't got out yet." Fat Lip again turned toward Egor. "He's still on his way."

Egor was still walking toward them, his boots continually sinking into the soft earth.

"He's even got a new walk now!" said Fat Lip with delight. "Like a real working man."

"Like a proletarian," mumbled the dull-witted Bulldog.

"Like a peasant—what do you mean 'proletarian'?"

"But the peasants are also the proletariat!"

"Bulldog! You only got through the fourth grade. Go read *Murzilka*—and wipe your mouth, you're drooling.[8] Hey, good boy, Gore!" Fat Lip loudly greeted Egor.

195

"And what else did they say?" Lyuba asked her parents in alarm.

"Nothing else... I told them how to get out there..."

"To Egor?"

"Well, yes.."

"Mother of God!" screamed Lyuba, and ran out of the house.

Just then Petro drove up to the fence.

Lyuba waved at him to stop.

Petro stopped.

Lyuba jumped into the cab, said something to Petro. The dump truck backed up, turned around and immediately sped off, bouncing and crashing over the pot holes in the road.

"Petya, dear brother, faster, faster! Oh Lord, I knew in my heart this would happen!" Tears rolled down Lyuba's cheeks. She didn't wipe them away, didn't even notice them.

"We'll make it," said Petro. "I just left him a little while ago..."

"They were just here... asking about him. And now they're already out there. Faster, Petya!"

Petro squeezed everything he could out of his humpbacked bogatyr.

The group that had been standing near the Volga moved toward the birch grove. Only the woman remained at the car—even crawling inside and slamming shut all the doors.

The group had not quite reached the birch trees when it stopped. They were evidently talking something over... Then two of the group stepped aside and returned to the car. The other two—Egor and Fat Lip—went into the birch grove and were soon hidden from sight.

... At that moment Petro's dump truck came into view far down the road. The two standing near the Volga gazed at the truck. They realized the truck was headed for them, shouted something in the direction of the trees. Immediately one man—Fat Lip—came running out of the grove, concealing something in his pocket. He also saw the dump truck and ran to the Volga. The Volga tore away and rapidly gathered speed as it shifted into higher gear...

... The dump truck pulled up to the birch copse.

Lyuba leaped out of the cab and ran toward the trees.

Walking slowly out to meet her, holding one hand over his stomach, came Egor. He staggered, clutching at the trees with his other hand. And on the white birches bright-red stains appeared.

196

Petro, seeing that Egor was wounded, jumped back into his truck, intending to chase down the Volga. But the Volga was already far away. He began to turn around.

Lyuba took hold of Egor's arms and supported him.

"I'll get blood on you," said Egor, wincing from the pain.

"Hush, don't speak." Lyuba was strong. She took him in her arms. Egor was about to protest, but another wave of pain passed over him. He closed his eyes.

Petro rushed up, took Egor carefully from the arms of his sister and carried him toward the truck.

"It's okay, it's okay now," he rumbled softly. "This is nothing... Men had bayonets run right through them during the war and still lived. In a week you'll be jumping around..."

Egor shook his head weakly and took a breath—the pain had subsided slightly.

"In there... the bullet..." he said.

Petro glanced down at him, at his white face, clenched his teeth and said nothing. He quickened his step.

Lyuba jumped into the cab first. She took Egor's hands. She held him in her lap, with his head resting on her breast. Petro cautiously put the truck into motion.

"Be patient, Egorushka darling. Soon we'll be at the hospital."

"Don't cry," said Egor quietly, not opening his eyes.

"I'm not crying."

"Yes, you are... your tears... on my face. Don't cry..."

"I won't, I won't..."

Petro spun the wheel this way and that, trying to avoid the bumps. But all the same the truck jolted. Egor winced in agony and groaned a couple of times.

"Petya..." said Lyuba.

"I'm doing the best I can. But I don't dare slow down. There's no time."

"Stop," said Egor.

"Why, Egor? We have to go as fast as we can."

"No... it's over. Take me... down... from the truck."

They lifted him out, placed him on the ground, on a shirt.

"Lyuba," called Egor, searching for her in the sky with unseeing eyes. He lay on his back. "Lyuba..."

"I'm here, Egor. I'm right here, see?..."

"Money..." Egor strained to get out his last words. "In jacket.. share it... with my mother..." A single tear squeezed out from under Egor's closed eyelids, rolled down his scalp toward his ear, hung there a minute, detached itself and fell into the grass.

197

Egor was dead.

And there he lay, a Russian peasant on his native steppe, not far from home... He lay with his cheek pressed to the earth, as though he were listening to something that only he could hear. That was how he had listened to telegraph poles in his childhood.

Lyuba fell on his breast and quietly, terribly, wept.

Petro stood above them looking down and also cried, without making a sound.

Then he raised his head, wiped away his tears with the sleeve of his jersey.

"No!" he said, letting out his breath, so that all his frightening strength could be felt. "They're not going to get away!" He circled around Egor and his sister and, not looking back, ran heavily toward the dump truck.

The truck gave a roar and rushed out over the open steppe, away from the main road. Petro knew perfectly every road and cart track in the region; he had suddenly come to the conclusion that it was possible to intercept the Volga by cutting across its path. The Volga would have to make a wide sweep around the forest that was visible in the distance as a dark blue band on the horizon... But passing through the forest was a lumber road used for hauling out timber on tractor sledges during the winter. Now, after the rain, the lumber road littered with branches and brush might even be better for the truck than the muddy main road. But the Volga, of course, would never go in there—and how could they know anyway where the road led?

... Petro intercepted the Volga.

The dump truck lurched out of the forest before the beige beauty was able to slip past. Its hopeless position immediately became apparent: it was too late to turn around, because the truck was racing toward it head on; and it was impossible to squeeze past the truck, because the road was too narrow. As for turning off the road: on one side was the forest, and on the other plowed ground soaked with yesterday's rain—out of the question for the small city vehicle. Yet that was the only chance the Volga had—to pull off into the field at full speed and try to jump back onto the road after it had passed the truck. The Volga turned off the hard road and immediately its rear wheels began to spin and skid. It slowed down to a crawl, though the engine roared at top speed. At this point Petro bore down on it. No one in the Volga even had time to jump out. The great toiler dump truck, like an infuriated bull, crashed into the side of the car, turned it over and reared up on top of it.

Petro climbed down from the cab...

From out of the field, jumping down from their tractors, people who had seen what happened came running up.

1973 —Translated by Donald M. Fiene

NOTES

1. Original Russian: "Kalina krasnaia," *Nash sovremennik,* 4(1973), 86-133. Reprinted in *Izbrannye proizvedeniia v dvukh tomakh* (1975), Vol. 1, pp. 417-492, and in *Kinopovesti* (1975) with only a few minor changes.

2. Egor is reciting a poem by Sergei Esenin written in 1922. The first stanza, which Egor omits (he also omits the fourth) is:

> Mir tainstvennyi, mir moi drevnii,
>
> Ty, kak veter, zatikh i prisel.
>
> Vot, sdavili za sheiu derevniu
>
> Kamennye ruki shosse.

> (My secret world of bygone days,
>
> You're cowering now like the dying wind.
>
> The countryside's been strangled
>
> By the highway's stony arms.)

The destruction of ancient rural culture by urban encroachment was a frequent theme with Esenin, as with Shukshin. The poetic line quoted two pages earlier by Egor, "Oh, my skies of May, and the long blue days of June," is also from Esenin (and not from Afanasy Fet as the old woman's remark might seem to imply). The line in Russian is: "Mai moi sinii! Iiun' goluboi!" It is from "Snova p'iut zdes', derutsia i plachut," 1923.

3. *Gore* in Russian means "grief, sorrow, woe, misfortune..." It has two syllables in pronunciation: Gór-ye. The hero's full given name is Georgii, pronounced Gi-ór-gi, with both G's hard; the version of the name he usually goes by, Egor, is pronounced Yegór. He is also referred to by such diminutives as Egorsha, Egorushka, Zhora and Zhorzhik. He even identifies himself once as "Dzhordzh", using the English pronunciation (spelled here: George).

4. Shukshin's phrase here is: "Rabota ne Alitet." [Work is not Alitet.] This is a reference to the colorful hero of a popular two-volume novel about a far-northern Siberian horseman of the Chukchi tribe by Tikhon Z. Semushkin: *Alitet ukhodit v gory* [Alitet flees to the mountains] (1947-48).

5. The name Pistonov rather remotely suggests *pizda* 'cunt'.

6. Kolenka is a diminutive of Nikolai, hence "saint" Nikolai (or Nicholas).

7. Egor is borrowing some words from a popular song. What he says is: "Chto zakruchinilas', zoren'ka iasnaia?" (literally: "Why have you begun to grieve, clear dawn?"). The actual title of the song is: "Chto zatumanilas', zoren'ka iasnaia?" ["Why have you become foggy, clear dawn?"].

8. *Murzilka:* monthly illustrated magazine for young school children.

199

Donald M. Fiene

VASILY SHUKSHIN'S "KALINA KRASNAIA"

"Kalina krasnaia ("Snowball Berry Red") is a work which loses much in the translation. In saying this, I do not want to seem to be excusing a mediocre translation by implying that no translator could have done justice to the supposed subtleties and nuances of the original. Shukshin's work is probably no "greater" in Russian than it appears to be in the present English text. However, it is the particular Russianness of "Kalina krasnaia" (as opposed to its potentially universal character) that contributes most to an appreciation of it as literature. And the ways in which this work is distinctively Russian need to be pointed out, I feel, to the American or English reader.

First about my translation: though it may not fully embody the original work, it has had the advantage of comparison against an earlier translation by Robert Daglish.[1] Both my translation and Daglish's fail, however, to render adequately the laconic style of the original—especially the laconicism of the speech of Egor Prokudin, the protagonist. For example, there is Egor's description to the prison superintendent of his correspondence with Lyuba:

> —Pishet, chto bedu moiu vsiu ponimaet... No, govorit, ne ponimaiu, kak ty dodumalsia v tiur'mu ugodit'. Khoroshie pis'ma. Pokoi ot nikh... Muzh byl p'ianchuga—vygnala. A na liudei vse ravno ne obozlilas'.

My translation:

> "She writes that she understands all my trials... 'But,' she says, 'I don't understand how you took the notion to land up in prison.' Nice letters. They make you feel peaceful... Her husband was a boozer. She kicked him out. And even so, she didn't get bitter at people."

Daglish's version is:

> "She writes that she understands all my troubles but can't understand how I managed to get into gaol... Lovely letters they are. Peaceful like. Her husband was too fond of the bottle so she chucked him out. But it hasn't made her bitter about people."

The original contains thirty-two words, my version forty-nine words, and Daglish's forty-five—indicating that a translation of Egor's speech into idiomatic English (whether British or American) may require up to half again as many words. Part of this discrepancy, of course, is due to basic

200

differences between English and Russian—such as the greater ease with which colloquial Russian dispenses with pronouns. But there is no doubt that Shukshin has given to Egor Prokudin a singularly terse manner of speaking which is very difficult to convey in English.

At the same time, there are defects in Shukshin's style that carry over only too well into English. Most of these have to do with unneeded descriptions of emotional states, movements of hands, feet, eyes and the like—as though the author is giving instructions to the actors who will eventually play the roles in his film script (or film-story). I doubt that the first publication of such a story requires so much instruction.

Another problem for the translator is Egor's speech at its most vivid and slangy, when he is excited, annoyed or frustrated. In Russian such speech (one of Shukshin's special successes as a writer) is convincing even though largely devoid of taboo words. This is due at least in part to the traditional reluctance of Russian literature (and film) to admit such words. Egor's speech would probably sound more authentic in English if it were packed with obscenities, but I decided to hold as closely as possible to the original. This in combination with Egor's frequent sentimentality, typified by his conversations with birch trees, lends to Shukshin's hero a degree of innocence that must seem at times in the English translation to be wholly unacceptable. This is only partly accounted for by the relatively less vicious life style of Soviet criminals and outlaws (who wickedly sip champagne from long-stemmed glasses) in contrast with their American counterparts. Egor's manner may seem more acceptable in the original Russian simply because that language (in my opinion) is somehow more "accommodating" to sentimentality than English, especially modern American English.

One of the most obvious losses in the English translation is the significance of the title to the reader. Quite apart from the song after which Shukshin's work is titled, there is the specific series of flora that the title identifies. The word *kalina* denotes the *Vibernum opulus*—vibernum being the second largest genus of the honeysuckle family, *Caprifoliacaea*. The species *Vibernum opulus* is native throughout the north temperate zone in both the old and new world. Common names for it in English are the guelder rose (named for its supposed origin in Guelderland or eastern Netherlands), the snowball or snowball bush, and the European cranberry bush or tree. It is a deciduous shrub up to twelve feet in height, with smooth, light gray branches; the leaves are maple-like, two to four inches long. It has white flowers with cymes three to four inches across (hence the name snowball). Its egg-shaped, bright red fruits, about one-third of an inch long, persist into the winter; birds avoid them because of their valeric acid content, but humans, especially in Europe, cook the berries to make tarts and sometimes steep them along with the wood to make a medicine effective against scrofula.

The second word of the title, *krasnaia*, 'red,' indicates that the title as a whole refers to the fruit of the *kalina* (not to the whole bush). Hence, Daglish's translation of the title as *Red Guelder Rose* is botanically incorrect and misleading anyway, in that it calls to mind only red roses; equally unsuitable are the following titles by which the work has been identified in various articles in English: "Red Snowball," "Red Snowball Tree," and "Red Vibernum." The title I selected, "Snowball Berry Red," undoubtedly means little more to the American or English reader than the titles here deemed unsuitable, but at least it focuses attention on the fruit of the tree and it preserves the alliterativeness and regular rhythm of the original (though reversing the iambic rhythm to trochaic); it is especially suitable as a poetic song title. But my title is not quite correct botanically either, since the snowball bush—the variety of *kalina* usually found in gardens in the United States—is actually sterile *(Vibernum opulus sterilis)* and bears no fruit. In England the same sterile, white-flowered shrub is more often called the guelder rose. The only accurate translation for *kalina* is 'European cranberry tree' (or bush) or simply 'cranberry tree.' But this name is unsuitable, since, being unknown to most American or British readers, only calls to mind the entirely unrelated cranberries that grow in bogs on low bushes *(Vaccinium macrocarpon)*. Another possible translation of *kalina* could be 'the wild guelder rose'—but this, or the full translation of 'the red berry of the wild guelder rose' is hopelessly unsuitable as the first line (and title) of the song that must be translated in the text.

While none of the above titles conveys much to the Western reader (beyond the possible vague image of a showy, cultivated shrub), *kalina krasnaia* is full of associations for the Russian reader, even if he should be a city dweller who has never actually seen the shrub growing and would not recognize it if he did see it. First of all, *kalina* calls to mind the deep provinces, where the bush grows wild and has long been used in various ways by Russian peasants. Old fairy tales and songs mention *mosty kalinovye*—bridges or causeways made of *kalina* brush wood laid down across a swamp. ["Est' li u tebia na mostakh na kalinovykh Spas, Bogoroditsa?"] There was an old custom in rural weddings of "breaking the *kalina* twigs" before passing around the wine at the wedding table. There were (probably still are) folk medicines made from the bark and berries of the *kalina*. Little pies made from the berries are called *kalinniki*. The *kalina*, as berry or bush, finds its way into proverbs ("Ne byvat' kaline malinoi" [The *kalina* can never be a raspberry]) and numerous folk songs, where it is often referred to by the affectionate diminutives *kalinka, kalinushka* or *kalinochka*.[2] A scanning of the tables of contents of only three or four Russian song books turned up the following titles or first lines: "Kalinka, kalinka, kalinka moia" (one of the most popular of all Russian folk songs); "Oi tsvetet kalina"; "Pri dolinushka stoit"; and "Kalina s malinoi da ne vovremia rastsvela." Some of these songs tell of unhappy love affairs. According to popular belief, the red *kalina* berry is a symbol of first love, more often than not, unhappy love.[3]

The typical Russian reader, upon hearing the poetic-sounding appellation *kalina krasnaia*, is likely to make many of the above associations subliminally, to experience a vague nostalgia for Russian rural life in bygone days.

Presumably, this is how Shukshin himself felt when hearing the popular song, "Kalina krasnaia," the one appearing several times in the text of his film script. It was evidently one of his favorite songs, for he had also quoted it in a story written six years earlier.[4] He obviously chose it as the basis for the title of his film script in order to reinforce the symbolic return of Egor Prokudin, corrupted by the evils of the city, to the pure, traditional life of the village. What Shukshin had not realized until well after the filming of the movie had begun was that "Kalina krasnaia" was not an old folk song but in fact a popular ballad composed in the 1950s.[5] Consequently, although the title of the film stayed the same, the song played only a minor role in the movie. It is not sung by Lucienne at all and is only barely mentioned by Egor in his next to last scene with Lyuba; in the script there is an elaborate duet here, but in the film Egor sings only a line or two at most. In a recent article on the film, Yuri Tiurin says "v fil'me etoi pesni fakticheski net"—"the song does not really appear in the film."[6] But an acquaintance of mine in Tallinn, Estonian SSR, Ursula Poks, editor of the journal *Sirp ja vasar* and a fan of Shukshin's, informs me that "the melody (so it is said, [Shukshin's] favourite folk tune) has been somewhat modified [for the movie] by Pavel Chekalov, the composer who made most of the music for his films."[7] Only once in the film do the red berries of the title appear—in a scene where a young boy tosses a handful of them into a stream. The camera focuses on one of the berries floating on the surface of the clear water, as little fingerling fish dart up to nibble at it.

In general, the movie is faithful to the script in that the psychology of the major figures is not seriously altered, although many scenes are greatly reduced in length. Of special interest to the Western reader of "Kalina krasnaia" seeking insight into the Russian responses to the work is the incredible popularity of the film in the Soviet Union (which in turn, especially after the untimely death of the author-actor-director, has led to the written version being vastly more popular now than when it first appeared in the widely distributed magazine *Nash sovremennik* [Our Contemporary]).[8] A note in *Soviet Literature*, 9(1975) observes that "the overwhelming majority of the readers of [the] very popular magazine [*Sovietsky Ekran* (Soviet Film-Screen)] who sent their replies to the [annual] questionnaire [of the magazine] in 1974 named *[Kalina krasnaia]* as the best Soviet film of that year, and Vasily Shukshin, who played the leading role in it, the best actor. Both the film and the actor received the Spectators' prizes" [p. 122]. The film also won first prize at the seventh annual (Soviet) National Film Festival in Baku in 1974.

I was able to gain some idea of the impact made by this film on ordinary Soviet citizens (Russians in particular) during a brief visit to the Soviet

Union in December of 1975, over eighteen months after the film was released. I was lucky in finding a theater showing the film—one in a worker's
club, Dom kul'tura tipografii "Krasnyi proletarii" [The House of Culture of
the "Red Proletariat" Printing Shop], on Delegatskaia Street in Moscow.
My taxi driver had difficulty finding the club on this narrow side street that
was really no more than an alley between high snow banks. It was well past
the scheduled starting time for the short subjects when I walked up to the
ticket window in the lobby of the club house, where a shrill argument was in
progress between a late-arriving Russian and the angry ticket seller, a stern
and adamant woman in her late fifties. She absolutely refused to sell the
latecomer a ticket. But when I approached and explained that I was just a
poor dumb American, very sorry for being late, she at once relented, sold
both me and the other latecomer a ticket, and quickly proceeded to close up
shop. Shortly after I was seated in the small, crowded theater, the ticket
seller entered and by chance took the seat next to mine, just as the feature
film was starting. The woman must have seen the movie many times, yet now
she was watching it again with rapt attention, respondingly animatedly to
every changing mood of the actors on the screen. Several minutes before the
death scene in the birch grove this sturdy Russian mother figure covered her
eyes with her hands and held her head down close to her knees. She remained in this position until well after the shooting (which took place off
screen in any case) had occurred. When she finally took her hands away
from her eyes to watch Egor breathe his last, tears came streaming down
her face.

That woman symbolizes to me not only the love of modern Russians
for Egor Prokudin, but, more significantly, the great innocence and simplicity that separates these Russians, both as artists and spectators, from modern
Americans.

On another occasion, a taxi driver in Leningrad whom I asked about
the film was so pleased that his foreign fare was familiar with his favorite
movie that he nearly crashed his cab into a lamp post as he turned around
in his seat to seriously discuss Shukshin with me. And once in Kiev, as I
arrived at my hotel after midnight, a young man approached me with the aim
of buying dollars from me. Instead of doing business with him, I chose instead to inquire of this technical criminal whether he liked the movie *Kalina
krasnaia*. His reaction was to put both his arms around me and kiss me
forcibly on the lips, as a comradely reward for my intelligence. One tries in
vain to imagine the American movie that would induce some petty criminal
in Manhattan or St. Louis—some casual marijuana or pornography peddler—
to embrace (let alone kiss) some fellow admirer of that movie from abroad.

Undoubtedly much of Shukshin's popularity is due to the more general
popularity now of rural romanticism in the Soviet Union—a romanticism
that strays far from the usual models of Socialist Realism and seems in fact
to be criticizing basic Marxist assumptions about the character of human

progress. One is tempted to see in the adulation of Shukshin a covert if not overt display of dissatisfaction with the current government. Yet it seems certainly to be true that Shukshin himself was not a conscious critic of the Soviet political system; he was in any case a member of the Communist Party. Furthermore, Shukshin's popularity extends not merely to the general run of Soviet intellectuals but also to conservative literary critics. Even if some of the latter object to Shukshin's excessive sentimentality, they do not as a rule question his objective political loyalty. It is evidently true, however, that the film *Kalina krasnaia* had some difficulty in passing the censors. Hedrick Smith remarks on this in his recent book, *The Russians,* speculating on the identity of the influential person who undoubtedly must have intervened in behalf of the author. Months after the film was released, notes Smith, "I was told by an intellectual with good friends at the Party Central Committee that Shukshin's mystery fan was Brezhnev himself. My friend said that while censors were holding *[Kalina krasnaia]* in limbo, Brezhnev had seen it at a private Kremlin showing and had been moved to tears by the authentic scenes of rural Russia, the well-told tragedy of the hero, and by the moving portrayal of simple people whose faith in Russia was unshaken by their hard lives. Brezhnev's tears, my friend said, 'guaranteed the film's success.' "[9]

Rather than repeat what has been written elsewhere about the current drift toward Russophilism in the Soviet Union, I should like to comment now on certain themes in "Kalina krasnaia" that, while still reflecting this new sentimental conservatism, are nevertheless subtle enough to resist obvious analysis.

Before I discerned these themes, I was in considerable doubt about the literary value of "Kalina krasnaia." Although it was easy enough to respond to the genuinely powerful scenes, it often seemed to me, as I translated this work, that certain passages were awkward, irrelevant or psychologically invalid with regard to the character and personality of the hero. These seemed to go beyond the mere "unevenness" that Shukshin's writing often exhibits. The author himself, incidentally, was well aware that his work was flawed. In his last interview, given a few months before he died, he reported that he considered himself to be a writer above all—and that he contemplated a drastic change in his life, perhaps giving up acting and directing. "If you are a writer," he said, "you must devote your whole life to literature. And literature calls for quiet concentration, study of life, knowledge of life, of the world we live in. . . . I see now that I have created practically nothing. One must probe very deeply into the essence of life, try to understand it in all its manifestations. Yet we look for multiformity, for immediate benefits, we waste so much energy on so many things and believe that we are dedicating our lives to art. But it is all hustle and bustle."[10] At the same time, one senses in the man a seriousness that prevents one from discussing his work without first examining it carefully.

Examining "Kalina krasnaia" with the special insights gained from translating it, I discovered that one of its most important unifying elements is that derived from pointed references to religion. These references seem on first reading to be few and haphazard at best, yet a definite religious or "spiritual" mood is established even at the very beginning of the tale, with the singing of "Evening Bells" by the prisoner's choir. The "bells" of this popular folk song (one very moving for Russians) are, of course, church bells, a point emphasized much later when the song is sung again at the "orgy." That Shukshin consciously intended such a mood is somewhat more obvious in the film: the close-up shots of the prisoners singing, with their sad eyes and shaven heads, impel the audience to see in those worn countenances one thousand years of Russian suffering—a suffering made to seem holy, as the prisoners are transformed by the camera into innocent souls who might well be chanting in a church. And soon after this, as Egor leaves the labor camp, the camera focuses on a ruined church in the background. The camera returns to this church (or one like it, in a long shot across the water) near the end of the film, and in three other important scenes pointedly lingers on village churches or icons—to point out for those who choose to perceive it the absence in modern Soviet society of something that might perhaps have been good in the old Russian spirituality. This is not, of course, a call for a return to Orthodox religion, but simply a tentative and melancholy observation. I believe it is this more than anything that Soviet (or Russian) audiences respond to in the film, though they are probably not precisely aware of it. It is true that the final scene of the film—in which Petro rams the murderers' car off a dock into the river (more melodramatic than the ending of the script)—brings a wild roar of audience approval. But this unfortunate though "necessary" warning to criminals is hardly the essential message of the film and I doubt that many ordinary Russian viewers seriously take it to be such. The somewhat more subtle treatment of Petro's vengeance in the script allows the perceptive reader to view the triumph of the truck over the Volga sedan as the ultimate triumph of rural values over city values. But it is the religious or spiritual theme, I believe, that is the key to understanding "Kalina krasnaia," or, more particularly, Egor. This may be demonstrated adequately enough by the script alone, without need for further references to the film.

It is my main contention that the story of Egor Prokudin makes sense psychologically and literarily only if we see it as a modern hagiography modeled on the ancient Russian saints' lives. What this means is that Egor's often strangely unaccountable pacifistic behavior is not to be seen as a wholly valid psychological portrait of a certain kind of victim of Soviet social forces, but rather as the embodiment of an ancient Russian ideal—the ideal of kenotic martyrdom exemplified by Boris and Gleb, the first saints canonized by the Russian Church (within a century after its founding in 988 AD). What is of interest in Boris and Gleb is not that the young princes were cruelly murdered by their elder brother in a feud over the throne, but that they *yielded voluntarily to death*. Ultimately, this act of nonresistance becomes a national Russian feature, which G.P. Fedotov in *The Russian Religious Mind* considers "an authentic religious discovery of the newly-converted Russian Christians."[11] This national religious ideal is something that many if not most Russians have always been able to respect, including even modern Soviet Russians completely lacking in religious education. This is not to say that many Russians actually follow this ideal, or that many Russians would even praise such behavior if they encountered it in daily life—but if this behavior is presented in the proper inspiring context, as I contend "Kalina krasnaia" to be, then these same ordinary Russians will respond to it with genuine admiration. But Americans, for instance, have no such national religious ideal, and for this reason would find the figure of Egor Prokudin rather difficult to accept as an archetype, to say nothing of his role at the literal level. Clearly, Egor could not be a popular hero in the United States.

I will not insist that this view of "Kalina krasnaia" is absolutely correct; I will say only that it provides an artistic justification for Shukshin's treatment of his hero. Thus, at the literal level, Egor seems oddly inconsistent in that he makes frequent threats against his enemies, yet never carries them out. He pushes Kolya off the porch, for instance—yet simply walks away from him when the latter wields a heavy stick. And Egor clearly is not a coward. He puts a wrench in his pocket before walking across the field toward the hated Fat Lip—yet never uses it (and this after the rather fierce threats he had conveyed earlier to Fat Lip's messenger). Shukshin finds it totally unnecessary to explain why Egor does not fight for his life. And Egor goes to his death literally without a word. At the literal level, Egor is inadequately accounted for; but at the allegorical or symbolical level he follows a recognizable pattern. Allegorically, he is a disciple of the Russian Christ—both as an innocent sufferer in the tradition of the suffering Russian people (the *narod*),[12] and as a voluntary sufferer in the kenotic tradition of Boris and Gleb. But in the Russian kenotic tradition, the Christian is not merely a follower of Christ, but an imitator of him. One is saved only through suffering in the image of a meek and suffering Christ.

Egor is thus additionally recognizable as a Russian Christ figure. Whether Shukshin consciously accorded him this final recognition is difficult to say; it would seem unlikely; yet, in its choice of language, Shukshin's story does convey that impression. For instance, at the end of the scene in the cemetery (following Egor's self-sacrificial flight to save two men he did not even like), Egor says, "I'll go off on my own, like an honest John. There's got to be some place where I can lay my head. There's just got to be, right? Right!" Shukshin then emphasizes the essential part of this utterance in a separate short paragraph: "So he set out to look for a place to lay his head." What is suggested here, of course, are the words of Jesus in Matthew 8:20: ". . . The foxes have holes, and the birds of the air have nests; but

207

the Son of man hath not where to lay his head." Furthermore, Shukshin had been careful to call attention earlier to the cemetery crosses lit up by the distant lights of vehicles, with "the shadows of the crosses, long and deformed," sweeping over the ground. Clearly, Egor is marked for symbolic crucifixion, a Christ-figure whose very name, *Gore* ('woe') marks him as "a man of sorrows, despised and rejected of men" (Isaiah 53:3) who will not in this allegory ever find a place to rest his head except in death.

In the original Russian, incidentally, Shukshin uses the verb *pritknut'* *(golovu)* or *pritknut'sia,* rather than *priklonit' (golovu)* [lay (his head)], which appears in the Russian translation of Matthew 8:20. Egor's speech should therefore be translated as "There's got to be some place where I can stick my head." I decided not to be quite that literal after reading Robert Daglish's astonishing translation of this passage: "There must be somewhere for the son of man to lay his head."

Though Daglish, living and working in the Soviet Union, seems clearly to have recognized Egor as a Christ figure, I doubt that many other Russian readers of Shukshin's text have been quick to see the parallel. Curiously, Daglish does not otherwise seem to emphasize this parallel when he has the linguistic opportunity to do so. For instance, when Lyuba is discussing Egor with Zoya and her parents (while Egor and Petro are bathing), she says to her mother and Zoya: "Ne pugaite vy menia, radi Khrista." I translated this, close to literally, as "Don't frighten me, for the love of Christ"; Daglish chose the much more commonplace, "For goodness sake, don't frighten me."[13] In the same scene, Lyuba's father denounces his wife and Zoya for wanting to send Egor away: "Vot tak da!... Sovsem uzh nekhristi kakie to." When I translated this passage, I seized upon the obsolete meaning of the word *nekhrist',* 'unbeliever' (literally, "not of Christ"), to have the old man say: "What a thing to do! It goes against Christ!" While Daglish leaned more toward the modern meaning ('brute, hard-hearted person') to produce: "How about that?... What kind of hell-hags are they!" In an earlier scene with Egor and Lyuba in the tearoom, just after Egor has reminded Lyuba of his sad nickname, Gore, he mentions how he completely detested the "stinking money" *(den'gi voniuchie)* that he stole.[14] Lyuba replies: "Preziraesh', a idesh' iz-za nikh na takuiu strast'." She uses the word *strast'* here in its secondary meaning of "horror." That is: "You hate it [the money], yet because of it you suffer such horror" [literally, "go to such horror"–to prison]. But *strast'* also means "passion"–or the Passion (the suffering and martyrdom) of Christ, as in English–so that Lyuba can very well be understood to say, as I have it in my translation: "You hate it, yet because of it you end up being crucified!" Daglish misses any opportunity to be interesting here by his flat interpretation: "You may scorn it [the filthy lucre], but look what risks you take to get it."

There are other, more obvious references to religion at interesting points in the narrative. For instance, at the onset of Egor's speech in praise of spring at the "orgy," one of his listeners remarks that "it won't be long until Trinity Sunday." This gives the whole affair a religious, indeed a Christian, context, so that Egor's drunken and sentimental declaration of love for his motley auditors is transformed into a Russian Sermon on the Mount. The curious debauchers, the "dregs" of a Siberian provincial city (who would not be thought of as sinners in any country except the USSR, probably) are made innocent in the presence of their unlikely jailbird Christ.

The continued emphasis on the season of spring by Egor continually puts before us the theme of regeneration, resurrection, Easter. There is no coherent presentation of Christian dogma, but most of its elements seem to be present. It is mixed in some degree with ancient Slavic animism (the feminine spirit of the birch trees); with old-Bolshevik enthusiasm (the loyalty and sacrifice of Lyuba's father); and with rural collectivism, which, for all the trauma of its modern inception in the form of the kolkhoz, has its roots in the traditional peasant commune. It is difficult to speak analytically of the Christian element in Shukshin's philosophy, since he presents this element almost exclusively through allusion, symbol, analogy and allegory. (The closest thing to a direct treatment of the meaning of Christ to Shukshin appears in the story " 'I Believe!' ")

Lyuba, of course, is also an allegorical, or at least symbolic figure. Her full name, Lyubov', in Russian means *love*. She may be seen in part as an idealized Russian feminine spirit, linked with the ancient figure of fertile mother earth; her relationship with Egor clearly contains a sexual element, although Shukshin adamantly withholds from both Lyuba and Egor, in all their human dealings, any true sexual embrace. We are left with chastity as an essential feature of Shukshinian (or Russian) Christianity. Lyuba may best be seen as symbolic of an idealized Russia—a Russia traditionally believed by Russian Christians to be the only nation where true Christianity exists. In her dealings with Egor, Lyuba explicitly follows the admonition of Jesus in Matthew 25:40 to do for every man as one would do for him; for "inasmuch as ye have done it unto one of the least of these my brethren, ye have done it unto me." That is, she came to Egor in prison through her letters; she comforted him in his sickness (seen as the exhaustion of a horse being driven up a mountain) when he arrived at her door seeking rest; he was truly a stranger to her, yet she took him in; she clothed him (one recalls the otherwise inexplicable scene where she insists he wear her husband's cast-off underdrawers); she gives him drink; she feeds him.

A Soviet critic named Konstantin Vanshenkin expresses amazement at Lyuba's behavior:

> This sober, intelligent village woman from a respectable home and a respectable family who refused to tolerate a drunken husband carries on a correspondence with a jailed criminal whom she doesn't know and invites him to join her when his sentence is up. For some reason most people accept this without question.

209

But only a woman in extreme circumstances, experiencing a woman's despair, could do such a thing, and undoubtedly such a woman would come from the town, from a different milieu, possessing some characteristics of former urban semi-educated lower middle classes. A village woman? Hardly credible.[15]

But of course her behavior is not credible, for she fulfills a sadly impossible Christian ideal:

When the Son of man shall come in his glory, and all the holy angels with him, then shall he sit upon the throne of his glory:

And before him shall be gathered all nations: and he shall separate them one from another, as a shepherd divides his sheep from the goats:

And he shall set the sheep on his right hand, but the goats on the left.

Then shall the King say unto them on his right hand, Come, ye blessed of my Father, inherit the kingdom prepared for you from the foundation of the world:

For I was an hungered, and ye gave me meat: I was thirsty, and ye gave me drink: I was a stranger, and ye took me in:

Naked, and ye clothed me: I was sick, and ye visited me: I was in prison, and ye came unto me.

Then shall the righteous answer him, saying, Lord, when saw we thee an hungered, and fed thee? or thirsty, and gave thee drink?

When saw we thee a stranger, and took thee in? or naked and clothed thee?

Or when saw we thee sick, or in prison, and came unto thee?

And the King shall answer and say unto them, Verily I say unto you, Inasmuch as ye have done it unto one of the least of these my brethren, ye have done it unto me. [Matthew 25:31-40]

Once one becomes convinced of Egor's identity with Christ, either as the least of men or the greatest of men, one is able to find many parallels wth the Biblical story of Jesus in Shukshin's tale. Petro, for instance, as Egor's loyal supporter, is easily recognized as the counterpart to Peter. And Egor's somewhat strange refusal to acknowledge his mother may be seen as paralleling a similar refusal by Jesus:

While he yet talked to the people, behold, his mother and his brethren stood without, desiring to speak with him.

Then one said unto him, Behold, thy mother and thy brethren stand without, desiring to speak with thee.

But he answered and said unto him that told him, Who is my mother? and who are my brethren? [Matthew 12:46-48]

But Lyuba's extraordinary compassion for Egor's mother, as well as for Egor, symbolizes the historical love of Russians for Mary no less than for her son. ("Lyuba leaned over and embraced him, as she had just embraced his mother, tenderly and capably... She laid his head on her breast. 'Oh, God!... Why are you like this? Why are you both so loveable?" She burst into tears . . . .") Lucienne, of course, corresponds to Mary Magdalene. And she is present at the shooting of Egor just as Mary Magdalene was one of those present at the crucifixion of Jesus. Doubtless many other parallels may be found. I leave them to others to discover—but with the warning that Shukshin's Christian allegory is neither exact nor complete. It is primarily a literary device, and much of it may be accidental. Though the parallels seem quite obvious to me now as I write about them, I recall only too clearly that I saw not a solitary one of them on my first reading of the script or my first viewing of the film. I found the film perfectly enjoyable and understandable at the simplest level of human interactions; I felt no need for saving symbolism.

The published scripts seems to require the symbolism for literary completeness, but one must resist seeing in Shukshin's Russian Christ figure a direct statement of religious doctrine or an implicit statement of political protest. Shukshin's basic message is little different from that of the great writers in the humanistic tradition over the past several centuries: all men are Christ; we must love one another or die. There is no particular reason why a modern writer from the Soviet Union who has chosen to dramatize this message in his last and greatest work should not be honored for it in his own country.

NOTES

1. "The Red Guelder Rose: The Story of the Film," *Soviet Literature*, 9(1975), 56-122.

2. Most of this information is given in Vladimir Dal', *Tolkovyi slovar'* (reprint of 1880-82 edition) at *kalina* and *most*.

3. According to Iurii Tiurin, " 'Kalina krasnaia'–kinopovest' i fil'm," *Moskva*, 4(1976), p. 199.

4. See "Nachal'nik," *Novyi mir*, 1 (1967), 158-162, which also concerns a former convict from a labor colony.

5. Information from Yuri Kuznetsov, curator of a film archive in Leningrad, letter to me of November 19, 1976; the composer was a man named Frenkel'. I asked a number of other Russians about the song; most were convinced it was an old folk tune.

6. " 'Kalina krasnaia'-kinopovest' i fil'm," *Moskva*, 4(1976), p. 198.

7. Letter to me of September 7, 1976. Like others, she seems not to be aware that the song is of recent origin.

8. For instance, 200,000 copies of the two-volume edition of Shukshin's works (1975), in which "Kalina krasnaia" appears, were printed.

9. *The Russians* (New York, 1976), p. 382. Even if Smith's report is not true, it still makes an interesting story: for if it is actually believed by Russians, it is no less useful than the purported fact would be in explaining current Russian attitudes.

10. "Vasili Shukshin's Last Interview," *Soviet Literature*, 4(1975), p.119.

11. *The Russian Religious Mind* (New York, 1960), p. 104.

12. Egor's role as a symbolic representative of the suffering *narod* is especially emphasized in the film, when Fat Lip says of Egor after the murder: "On chelovekom

i ne byl. On byl muzhik. A ikh na Rusi mnogo." [He was not even a man. He was a muzhik. And of these Russia has many.] This speech does not appear in the published film script. It is interesting that Fat Lip uses the ancient word *Rus'* here rather than the more modern word *Rossia* (to say nothing of "Soviet Union"). (I have used as the text for this speech the version of it quoted by Iurii Tiurin in " 'Kalina krasnaia'—kinopovest' i fil'm,' " *Moskva*, 4[1976], p. 194.)

13. I chose the same words, "for the love of Christ," to translate Lyuba's expletive "Khristom bogom," in her plea near the end of the narrative (just after she and Egor had sung "Kalina krasnaia" together for the first time), that Egor be frank with her: "Please, for the love of Christ, tell me they're not going to do anything to you." Daglish renders this (more appropriately now) as: "Please, for Jesus Christ's sake, tell me they won't do you any harm."

14. Here Daglish chooses to be Biblical (while I do not) by translating *den'gi voniuchie* as "filthy lucre" (See I Timothy 3:3, 8; Titus 1:7; I Peter 5:2, etc.)

15. K. Vanshenko, "A Few Criticisms," *Soviet Literature*, 9(1975), p. 130 (translation of his article "Nekotorye proschety," *Voprosy literatury*, 7[1974], 70-74). Vanshenko has the perception to realize that Egor is "surrounded by strange, half-real personages"; he finds the gang of thieves to be portrayed so "grotesquely," that they ought not to be capable of committing murder. (Here again, Fat Lip is indeed not real, but allegorical, evidently a personification of Evil, over which even Christ may not triumph, except through his death.) Despite his prodigious grumblings, Vanshenko is able to praise Shukshin: "Not the Shukshin who stands behind [the film], but the Shukshin who is on the screen. His acting is brilliant, he takes the whole thing in hand, often taking in hand the director and script-writer who, as often happens, stand in his way. The marvel is that he himself is all three." [pp. 130-131] As for "the many faults so rarely to be found in the work of this outstanding artist," Vanshenko suggests that "perhaps the author wanted to present and seek the answer to questions troubling him, and to do it on the basis of country people and country life. But the scope of the problem is too great to fit into the narrow framework of country life. This causes general distortion." [p. 131]

Michel Heller

VASILY SHUKSHIN: IN SEARCH OF FREEDOM[1]

In an interview published after the writer's death, Vasily Shukshin, summarizing what he had done, said somewhat disparagingly: "Well, what a result! For fifteen years of work, several slight little books, eight or nine printers' sheets apiece... this isn't the work of a professional writer." Today, now that death has called for a summary, one can say after surveying, even superficially, all that Shukshin did, that he was unfair to himself. He was unfair not only because in speaking about the "result," his creative work, he put between brackets, as it were, his cinematographic work, which is inseparably linked with his literary activity.

In one of the articles which appeared after his death (criticism had treated the writer with complete indifference, but grew passionately fond of him after his death), is the following: "For some reason we were ashamed to apply to the best books of Shukshin the same standards we apply, let us say, to Leskov, Bunin, and even Chekhov. Only now, when Shukshin is not here with us, are we beginning to realize that the highest standards are appropriate and not beyond Vasily Shukshin's power."[2]

It is totally obvious that in Soviet criticism, which observes with undue strictness the Table of Ranks, a comparison of Shukshin with the "classics" cannot be an accident explained only by the death of the writer. The publication in 1975 of a two-volume collection of Shukshin's works (an edition of 200,000 copies), the one-volume *Brat moi* [Brother of mine] (an edition of 300,000 copies), the dedication of two issues of *Roman-gazeta* (editions of two million each) to stories by the writer, the separate publication of film scripts, and finally, the award of the highest state prize, the Lenin Prize, for the film "Kalina krasnaia" ["Snowball Berry Red"] bears witness to the interest of leaders of Soviet culture in the work of Vasily Shukshin. On the other hand, the exceptional popularity of "Kalina krasnaia," which was completed by Shukshin shortly before his death, has drawn readers' attention to his prose.

A rare phenomenon is before us—a Soviet artist esteemed simultaneously by authorities and readers alike. An explanation must be sought both in the writer's work and in his biography.

In Soviet literature at the very end of the 1950's and the beginning of the 1960's, a genre was revived, it would seem, that had been buried a long time ago: rural prose. In the middle of the 1930's rural literature lost its right to exist (for many rural writers this literally meant death) and its place was taken by kolkhoz literature. The rebirth of the genre was unexpected. The lexicon was unexpected, coming from another epoch: muzhik, village, land, church, soul. One of the important factors which supported the

213

development of rural prose was the desire of leaders of Soviet literature to find a remedy for the so-called young people's prose which was engendering fear by its "modern" form, the visibility of its search for new, unconventional paths in life, and its enthusiasm for jazz and jeans.

Vasily Shukshin was one of those new young authors who arrived with a hero unlike the popular "city boys" of Aksenov, Gladilin, and Bitov. Vasily Shukshin was thirty when his first stories appeared (1959). By this time he had been able to work a little on a kolkhoz in his native village, Srostki, to serve in the navy (1949-53), and to work a short time as director of an evening school for village young people (1953-54). Legends circulate today about Shukshin's appearance in Moscow and entrance into the Faculty of Directing at the State Institute of Cinematography, and these legends recall legends about young Esenin's appearance in St. Petersburg salons on the eve of World War I. They say—no doubt Shukshin himself said all this first—that during the entrance exam he declared that he saw the word "director" *(rezhisser)* for the first time, and they also say that his choice of the institute was explained by the persistent persuasion of a person he accidentally met on the street who maintained: "You have a social look, the rest will come."

Shukshin indeed had a "social look" (he said to himself: "I have a soldier's face."). This became obvious when viewers saw him for the first time on the screen in the role of a driver and demobilized soldier, Fedor, in Marlen Khutsiev's film, "Dva Fedora" [Two Fedors]. The film came out in 1959. Simultaneously, the writer's first stories were published. It is worth noting that Shukshin would give his stories both to *Novyi mir* [New World], the stronghold of liberalism, and to *Oktiabr'* [October], the organ of conservative forces. This practice of simultaneously publishing in rival journals was very rare at that time, and testifies to the need for "writers from the people," and to the indefiniteness of Shukshin's position.

Shukshin finished at the Faculty of Directing in 1960, but worked the following four years in the movies as an actor. In 1964 he shot his first full-length film, for which he himself wrote the script, using a situation taken from his published short stories. The hero of the film—Pashka Kolokolnikov—was the first draft of a common Shukshin character: the young driver, a person (in the words of the writer) with an "elemental way of life," moved by immediate feelings and not by what is rational. By naming his film "Zhivet takoi paren' " [There lives such a fellow], Shukshin wanted to signify the typicality of his hero. Ten years later, surveying what he had accomplished, Shukshin referred to his first film negatively, saying of the hero: "Too happy *[blagopoluchen]."* This attribute relates fully as well to the heroes of short stories Shukshin wrote in the first half of the 1960s. Before us are stories fresh in language, sharp-sighted, with details noticed in everyday life, but also traditional, about "rural dwellers" who overcome, without special effort, several still uneliminated difficulties of kolkhoz life.

Shukshin's uniqueness in Soviet literature lies primarily in the organic relationship of his purely literary and cinematographic activity. What immediately stands out in his literary works is the visual, cinematographic concreteness, and, in his films, the literary quality: the desire and ability to render the character of personages first and foremost by the word. The writer Shukshin's uniqueness is that he saw his hero not only in himself, but also outside of himself, not only on paper, but also on the screen. It is not surprising, therefore, that he expressed his main ideas and his central hero best of all in his two final films, in which he was simultaneously author of the script, director, and leading actor.

The year Shukshin died—1974—was also the year that his collection of short stories, *Besedy pri iasnoi lune* [Conversations under a clear moon], was published and "Kalina krasnaia" [Snowball berry red] opened. The year of his death saw the birth of a great writer. *Besedy pri iasnoi lune* and "Kalina krasnaia" allowed one to see all of a sudden, as it were, that everything written and filmed earlier was part of a vast canvas, the meaning of which was unclear without the final works: his last book and his last film. The artist's death, which forced us to sum up his career, allowed us to see in his works that which critics and readers acquainted with Shukshin's short stories and films had not noticed in them one by one, separately. It became evident that Shukshin had arrived in Soviet literature with a new, or perhaps it is better to say, unexpected hero. Analyzing this hero permits us to understand the reasons for his popularity and to see the place which Shukshin will occupy in Russian literature.

Vasily Shukshin draws one and the same character; he always has one hero. This hero is a Russian muzhik in search of freedom. Freedom, *volia,* is the writer's key word. We practically never encounter the other word for freedom, *svoboda.* It is always *volia.* One cannot consider these words fully synonymous in Russian. In Dal''s dictionary, *Tolkovyi slovar'* (1880-82), the word *svoboda* occupies less than one half of a page, while the word *volia* has two full pages. In Ozhegov's contemporary dictionary, *Slovar' russkogo iazyka,* a note is given for the expressions *na voliu* and *na vole* [at liberty]: "colloquial." This should signify that these expressions have a "non-literary" character. The word *volia,* which almost disappeared from the contemporary Russian literary language, returns in the works of Shukshin as a symbol of disappearing features of the Russian national character. The word *svoboda,* in those cases where it appears, carries signs of its urban origin, while the word *volia* [which now has the primary denotation of "will"] enters as a rural, Russian word.

Shukshin's hero searches for "freedom" *(volia).* Seeking to understand the sense of this word, the reason a muzhik strives for it, Shukshin is not limited to the contemporary scene. He turns to history. And his hero acquires two hypostases. We meet two different embodiments of him—one in the short stories and the other in the larger works.

In 1965 Shukshin wrote the historical novel, *Lyubaviny* [The Lyubavin family], the action of which takes place in the Altai region in the 1920s, right after the end of the Civil War. In 1968, the journal *Iskusstvo kino* [The art of film] published Shukshin's film script, "Ia pereshel dat' vam voliu" [I have come to give you freedom], which deals with Stepan Razin, the Don Cossack who headed the 1667 revolt and was quartered in Moscow on Red Square in June of 1671. A favorite hero of Russian folklore who became a symbol, in the Russian consciousness, of a rebel and free man, Stepan Razin did not release Shukshin till the end of his life. Up to his last days Shukshin thought about the film which he was not allowed to make. In 1971 he reworked the script into a novel, strengthening in the image of the rebellious leader the tragic features of a free man who sees himself surrounded by slaves. The film-narrative, "Kalina krasnaia," which is set in the late 1960s, transfers Shukshin's favorite hero to our own days. The robber and insurgent Stepan Razin becomes the recidivist thief Egor Prokudin.

The seventeenth century; a peasant revolt on the Volga; the 1920s: the Civil War is over, but Soviet authority must still be consolidated in the remote Altai taiga; finally, our own days—a labor camp, a community of thieves, an Altai village. And there is always the quest of the Russian muzhik for "freedom," for what he considers freedom.

Stepan Razin in Shukshin's novel is a free person for whom freedom is an absolutely indispensable feeling, for whom freedom is a holiday for the soul: "If I were a faithful comrade, then my conscience would rest easy. Then I would be free. And that's all there is to it." Stepan is free, but around him are slaves. The ataman tells his cousin Frol: "You, Frol, are a slave... You were already a little slave when you were still sitting in your mother's arms. And you have servile thoughts, although they seem true. They are true, but they are servile. And you don't know any others." "I have come to give you freedom," announces Stepan. And he discovers that slaves do not need freedom. Doubting, torn by contradictory thoughts, tormented by grief, drowning the grief in vodka, Shukshin's Stepan Razin presents a tragic and very contemporary image. Stepan's tragedy is in feeling the impossibility of giving others freedom. Stepan Razin finds absolute freedom on the block, quartered by the executioner. He turns out to be stronger than the executioner. In a surprising way, the hero of Shukshin's novel, a Russian rebel from the seventeenth century, turns out to be similar to an American rebel of the twentieth century, the hero of Ken Kesey's novel, *One Flew Over the Cuckoo's Nest.*

In the novel *Lyubaviny,* the rebel Razin, while searching for freedom, is transformed into the Lyubavin family, Siberian muzhiks who are defending their property against Soviet authority. The Lyubavins are bandits, plunderers, and killers. Many similar Siberians inhabit many Soviet novels.

Shukshin wrote *Lyubaviny* in the tried and tested tradition of the Soviet "Siberian" novel. He condemns his heroes. But in contrast with other writers, he simultaneously shows that the Lyubavins—bandits and murderers—also are searching for freedom, a holiday for the soul. It is just that they have lost their way on this search. They got lost, they perished, and they are condemned. But the writer gives one of the bandits his father's name, Makar. The name of another—Egor—he took for the hero of "Kalina krasnaia," a role he played himself.

The "story" (the writer called it a *kinopovest'*) begins with a scene in the camp from which Egor Prokudin is escaping. The scene closes with the words: "Ahead—is freedom." And again—a search for freedom, a search for the soul's holiday: in the company of thieves, in drunken revelry, in pitiable depravity, in the love of good, dear Lyuba, and, finally, in kolkhoz work. Egor does not find freedom. He does not find it in the old life of a thief, which seemed free before. Nor in the new life of a kolkhoz tractor driver. In discussing "Kalina krasnaia," the film's author admitted: "It's horrible for Egor to believe that till the end of his days there'd be only one course—plowing and planting; for Egor this was perhaps more horrible than prison."[3] Egor ends it all with suicide. The writer uses a banal narrative device: the bandits, whom Egor leaves after deciding to lead an honorable life, are trying to kill him out of revenge. But Egor actually commits suicide. And concerning this, Shukshin says: "I assume that Egor himself was seeking death. I simply lacked the daring to present this unambiguously... What is more, by virtue of a concrete soul's own laws, life loses its sense."[4]

"Kalina krasnaia," a story of yet another unsuccessful attempt to find freedom, ends with a symbolic scene: "Egor died. And there he lay, a Russian peasant, on his native steppe, not far from home... He lay with his cheek pressed to the earth, as though he were listening to something that only he could hear." He returns to the land, he returns to the land—the Russian peasant, Egor Prokudin, killed by the city.

In the film, the murderer of Egor, the bandit Guboshlep [Fat Lip], says even more succinctly: "Egor never was a real bandit, he always remained a muzhik, and there are a lot of muzhiks." At the beginning of the story, Egor, who has left the camp, is reciting Esenin's verses: "Thou hast come, my black destruction—Unafraid I rush to meet theee.... O city, in your discord cruel, You called us filth and liars.... As hunters torture a wolf, While the beaters close in like a vise..." These lines, written in 1922 by the "last poet of the village," are recited fifty years later by a peasant's son who has become an urban bandit—as his own epitaph, as a prophecy of his death.

Egor Prokudin occupies a special place in Shukshin's creative work. He is not only a man "at the turning point," a rural muzhik who has left for the city, but having preserved a peasant's dream about freedom, he is also a "character at the turning point," and in him features of Razin and Makar Lyubavin are combined with features of heroes of Shukshin's short

217

stories.

This is the second hypostasis of the hero. Rereading Shukshin's short stories, one cannot help attending to the evolution of their main character: the happy hero of mediocre rural prose acquires tragic features. The Soviet critic Lev Anninskii even tried to identify precisely the "date when the new Shukshin, or better, the real Shukshin, cut through the fabric of the first short stories."[5] Anninskii considers February of 1964 the birth-date of the "real Shukshin," when on the pages of the journal *Iskusstvo kino* there appeared a pivotal and extremely significant story, "Kritiki" [The critics].

The story is interesting: an old man from the country, who has seen an actor on television portraying a carpenter, cannot bear "untruth," is indignant that the actor does not "even know how to hold an axe," and breaks the television with his boot. As a preliminary, he has done some heavy drinking. There are actually many features of the Shukshin hero in this character: passion, which makes life colorful, love for film, love of truth, and the feeling that falsehood is "urban deception." But the old man of "Kritikii" is only a particle of the Shukshin hero. A feature of this hero is his many-sidedness. He is formed from characters of dozens of stories, as a mosaic portrait made up of a multitude of little stones. Similar features are essential to each of these characters, but only all together can they create Shukshin's hero. The first time this becomes evident, I think, is in the collection of short stories, *Kharaktery* [Characters]. The next collection— *Besedy pri iasnoi lune* [Conversations under a clear moon] (1974)—marks the highest attainment of Shukshin; in this collection are the best stories of this writer, and his main ideas are set forth. Shukshin chose the title of his last book apparently through association with the title of a film by the Japanese film director, Mizoguchi: "Skazki tumannoi luny posle dozhdia" [Tales of a misty moon after a rain]. Shukshin replaced "tales" *(skazki)* with the more prosaic "conversations" *(besedy),* but in the first story there is talk of a tale. He replaced "misty moon" with "clear moon," but in the story which gives the collection its name we read: "There was such clarity around, such silence and clarity, that you don't feel quite yourself if you take a good look and listen carefully. It's unsettling somehow. In your chest there's something... As if something hot would roll up toward your heart from below and beat softly in your temples. And in your ears the blood would pound with each beat." And under the "clear moon" Shukshin's hero is restless, he listens carefully, he takes a good look into his inner world, into an anxiety he cannot understand that is inexplicably rising in his chest.

In 1972 Shukshin produced a film based on his own short stories and called it "Strannye lyudi" [Strange people]. The hero of the writer's short stories is first and foremost a strange person—separated from others by his "strangeness," or as Shukshin expresses it, by his "fancy" *(prixot').* The strangeness of Shukshin's hero is in his constant search for something elusive, unclear, perhaps non-existent, but painfully needed. The failure of the search engenders dissatisfaction, loneliness, grief—the feelings tormenting the heroes of Shukshin's short stories.

They suffer because they feel out of place—out of place in the city where they arrived only yesterday, leaving all their roots in the country. And out of place in the country, poisoned by their stay in the city, even if it was only temporary, or poisoned by the urban word: this hell is spread by the newspapers, radio, and television. "Vanya, why are you here?" ["Vania, ty kak zdes'?"] is the title of one of Shukshin's short stories about a country lad in the city. The writer addresses this question to all of his characters: why are you here? what are you doing here? "Here" means "in life," or "on earth." Shukshin shows the clash of two different and, in principle, antagonistic civilizations: the rural and the urban. Rural civilization resists: in the story "Kritiki," the old man breaks the television with his boot. In the story "Srezal" [Flunked] (1970), the hero, a rural muzhik, Gleb Kapustin, defeats city dwellers in a verbal duel. But he defeats them with an urban weapon—the senseless urban word. And the victory turns into defeat.

Shukshin's hero is related to the hero of Mikhail Zoshchenko's stories of the 1920's: thrown into the city by the Revolution, Zoshchenko's heroes painfully felt the loss of their roots and they sensed their own imaginary (as the writer shows and the characters subconsciously feel) movement up the social ladder. The comic in the situation of Zoshchenko's characters is also tragic, just as the comic in the situation of Shukshin's characters is tragic. Shukshin's heroes, like Zoshchenko's heroes, live in a world of changing values. In this world Shukshin's heroes represent values which have died out: honor, the good, and goodness. Shukshin does not idealize his hero. He does not look for positive or negative features in him—a unique trait in Soviet literature. The writer shows a person who senses an emptiness in his chest. It is said that people who have lost an arm or a leg feel a pain in the amputated part of their body till the end of their life. Shukshin's hero feels a pain in the place where man used to have a soul.

The "strangeness" of the characters in the short stories—this is their search for a soul. Discovering it should give one freedom. The "fancies" of Shukshin's heroes are strange. Nikolai Grigorevich Kuzovnikov (" 'Vybiraiu derevniu na zhitel'stvo' " ["I am choosing a village to live in"]) is a storekeeper in a big city, living well, in good circumstances. Several years before, he has suddenly begun to go to the train station each Saturday after work, where he talks with the muzhiks, asks them about a good village to move to. Then there is Bronka Pupkov (" 'Mil' pardon, madam!' " [" 'Mille pardons, Madame!' "]), the rural hunter who, each time city dwellers arrive to do a little hunting, tells a shocking story about how he, Bronka Pupkov, tried to kill Hitler. Monya Kvasov ("Upornyi" ["The Obstinate One"]) builds a perpetuum mobile. The drunkard and remarkable joiner Semka Rys ("Master") suddenly discovers for himself the surprising beauty of an abandoned church. Nikolai Grigor'evich Kuzovnikov does not intend to move anywhere. Bronka Pupkov has completely invented the story about the attempted assassination. It is proven to Monya Kvasov that eternal motion is unrealizable. Papers are shown to Semka Rys which maintain that the church which stunned him with its beauty is only a copy of ancient temples. But for Shukshin's heroes, the boring reality of everyday life has no meaning. Each of them gets for himself—for an instant, even an hour or two a week or a month—a holiday of the soul, freedom. Nikolai Grigorevich always returns from the station on foot, "He walked away after great agitation. Ever so quietly his soul still ached, and he felt fatigue." And, after all, he was only "choosing a village to live in." Bronka Pupkov, after the story, "walked off to the water. And there he sat for hours, alone on the bank, in the grip of his traumatic experience." But, after all, he had only told a funny story about an imaginary attempt to assassinate Hitler. In like manner, Gleb Kapustin ("Srezal") experiences an "instant of freedom"; for him the duel with city dwellers was also a "holiday for the soul." And telling the surprising story of how the director of a city restaurant fell in love with him, Sanka Zhuravlev ("Versiia" [Version]) "was nervous, irritated, and anxious."

" 'Vybiraiu derevniu na zhitel'stvo' " ends with the words: "He could no longer help going to the train station—it became a need. If someone would make him feel ashamed, his oldest son, for example, or forbid him to go there, forbid him to write down addresses, to speak with muzhiks... But no, how could you forbid him? He would only begin to go there on the sly. Now he couldn't get along without it." Bronka Pupkov "could not get along without it" as well—even though he was vaguely threatened with being held criminally responsible "for the distortion of history." And other characters of Shukshin's short stories cannot get along without their "fancies," or "strangeness."

The "strangeness" of Shukshin's heroes, of his hero, is that he is a story-teller, that he tells those around him—and himself—a tale *(skazka)*. The hero of the short stories lives simultaneously in real life and in an imaginary life. Moreover, the imaginary life can be more important to him than real life. Only in his imagination, only in his tale, can he become the person he wants to be, can he find his own real self, can he find what he is looking for. The tale gives him a chance to break away—for a moment, for a day, for an hour or two a week—to freedom. The tale becomes a surrogate for freedom, a semblance of freedom, without ceasing to be indispensable to the heroes of the short stories. The short stories become tales told by Shukshin's hero, searching for a holiday of the soul, searching for freedom.

Vasily Shukshin wrote more than one hundred short stories, and populated them with hundreds of characters. Only one of them got a firm hold on freedom, only one of them was happy. Kostya Valikov ("Alesha Beskonvoinyi") was called Alesha Beskonvoinyi ("Alesha Without-Escort") in the country. In the sharp struggle with kolkhoz authorities, in the cruel war with his wife, Alesha fought for the right, for himself, not to work on Saturday and Sunday. "What did he do on Saturday? On Saturday he heated the bathhouse. That's all. Nothing else." But this is quite a bit. To Alesha Beskonvoinyi the Saturday bath becomes a tale. For one day a week the tale becomes a fact. This is enough, however, for the muzhiks to nickname their fellow-villager "Alesha Beskonvoinyi": "for his rare, in our days, irresponsibility and unmanageability." Alesha was not liberated, but he became "escortless," i.e., conditionally free for a short time. Then he had to return to custody, to bondage.

There are two embodiments of Shukshin's hero. The first type: Stepan Razin, Makar Lyubavin, and Egor Prokudin, who give their life in search of freedom, in search of the holiday that burns the soul. The other: Alesha Beskonvoinyi, escaping from custody for two days a week, arranging a holiday of the soul in the bathhouse. The comparison can seem comic. It is tragic. The comic element is a result of the contrast between efforts spent and the results. The tragedy is in the outcome of the story: even for the "free" Saturday bath, you have to wage a battle: moreover, this battle ended with Alesha's victory only because his brother, waging war for "freedom," committed suicide. The tragedy is also that of all the characters of Shukshin's stories; only one, Kostya Valikov, succeeds in going "unescorted."

The role which the tale plays in the life of Shukshin's heroes, the intensity with which they live through it, the excitement that they experience in telling it, allows us to compare the tale to a prayer. It is a strange prayer, but the heroes, after all, are also strange. Nikolai Grigorevich "prays" at the station, in its dirtiest corner, Bronka "prays" on the river bank, Alesha Beskonvoinyi "prays" in the bathhouse. Semka Rys discovers his tale, beauty in a real temple, in an inactive, destroyed church. Maksim Yarikov (" 'Veruiu!' " ['I Believe!']) prays in his neighbor's house, but with a real priest, except that, instead of singing church music, the priest sings a poem by Esenin. Having been drinking himself, and having given a drink to Maksim, the priest forces the man who has come to him with a question about life's meaning to repeat: "I believe!" Maksim repeats: "I believe! In aviation, in the mechanization of agriculture, in the scientific revolution! In space and weightlessness.... I believe! I believe that soon everyone will gather in huge stinking cities! I believe that they will suffocate there and rush back to the open fields... I believe!" There is an inexorable logic in the enumeration of objects of "faith": one can believe in a lot, but in the final analysis you arrive in open country. And it is no accident that the priest sings a poem by Esenin about the maple covered with ice: written a month before the poet's suicide, it is a declaration of love to trees, to the birch. In "Kalina krasnaia," Egor Prokudin addresses the birches four times: he can tell only them about his loneliness. And only to them does he say farewell when he leaves to die.

The short story is called " 'Veruiu!" Drunken muzhiks, after drinking, dance, screaming out: "Hey, I believe! I believe!" All of Shukshin's heroes would like to scream out these words, for they are all looking for a foothold, alleviation of their grief, a holiday for the soul. Their prayer is about this. "Strangeness," "fancies" become for the characters of the stories a means of expressing their feelings, a language, an appeal to someone who can understand, explain, and help. The tale becomes a prayer of faith, of the soul. Shukshin's single happy character—Alesha Beskonvoinyi, finding freedom in the bathhouse, finds his soul: "Last time Alesha began to notice, in a fully conscious way, that he loved. He loved the steppe beyond the village, the dawn, the summer day.... That is, he fully understood that he loved. Peace began to enter his soul—he began to love. It was harder to love people, but children and the steppe, for example, he loved more and more."

The writer asserts an equivalence: peace began to enter his soul—he began to love. True, Alesha admits that it is difficult for him to love people, but when the soul finds peace, a support, when a person finds freedom and realizes the presence of his soul, love for children and nature is awakened inside.

Shukshin does not idealize his heroes: I already spoke about this. He shows their distinctive character. It is the distinctive character of representatives of a dying civilization. The story, "Kak zaika letal na vozdushnykh sharikakh" [How the bunny rabbit flew in balloons], which opens the book *Besedy pri iasnoi lune,* is symbolic. The older brother, a big boss living in the city, calls a faraway Altai village and asks his younger brother to fly 1500 kilometers so that he can tell his sick daughter a tale. A tale can save the sick child, but in the city people no longer know how to tell stories. Tales are not necessary to city people, they do not need freedom, they do not need souls. Only children still need a tale. Perhaps it can still save children.

Even in the country, not everyone knows how to tell tales. Vodka replaces the tale as a surrogate for the soul's holiday. Shukshin's heroes fill with vodka the emptiness which was there after the amputation of their souls. Vodka is an obligatory accessory of Shukshin's stories. No, it seems there is not one in which people do not drink. Or, at least, in which they do not talk about vodka. Shukshin's favorite poet, Esenin, explained his drunkenness: "And I, myself, dropping my head, fill my eyes with wine so as not to see fate's face, so as to think, at least for a moment, about something else." Shukshin's characters give two explanations for drunkenness. The old man, Naum Evstigneich ("Kosmos, nervnaya sistema i shmat sala" ["Outer Space, the Nervous System and a Slab of Bacon Fat"]) gets drunk regularly, once a month, in order to feel like a person. Timofei Khudiakov "Biletik na vtoroi seans" [A ticket for the second show]) drinks, for he has "something wrong in his soul": "he drank with the watchman in the warehouse... it didn't work. No, not that it didn't work—it didn't make him feel easier." Vodka as medicine for spiritual pain. And vodka as the single means of permitting one to feel like a person. And vodka as a means of going out "to freedom."

Shukshin's heroes are looking for freedom, are looking for their soul. And woman is the main obstacle in their path. Woman in Russian literature has always been a positive force. Even Dostoevsky's women, who carry death, attract with their devilish beauty. In Shukshin's world, woman is disgusting, evil, cruel, and greedy.

The arrangement of forces is determined in one of the first stories. The harnessmaker Antip ("Odni" [Alone]) says, addressing his wife: "What is it you want? That I sew and sew, day and night: But I have a soul too. Doesn't it want to have a good time too? My soul wants to play too." The arrangement of forces is obvious: on the one hand, a soul is looking for a holiday, freedom, and on the other, a woman, always personifying greed for material wealth. As a rule the woman is a wife, and is usually described in the same way: "She lies there filled, fat" ("Dva pis'ma" [Two letters]), possessed by "proprietary lust" ("Chudik" ["Quirky"]), by a greed for things, for a post, for a position in society. In several stories the writer considers the same situations: two brothers and their wives. And always—"Kak zaika letal na vozdushnykh sharikakh," "Chudik," "Alesha Beskonvoinyi"— the wives are alike: malicious, quarrelsome, and, the main thing, greedy. The writer insists that it is not a matter of the men, or even the place of residence of the women—city or country; woman is always the same.

In "Stradaniia molodogo Vaganova" [The sufferings of young Vaganov], the philosophy of Shukshin's heroes is set forth: "In that respect, from women there is nothing to expect. It's sheer deception.... Go ahead and look: every family is a mess. Every family is screwed up. Why is it that way? Because you can't expect anything from a woman.... A woman is a woman." Startled by this philosophy, the young Vaganov—who still doesn't know any women!—asks the fifty-year old country driver: "Why the hell get married then?" The driver thinks that this is a completely different question. A man needs a family, for without it he is completely alone. But to endure a wife is unusually difficult. To help him, man is given a love for children. Love for children gives the strength to endure "women's tricks." "But surely there are normal families," insists Vaganov, amazed. And he receives a categorical answer: "Where, then?! All they do is pretend... While everywhere they rage at each other." The shaken young Vaganov asks, "How should we live then?" And he hears in reply: "You just live: you get stronger and you live. And don't go fooling yourself. There's no need to resent them for all this—since that's the way they're made."

And there is no need to resent...

Shukshin's heroes are not resentful: They suffer from betrayed love, from faithlessness, and from the treachery of women ("Bespalyi" ["Two fingers"], " 'Raskas' " [" 'A Storey' "]). They weep from being hurt: "But something happened with his brother Dmitry: he began to weep and began to beat his fist on his knee. 'What a life I have! Did you see? How much malice there is in people!.... How much malice!' " One of the heroes of the story "Chudik" cannot endure the persecution of his wife. Shukshin's heroes do not simply suffer, do not just weep, unable to endure the female nature, but they commit suicide.

In Soviet literature suicide is met exceptionally rarely: it is always a sign of shameful weakness, evidence of degeneration. With Shukshin, peasants kill themselves. The handsome Spirka Rastorguev ("Suraz" ["The Bastard"]) shoots himself after misunderstanding the intentions of a young teacher. Alesha Beskonvoinyi's brother Ivan kills himself: "And his wife joined in: and they swore at each other, and swore at each other, and swore at each other to the point where brother Ivan began to beat his head against the wall and say again and again: 'How long will I be tormented?! How long?! How long?!' " Kolka Paratov (" 'Zhena muzha v Parizh provozhala' " [" 'Oh, a wife saw her husband off to Paris...' "]) kills himself with gas. And again the familiar explanation: Their mistery began "with Kolya's swift discovery of his wife's boundless appetite for money." When the body of Kolka was found, on his face, his "tears were not yet dry." Before death he had begun to weep, for he remembered his daughter, for whom he left a note "on the margin of the newspaper: 'My dear little daughter, your daddy's gone on a business trip.' " This time his love for his daughter was not enough to help him "endure his wife."

The writer's attitude toward women is a constant which does not change from the first short stories to his last works. There is the story "Odni," written in 1963, " 'Zhena muzha v Parizh provozhala,' " written in 1971, and "Stradaniia molodogo Vaganova," written in 1972. If we consider the "first embodiment" of Shukshin's hero, then we shall see that even Stepan Razin falls into conflict with his militant comrades over a woman, that Makar Lyubavin behaves like a madman—and ultimately dies—because of a woman, and we shall see that even Egor Prokudin's death, his "suicide," is a chance to escape the good—but for him impossible—advice of dear Lyuba.

Shukshin's heroes suffer, weep, kill themselves, and do not have the strength to endure women. The writer does not forgive. The story, "Tri gratsii" [Three graces], in which Shukshin uses a first-person narrator, begins with the words: "Sunday. Today in the course of the day I will hate. It's about two months since I moved to a new apartment, and each Sunday, all day long, I hate. It happens like this. From about nine o'clock in the morning, three graces sit on a bench under my balcony talking. About everything: about the husbands of others, about politics, about passers-by.... I place a chair out on the balcony, smoke, and listen to these three—and I hate. All humanity. I even get tired by evening."

Three "graces," three women, evoke in the writer a feeling of hatred for humanity. And for this he hates women. The story's subtitle is: "a joke." But Shukshin is not joking when he speaks about his feeling of hatred. His heroes in search of freedom, a holiday for the soul, leave the real world for an imaginary, fantastic, and poetic world. They find freedom in a tale:

224

Bronka Pupkov, who thought up the story of his attempt to kill Hitler, Kolka Paratov, who arranged a concert in the courtyard on Saturday night, the joiner Andrei Erin, who bought with a whole month's salary a microscope ("Mikroskop"), knowing that he could not avoid the beatings of his wife, but passionately wishing to see microbes with his own eyes. Woman—in Shukshin's world—always lives in the real world. Hence her anger, her hatred for her husband who lives in the world of a tale, in the world of poetry, for her husband who slips away—if only for a moment—to freedom. Woman always tries to bring the husband down to earth. For Shukshin, woman is—even in the country—the bearer of urban civilization, the civilization of material wealth, of things hostile to the tale, and therefore hostile to freedom.

Shukshin's hero is looking for freedom. His search carries not just an active character: a struggle with his wife, resentment against all-powerful bureaucrats ("Nol'-nol' tselykh" [Zero-zero and something], " 'Moi zyat' ukral mashinu drov' " ["My son-in-law stole a load of wood"], "Oratorskii priem" [Oratorical device]). The search also bears a speculative character, a philosophical character. In Shukshin's world an answer to the "main questions" is sought with unusual intensity, with a powerful passion: In what is the meaning of life, what is death, what is God?

Stepan Voevodin ("Stepka"), three months before his release from camp, runs home to his native village. He knows they will arrest him immediately, that he will have to spend several years in camp for his flight. But he ran away, for "dreams were torturing" him. His longing for freedom was so strong that Stepka could not help running away. So that he could at least "take a stroll once more" over his native earth in spring. Muzhiks ask "eternal questions" with such tormenting intensity, hoping to get an answer and, with it, to be saved from "grief," to escape to freedom. Only in the heroes of Andrei Platonov do we find a similar thirst for an answer to "eternal questions." The fisherman, Dvanov ("Proiskhozhdenie mastera" [The master's origin]), jumps into the water, after first tying his legs, in order to discover the secret of death. With such poignancy, with such pain, Shukshin's heroes look for the answer. They feel, as a pain, the need, physical and insistent, to discover the secret: "Every Sunday a mood of depression would descend upon him. Real, deep-down... depression." The comparison which Shukshin finds discloses better than anything his attitude toward women: "Maksim could feel [the depression] physically, as if a slovenly, slightly diseased peasant woman with bad breath were pawing him shamelessly all over, caressing him and trying to kiss him." (" 'Veruiu!' ") "Recently something had gone wrong in Timofei Khudiakov's soul—everything in the world grew hateful. So that he would get down on all fours, and would growl, and would begin to bark, and would twist his head. Perhaps he'd begin to weep." ("Biletik na vtoroi seans")

When the horrible question is raised: "With what can the soul be calmed?" ("V profil' i anfas" ["In Profile and Full Face"]), when it is not known: "Where can a person go with an anxious soul? After all, it hurts, that soul. Teeth will begin to hurt at night, and then we run like mad.... But where do you go when it's your soul that hurts?" ("Noch'iu v boilernoi" [At night in the boiler room])—Shukshin's heroes go off to "learned people."

Andrei Platonov saw the main conflict of life in the collision between the "thinkers" (umniki), leaders with heads filled with paper, and "fools" (duraki), people with souls. Shukshin's "learned people" are the "fools": "Who knows, perhaps Sanya had seen and learned a lot in the course of his life. . . He was a genuinely kind man, too." ("Zaletnyi" ["A Bird-of-Passage"]). Sanya Neverov, a man who is mortally ill, after accidentally wandering into a village, attracts the peasants to himself. Being next to him, "you felt better, more clear in your head, as though you had suddenly become an immense, free being, able to fathom the beginning and end of your life, or as though you had taken the measure of priceless things and understood them all."

You became free and you understood everything. You understood everything—and became free. This is what Shukshin's heroes are looking for. And the lack of convergence between the complexity of the problems of existence which torment the muzhiks, and the concreteness, the ordinariness, the primitiveness of the language which they use for the expression of their thoughts, often creates a comic effect. The comic in this case, however, never can overshadow the tragic in the situation: the helplessness of the man who has lost his soul while looking for freedom.

In their search for freedom Shukshin's heroes run up against the queston of death, the meaning of death. For a long time in Soviet literature death has always been only "useful death": for one's country in war, for the sake of fulfilling the plan or strengthening the state. Soviet writers have not spoken about death as the unavoidable end of life. "We Will Never Die" is the title of one of Solzhenitsyn's Prose Poems. Solzhenitsyn: "Above all else, we have grown to fear death and those who die. If there is a death in a family, we try to avoid writing or calling, because we do not know what to say about death." For Solzhenitsyn this fear of death was engendered by Soviet ideology, which cannot explain the secrets of death and hence announces in a cowardly way: "Don't disturb our lives! We will never die."

Shukshin's hero knows that he will die. Transfixed by the thought of an inescapable death, Matvei Riazantsev wakes his wife to ask: "Do you fear death?" ("Dumy" [Thoughts]); at the thought of death, "all the hidden, wonderful, eternal beauty of Life is disclosed to a person." With special sharpness people, whom the writer intently observes, perceive the beauty of life on the eve of death. "Kak pomiral starik" ["How the Old Man Died"] is a clinical study of death. Shukshin bends over the dying man, notes his gestures, words, attempting to discover through them the terrible secret of death. The heroes of his stories, "Zarevoi dozhd' " [Rain at dawn] and "Zaletnyi" are dying. They literally say the same thing, uttering identical words: "Why?... I know! I know everything...." ("Zarevoi dozhd' "), "I don't want to.... I know everything... I don't want to! I don't want to!" Even the old man ("Kak pomiral starik"), dying without complaints, without groans, with unusual dignity, says all the same, he would prefer to wait until summer. When death stops at the head of a person's bed, the person suddenly understands something unusually important and then asks for "a ticket to the second showing"; he asks—only, whom?—about the possibility of living a new life.

The theme of death runs through the entire creative work of Shukshin, occupying a larger and larger place to the degree that the writer's stories become more and more sad and hopeless. In the stories about death, one can consider the indispensable presence of the author, who often plays the role of narrator, as a distinctive feature. The beginning of the cycle apparently dates back to 1967. In the story, "Gore" [Misery], Shukshin shares recollections of his childhood: as a twelve-year old boy he saw one night at a cemetery his grandfather Nechaev's neighbor, and heard the old man conversing with his wife, who had died three days before. This was his first encounter with death, with real misery. The nickname of the hero of "Kalina krasnaya," who did not find freedom—is Gore ("misery"). The cycle of stories about death ends with the story, "Zhil chelovek" ["There Was a Man Living"], which was published in Nash sovremennik in the September, 1974, issue. Vasily Shukshin died in October of 1974. The journal with the writer's last story about death went on sale after Shukshin's death.

The story is called "Zhil chelovek." The writer lies in the hospital next to a man, and he speaks with him. At night his neighbor is dying: "The man passed away. After that, all night long I lay there with an empty soul: I wanted to concentrate on some kind of central thought, I wanted—not to understand, no, I had tried to understand before and couldn't—but to feel, even if only for a moment, even briefly, at least like a faint little track, so that in my mind or soul just a tiny bit of light should be thrown on what it was then—there was a man living.... Does it mean that it's necessary, perhaps, that we live? Or what? Let's allow that we should live, but then why hasn't that accursed gift been taken from us—to try forever, agonizingly and fruitlessly, to understand: What is the point of everything?"

Agonizing—and fruitless, by the author's admission—reflections about the meaning of life and the meaning of death could not help but prompt Shukshin to think about God. "And what's the point of everything, the point!" thinks the writer. "And no matter where you shout it, no one will hear." Carefully, groping his way along, he looks for it: but perhaps there is someone who hears? To whom can one "shout"?

The difficulties of searching for God in Soviet literature are obvious. Shukshin's hero only asks, very cautiously: "What do you hear said about him?—About whom?—About God?—Nothing—nothing about him." This is the old man, Naum Evstigneich, questioning his tenant, the eighth-year student Kolka ("Kosmos, nervnaya sistema i shmat sala" ["Outer Space, the Nervous System and a Slab of Bacon Fat"]). Kolka's answer is not very convincing to the old man, who then asks another question: "And why then do so many people pray?"

Shukshin's hero is very troubled by this question: why do so many people pray, why do people believe? He himself—the hero of the short stories—is an unbeliever. He is looking for faith. Hence he is so strict with believers, and he keeps thinking that believers do not really believe, but are pretending. He needs an all-consuming faith, and the main thing is that it be completely unselfish, not evoked, for example, by fear before death, which, as it seems to Shukshin's truth-lovers, often prompts a turn to God. The hero of the short stories is irrepressibly drawn to the wonderful secret of faith, of God. The church becomes a symbol of faith in Shukshin's stories. If the "strange people" express themselves with distrust, sometimes with irony (with the obligatory, one could say, irony of Soviet literature) about God and about faith, they speak about the church with love and delight.

The drunkard and remarkable master, Semka Rys, is struck by the beauty and mystery of the church: "Semka remembered from childhood that if you were going to Talitsa and got lost in your thoughts, then at the turn of the road, near the hillside, you'd start up at the sudden appearance of the church; it was white and seemed to float amidst the heavy greenery of the poplars." ("Master"). The wondrous beauty of the church is confided to Semka, like a word addressed to him by a seventeenth-century master. And the uneducated, dissolute Semka goes through numerous departments, trying to obtain permission to restore the beauty of ancient days with his own hands: "No, not to pray in," he explains to the authorities. "It's valuable, but not from the religious point of view," Semka naively tries to persuade them. The authorities turn him down, understanding better than he does that admiration of the church's beauty is the beginning of accustoming people to faith. The connection between the church and faith is distinctly apparent in the tragic history of the death of a church ("Krepkii muzhik" [The strong muzhik]). The church in the country had long ago been converted into a storehouse, and its cross had been taken off. But all the same it was there. The foreman, Shurygin, did not decide to destroy the church until a new storehouse had appeared. For a long time people who lived in the area had not prayed in the church, but when tractors began to stretch the ropes, the crowd which had gathered "quietly, with horror, sighed." People had grown accustomed to seeing the church, as they had grown accustomed to seeing the sky every day. Shurygin's actions evoke authentic hatred. "The people went crazy," notes the "strong muzhik" in bewilderment.

The white church—and the white birches—appear on the screen each

228

time Egor Prokudin ponders the meaning of his life.

The theme of faith and God—which parallels the theme of death—occupies a place in Shukshin's short stories that gradually becomes more and more noticeable. The last book published in the writer's lifetime, *Besedy pri iasnoi lune,* ends with the story, "Na kladbishche" [At the cemetery] (1973). It can be considered the final work on the theme of faith and God. It is perhaps the most unexpected short story in Soviet literature. The writer—the story is narrated in the first person—has come to the cemetery to think: "A very definite desire atracts me, personally, to the cemetery: I love to think there. One can think freely and somehow unexpectedly amidst those little mounds." The writer thinks *freely* amidst the dead. The writer comes to the cemetery seeking "freedom to pray," just as his "strange" heroes visit strange places in order to "pray." At the cemetery he meets an old woman who is visiting the grave of her son.

When speaking of Shukshin's hatred for women, I had in mind women as wives.[6] The writer has a complete different attitude toward women as mothers. At the cemetery he meets a mother. And she tells him about an extremely surprising (for Soviet literature) story about the appearance of the Virgin to a Soviet soldier. The soldier, standing guard one night, hears a woman crying at a nearby cemetery. He goes toward the sound and sees the woman: "The soldier became frightened.... 'Were you the one crying?—'I was crying'—'Why are you crying?'—'I am crying over you, over the young generation,' she said. 'I am the earthly Mother-of-God and I weep for your good-for-nothing life. I feel sorry for you. Go out and tell what I've told you.'—'But I'm a komsomolets!.. Who will believe that I saw you? And even I don't believe you.' And then the Mother-of-God touched with her palm the soldier's field-shirt, and when he returned to the barracks, he discovered on his field-shirt the image of the Mother-of-God."

The writer not only tells this story without the slightest trace of irony, but he adds: "[The old woman] concluded her story so forcefully and persuasively that, if she had got up then and left, I would have taken off my jacket to see if anything had appeared on it."

The old woman walks away. "I followed her with my eyes, and then set off on my own path." Where was Shukshin going?

The stories of 1973-74 marked the completion of one stage and the beginning of a new one—which remains unknown. One can consider, as a summary, the "tale of Ivan-the-fool, and how he walked to the end of the earth to acquire wisdom." The tale is called, "Do tret'ikh petukhov" [Till the cock crow thrice]. It was published after the author's death in *Nash sovremennik* (No. 1, 1975).

For the first time Vasily Shukshin pronounces a word that is extremely important to him: the tale *(skazka).* For the first time he explicitly points to the tale in his naming of the hero: Ivan-the-fool. For the first time he openly speaks of his dream: the third cock's crow will resound, it is dawn, and the evil spirit that has cast a spell on Russia will disappear. And, finally, for the first time, it is told where this evil spirit has nestled—"at the end of the world" ("za trideviat' zemel' "), in the city.

In 1973 Shukshin produced his first "author's film," "Pechki—lavochki" [Happy-go-lucky]: he played the main role and produced it according to his own filmscript. It is the realistic story of the journey of an Altai tractor driver, Ivan, from the village of Srostki (the writer's place of birth) to the city. He encounters numerous difficulties on his trip. He returns from the city to his home with relief. In the last sequence of the film, Ivan— barefoot, shirt unbuttoned, sits on the ground in a field and says: "That's all fellows, the end." This is a Russian muzhik who has returned to the land; that's all, the end of a frightening story of the city.

"Do tret'ikh petukhov" does not try to pass for a realistic work; it is a tale; it has a fairy-tale situation and the heroes have fairy-tale names. In reality, "Do tret'ikh petukhov" will pass for a tale enclosed in a fairy-tale form, but the writer says openly all that he has expressed allegorically earlier.

The tale begins in a library. At night the heroes emerge from books and begin to live their own lives: Onegin, Chatsky, Oblomov, Poor Liza. At their night meeting the literary heroes, at the urging of Poor Liza, demand that Ivan set out for the city to get a certificate testifying to the fact that he is intelligent. Intelligent heroes of intelligent books do not want to be the neighbors of a fool. Only the hero of Russian *byliny*—the bogatyr' Il'ya Muromets—and the hero of Russian folk songs—the Don Ataman—are on Ivan-the-fool's side. They sit together on the highest shelf in the library. At the insistence of the smart ones, Ivan goes to the Wise Man in the city for a certificate.

The initiator of the mission for the document is a woman—"progressive Poor Liza," as the writer terms her. And the first danger Ivan meets on his trip to the city is women: Baba-Yaga and her daughter. Later, paper is Ivan's enemy: a document with a stamp which he must present by a specified date, by a specified time. His enemy is Zmei-Gorynich, the censor-tyrant, who forces him to throw out "words from songs" in the name of the struggle with "bad esthetics," "sexuality," and "cruelty." The reader of Shukshin's stories is acquainted with these elements of his world. Two new, important ones appear in the tale.

Evil, with which Shukshin's heroes fought while looking for the way to freedom, receives a new personification in "Do tret'ikh petukhov." Evil is embodied by devils who are striving to enter a monastery, and by Soviet youth, by young men and women from the city who have acquired Western manners, who dress in Western styles, and even drink, not their native vodka, but cognac. In the short stories of his last years ("Drug i igrishch i zabav" [Friend of games and amusements], and "Privet Sivomu" [Greetings to Sivoi]) one can detect this tendency. In the film "Pechki-lavochki" Shukshin portrays the activities of "contemporary" Soviet youth, which Ivan sees as devils' games. In the tale, the writer has his say up to the end: the young bearers of Western influences storm the monastery, the last stronghold of the Russian spirit.

Having lost their faith, having lost their souls, young people, who have turned into "devils," are not content with their fall. After taking the monastery the devils want to efface the icons and to hang their own portraits in place of them.

In the city there is no tale, no song; this is still preserved only in the country, Shukshin maintains in his stories. In "Do tret'ikh petukhov"—and this is a completely new theme—Ivan-the-fool, who possesses the gift of song and wishes to get the help of the devils, helps them into the monastery. The tale and the song serve the devils in their work. For the sake of an unnecessary document—a piece of paper—Ivan helps the devils.

In the short story "Kritiki," an old man in the country smashes with his boot the television which is spreading the urban lie. In "Srezal" [Flunked], the muzhik Gleb Kapustin exposes urban pseudo-culture, which is incomprehensible to muzhiks. "Vanya, what are you doing here?"—exclaims the film director, attempting to teach the country lad how to play a country lad. In his last work, his satirical tale, Vasily Shukshin asks himself this question: "Vanya, what are you doing here?" And answers in complete sincerity: I too am taking part in the poisoning of culture, I too am betraying the tale and the song. I am helping those who want to destroy the human soul. Ivan-the-fool listens to the song: "And the song flowed, tore the soul, destroyed the vanity and triviality of life—it summoned one to spaciousness, to unrestricted freedom." This song opens the gates of the monastery to the devils.

The sabre of the Don Ataman saves Ivan-the-fool from death. It is a happy ending. A fairy-tale ending. "And here, too, is the end of our tale," Vasily Shukshin concludes. "Perhaps there'll be another night... Perhaps something else will happen here. But that will be another tale. For this one— it is the end."

There was not to be another tale by Shukshin. He had sung his song.

"Do tret'ikh petukhov" is the end of a stage which marked the end of the writer's creative work. The tale becomes a synthesis of his weak and strong sides, his merits and shortcomings. The main thing is that in the tale we are given a summarized portrait of Shukshin's hero. This hero is the new element Shukshin brought to literature. This hero is the writer's contribution to literature. Of course, this hero by himself is not new in Russian literature. What is new is his appearance in today's Soviet literature. What is new is his coming to light in today's Soviet reality.

Vasily Shukshin portrayed, with remarkable talent, Soviet man one-half century after the Revolution. Shukshin's "strange person" is stunned by urban civilization, looks for aplace in it, and looks for an exit from it. He has "everything there is," i.e., no material need. And finding this "everything," he suddenly senses that he lacks something important, that his "soul hurts." The emptiness in his chest, which he cannot account for, makes him dissatisfied, displeased, and—unhappy. And—alone. For by his "strangeness" and "fancies" he expresses what those around him do not want to feel, what they laugh at, what they fear. A representative of a dying civilization, he is tormented by that emptiness which comes to replace what is dying. Urban civilization is to him not only empty, but hostile. Hence his enmity toward and distrust of the city and everything connected with the city.

The joiner Erin ("Mikroskop"), after seeing mircrobes under the microscope, is shaken first of all by the perfidy of scientists who keep hidden from the people the presence of harmful creatures which are everywhere—in the water, in soup, in blood. The village mechanic, Roman Zviagin, having suddenly understood that in the famous section of Gogol's *Dead Souls* about the winged-troika personifying Russian, in the section which he memorized in school, his son memorized, all Soviet children memorized and will memorize, there is a strange incongruity: in the "winged-troika" rides the rogue Chichikov; Zviagin does not find an ally in the teacher ("Zabuksoval" [Skidding]). The reverse is true; the teacher recommends to Roman that he not talk about his discovery (not once in his life had the teacher thought about the incongruity) to his son: "You shouldn't. Or else... You shouldn't."

Shukshin's hero is promoting evolution—it is undoubtedly the evolution which the writer was promoting. The hero's "strangeness"—the tale which he tells—reminds us more and more of a prayer. He fills the emptiness in his soul with a faith in Russia which is more and more often symbolized by the church.

Shukshin spoke about his evolution: "By my forties I was neither completely, urban, nor any longer rural. A horribly uncomfortable position. It's not even like being between two stools, but rather like having one leg on the shore and the other in the boat... But even in this situation there are 'pluses'... From comparisons, from all kinds of from-there-to-here's and from-here-to-there's, thoughts come automatically, not only about the 'country' and the 'city,' but also about Russia."[7] Faith in Russia represents to the writer a way out to freedom. This faith in several of the last short stories, in "Do tret'ikh petukhov," assumes the form of neo-Slavophilism—fashionable in certain Moscow circles, with its unfounded connection of the "noxious West" and its spreading influence.

In his search for freedom Shukshin made concessions. To fashion: evil is personified by longhaired lovers of Western pants and jazz. To the censor: Egor Prokudin ("Kalina krasnaia") dies at the hands of bandits, which allows the viewer to draw the conclusion: only bandits prevented Egor from becoming an exemplary tractor driver, a hero of labor.

Despite these concessions, despite the many weaknesses of the writer, his sincerity remains his most important merit. Sincerity in his search, in his errors, and in his discovery.

Shukshin's hero looks for freedom. The writer's service here was first of all that he showed how his hero changed, for his concept of freedom changed. The soul's holiday is displaced by a mouse-hole. A bathhouse becomes freedom. The writer warns us: this is not freedom, this is only a lack of escort. But his hero no longer knows any other kinds. And for this he exhausts an incredible amount of spiritual strength. The introduction of such a hero allowed Shukshin to depict a broad picture of life—colorless, dim, devoid of the spiritual, in which the tale—the ersatz prayer, becomes an ersatz freedom. This life seems still more joyless, more dim, for Shukshin demonstrates that in the city there is not even a substitute for freedom, as there is in the country.

The tale of a writer is determined by his ability to create his own special world, a world which he has seen. Shukshin succeeded in creating his own Shukshin world. And this defines his place in literature. Still more important: Shukshin's world is a truthful world.

The reader recognizes himself in the portrait of Shukshin's hero. And he accepts this portrait: a weak man, lonely, tormented by his wife and by life, but overcome by existential anguish, tortured by questions about the meaning of life, and looking for freedom. The reader recognizes himself in the hero, who drowns his grief with vodka or with a tale. It is vodka that gives birth to the tale. And it is the tale that becomes vodka.

This hero—weak and, in the final account, satisfied with very little, has suited the taste of literary authorities who see in him an ideal portrait of the Soviet citizen. Was it not the Grand Inquisitor who said: "Then we shall give them the quiet, humble happiness of weak creatures such as they are by nature."[8]

Shukshin's remarkable talent depicts the present period of Russia, the present period of its inhabitants. It is a portrait of the times and of the hero of the times. The portrait is both comic and tragic. The portrait is true.

—Translated by George Gutsche

NOTES

1. Original Russian: Mikhail Geller, "Vasilii Shukshin: V poiskakh voli," *Vestnik Russkogo Khristianskogo Dvizheniia*, 120(1977), 159-182.

2. Gleb Goryshin, "Gde-nibud' na Rusi...." *Avrora*, 6(1975).

3. *Voprosy literatury*, 7(1974).

4. Ibid.

5. "Put' Vasiliia Shukshina," *Nedelia*, 15(1976).

6. Lyuba in "Kalina krasnaia" is sooner a mother for Egor than a wife.

7. See *Nedelia*, 15(1976).

8. F.M. Dostoevsky. *Sobranie sochinenii v 10 tomakh*. Vol. 9, p. 325.

V. M. SHUKSHIN: A FILMOGRAPHY

—Compiled by Boris N. Peskin

Dates given indicate, as far as is known, year of release of films. Indication is given of roles played by Shukshin both in his own films and those directed by others; of films directed by him, whether written by him or others; of scenarios written by him, whether directed by him or others; and of films based on writings by Shukshin other than scenarios. For scenarios or "film-stories *[kinopovesti]*, as Shukshin sometimes calls them, published in journals or as books, see items numbered 42, 93, 110, 117, 121 and 130 in the bibliography following this section. Note that several of Shukshin's scripts for films actually made were never published, while several of his published film scripts were never filmed. The information given here is as complete as possible based on somewhat limited resources; probably there are a few omissions of minor roles and the like.

1959   Role: Big Fedor. "Dva Fedora" [Two Fedors], Odessa Film Studio. Scenario, V. Savchenko; director, M. Khutsiev; camera, P. Trudovskii; other actors: Kolia Chursin, T. Semina.

Role: Andrei Nizovtsev. "Zolotoi eshelon" [The golden echelon], Gorky Film Studio (Moscow). Scenario by the brothers Tur; director, I. Turin; camera, M. Bogatkova; other actors: E. Dobronravova, S. Krylov.

1960   "Iz Lebiazh'ego soobshchaiut" [Report from Lebiazh'e], State Institute of Cinematography (Moscow). Written and directed by Shukshin and main role acted by him; short film submitted for diploma.

1962   Role: Chairman of Kolkhoz. "Kogda derev'ia byli bol'shimi" [When the trees were tall], Gorky Film Studio. Scenario, N. Figurovskii; director, L. Kulidzhanov; other actors: Iu. Nikulin, I. Gulaia.

Role: Stepan. "Alenka," Mosfilm. Scenario, S. Antonov; director, B. Barnet; camera, I. Chernykh; other actors: V. Ushakova.

Role: Gennadii Nikolaevich. "Mishka, Serega i ia" [Mishka, Serega and I], Gorky Film Studio. Scenario, N. Zeleranskii and B. Larin; director, Iu. Pobedonostsev.

Minor role. "Komandirovka" [Mission], Gorky Film Studio. Scenario, N. Figurovskii; director, Iu. Egorov.

1963   Role: Gorlov. "My, dvoe muzhchin" [We, two men], Dovchenko Film Studio (Kiev). Scenario, A. Kuznetsov; director, Iu. Lysenko.

1964   "Zhivet takoi paren' " [There lives such a fellow], Gorky Film Studio. Scenario and director, V. Shukshin; camera, V. Ginzburg; music, P. Chekalov; actors: L. Kuravlev, L. Aleksandrova.

1965   Role: Zhorka. "Kakoe ono, more?" [What is it like, the sea?], Gorky Film Studio. Scenario, N. Dubov; director, E. Bocharov; other actors: A. Bukharov, N. Kriuchkov, L. Fedoseeva.

1966   "Vash syn i brat" [Your son and brother], Gorky Film Studio. Scenario and director, V. Shukshin [scenario based on three stories by Shukshin; see Bibliography: 13, 20, 21); camera, V. Ginzburg; music, P. Chekalov; actors: V. Sanaev, M. Grakhova, L. Kuravlev, A. Filippova.

"Odni" [Certain people] (short film based on story by Shukshin; see Bibliography: 14), Mosfilm. Written and directed by A. Surin and L. Golovnia; camera, M. Korobtsov and M. Suslov; actors: M. Vinogradova, P. Kormunin. (Film submitted for diploma by students graduating from Faculty of Directing, State Film Institute.)

1967	Role: Korpachev. "Zhurnalist" [Journalist], Gorky Film Studio. Written and directed by S. Gerasimov; other actors: Iu. Vasil'ev, G. Pol'skikh.

1967   Role: Korpachev. "Zhurnalist" [Journalist], Gorky Film Studio. Written and directed by S. Gerasimov; other actors: Iu. Vasil'ev, G. Pol'skikh.

1968   Role: Kravchenko. "Tri dnia Viktora Chernysheva" [The three days of Viktor Chernyshev], Gorky Film Studio. Scenario, E. Grigor'ev; director, M. Osep'ian; other actors: G. Korol'kov, V. Vladimirova.

1969   Role: Sasha's father. "Muzhskoi razgovor" [Talk between men], Gorky Film Studio. Scenario, V. Ezhov, V. Frolov; director, I. Shatrov; other actors: K. Iakhontov, N. Myshkova.

1971   "Strannye liudi" [Strange people], Gorky Film Studio. Written and directed by V. Shukshin; camera, V. Ginzburg; actors: S. Nikonenko, E. Evstigneev, L. Fedoseeva, E. Lebedev. V. Sanaev.

        Role: Chernykh. "U ozera" [At the lake], Gorky Film Studio. Written and directed by S. Gerasimov; camera, V. Rapoport; other actors: O. Zhakov, N. Belokhvostikova.

1970-72   Role: Marshal Konev. "Osvobozhdenie" [Liberation], Mosfilm. Scenario, Iu. Bondarev, O. Kurganov, Iu. Ozerov; director, Iu. Ozerov; other actors: N. Olialin, M. Ul'ianov, N. Rybnikov.

1972   "Konets Liubavinykh" [End of the Liubavins] (based on novel by Shukshin; see Bibliography: 122) Mosfilm. Scenario, L. Nekhoroshev, L. Golovnia; director, L. Golovnia; actors: A. Akchurin, M. Vertinskaia.

        "Prishel soldat s fronta" [A soldier has come from the front], Mosfilm. Scenario, V. Shukshin; director, N. Gubenko; actors: N. Gubenko, M. Gluzskii.

1973   "Pechki-lavochki" [Happy-go-lucky], Gorky Film Studio. Written and directed by V. Shukshin; camera, A. Zabolotskii; music, P. Chekalov; actors: V. Shukshin, L. Fedoseeva, V. Sanaev, G. Burkov.

1974   "Kalina krasnaia" [Snowball berry red], Mosfilm. Written and directed by V. Shukshin; camera, A. Zabolotskii; music, P. Chekalov; actors: V. Shukshin (Egor Prokudin), L. Fedoseeva (Lyuba), I. Ryzhov, M. Skvortsova, L. Durov, O. Korchikov, G. Burkov, T. Gavrilova, A. Banin.

        Role: The happy husband (with wife played by L. Fedoseeva). "Esli khochesh' byt' schastlivym" [If you want to be happy], Mosfilm. Scenario, N. Gubenko, V. Solov'ev; director, N. Gubenko; camera, O. Karavaev; other actors: Zh. Bolotova, N. Gubenko.

1975   Role: Lopakhin. "Oni srazhalis' za Rodinu" [They fought for the Motherland] (based on M. Sholokhov's unfinished novel), Mosfilm. Written and directed by S. Bondarchuk; camera, V. Iusov; other actors: S. Bondarchuk, V. Tikhonov, Iu. Nikulin, G. Burkov, L. Fedoseeva, I. Lapikov. (A double was used successfully in the few scenes in which Shukshin had yet to appear.)

        "Zemliaki" [Fellow countrymen], Mosfilm. Scenario by V. Shukshin and V. Vinogradov (based on Shukshin's "Brat moi" [Brother of mine] ; see Bibliography at 110); director, V. Vinogradov; camera, R. Veseler; actors: G. Nekasheva, S. Nikonenko, L. Nevedomsky. (Title was changed by Vinogradov after Shukshin's death to that of an earlier story; see Bibliography at 41a and 124.)

1976   Role: The dramatist Fedia. "Proshu slova" [I beg a word], Lenfilm (Leningrad). Written and directed by G. Panfilov; camera, A. Antipenko; other actors: I. Churikova, N. Gubenko, L. Bronevoi. (Filmed in 1973; working title was "Elizaveta Uvarova.")

VASILY SHUKSHIN: A PRELIMINARY BIBLIOGRAPHY

—Compiled by Geoffrey A. Hosking

Although an effort was made to compile a complete list of works by and about Shuk-shin based on standard reference sources, this preliminary bibliography may well be incomplete. Nevertheless, it should prove useful to readers who would like to explore Shukshin further.

I. Fiction: A Chronological List of Works Appearing in Periodicals
1. "Dvoe na telege," SMENA, 15 (1958).

"Tri rasskaza," OKTIABR', 3 (1961), 91-103.
2. "Pravda"; repr.: 120.
3. "Svetlye dushi"; repr.: 120.
4. "Stepkina liubov' "; repr.: 120; tr.: 131, 134.

4a. "Ekzamen," OKTIABR', 1 (1962), 133-7; repr.: 120; tr.: 131, 134.

MOLODAIA GVARDIIA, 3 (1962), 111-24:
5. "Len'ka"; repr.: 120.
6. "Demagogi"; repr.: 120.

"Tri rasskaza," MOSKVA, 4 (1962), 123-35:
7. "Artist Fedor Grai"; repr.: 120.
8. "Plemiannik Glavbukha"; repr.: 120; tr.: 131.
9. "Sten'ka Razin"; repr.: 120.

"Sel'skie Zhiteli," OKTIABR', 5 (1962), 113-32:
10. "Kolenchatye valy"; repr.: 120.
11. "Sel'skie zhiteli"; repr.: 120, 127, 129; tr.: 134, 137.
12. "Lelia Selezneva s fakul'teta zhurnalistiki"; repr.: 120; tr.: 137.

"Oni s Katuni," NOVYI MIR, 2 (1963), 76-106:
13. "Ignakha priekhal"; repr.: 120.
14. "Odni"; repr.: 120, 129.
15. "Grin'ka Maliugin"; repr.: 120.
16. "Klassnyi voditel' "; repr.: 120; tr.: 131, 134.

17. "Kritiki," ISKUSSTVO KINO, 2 (1964), 59-62.

18. "Baklan' " (otryvok iz romana), MOSKOVSKII KOMSOMOLETS (5 & 7 IV 1964).

19. "I razygralis' zhe koni v pole," LITERATURNAIA GAZETA (22 X 1964), 2-3; repr.: 123, 124, 129; tr.: 134.

"Rasskazy," NOVYI MIR, 11 (1964), 58-72:
20. "Zmeinyi iad"; repr.: 123, 128.
21. "Stepka"; repr.: 123, 124, 129.

22. "Liubaviny," SIBIRSKI OGNI, 6 (1965), 3-39; 7 (1965), 24-71; 8 (1965), 28-102; 9 (1965), 76-110; repr.: 122, 129.

22a. "Okhota zhit'," NEDELIA, 28 (1966), 6-9; repr.: 123, 130 d; tr., 124.

23. "Nechaiannyi vystrel," MOSKOVSKII KOMSOMOLETS (27 VII 1966); repr.: 123, 124; tr.: 134.

24. "Kosmos, nervnaia sistema i shmat sala," LITERATURNAIA ROSSIIA (29 VII 1966); repr.: 123, 124, 129; tr.: 134.

25. "Svad'ba" (otryvok iz povesti "Tam vdali"), MOSKOVSKII KOMSOMOLETS (26 X 1966).

26. "Tam, vdali," MOLODAIA GVARDIIA, 11 (1966), 98-127; 12 (1966), 226-54; repr.: 123.

26a. "Kapronovaia elochka," SEL'SKAIA MOLODEZH', 12 (1966); repr.: 123.

SIBIRSKIE OGNI, 12 (1966), 3-15:
27. "Dozhd' na zare"; repr. in KAZAKHSTANSKAIA PRAVDA (25 XII 1966), 3; repr.: 123; repr.: 128, under title "Zarevoi dozhd'."
28. " 'Vania, ty kak zdes'?"; repr.: 123, 128.
29. "Kukushkiny slezki"; repr.: 123; tr.: 134, 137.

"Tri rasskaza," NOVYI MIR, 1 (1967), 154-66:
30. "Volki"; repr.: 123, 124, 127, 129; tr.: 134.
31. "Nachal'nik"; repr.: 123.
32. "Vianet, propadet"; repr.: 123, 124, 127, 129; tr.: 137.

MOSKVA, 3 (1967), 140-53:
33. "Sluchai v restorane"; repr.: 123, 127; tr.: 137.
34. "Vnutrennee soderzhanie"; repr.: 123; tr.: 132, 134, 140.
35. "Gore"; repr.: 123, 127, 128, 129.

36. "Dva pis'ma," SOVETSKAIA ROSSIIA (17 V 1967), 3; repr.: 123, 129.

"Novye rasskazy," NOVYI MIR, 9 (1967), 88-108:
37. "V profil' i anfas"; repr.: 123, 124, 129; tr.: 140.
38. "Dumy"; repr.: 123, 124, 129; tr.: 134.
39. "Kak pomiral starik"; repr.: 123, 124, 127, 129.
40. " 'Raskas' "; repr. in SOVETSKAIA KIRGIZIIA (5 XII 1967), 3 and: 123, 124, 127, 129.
41. "Chudik"; repr.: 123, 124, 127, 129; tr.: 134.

41a. "Zdeshnii," SEL'SKAIA MOLODEZH', 5 (1968); repr. under title "Zemliaki": 124, 129; tr.: 134.

42. "Ia prishel dat' vam voliu" (kinostsenarii), ISKUSSTVO KINO, 5 (1968), 143-87; 6 (1968), 131-85. [See novel of same title: 60. 126.]

NOVYI MIR, 11 (1968), 98-115:
43. "Iz detstva Ivana Popova"; repr.: 124.
44. " 'Mil' pardon, madam!' "; repr.: 124, 127, 129.

44a. "Mikroskop," SEL'SKAIA MOLODEZH', 1 (1969); repr.: 124, 129.

"V sele Chebrovka," NOVYI MIR, 10 (1969), 67-94:
45. "Sud"; repr.: 124, 129.
46. "Khakhal' "; repr.: 127.
47. "Makar Zherebtsov"; repr.: 124; repr.: 125, 128, 129 under title "Neprotivlenets

Makar Zherebtsov."
48. "Materinskoe serdtse"; repr.: 127, 128, 129.
49. "Svoiak Sergei Sergeich"; repr.: 125, 128; tr.: 136.

50. "Cherednichenko i tsirk," LITERATURNAIA GAZETA (15 VI 1970), 7; repr.: 128.

"Rasskazy," NOVYI MIR, 7 (1970), 42-73:
51. "Svatovstvo"; repr. under title "Bessovestnye": 125; repr.: 134.
52. "Shire shag..."; repr.: 125; repr.: 127, 128 under title "Shire shag, maestro."
53. "Srezal!"; repr.:125, 127, 128, 129.
54. "Mit'ka Ermakov."
55. "Krepkii muzhik"; repr.: 125, 127, 128.
56. "Krysha nad golovoi"; repr.: 125, 128.

57. "Garmonist," SEL'SKAIA ZHIZN' (19 IX 1970), 4; repr. under title "V voskresen'e mat'-starushka...": 124, 127.

LITERATURNAIA ROSSIIA (16 X 1970), 12-13:
58. "Sapozhki"; repr.: 125, 128; tr.: 133, 134.
59. "Petia"; repr.: 125, 128, 129; tr.: 133.

60. "Ia prishel dat' vam voliu" (roman), SIBIRSKIE OGNI, 1 (1971), 3-95; 2 (1971), 3-122; repr.: 126, 129. [See screenplay of same title: 42.]

61. "Obida," LITERATURNAIA ROSSIIA (12 II 1971), 18-19; repr.: 125, 127, 128, 129.

62. "Na kurorte," SOVETSKAIA ROSSIIA [periferiinyi vypusk] (16 VI 1971).

"Rasskazy," ZVEZDA, 9 (1971), 24-40:
63. " 'Veruiu!' "; repr.: 125, 127, 128.
64. "Lesia"; repr.: 128.
65. " 'Debil' "; repr.: 125, 128.
66. "Biletik na vtoroi seans"; repr.: 125, 127, 128.

"Kharaktery," NASH SOVREMENNIK, 9 (1971), 56-81:
67. "Diadia Ermolai"; repr. in TURKMENSKAIA ISKRA (9 IX 1971), 4 and: 125, 128, 129.
68. "Khoziain bani i ogoroda"; repr.: 129.
69. "Khmyr' "; repr.: 129.
70. "Nol'-nol' tselykh"; repr.: 125, 127, 128, 129.
71. "Pis'mo"; repr.: 127, 129.
72. " 'Zhena muzha v Parizh provozhala...' "; repr.: 129.
73. "Oratorskii priem"; repr.: 127.

74. "Tri gratsii," LITERATURNAIA ROSSIIA (24 XII 1971), 14-15; repr.: 129.

"Rasskazy," SIBIRSKIE OGNI, 12 (1971), 11-23:
75. "Master"; repr.: 125, 127, 128, 129.
76. " 'Moi ziat' ukral mashinu drov!' "; repr.: 125, 128.

"Rasskazy," SEVER, 3 (1972), 3-15:

77. " 'Post skriptum' "; repr.: 127, 128, 129.
78. "Tantsuiushchii Shiva"; repr.: 127, 129.
79. "General Malafeikin"; repr.: 129.

"Rasskazy," NASH SOVREMENNIK, 10 (1972), 39-64:
80. "Stradaniia molodogo Vaganova"; repr.: 127, 128, 129.
81. "Besedy pri iasnoi lune"; repr.: 127, 129.
82. "Mnenie"; repr.: 129.
83. "Bespalyi"; repr.: 127, 129; tr.: 137.
84. "Kak zaika letal na vozdushnykh sharikakh," LITERATURNAIA ROSSIIA (27 X 1972), 18-20; repr.: 127.

"Rasskazy," ZVEZDA, 12 (1972), 17-26:
85. "Nakaz"; repr.: 127.
86. "Medik Volodia"; repr.: 127.

87. "Alesha beskonvoinyi," LITERATURNAIA ROSSIIA (19 I 1973), 18-19; repr.: 127, 129.

"Rasskazy," ZVEZDA, 2 (1973), 3-19:
88. "Van'ka Tepliashin"; repr.: 127.
89. "Gena Proidisvet"; repr.: 128.
90. "Versiia"; repr.: 127, 129.

91. "Upornyi," LITERATURNAIA ROSSIIA (2 III 1973), 18-20; repr.: 127, 129; tr.: 135.

92. "Vladimir Semenych iz miagkoi sektsii," LITERATURNAIA ROSSIIA (30 III 1973), 18-20.

93. "Kalina krasnaia" (kinopovest'), NASH SOVREMENNIK, 4 (1973), 86-133; repr.: 129, 130; tr.: 138. Excerpt pub. in V MIRE KNIG, 3 (1973), 57-61.

94. "Doroga k domu," SEL'SKAIA ZHIZN' (19 IV 1973), 3.

95. "P'edestal," SEL'SKAIA MOLODEZH', 5 (1973).

95a. "Vybiraiu derevniu na zhitel'stvo," NEDELIA, 19 (1973), 6-7; repr.: 127.

96. "Shtriki k portretu (nekotorye konkretnye mysli N. N. Kniazeva, cheloveka i grazh-danina)," NASH SOVREMENNIK, 9 (1973), 2-20; repr.: 129.

97. "Osen'iu," AVRORA, 7 (1973), 38-41; repr.: 127, 129, 130b.

98. "Psikhopat," LITERATURNAIA ROSSIIA (28 XII 1973), 12-13; repr.: 129; tr.: 139.

"Vnezapnye rasskazy," SIBIRSKIE OGNI, 11 (1973), 90-106:
99. "Mechty."
100. "Pet'ka Krasnov rasskazyvaet."
101. "Kak muzhik perepravlial cherez reku volka, kozu i kapustu"; repr.: 128.
102. "Son materi"; repr.: 128, under title "Sny materi."
103. "Boria"; repr.: 128.
104. "Na kladbishche"; repr.: 127, 129.

"Dve sovershenno nelepye istorii," LITERATURNAIA ROSSIIA (22 III 1974), 8-10:
105. "Kak Andrei Ivanovich Kurnikov, iuvelir, poluchil piatnadtsat' sutok."
106. "Noch' v boilernoi."

107. "Energichnye liudi," LITERATURNAIA ROSSIIA (7 VI 1974), 18-19; (14 VI 1974), 12-13; (21 VI 1974), 18-20.

108. "Tochka zreniia," ZVEZDA, 7 (1974), 108-35.

109. "Ryzhii," AVRORA, 7 (1974), 50-1; repr.: 129.

110. "Brat moi..." (kinostsenarii), ISKUSSTVO KINO, 7 (1974), 169-92; repr.: 128, 129.

110a. "Kliauza," AVRORA, 8 (1974); repr.: LITERATURNAIA GAZETA (4 IX 1974), 11.

NASH SOVREMENNIK, 9 (1974), 2-25:
111. "Drugi igrishch i zabav"; repr.: 128.
112. "Muzhik Deriabin"; repr.: 129.
113. "Zhil chelovek..."; repr.: 128; tr.: 137.
114. "Chuzhie"; repr.: 128.
115. "Privet Sivomu!"; repr.: 129.

116. "Do tret'ikh petukhov (skazka pro Ivana-duraka, kak on khodil za trideviat' zemel' nabirat'sia uma-razuma)," NASH SOVREMENNIK, 1 (1975), 28-61; repr.: 128, 130c.

117. " 'Pozovi menia v dal' svetluiu'," ZVEZDA, 6 (1975), 3-38 (untitled biographical note by L. Fedoseeva-Shukshina, pp. 3-4); repr.: 130.

118. "A poutru oni prosnulis'," NASH SOVREMENNIK, 6 (1975), 63-82.

119. "Priezzhii," AVRORA, 6 (1975), 19-23.

Note: Shukshin's collections of stories contain a few works not previously published. See next section.

II. Fiction: Works Published in Book Form
Note: stories are often reprinted with changes.

120. SEL'SKIE ZHITELI. Moscow: Molodaia gvardiia, 1963. Contains "Dalekie zimnie vechera," "Solntse, starik i devushka," "Voskresnaia toska" and 2, 3, 4, 4a, 5, 6, 7, 8, 9, 10, 11, 12, 13, 14, 15, 16.

121. ZHIVET TAKOI PAREN' (kinoststenarii). Moscow: Iskusstvo, 1964. Repr.: 130.

122. LIUBAVINY (roman). Moscow: Sovetskii pisatel', 1965. Reprint of 22; reprinted in 129.

123. TAM, VDALI (povest' i rasskazy). Moscow: Sovetskii pisatel', 1968. Contains 19, 20, 21, 22a, 23, 24, 26, 26a, 27, 28, 29, 30, 31, 32, 33, 34, 35, 36, 37, 38, 39, 40, 41.

124. ZEMLIAKI. Moscow: Sovetskii pisatel', 1970. Contains "Zaletnyi" (1970), "Suraz" (1970), "Daesh' serdtse!" (1970), "Operatsiia Efima P'ianykh" (1970) and 12, 21, 23, 24, 30, 32, 37, 38, 39, 40, 41, 41a (under title "Zemliaki"), 43, 44, 44a, 45, 47, and 57 (under title "V voskresen'e mat'-starushka...").

125. KHARAKTERY. Moscow: Sovremennik, 1973. Contains "Suraz" (1970),

"Daesh' serdtse!" (1970), "Zabuksoval" (1970) and 47 (under the title "Nepro-tivlenets Makar Zherebtsov"), 49, 51 (under title "Bessovestnye"), 52, 53, 55, 56, 58, 59, 61, 63, 65, 66, 67, 70, 75, 76.

126. IA PRISHEL DAT' VAM VOLIU (roman). Moscow: Sovetskii pisatel', 1974. Reprint of 60; reprinted in 129; see also film script of same title: 42.

127. BESEDY PRI IASNOI LUNE. Moscow: Sovetskaia Rossiia, 1974. Contains "Zaletnyi" (1970), and 11, 30, 32, 33, 35, 39, 40, 41, 44, 46, 48, 52 (under the title "Shire shag, maestro!"), 53, 55, 57 (under title "V voskresen'e mat'-starushka..."), 61, 63, 66, 70, 71, 73, 75, 77, 78, 80, 81, 83, 84, 85, 86, 87, 88, 90, 91, 95 (under title "Vybiraiu derevniu na zhitel'stvo"), 97, 104.

128. BRAT MOI. Moscow: Sovremennik, 1975. Contains 20, 27 (under the title "Zarevoi dozhd' "), 28, 35, 47 (title as in 125), 48, 49, 50, 52 (title as in 127), 53, 55, 56, 58, 59, 61, 63, 64, 65, 66, 67, 70, 75, 76, 77, 80, 89, 101, 102 (under the title "Sny materi"), 103, 110, 111, 113, 114, 116.

129. IZBRANNYE PROIZVEDENIIA V DVUKH TOMAKH. Moscow: Molodaia gvardiia, 1975. Vol. 1 contains "Zaletnyi" (1970), "Suraz" (1970), "Operatsiia Efima P'ianykh" (1970) and 11, 14, 19, 21, 24, 30, 32, 35, 36, 37, 38, 39, 40, 41, 41a (under title "Zemliaki"), 44, 44a, 45, 47 (title as in 125), 48, 53, 59, 61, 67, 68, 69, 70, 71, 72, 74, 75, 77, 78, 79, 80, 81, 82, 83, 87, 90, 91, 93, 96, 97, 98, 104, 109, 112, 115. Vol. 2 contains 122 and 126.

130. KINOPOVESTI. Moscow: Iskusstvo, 1975. Contains "Pechki-lavochki" (1972) and 93, 110, 117, 121.

Note: Have not seen the following recent collections of stories

130a. RASSKAZY. Moscow: Khudozhestvennaia literatura, 1975 (ROMAN-GAZETA, 17)

130b. OSEN'IU (rasskazy). Barnaul: Altaiskoe knizhnoe izdatel'stvo, 1976 [?].

130c. DO TRET'IKH PETUKHOV (povesti, rasskazy). Moscow: Izvestiia, 1976.

130d. OKHOTA ZHIT' (rasskazy). Kazan': Tatknigoizdat (Tatarskoe knizhnoe izdatel'-stvo), 1977.

III. Fiction: Works Published in English Translation
(The figures in brackets after the titles refer to Section I.)

131. "The Chief Accountant's Nephew" [8], "A Classy Driver" [16], "The Exam-ination" [4a], "Stepan in Love" [4], SOVIET LITERATURE, 5 (1964), 82-114; tr. Ralph Parker.

132. "Inner Content" [34], SOVIET LITERATURE, 6 (1968), 138-145; tr. Avril Pyman.

133. "Petya" [59], "Boots" [58], SOVIET LITERATURE, 12 (1971), 102-15; tr. Robert Daglish.

134. I WANT TO LIVE. Moscow: Progress, 1973. Contains "The Classy Driver" [16], "Country Dwellers" [11], "Stepan in Love"[4], "The Examination" [4a], "Men of One Soul" ["Zemliaki"; see 41a], "I Want to Live" [22a], "Cuckoo's Tears" [29], "See the Horses Gallop" [19], "Wolves" [30], "Outer Space, the Nervous System, and a Slab of Bacon Fat" [24], "Inner Content" [34], "Thoughts" [38], "A Matchmaking" [51], "An Accidental Shot" [23], "Quirky" [41] and "Boots" [58]; tr. Robert Daglish.

135. "The Obstinate One" [91], SOVIET LITERATURE, 10 (1974), 3-17; tr. Na-tasha Johnstone.

136. "The Brother-in-Law" [49], RUSSIAN LITERATURE TRIQUARTERLY, 12 (1975), 168-74; tr. D.M. Fiene and B.N. Peskin.

137. "Country Folk" [11], tr. Hilda Perham; "Two Fingers" [83], tr. H. Perham; "Happening at the Restaurant" [33], tr. H. Perham; "Olga Selezneva of the

School of Journalism" [12], tr. Robert Daglish; "Sunday Boredom" ["Vos-kresnaia toska"], tr. R. Daglish; "Cuckoo's Tears" [29], tr. R. Daglish; "Fading Blossoms" [32], tr. R. Daglish; "There Was a Man Living" [113], tr. Keith Hammond, SOVIET LITERATURE, 9 (1975), 3-55.

138. "The Red Guelder Rose" [93], SOVIET LITERATURE, 10 (1976), 56-122; tr. Robert Daglish.

139. "The Odd-Ball" [98], SOVIET LITERATURE, 10 (1976), 130-138; tr. Margaret Wettlin.

140. "In Profile and Full Face" [37], "Depth of Character" [34] in M. Dewhirst and R. Milner-Gulland, eds. SOVIET WRITING TODAY. Harmondsworth: Penguin Books, 1977; tr. G.A. Hosking [37] and R. Daglish [34].

IV. Miscellaneous Publications: Articles, Interviews, etc.

141. "Kak ia ponimaiu rasskaz," LITERATURNAIA ROSSIIA (20 XI 1964), 15.

142. "Priglashenie v soavtory (o rabote v kino)," VODNYI TRANSPORT (17 XII 1964).

143. Contribution to discussion on film MNE DVADTSAT' LET, ISKUSSTVO KINO, 4 (1965), 27-46.

144. "Voprosy samomu sebe," SEL'SKAIA MOLODEZH', 11 (1966).

145. "Epigrammy," LITERATURNAIA GAZETA (17 V 1967), 6-7.

146. Contribution to "Literatur i iazyk," VOPROSY LITERATURY, 6 (1967), 148-150.

146a. "Monolog na lestnitse," pp. 114-128 in KUL'TURA CHUVSTV, ed. V. Tolstykh. Moscow: Iskusstvo, 1968.

147. "Nasushchnoe, kak khleb (problemy kul'tury i byta sela: beseda s pisatelem V. Shukshinym)," SOVETSKAIA KUL'TURA (18 I 1969), 4.

147a. "Nravstvennost' est' pravda," pp. 136-144 in ISKUSSTVO NRAVSTVENNOE I BEZNRAVSTVENNOE. Moscow: Iskusstvo, 1969.

148. "Stepan Razin—legenda i byl' (beseda o rabote nad novym fil'mom)," LITERATURNAIA GAZETA (4 XI 1970), 8.

149. "Edin v trekh litsakh (beseda s V. Shukshinym)," MOSKOVSKII KOMSOMO-LETS (11 III 1971).

150. "Mikhail Il'ich Romm (pamiati kinorezhissera)," ISKUSSTVO KINO, 2 (1972), 125-8.

151. "Sud'bu vystraivaet kniga (beseda s V. Shukshinym)," KOMSOMOL'SKAIA PRAVDA (27 IV 1973), 2.

152. "Geroi Vasiliia Shukshina (beseda s pisatelem i kinoartistom)," VODNYI TRANS-PORT (15 I 1974).

153. "Samoe dorogoe otkrytie (postanovshchik i stsenarist o svoei rabote v kino i literature)," PRAVDA (22 V 1974), 6; repr. pp. 77-78 in EKRAN, 1974-1975. Moscow: Iskusstvo, 1976; (see 238a).

154. "Vozrazheniia po sushchestvu," VOPROSY LITERATURY, 7 (1974), 84-88; trans.: "Fundamental Objectives," SOVIET LITERATURE, 9 (1975), 135-138. See item 212.

155. Contribution to "Zdravstvui, festival'," BAKINSKII RABOCHII (12 IV 1974), 3.

156. "Vasilii Shukshin: poslednie razgovory," LITERATURNAIA GAZETA (13 XI 1974), 8. Most of this same material appears in English in: "Vasili Shukshin's Last Interview," SOVIET LITERATURE, 4 (1975), 124—a translation by Rose Prokofieva of an interview of Shukshin on July 16, 1974 by Bulgarian journalist Spas Popov, published in NA RODA KULTURA.

157. "Pis'ma V.M. Shukshina k materi,' ALTAI, 3 (1975), 82-83. Notes by B. Iudale-

vich.

158. "Ot prozy k fil'mu: beseda," pp. 252-277 in collection of articles, KINOPANO-RAMA (SOVETSKOE KINO SEGODNIA). Moscow: Iskusstvo, 1975.

159. " 'Govorit' pravdu kakoi by gor'koi i zhestokoi ona ni byla': Interv'iu Shukshina," by V. Fomin, p. 117 in book EKRAN, 1973-1974. Moscow: Iskusstvo, 1975 (see 220a).

159a. "Nenapisannaia avtobiografiia," SMENA, 19 (1975), 26-7.

159b. "Milaia moia rodina," LITERATURNOE OBOZRENIE, 12 (1975), 99-101.

159c. "Predislovie" [foreword to stories by E. Popov], NOVYI MIR, 4 (1976), 164.

V. Critical and Biographical Articles on Shukshin

159d. "Ob avtore," pp. 3-4 in SEL'SKIE ZHITELI, by Shukshin. Moscow: Molodaia gvardiia, 1963.

160. M. Klimakova, "Zhivet takoi paren' (o kinorezhissere V. Shukshine)," MOSKOV-SKII KOMSOMOLETS (7 VI 1964).

161. Ia. Varshavskii, "Dobro pozhalovat' na komediiu," KOMSOMOL'SKAIA PRAV-DA (24 VI 1964), 4.

162. M. Berestinskii, "Zhivet takoi paren' (o kinodramaturge V. Shukshine)," LITERATURNAIA ROSSIIA (24 VII 1964).

163. N. Pashkevich, "Doroga u kazhdogo svoia (tvorcheskii portret dramaturga, kino-rezhissera i aktera V. Shukshina)," SOVETSKAIA KUL'TURA (14 XI 1964).

164. N. Kovarskii, "U sebia doma (khudozhestvennyi fil'm 'Vash syn i brat')," SO-VETSKAIA KUL'TURA (7 V 1966), 3.

165. V. Orlov, "Strela v polete," LITERATURNAIA GAZETA (10 III 1966), 3.

166. G. Chukhrai, "Na svoei zemle (otklik na stat'iu V. Orlova)," KOMSOMOL'-SKAIA PRAVDA (12 V 1966), 3.

167. L. Anninskii, "Ne v etom delo, tiatia! (o khudozhestvennom fil'me 'Vash syn i brat')," ISKUSSTVO KINO, 7 (1966), 15-20.

168. N. Klado, "Tak, v chem zhe delo?" ISKUSSTVO KINO, 7 (1966), 21-5.

169. V. Kamianov, "Zhivut sebe parni (molodoi geroi V. Shukshina segodnia i zav-tra)," LITERATURNAIA GAZETA, (7 VI 67), 6-7.

170. V. Iavinskii, "Pisatel', akter, rezhisser," ALTAI, 1 (1968), 107-14.

171. Iu. Skop, "V Sibiri dobro — sibirskoe: v gostiakh u V. Shukshina," LITERA-TURNAIA GAZETA (3 VII 1968), 3.

171a. N. Rubetskaia, "Tri professii Vasiliia Shukshina, SOVETSKOE KINO (10 VIII 1968).

172. L. Anninskii, "Vasilii Shukshin i ego geroi: zametki kritika," MOSKOVSKII KOMSOMOLETS (27 XII 1968).

173. E. Shubin, "Rasskaz 60 godov," pp. 636-9 in book RUSSKII SOVETSKII RASS-KAZ: OCHERKI ISTORII ZHANRA. Leningrad: Nauka, 1970.

174. I. Levshina, "Shukshin protiv... Shushina (o khudozhestvennom fil'me 'Strannye liudi')," ISKUSSTVO KINO, 2 (1970), 40-9.

174a. Iu. Smelkov, " 'Strannye liudi' V. Shukshina," KOMSOMOL'SKAIA PRAVDA (16 IX 1970).

175. Iu. Skop, "Segodnia ia shchastliv," SOVETSKII EKRAN, 1 (1971), 6-7.

176. Iu. Nikishov, "Ot ulybki do ironii (o tvorchestve pisatelia V. Shukshina)," LITERATURNAIA ROSSIIA (28 V 1971).

177. V. Kantorovich, "Novye tipy, novyi slovar', novye otnosheniia," SIBIRSKIE OGNI, 9 (1971), 176-80.

178. M. Chudakova, "Zametki o iazyke sovremennoi prozy," NOVYI MIR, 1 (1972), 212-45.

179. S. Borovikov, "Kharaktery Vasiliia Shukshina," VOLGA, 1 (1972), 183-6.
180. I. Aleksandrova, "Mir rasskazov Shukshina," LITERATURNAIA ROSSIIA (14 I 72).
181. V. Petelin, "Stepan Razin — lichnost' i obraz: tri romana o Stepane Razine," VOLGA, 3 (1972), 157-83.
182. A. Zorkii, "Na tom stoit zemlia (o khudozhestvennom fil'me 'Prishel soldat s fronta')," ISKUSSTVO KINO, 3 (1972), 21-32.
183. G. Kapralov, "Istoki geroicheskogo," PRAVDA (2 IV 1972), 3.
184. A. Medvedev, "Soldat — stroitel'," IZVESTIIA (11 IV 1972), 5.
185. M. Makina, "Na konchike lucha," MOSKVA, 6 (1972), 207-13.
186. A. Klitko, "Osmyslenie kazhdodnevnosti (o proze V. Shukshina)," SIBIRSKIE OGNI, 7 (1972), 157-66.
187. V. Chalmaev, "Poryv vetra (molodye geroi i novelisticheskoe iskusstvo V. Shukshina)," SEVER, 10 (1972), 116-26.
188. B. Iudalevich, " 'Da' plius 'net' Vasiliia Shukshina," ALTAI, 3 (1973), 91-8.
189. T. Bachelis, "Kharakter spektaklia (spektakl' 'Kharaktery' po rasskazam V. Shukshina v Moskovskom Teatre imeni Maiakovskogo)," KOMSOMOL'SKAIA PRAVDA (31 V 1973), 2.
190. G. Belaia, "Iskusstvo est' smysl," VOPROSY LITERATURY, 7 (1973), 62-94.
191. M. Velikhova, "Spektakl' — 'ekzamen," MOSKOVSKAIA PRAVDA (4 VII 1973).
192. L. Emel'ianov, "Edinitsa izmereniia: zametki o proze V. Shukshina," NASH SOVREMENNIK, 10 (1973), 176-87.
193. V. Fedorova, "Kharaktery, kharaktery... (o spektakle 'Kharaktery')," MOSKOVSKII KOMSOMOLETS (11 X 1973).
194. V. Ivanova, "Talant Vasiliia Shukshina (o spektakle 'Kharaktery')," ZARIA VOSTOKA (24 X 1973), 4.
195. R. Iurenev, "Talant obeshchaet mnogoe (o khudozhestvennom fil'me 'Pechki-lavochki')," ISKUSSTVO KINO, 12 (1973), 97-103.
196. M. Makina, "Uderzhat'sia na grani," MOSKVA, 12 (1973), 191-5.
197. Iu. Khaniutin, " 'Da' i 'net' Vasiliia Shukshina," SOVETSKII EKRAN, 12 (1973), 4-5.
198. I. Solov'eva, V. Shitova, "Svoi liudi—sochtemsia," NOVYI MIR, 3 (1974), 245-50.
198a. " 'Kalina krasnaia,' " SPUTNIK KINOZRITELIA, 4 (1974), 6-7.
198b. G. Kapralov, "Berezy Egor Prokudina," PRAVDA (1 IV 1974); repr.: 238a.
199. S. Gerasimov, "Pravda zhizni (o 'Kaline krasnoi')," SOVETSKAIA KUL'TURA (9 IV 1974), 3.
200. Z. Kedrina, "Postizhenie sovremennosti: udachi i proschety," LITERATUR-NOE OBOZRENIE, 5 (1974), 11-18.
201. M. Van'iashova, "Karnaval Vasiliia Shukshina," LITERATURNAIA ROSSIIA (17 V 1974).
202. K. Rudnitskii, "Prostye istiny (o 'Kaline krasnoi')," ISKUSSTVO KINO, 6 (1974), 36-51.
203. S. I. Gimpel', "Problema lichnosti v romane V. Shukshina 'Liubaviny'," IZ-VESTIIA SIBIRSKOGO OTDELENIIA ANSSSR (seriia obshchestvennykh nauk, vypusk 2), 6 (1974), 125-30.
204. "Fil'm vzial za zhivoe (o 'Kaline krasnoi')," SOVETSKII EKRAN, 13 (1974), 1-3.

"Zhiznennyi material, poisk khudozhnika, avtorskaia kontseptsiia (Obsuzhdaem 'Kalinu krasnuiu': Kinopovest' i fil'm V. Shukshina)," VOPROSY LITERA-TURY, 7 (1974), 28-90 [partially translated by Margaret Wettlin: "Reality and

the Writer's Vision," SOVIET LITERATURE, 9 (1975), 123-138] :
205. B. Rudin, "Dialektika kharaktera i eklektika stilia," 29-37.
206. G. Baklanov, "Chto daet nam iskusstvo?" 37-46; tr.: "What Does a Work of Art Give Us?" 123-127.
207. S. Zalygin, "Opiraias' na traditsiiu," 46-53.
208. V. Baranov, "Vragi Egora Prokudina," 53-62.
209. L. Anninskii, "Mezh dvukh opor," 62-70.
210. K. Vanshenkin, "Nekotorye proschety," 70-74; tr.: "A Few Criticisms," 128-31.
211. V. Kisun'ko, "Vstrecha 'vtoroi i 'tret'ei' zhizni," 75-84; tr.: "The Encounter of the 'Second' and 'Third' Lives," 131-35.
212. V. Shukshin, "Vozrazheniia po sushchestvu," 84-88; tr.: "Fundamental Objections," 135-8.
213. K. Shcherbakov, "Pravo na risk: zametki kritika," KOMSOMOL' SKAIA PRAVDA (7 VIII 1974), 2.
214. A. Kapler, "Iasnye dali talanta," LITERATURNAIA GAZETA (14 VIII 1974), 8.
215. N. Leiderman, "Trudnaia doroga vozvysheniia (o novykh proizvedeniiakh V. Shukshina)," SIBIRSKIE OGNI, 8 (1974), 163-9.
216. I. Luk'ianova, " 'Energichnye liudi'," PRAVDA VOSTOKA (27 IX 1974), 4.
217. N. Lordkipanidze, "Shukshin snimaet 'Kalinu krasnuiu'," ISKUSSTVO KINO, 10 (1974), 113-32.
218. B. Metal'nikov, "Blagodarnost'," SOVETSKII EKRAN, 23 (1974), 20.
218a. G. Bocharov, "Esli govorit' o Shukshine," KOMSOMOL'SKAIA PRAVDA (24 XI 1974).
219. O. Mitskevich, "S veseloi i zloi ironiei (o p'ese 'Energichnye liudi')," KAZAKH-STANSKAIA PRAVDA (25 XII 1974), 4.
219a. Ia. El'sberg, "Smena stilei v Sovetskom russkom rasskaze 1950-60 gg. (Antonov, Kazakov, Shukshin)," pp. 178-98 in SMENA LITERATURNYKH STILEI, Ed. V. Kozhinov. Moscow: Khudozhestvennaia literatura, 1974.
220. G. A. Belaia, "Shukshin, Vasilii," KRATKAIA LITERATURNAIA ENTSIKLO-PEDIIA, Vol. 8. Moscow: Sovetskaia entsiklopediia, 1975, 808-809.
220a. V. Fomin, "Doma i v gostiakh ('Pechki-lavochki')," pp. 28-31 and "V. Shukshin: Strasti po Egoru," pp. 113-116 in book EKRAN, 1973-1974. Moscow: Iskusstvo, 1975. [Book also includes entry 159.]
221. A. Ovcharenko, "Sovetskaia khudozhestvennaia proza 70-ykh godov," MOSKVA, 1 (1975), 202-212; 2 (1975), 202-212.
222. L. Mikhailova, "Pronitsatel'nost' talanta," LITERATURNOE OBOZRENIE, 1 (1975), 31-6.
"Pamiati tovarishcha," ISKUSSTVO KINO, 1 (1975), 146-152:
222a. S. Gerasimov, "Zaveshchanie,"; repr.: 238a.
222b. G. Baklanov, "On byl i ostanetsia."
223. N. Pervusin, "Vsia zhizn' pisatelia (Vasilii Shukshin)," NOVOE RUSSKOE SLOVO (New York), 5 I 1975.
224. F. Kuznetsov, "S vekom naravne," NOVYI MIR, 2 (1975), 229-53.
225. I. Bodrov, "Vasilii Shukshin, khudozhnik i chelovek," ZHURNALIST, 2 (1975), 63-5.
226. I. Dedkov, "Poslednie shtrikhi," DRUZHBA NARODOV, 4 (1975), 254-62.
227. V. Sakharov, "Zhizn', oborvavshaiasia na poluslove," MOSKVA, 6 (1975).
227a. G. Goryshin, " 'Gde-nibud' na Rusi...'," AVRORA, 6 (1975), 24-28.
228. S. Zalygin, "Geroi v kirzovykh sapogakh," in V. Shukshin, IZBRANNYE PRO-IZVEDENIIA V DVUKH TOMAKH. Moscow: Molodaia gvardiia, 1975, Vol. 1, 5-12.
229. I. Dedkov, "Vozvrashchenie k sebe," NASH SOVREMENNIK, 7 (1975), 174-85.

230. G. Kapralov, "Zhizn' i smert' Egora Prokudina," SOVETSKII FIL'M, 7 (1975), 13-15.
230a. V. Novikov, "Vstrechi v Srostkakh (Iz vospominanii o V.M. Shukshine)," SIBIR-SKIE OGNI, 7 (1975), 136-43.
231. I. Zolotusskii, "Poznanie nastoiashchego," VOPROSY LITERATURY, 10 (1975), 3-37.
232. F. Kuznetsov, "Dvizhenie prozy i 'problema galuzo'," LITERATURNOE OBO-ZRENIE, 11 (1975), 8-15.
233. D.M. Fiene and B.N. Peskin, "The Remarkable Art of Vasily Shukshin, " RUS-SIAN LITERATURE TRIQUARTERLY, 11 (1975), 174-178.
234. V. Solov'ev, "Fenomen Vasiliia Shukshina," ISKUSSTVO KINO, 10 (1975), 16-29; 12 (1975), 33-43.
234a. V. Korobov, "Vkliuchit'sia v narodnuiu zhizn'...," SOVETSKAIA ESTONIIA (15 X 1975); reprinted: MOSKOVSKII KOMSOMOLETS (6 XI 1975).
234b. D. Manaeva, "Razgovor pri svideteliakh," SOVETSKAIA BELORUSSIIA (11 XI 1975). [On play "Kharaktery."]
234c. N. Putintsev, "Iumor ili satira?" MOSKOVSKAIA PRAVDA (5 XI 1975). [On play "Energichnye liudi."]
234d. N. Tolchenova, "V Srostkakh, u Shukshina," LITERATURNAIA ROSSIIA (21 XI 1975).
234e. "Spektakl'" okonchen. Spor prodolzhaetsia," SOVETSKAIA ESTONIA (23 XI 1975). [Round-table discussion of play "Energichnye liudi"; includes remarks by I. Repina and V. Kubi.]
235. L. Anninskii, "Volia. Put'. Rezul'tat," NOVYI MIR, 12 (1975), 262-4.
236. V. Chalmaev, "Obnovlenie perspektivy," MOSKVA, 12 (1975), 182-93.
237. A. Khailov, "Svet 'Sibirskikh ognei,' " LITERATURNOE OBOZRENIE, 12 (1975), 17-21.
238. A. Bocharov, "Sila dukhovnogo izlucheniia," OKTIABR'!, 12 (1975), 172-84.
238a. EKRAN, 1974-1975. Moscow: Iskusstvo, 1976; contains reprints of 222a, pp. 72-74; 198b, pp. 74-76; and 153, pp. 77-78.
238b. V. Fomin, "V. Shukshin: 'Govorit' pravdu, kakoi by gor'koi ona ni byla,' " pp. 291-358 in Fomin's PERESECHENIE PARALLEL'NYKH. Moscow: Iskusstvo, 1976.
238c. B. I. Bursov, KRITIKA KAK LITERATURA. Leningrad: Lenizdat, 1976. Contains three subchapters dealing with Shukshin:
"Nesostoiavshiisia dialog," 113-118;
"Literaturnaia sud'ba Shukshina," 165-170;
"Vechernie dumy," 287-300.
238d. L. Belova, "Tri rusla odnogo puti (O tvorchestve Vasiliia Shukshina)," in the annual VOPROSY KINOISKUSSTVA (No. 17). Moscow: Nauka, 1976.
239. Hedrick Smith, THE RUSSIANS. New York: Quadrangle, 1976. See pp. 381-3.
239a. A. Romanov, "On iskal ne skhodstva, a pravdy," ISKUSSTVO KINO, 1 (1976), 123-31.
240. B. Anashenkov, "Istselisia sam...," VOPROSY LITERATURY, 1 (1976), 43-78.
240a. A. Ovcharenko, "Rasskazy Vasiliia Shukshina," DON, 1 (1976), 155-66.
240b. L. Korneshov, "Mezhdu proshlym i budushchim," KOMSOMOL'SKAIA PRAV-DA (18 I 1976).
241. Miroslav Drozda, "Novele Vasilija Suksina: Karakterizacija umjetnicke strukture," UMJETNOST RIJECI (Zagreb), xx, 2 (1976), 217-37.
241a. "Ego geroi—sredi nas," SOVETSKAIA KUL'TURA (17 II 1976). Three separate articles by T. Roganova, E. Sokolova and N. Smirnova.
241b. V. Kunitsyn, "Glubokoe rodstvo (O romane V. Shukshina 'Ia prishel dat' van voliu')," ALTAI, 3 (1976), 86-90.

242. A. Lanshchikov, "Razmyshleniia o 'Kaline krasnoi,' " VOLGA, 3 (1976), 145-58.

242a. Galina Kozhukova, "Imia sobstvennoe (Vasilii Shukshin—pisatel', rezhisser, akter)," LITERATURNAIA GAZETA (31 III 1976), 8.

242b. V. Grishaev, "Liubov' liubov'iu otzovetsia (K biografii V. Shukshina)," ALTAI, 4 (1976), 64-72.

243. Iu. Tiurin, " 'Kalina krasnaia: Kinopovest' i fil'm," MOSKVA, 4 (1976), 193-9.

243a. E. Solov'eva, "Bez Shukshina...," ISKUSSTVO KINO, 4 (1976), 63-66.

243b. Vladimir Solov'ev, "Poisk khudozhnika," PRAVDA (12 IV 1976).

243c. A. Kuksin, "Pis'mo iz detstva," KOMSOMOL'SKAIA PRAVDA (18 IV 1976).

243d. L. Anninskii, "Put' Vasiliia Shukshina," NEDELIA, 15 (1976); repr.: SEVER, 11 (1976), 117-28.

244. E. Liubareva, "Chelovek deistviia, chelovek mysli," LITERATURNOE OBOZRENIE, 5 (1976), 9-13.

245. S. Freidlikh, "Ekran i sovremennost'," NOVYI MIR, 5 (1976), 250-63.

245a. V. F. Gorn, " 'Nado chelovekom byt',' " LITERATURA V SHKOLE, 5 (1976), 9-16.

246. N. Mashovets, "Obshchnost' tseli," VOPROSY LITERATURY, 5 (1976), 48-76.

246a. N. Iakovleva, "Dumaia o Shukshine," MOSKVA, 6 (1976), 196-7.

247. B. Pankin, "Vasilii Shukshin i ego 'chudiki'," IUNOST', 6 (1976), 74-80.

247a. V. Sanaev, "Tri zhizni Vasiliia Shukshina," ISKUSSTVO KINO, 6 (1976), 83-90.

248. E. Sidorov, "Prodolzhenie sleduet," VOPROSY LITERATURY, 6 (1976), 33-49.

249. "Luchshie—na moi vzgliad (otvety chitatelei)," LITERATURNOE OBOZRENIE, 6 (1976), 10-11, 18-19.

249a. K. Dmitriev, "Smekh—delo ser'eznoe," SOVETSKAIA KIRGIZIIA (4 VI 1976). [On play"Energichnye liudi."]

249b. S. Grigor'ev, " 'Energichnye liudi,' " SOVETSKAIA LITVA (7 VI 1976).

249c. Lev Anninskii, "Pisatel', rezhisser, kinoakter," MOSKOVSKII KOMSOMOLETS (9 VI 1976); repr.: KOMMUNIST TADZHIKISTANA (13 VII 1976).

250. A. Bocharov, "Skvoz' prizmu polikonfliktnosti," OKTIABR', 7 (1976), 176-194.

250a. A. Tamme, "S beloi ptitsei v serdtse," SOVETSKAIA ESTONIIA (6 VII 1976). [On play "Kharaktery."]

250b. I. Valin, "Na stsene—geroi Shukshina i Vampilova," SOVETSKAIA LATVIIA (10 VII 1976). [On play "Kharaktery."]

250c. L. Sergeev, "Takie raznye prem'ery," MOSKOVSKAIA PRAVDA (18 VIII 1976). [On stage adaptation by E. Elanskaia of "Tam, vdali."]

250d. M. Svarinskaia, "Vstrecha s geroiami Shukshina," SOVETSKAIA LATVIIA (19 IX 1976). [On the play "Energichnye liudi" and the dramatic adaptation of "Tochka zreniia" as performed in Griboedov Theater, Tiflis.]

251. N. Leikin, "Proza prikhodit na stsenu," LITERATURNAIA ROSSIIA (29 X 1976), 11.

252. L. Ershov, "Sotsial'noe i nravstvennoe," ZVEZDA, 10 (1976), 209-17.

253. I. Grinberg, "Strogaia chelovechnost' epokhi, OKTIABR', 11 (1976), 186-99.

254. Iu. Sokhovich, "A ia nashel u Shukshina," KOMSOMOL'SKAIA PRAVDA (8 XII 1976). (In "Chitaia knigu zhizni.")

255. Sergei Zalygin, VASILII SHUKSHIN: LITERATURNYI PORTRET. Moscow: Sovetskaia Rossiia, 1977.

256. V. Sakharov, "Vlast' kanona (Zametki o rasskaze)," NASH SOVREMENNIK, 1 (1977), 156-64.

257. V. F. Gorn, "Pereizdaniiam V. Shukshina—podlinno nauchnyi uroven'," VOPROSY LITERATURY, 1 (1977), 248-52.

258. V. Korobov, "Pisatel', akter, rezhizzer Shukshin," SMENA, 1-5 (1977).
259. Iu. Seleznev, "Fantasticheskoe v sovremennoi proze," MOSKVA, 2 (1977), 198-206.
260. V. F. Gorn, "Zhivoi iazyk Vasiliia Shukshina," RUSSKAIA RECH', 2 (1977).
261. Viktor Nekrasov, "Vasia Shukshin," NOVOE RUSSKOE SLOVO [New York] (27 II 1977), 2. Repr.: 265.
262. G. Belaia, "Antimiry Vasiliia Shukshina," LITERATURNOE OBOZRENIE, 5 (1977), 23-26.
263. V. Kaverin, "Rasskazy Shukshina," NOVYI MIR, 6 (1977), 261-66.
264. M. Geller, "Vasilii Shukshin: V poiskakh voli," VESTNIK RUSSKOGO KHRISTIANSKOGO DVIZHENIIA [Paris], 120 (1977), 159-82; appears in English translation in present volume.
265. Viktor Nekrasov, "Vzgliad i nechto," KONTINENT, 12 (1977). See pp. 112-119 (repr. of 261).

ALPHABETICAL INDEX OF TITLES OF FICTIONAL WORKS BY SHUKSHIN